The Mystery of Leopold Stokowski

February, 1971 Stokowski rehearsal of the American Symphony Orchestra Carnegie Hall, New York City. © Paul Hoeffler.

The Mystery of Leopold Stokowski

William Ander Smith

Rutherford • Madison • Teaneck
Fairleigh Dickinson University Press
London and Toronto: Associated University Presses

Associated University Presses
440 Forsgate Drive
Cranbury, NJ 08512

Associated University Presses
25 Sicilian Avenue
London WC1A 2QH, England

Associated University Presses
P.O. Box 488, Port Credit
Mississauga, Ontario
Canada L5G 4M2

The paper used in this publication meets the requirements of the American National Standard for Permanence of Paper for Printed Library Materials Z39.48-1984.

Library of Congress Cataloging-in-Publication Data

Smith, William Ander, 1931–
The mystery of Leopold Stokowski / William Ander Smith.
p. cm.
Includes bibliographical references.
Discography: p.
ISBN 0-8386-3362-5 (alk. paper)
1. Stokowski, Leopold, 1882–1977. 2. Conductors (Music)—United States—Biography. 3. Conductors (Music)—United States—Discography. I. Title.
ML422.S76S6 1990
784.2'092—dc20
[B] 88-46154
CIP
MN

PRINTED IN THE UNITED STATES OF AMERICA

Contents

In memory of historian Douglass Adair:

artist, teacher, and mystery story buff

Foreword

I have a friend who thinks Toscanini the greatest conductor that ever lived. Like all fanatics, he feels he has to convert me, and accuses me of stubborn refusal to yield to the Truth. But I do listen to the recordings and read the books he gives me—and they all just confirm my lifelong antipathy for Toscanini. I have always heard in the music what I am finding out from the books: the man was a tyrant who beat his musicians into submission with insults and temper tantrums. He never smiled when conducting (not even at rehearsals!), never thanked or complimented his men, never made them feel they were valuable partners or had even done a creditable job. He would fail to give them cues, then blame them with curses and insults for needing them! Besides being a compulsive perfectionist, he was childish, petulant, inconsiderate, monomaniacal, and monstrously self-centered. His technique was *fear*, and I had always heard that fear in his music. The tension in a Toscanini performance is palpable. The musicians certainly don't seem to be enjoying it.

I'm sure I'm not the only American who is constitutionally incapable of "obedience", who hates tyranny and authoritarianism. I had been instinctively reacting to Toscanini's recordings the way I react to police states and radar traps! Reading about him—especially books by people who worked with him—strongly confirmed what I had felt in my bones.

But then there's Stokowski. I had always responded warmly to his music-making. I attended many of his concerts, and it was clear that he, like Toscanini, always conquered his audience. But the latter did so as a priest of the God of Wrath, while Stokowski acted upon us like a magician. He did not evoke trembling respect; he *seduced* us—often, it seemed, against our wills. Our defenses crumbled in the face of irresistibly attractive sounds. I talked with musicians in Philadelphia who described how the whole orchestra had again "come under his spell" after his 20 year absence. He never beat his musicians into submission; he was able to make them *want* to cooperate. They did so gladly. And together they bewitched the audience—above all, with gorgeous sound. He was a wizard and we responded to his magnetism; he was a sensualist and we were seduced by the sheer beauty of what he put before our ears.

And now there is a book to explain him, too. All that I had felt in the music seems to have a basis in the man himself. Perhaps "explain" is too strong a word, for we are dealing with mysteries here; but Professor Smith has at least *named the mystery* where others have skirted the issue. Because of the light it sheds on the personality of Stokowski, this book is seductive too. Its central thesis, that the man had parapsychic gifts, strikes me as a perfectly reasonable interpretation of the evidence. Some will refuse the seduction—largely out of prejudice against the whole realm. But I can only say that I am convinced I understand Stokowski—and music—better after reading this mind-opening book.

DONALD R. VROON

Editor, *American Record Guide*

Preface

Since his death in 1977 at the age of ninety-five, several books have been written about conductor Leopold Stokowski, most notably biographies by the late Abram Chasins and by Oliver Daniel revising the traditional interpretation of the musician and conductor. Yet revisionist accounts incorporating additional material on the life and works of the maestro have raised as many questions as they have answered about their enigmatic subject.

In his *Leopold Stokowski: A Profile* (1979), Abram Chasins actually used the paradoxical nature of the man as the single most important theme of his book, with Stokowski described again and again as a creature of contrasts and contradictions and, therefore, inexplicable in many ways. William Trotter, writing a serialized account of Stokowski's professional life for the English Stokowski Society's journal, *Toccata*, echoed Chasins in noting that Stokowski was a human kaleidoscope of "enigmas, contradictions, ambiguities and paradoxes"; so much so that he showed no central "essence" nor "nucleus" needful for a better understanding of the man and of the musician. The richest and most valuable biography by far is Oliver Daniel's fine *Stokowski: A Counterpoint of View* (1982). While Daniel has not used the Stokowski-as-paradox-and-enigma theme employed by Chasins and Trotter, his findings have actually multiplied the number of paradoxes in the nature of the man even as his prodigious research has added much new and reliable information about his subject. *New York Times* critic Richard Dyer called attention to this fact in his laudatory review of Daniel's book, ending his critique by pointing out that with all of the new information provided in Daniel's thousand-page biography, Stokowski yet remained elusive.

While I believe I have indicated the maestro's important place in modern American musical life, my own primary interest in Stokowski has been with the aforementioned enigmas and paradoxes of the man and of the musician; hence the word mystery used in the title. What I have tried to do, using an interdisciplinary approach, is consider the contradictions of the maestro as parts of a very human puzzle—a puzzle made difficult to figure out by Stokowski himself, both intentionally and unintentionally, as a result of his unusual gifts and philosophy.

In short, my work is not a biography, but a biographical mystery story about a most puzzling musical figure. Its subject matter often deals with the biographical material that has appeared since the conductor's death in 1977 and without which my own work would have been impossible. All hail, then, to Daniel, to Chasins, Trotter, Robinson, and Opperby, and to that earlier and most astute Stokowski watcher of the thirties and forties, Charles O'Connell.

I have tried here to examine this material in conjunction with Stokowski's own writing, with interviews given by him over the years, and with a variety of other evidence, in order to resolve some of the contradictions of the man and to uncover his identity—or, more appropriately in Stokowski's case, *identities*.

Elements of Stokowski's mystery include the maestro's strange verbal accents, which came and went in ways most unusual: his stories—fantasies—about a childhood and family that never were; his sense of his own artistic identity, which was largely self-constructed, romantic, and psychologically defensive—playing hob with Stokowski's personal relationships in the process; his linkage of that identity to his unusual approach to music; and, finally, his unique paranormal gifts, which were also turned by Stokowski toward musical ends. This kind of approach is the stuff of chapters 1 and 2, and of the Appendix, "Stokowski and the Family Romance."

I have also included chapters on Stokowski's Philadelphia years and on his penultimate career stage with the American Symphony Orchestra by way of illustrating how his unusual identity and approach to music worked out in a concert world dominated by a strong sense of convention and traditionalism.

Closing the work is a chronological discography linking Stokowski's career and individual approach to music with his work in the recording studio and its often idiosyncratic results. These recordings are linked very much, I believe, to the unique gifts and psyche of the maestro considered in earlier portions of the book.

Over the course of my work I have been indebted to a number of individuals who have provided invaluable information and/or criticism. I am grateful to the first biographer of Stokowski, his friend and fellow musician, the late Abram Chasins, for early encouragement and the opportunity to interview him. Sylvan and Elizabeth DeYoung Levin not only talked with me about the Stokowski they knew, but Mr. Levin, musical collaborator with the maestro for twenty years, generously made available his correspondence with the conductor as well as materials from his own Stokowski collection. Dr. Edwin Heilakka, curator of the Stokowski collection at Curtis Institute of Music, was a gracious host showing me through Philadelphia's Academy of Music and through manuscript materials and memorabilia in the Stokowski collection. Since that time, he has continued his help with updated information on Stokowski manuscript materials and with discoveries made in the collection. Mr. Oliver Daniel, Stokowski's friend and author of *Stokowski: A Counterpoint of View*, read my manuscript, offering corrections, valuable criticism, and very practical suggestions on how to strengthen the book. Mrs. Louisa Miller née Knowlton, who studied at Curtis during its first year, 1924, played under Stokowski in the Curtis Institute Orchestra, and studied cello as protégée of the Philadelphia Orchestra's first cellist Michel Penha, was kind enough to share her recollections of Stokowski both as conductor and during off duty hours. Mr. Paul Hoeffler, free-lance photographer, was, in his twenties, responsible for recording on tape many of the Stokowski-led American Symphony Orchestra concerts during the sixties. Close to Stokowski at the time, Mr. Hoeffler was also able to take a number of photographs of the maestro and has permitted me to use several of them in this book.

Nancy Shear and Marguerite Friedeberg shared impressions of the Stokowski they knew in phone conversations with me and Mrs. Friedeberg provided her own 1939 caricature of the maestro for use on the dust jacket of this book. Gustav Janossy, a member of Stokowski's All American Youth Orchestra in 1941, graciously gave me materials covering the American tour of that orchestra with permission to use the account in the book. Poet Richard Howard shared his sense of Stokowski's meaning in recollecting his own boyhood reaction to Stokowski performances generally and to the maestro's performances of pre-Baroque Italian music at a time—as Mr. Howard put it—when no other major conductors were performing it.

Harpsichordist Igor Kipnis shared his memories of working with the conductor, as well as pictures of Stokowski taken at their 1967 joint recording session. Elizabeth Neuburg, who played in the American Symphony Orchestra from 1962 to 1964, told me about Stokowski's unique ear when it came to orchestral sound. To Don Vroon, editor of the *American Record Guide*, and to Ezra Schabas, professor of music at the University of Toronto, I am grateful for their insights into Stokowski's place in American music.

Since so much in the research and writing of this book has depended on the alliance of historical and psychological interpretation, I owe a special debt of thanks to the psychoanalytic community, above all to Martin Silverman, M.D., who shared with me key insights centering on the concept of the "family romance" in relationship to my work on the conductor. No less important was the charm and humor of Mrs. Lila Silverman, who shared our talks and created a warm ambience for them. My thanks to the New York Psychoanalytic Association for inviting me to share my research with its members at a 1984 meeting. Special thanks to analyst Charles Entellis, M.D., chairman and transcriber of the meeting I addressed, to Stuart Feder, M.D., and Jules Glenn, M.D., who acted as commentators on my presentation to the association, and to psychiatrist John Diamond, M.D., who joined us with his own interpretation of Stokowskiana. Although she could not be at the meeting, Bettina Warburg, M.D., shared by mail memories of personal encounters with Stokowski that both she and her husband, Samuel Grimson, had. From all of the above I gained insights about my subject and valuable criticism.

On a day to day basis I have been indebted to my colleagues and students, upon whom I periodically tried out materials from work in progress. They gave me encouragement, ideas, and criticism in return. I am particularly grateful to Anthony Brundage and William Fawcett Hill for encouraging me and helping me in matters of fact and interpretation. To Jacqueline Ryan, Katherine Selke, Sandy Sharp, and Joan Carter, loving thanks for what each knows she has meant to me and contributed to in this work.

I owe a debt of thanks to the following institutions and organizations for making my work possible and enjoyable. For sponsored public presentation of my research I wish to thank the California American Studies Association, the Western Social Sciences Association, the Sonneck Society, the Mid-Continent American Studies Association, the Phi Alpha Theta Society, and Donald Fritz, organizer of the "World As Mirror" conference at Miami University in 1983. To the journals *Biography, American Music*, and the *South Atlantic Quarterly* my thanks for first publishing my research on the maestro. Thanks as well to their sponsoring university presses for permission to include material from those essays in the present book. In my research, I have been indebted to the work of the English Stokowski Society and to that of the Stokowski Society of America, led by its president, Robert Stumpf. The two societies not only contributed materials for research, but reprinted two of my pieces in, respectively, *Toccata* and *Maestrino*.

Research trips, conference presentations, and a research sabbatical leave would not have been possible without the generous financial support of my department, the California State Polytechnic University, College of Arts, and the university itself, through the President's Fund for Travel. No one could have asked for warmer support than I have received from my colleagues at Cal Poly.

As a largely longhand manuscript, replete with carets, arrows, and cross-outs, the original of this book would not have made half the journey toward publication without the work of Ms. Diana Martin and her word processor. For the last half of that journey I am indebted to my editors, Thomas Yoseloff, Lauren Lepow, and Leslie Foley.

Much of my research and writing has been done at the Honnold Library for the Associated Colleges of Claremont. I am grateful to the Honnold staff for their help and for the research facility that is Honnold.

Acknowledgments

The author is grateful to the following for permissions of several sorts: permission to quote excerpts from copyrighted written material; permission to reproduce photographs and drawings; permission to use material from my own previously published journal articles on Stokowski; and permission to quote from recorded material.

American Record Guide, Record Guide Productions. Permission to quote editor, Don Vroon from *American Record Guide* 51, no. 3 (May–June 1988) and from vol. 5, No. 5 (September–October 1988).

Biographical Research Center. Permission to use material from an earlier version of chapter one, which appeared in *Biography: An Interdisciplinary Quarterly* 7, no. 3 (summer 1984).

Consumers Union of the United States. Permission to quote from *Consumers Union Reviews Classical Recordings*, © 1978 by Consumers Union of the United States Inc., Mount Vernon, N.Y. 10553. Excerpted by permission from Consumers Reports Books, 1978.

Curtis Institute of Music, Dr. Edwin Heillakka, Curator of the Stokowski Collection. Permission to quote from "The Stokowski Collection", *Maestrino* (fall 1987) and to reproduce a drawing and photographs from the Curtis Institute's Stokowski Collection.

Oliver Daniel. Permission to quote from Oliver Daniel, *Stokowski: A Counterpoint of View* (1982), © Oliver Daniel.

John Diamond M.D. Permission to quote from John Diamond, *Life Energy in Music* (1981), © John Diamond M.D.

Duke University Press. Permission to use material from an earlier version of chapter three, which appeared in *The South Atlantic Quarterly* 81, no. 3 (summer 1982).

Marguerite Friedeberg and *Westways* magazine. Permission to reproduce Mrs. Friedeberg's 1939 caricature silhouette of Stokowski on the dust jacket of this book.

Paul Hoeffler. Permission to reproduce pictures of Stokowski taken by Mr. Hoeffler, © Paul Hoeffler, and one 1922 picture of the maestro with chorus, soloists and orchestra, courtesy of Paul Hoeffler.

Igor Kipnis. Permission to reproduce pictures taken by Mr. Kipnis of Stokowski in the recording studio and permission to quote from Mr. Kipnis's taped reminiscences of the maestro.

Sylvan Levin. Permission to quote from Leopold Stokowski's correspondence with Mr. Levin, 1929–51 and to reproduce Mr. Levin's 1934 picture of Stokowski in Havana, Cuba.

The estate of Leopold Stokowski, Herman E. Muller, Executor. Permission to quote from Leopold Stokowski, *Music for All of Us* (1943), © Leopold Stokowski.

Leopold Stokowski Society, A. R. Teal President. Permission to quote from recorded rehearsal comments by Stokowski to the 1973 International Festival Youth Orchestra, © Indigo Records Cameo Classics GOCLP 9007 in association with the Leopold Stokowski Society.

William R. Trotter. Permission to quote from Mr. Trotter's serialized biography of Stokowski, *The Conductor as Musical Hobo, Toccata* (winter 1982–83).

University of Illinois Press. Permission to use material from an earlier version of chapter four, which appeared in *American Music* 1, no. 3 (fall 1983).

Viking Penguin, a division of Penguin Books USA, Inc. Permission to quote from Jerome Toobin, *Agitato* (1975) © Jerome Toobin. All rights reserved.

The Mystery of Leopold Stokowski

1

Of Sonya's Doll, Grandfather's Fiddle, and the Changeling: The Fantasy Childhood of Leopold Stokowski

Robert Gomberg, violinist in the Philadelphia Orchestra from 1931 to 1940, played with Stokowski many times and remained, over the years, fascinated by both the conductor's brilliant music making and his strange personality. While Stokowski could be arrogant to the point of cruelty, he also involved his musicians, more than any other conductor in Gomberg's experience, in the shared excitement of realizing a musical vision with each performance. As Gomberg recalled, the musicians were psychologically galvanized by the maestro. He made each of them feel his or her importance in the success of the orchestra at each performance. They knew they were responsible. Although Stokowski was a gifted psychologist at involving the orchestra's members and literally convincing them of their mission, it was more esoteric than that. Echoing Morton Gould, who found that Stokowski's rehearsals and performances added up to a "magic" that was far more than the discernible sum of their musical parts, Gomberg described performance eye contact with Stokowski as the ultimate and near eerie explanation of Stokowski's magic with an orchestra. Gomberg wrote that there was in Stokowski's eye contact with his musicians an imperative message nonverbally carrying musical intent, conveying strength and an intense focus on the work in progress.

The musicians played beyond themselves as a result, recalled Gomberg, breathing life into the manuscripts of Bach and Beethoven as they could with no other conductor. And what strange Stokowski paradoxes were involved. Gomberg remembered the conductor as a man who could be so petty as to fire a good musician because, in the conductor's judgment, he had on inappropriate dress for rehearsal. Minutes later, he could make the musicians feel as one in the beauty and emotional power of the music being played. To understand Stokowski, wrote Gomberg, one would have to feel through his contradictions psychologically and trace his complexity back to his origins and youth.[1]

And there is the nub of this chapter as an attempt to get a perspective on Stokowski. By examining episodes from the maestro's life for those paradoxes and by attempting to see what sort of pattern they form, I propose to establish something of Stokowski as a person—not in spite of those contradictions, but by explaining them. Much popular writing about Stokowski—and I am thinking of those critics, ostensibly dealing with the conductor's music making, who have concentrated anecdotally on his hands, his hair, his eroticism, his strange accents, his untruths about his own age, childhood origins, and so forth—misses the mark. This kind of nonanalytical criticism loses Stokowski, not because it is critical of the conductor, but because it often ignores the music making and focuses on only the eccentricities of the man, and then with no interest in what those eccentricities, when linked in psychological pattern, can tell us about the maestro. These critics' choices of Stokowskiana are picked carefully with an eye for the seemingly ridiculous. One can be positive or negative about the man and his musical legacy, depending upon one's taste, point of view, and sense of style, but to make Stokowski look absurd or seem an object of fun is proof of failure to deal with what the knowledgeable Mr. Gomberg and others have noted as the musical magic of this longest-lived and most enigmatic of modern conductors. Ludicrous he wasn't. Complex and controversial he was. Barbed and misleading critiques have already been met by the thoughtful appraisals of Abram Chasins, Charles O'Connell, Preben Opperby, and Oliver Daniel. Still questions remain unanswered, and Stokowski's peculiarities of accent and memory remain enigmatic.[2]

Given Robert Gomberg's emphasis on the maestro's seeming inner contradictions and the need for psychological context in understanding them, it is quite possible that historical and psychological approaches to the conductor will offer some conclusions about Stokowski's idiosyncracies. Such an approach will, in turn, bring us closer to the real man and thus eventually to the musician. By opening with such concerns, I gain another advantage. The author is spared writing later repetitious comments on these idiosyncracies. The reader is spared the need to recross this biographical territory, and the text will be less cluttered with seeming Stokowskian mysteries.

I am referring to psychological characteristics in the manner of the youth and the man rather than to musical traits as such. Stokowski's musical innovations, his professional risk-taking, and his orchestral work toward sometimes eccentric live performances or recordings owed much to his personality, his romanticism, and his intuition. I believe, however, that these should be considered separately and later if only to allow for first establishing needed clarity on what manner of person Stokowski was and only then what this meant in terms of his musical style.[3]

Among the most often cited and most peculiar characteristics of the man were his tendency to mythologize his own origins and ethnic background coupled with his sense of his own special place in music, an art form that he chose in turn to describe cosmically as "Music, the voice of the All."[4] In tandem, too, was his coupling of exotic spoken accents with a gift for psychological free association that mystified both friends and casual acquaintances. Conversationally he often moved—on occasion playfully, seriously, ironically, irreverently, and yes, erotically—from one subject to another without any observable transition made between them. Stokowski did this with some internalized and freely associative logic of his own that also included a delight in shocking those close to him.[5]

The binding agent, the glue holding these traits together, was a strong and lifelong romanticism.[6] Stokowski could be tough, shrewd, realistic, and practical, but overarching and underpinning such survival and success skills was an ardent romanticism, which early on carried him beyond rationalism's imperatives in daily life even as it established him outside concert hall norms in his musical career. Where the rationalist in everyday life and the literalist or classicist in music stresses established principles, tradition, seriousness, reason, and regularity, Stokowski practiced and stressed imagination, playfulness, experimentation, and intuitive judgment as guides through a musical life.[7]

In my wonder at this strange man and in my need to put him in focus, let me present him, in a series of illustrative vignettes, in the context of his life as he lived it.

* * *

Edgard Varèse, composer and iconoclast, had every reason to consider Leopold Stokowski a musical friend and comrade during the 1920s. Varèse, composing with masses of sounds carefully reckoned and poised against each other, created music that had little of conventional harmony and melody about it. For this reason his works had received few performances and little critical support since he had emigrated to the United States in 1915. Persuaded by his friend, harpist Carlos Salzedo, that he should send a score to Stokowski for consideration, Varèse did so in 1922. But he expressed his doubts about Stokowski and all of the conducting notables who made careers of playing the same music over and over again without providing sponsorship for new and controversial works. To Varèse, such conductors seemed more concerned about image and success than about music. To them, his work was not music but an aberration in sound, and he was a "freak."[8]

Yet Stokowski did respond favorably, promising to play Varèse's *Hyperprism* with the Philadelphia Orchestra as soon as his schedule permitted. This he did in Philadelphia and in New York's Carnegie Hall in 1924, to the boos and hisses of detractors and the cheers of the composer's supporters. In successive years Stokowski, conducting the Philadelphia Orchestra, premiered *Integrales* (1925), *Ameriques* (1926), and *Arcana* (1927). During these years Stokowski became Varèse's most effective partisan, and Stokowski, loner though he was, came close to friendship with the combative individualist. Stokowski, the more serene and centered of the two, took philosophically the concert hall controversy over the performances of Varèse—including the boos and catcalls—although he worried about their effect on the composer's health. Varèse had a hot temper and was given to frequent rages, even as he complained of a variety of physical ailments. Contemporary medicine and the Stokowski of the twenties would relate these ailments to stress and psychological pressure. Stokowski advised Varèse to get out of the musically contentious atmosphere of New York, to change his diet, to get more exercise, and to learn, or relearn, how to play, noting that children should be his models for the recovery of a real sense of delight. When the composer did finally decide to leave the traumas of New York to return to France in 1928, Stokowski added two thousand dollars to Varèse's meager assets to make the trip and a return to Paris possible.[9]

The French composer came to appreciate Stokowski's personal concern and certainly admired the conductor's courage on his behalf and for the cause of contemporary music generally. On a limited budget Varèse in turn showed his appreciation by giving Stokowski small presents of all sorts. Of these, the most interesting, in view of the maestro's reaction to it, was a doll sent by Varèse to Stokowski's daughter Sonya. It was no ordinary doll because Varèse, aware of Stokowski's intense feelings about his

Polish heritage, had professional dressmaker Franka Gordon design an authentic Polish costume for the doll. The doll was delivered, and Stokowski responded with a delighted thank you note in Sonya's name. Shortly after receiving the doll, Stokowski invited the Varèses, Louise and Edgard, to a luncheon he was giving for the Polish ambassador to the United States at his Philadelphia home. After lunch, host Stokowski asked the Varèses, other guests, and the ambassador to join him for a moment in his upstairs study. There, propped in the middle of his desk, was Sonya's doll. With the composer scant feet away, the ambassador in close tow, and Louise Varèse at his elbow, Stokowski held up the doll for inspection by the guest of honor, saying that the doll had been sent by villagers from the Stokowski family's home village in Poland. The bogus claim was made in Stokowski's most convincing and honeyed voice, with an accent not heard during lunch. While Louise Varèse, the keeper of the family diary, did not record the Polish ambassador's reply, she did record in her diary, that of the doll's senders to the effect that Stokowski on a moment's notice could be outrageous in his obfuscations and for no observably good reason.[10]

Over the years from the teens of the twentieth century to the late seventies, Stokowski's mystifications—Sylvan Levin, his friend and close associate for twenty years, described them as "idiosyncracies and oddities,"—were the subject of both friendly wonder and hostile jibes, with as much space in print devoted to them as to his music making.[11] Now the norms of society dictate that the assumption of a manner, accent, and family background not assumed by an observer to be one's own, coupled with a tendency to distort the truth or wholly fabricate it in line with strange and inexplicable changes of personal manner and accent, brand one—by definition—as a poseur, charlatan, or phony. Yet norms are based on a normality rooted in the *ordinary* behavior of *ordinary* persons, as true for conductors as for carpenters. Stokowski was an unusual conductor, but more fundamentally he was a very unusual human being in many ways.

Abram Chasins, Stokowski's able biographer and a friend for fifty years, described something of this to me. His eyes widening in wonder, Chasins said that most observers talk about Stokowski's strange accent. The truth is, he had, "accents not an accent." There were several distinct accents. Stokowski could and did speak with no discernible accent at all, but, invoking remembrance or imagination, he would change both his mood and his accent in an instant, employing some intellectual-emotional set unique in Chasins's experience. Stokowski spoke excellent German and indifferent French, in addition to English, but, continued Chasins, if Stokowski were talking about Prague—*Praga* in the maestro's terminology—a different accent, one suitable to the discussion and to Stokowski's feeling for the Czech capital at that moment, would appear and would disappear with a change of topic or mood. The same was notably true in discussion of Stokowski's Polish heritage. Even the lower-middle-class London accent, his true accent as a child born in the Marylebone district of that city, would on occasion become Stokowski's vehicle for expression, particularly in moments of stress. In much the same way, Stokowski's mood and train of thought could alter inexplicably. From rhapsodizing about Chopin as a composer who truly represented the Polish spirit. Stokowski could in an instant turn practically shrewd in discussing financial matters. He could further shift tone and mood to irony in assessing the state of the arts in America and the conductor's role in that context, or demonstrate realistic understanding of scientific matters centering on acoustics, recording, or the nature of sound. These shifts of subject and emotional tone—and there were many of them—might occur abruptly and without seeming transition from earlier conversational subject matter. The appearance and change of vocal accents further complicated matters. In Chasins's experience, Stokowski was unique as a human being in his emotional-intellectual changes of tone and manner, including verbal accent; the claim was not unlike that of music critics faced with the interpretive surprises of Stokowski in symphonic performance.[12] This lifelong tendency was so marked in the man that an interested observer would expect this mode to show its roots in Stokowski's sense of his own place in the world and in his own sense of identity. If it did, it might make those Stokowski mystifications less mystifying and help resolve the seeming contradictions of character noted over the years.

Musicians and nonmusicians have long recorded the inexplicable behavior of conductor Leopold Stokowski when it came to discussing his personal life, origins, and namesake grandfather Leopold Stokowski. When Herbert Kupferberg interviewed Stokowski in 1968 as part of his research for *Those Fabulous Philadelphians*, an account of Stokowski's own Philadelphia Orchestra, the maestro described his first interest in music as generated by his beloved Polish grandfather, who, when Stokowski was seven or thereabouts, took the boy to his London club. The experience was touchingly recounted by the eighty-six-year-old conductor, who described the club as an 1880s ethnic meeting ground for European émigrés in London—Poles, Russians, and Germans in the main. Talk, drink, laughter, much open emotion, and wonderful music made this ethnic center a wonderland for the seven-year-old. Loud and boisterous folk songs from the old country, sung with great feeling and intensity, alternated with songs of sadness and longing. Stokowski recalled that these sad songs wrought so much emotion among those present that he could see tears streaming down into their whiskers. In recollection, what attracted him most in this magic place was the beauty of the violin playing. For Stokowski it was the stuff of the old country, of Central European life and culture, centering on the poignant beauty of sound created by a fiddler strolling through the room. In remembrance, so entranced was the little boy that he turned to his grandfather and asked him if he might have such a violin to make beautiful music on. The story ends with an understanding grandfather presenting little Leopold with a quarter-size violin of his own, the first instrument he claimed to have played; it was his entrée to the world of music and still, he told Kupferberg, his favorite instrument.[13]

This story, however, is really only a beginning to a much stranger story, since maestro Leopold Stokowski was born in 1882, three years *after* his grandfather Leopold's death. The same interview with Mr. Kupferberg netted a brief biographical account of the Stokowski family, of how his grandfather, a sturdy Polish farmer and patriot of the village of Stokki, had been forced off his land by agents of the Czar, who awarded the land to Russian tenants—a practice, continued the conductor, which cost many Poles their land in the nineteenth century. According to Stokowski, his grandfather lost several farms in succession to the Russians before he left his native land, taking his family to Vienna, to Paris, and finally to London.[14]

Was grandfather Leopold of sturdy land-owning peasant stock? If so, how could *his* own father have been the aristocratic General Stokowski who marched with Napoleon into Russia—a story maestro Stokowski told on another occasion. Philadelphia rumor even had it once that he was a descendant of Richard Wagner. This last is a story that Stokowski would neither refute nor admit.[15]

Radio listeners in the Miami area were treated to another episode of Stokowski family mystification when, in 1955, Stokowski agreed to be interviewed on the air prior to a concert with the Miami University Symphony Orchestra. His interviewer opened by describing the conductor as born in 1882. He got no further because of Stokowski's interruption to the effect that he was born in 1887. Trying once more, he ventured the notion that Stokowski was born of a Polish father and an Irish mother. Again Stokowski interrupted, denying Irish ancestry and demanding to know where the interviewer had gotten his information? As it turned out, the interviewer had gotten his data from the *World Almanac*, and with only one minute used out of a scheduled thirty minute interview, that is all he did get. Stokowski stalked out of the studio to the sound of recorded music used to fill in the dead air. Much the same thing happened on Chicago radio twelve years later when Stokowski corrected an announcer, who had described his mother as English, with the statement that she was a Pole. But then she would have been Polish if what Stokowski told the Royal Philharmonic Orchestra's first flutist, Gerald Jackson, had been true. On first meeting guest conductor Stokowski and trying to make conversation, Londoner Jackson innocently mentioned London as the conductor's birth place. Stiffening, Stokowski replied that he was born in Poland and quickly turned away from Jackson. He also reported the story of his Polish birth to sweetheart Gloria Vanderbilt in 1945, adding that he was sent to England to live after the death of his Polish mother, Maria.[16]

The truth is that Stokowski's grandfather Leopold was neither a sturdy peasant nor landed gentry. He was an artisan, a cabinet maker who had emigrated to England and there married Jessie Sarah Anderson. Their one son, the conductor's father, Joseph Kopernik Stokowski, was born in London and followed his father's trade of cabinet-making. Two years after grandfather Leopold's death, Joseph married Annie Marion Moore, the daughter of an Anglo-Irish bootmaker. One year later, in 1882, their first son, named Leopold after his grandfather, was born in a poor to middling section of London. Two more children, Lydia, who died young, and Percy John, were born to the couple by the end of the decade. The second of the two, Percy John, would follow the family's bent for trade by selling cars and also real estate for a living, changing his name to Stock for business reasons.[17]

There were no generals, aristocrats, nor sturdy peasant patriots, no musical evenings with grandfather at his club, no Polish mother nor proud heritage from the village of Stokki, the mythical point of origin for Sonya's doll. Instead, there was a Polish immigrant with Scottish and Irish-Anglo mix over two generations, with emphasis on handicrafts, hard work, and survival, but not on music. At best, the Stokowskis had to a degree improved their social and economic position within the confines of central London during that time, moving up from a working class ghetto of the foreign-born to modest middle-class lodgings. Even the original accent of grandfather Leopold would give way to central London lower-middle-class phrasing by the time of our Leopold's birth in a home where Polish was never spoken, according to his brother's testimony. When under stress or excited, Stokowski's voice sometimes returned to this original London accent off and on throughout his life.[18]

On rare occasions the mature Stokowski veered away from the ethnically romantic family fantasy and would describe his childhood in almost Dickensian terms. Some forty years beyond the small boy in grimy London town, a now famous Leopold Stokowski taxied through the streets of Philadelphia with his friend Charles O'Connell. O'Connell, supervisor for RCA's classical Red Seal record division, was complaining about his own lack of money and the natural advantages of wealth. When Stokowski responded that he liked O'Connell the way he was, O'Connell answered heatedly that Stokowski wouldn't talk that way if he had ever been poor. At that, Stokowski pulled up his trouser leg to expose a swollen and misshapen ankle—in sharp contrast to his image of comeliness. The conductor asked O'Connell if he recognized the condition. O'Connell answered that it looked like the result of "malnutrition or rickets." Stokowski, smiling bitterly, answered that O'Connell had made a perfect diagnosis, and, with it in mind, hoped he would never again suggest that Stokowski had no experience with poverty.[19]

After three more decades of publicly romanticizing his Polish background, a newly divorced Stokowski vented his anger over what he considered the loss of his two boys to ex-wife Gloria Vanderbilt. To Jerome Toobin, general manager of the Symphony of the Air, Stokowski complained that even the Vanderbilt wealth worked against Gloria's ability to raise the boys in the right way, adding for emphasis that he had been poor when the same age as his sons. Rhetorically querying Toobin as to whether he had ever been poor, Stokowski continued without waiting for an answer that he had known poverty; he had been poorer than anyone Toobin had ever known.[20]

It is clear that whatever the socioeconomic specifics of the maestro's childhood were, he remembered them with some bitterness. When forced to deal with his childhood publicly, he substituted fantasized and romanticized variants on the grandfather story. However, from young adulthood on Stokowski generally avoided all mention of his childhood—whether real or fantasized—with remarks to the effect that he lived in the present and for the future, not in the past. Thus he explained his 1955 blowup with the Miami radio interviewer to his friend and colleague Oliver Daniel by saying that he didn't like personal information about his background brought up. But if put on the spot, as he was in the Kupferberg interview, Stokowski shared a vision of his early life in which accent matched myth concerning that "wahn-dah-fool" childhood with grandfather in a little cottage where life was simple and serene.

Appearing somewhere between the realm of myth and that of late nineteenth-century London reality was the apple tree Stokowski remembered as his own when a small boy. No fruit was ever sweeter, but then small boys and girls are always enchanted by a climbable tree for reasons far beyond luscious fruit. Surrounded by the airborne world of leafy foliage, they can live in fantasy and imagination much more safely than is possible on a ground level rooted in mundane daily cares and the struggle to simply live. The tree Stokowski remembered into his nineties was probably real. Its remembered context as part of a secure and comfortable home life was not. Strangely, the aged maestro actually did manage to find that childhood setting on his final return to England in 1972, but only when over ninety, and then he found it by creating it in Place Farm House, remodeled to his specifications and set in the little village of Nether Wallop. There in the English countryside sat the comfortable cottage of memory with a one-acre backyard, complete with brook, waterfall, and an apple orchard with enough trees to transplant any number of children to that airy world beyond reality.[21]

Living out a romance was much more difficult for a London boy in the 1880s and 1890s than creating one was for the world-famous maestro in the 1970s. But life-long romantic that he was, his early feeling for that apple tree was matched by his early passion for music. Recalled Stokowski for BBC's Sandra Harris in 1974, he was a musician from the beginning, from as far back in childhood as he could remember. Why this was so he didn't know, but with his first thoughts also came music.

His early childhood passion for music first led him into the choir of central London's St. Marylebone's Anglican Church. Choirboy Stokowski at seven took up the piano in his passion for music. But before his legs were long enough to reach the low c and high f pedals, Stokowski had also become enamored of the enthralling music of the church's organ and took that instrument up too, playing only the manuals until his legs grew long enough to reach each pedal in succession. With only a grade school education and elementary musical instruction, the boy yearned to conduct as well. He got his chance at the age of twelve. Already earning money in a music hall where he played piano for chorus rehearsals, Stokowski at twelve, like Toscanini at nineteen, seized the opportunity to conduct when the band's regular conductor failed to show up for a performance. Years later, maestro Stokowski would confide to Abram Chasins that in this event he had discovered his "real identity." He further recalled that the experience was so consuming that he couldn't sleep all night for thinking about becoming a conductor. Within a year of this incident, Stokowski was accepted at the Royal College of Music. And at age thirteen, he was one of the youngest students ever accepted by the RCM.[22]

Upon graduation in 1900, an eighteen-year-old Stokowski, with the sponsorship of his teacher, Henry Walford Davies, became choirmaster and organist at St. Mary's Anglican Church, and by 1902, again with Davies's help, had moved up to St. James Church in Piccadilly. By this time he was a strikingly handsome young man. He also clearly knew what he wanted to be and do.

"Conductors are born not made," a sixty-one-year-old Stokowski would write in 1943, echoing the six-year-old of 1888 who at Christmas time had asked his mother for a "magic wand." At twenty-one he had neither wand nor his own orchestra, but, closer to music than to human kind, he was mesmerizing St. James Church audiences with his organ playing while looking beyond those concerts for his magic wand. During his short tour of duty at St. James, Stokowski became engaged to the rector's daughter even as he persuaded his future father-in-law to hire an orchestra for special church performances with himself as conductor, only to break his engagement after he moved across the Atlantic to New York's St. Bartholomew's Church. Again in New York, there was at least a hint of romantic attachment between Stokowski and the rector's daughter, Ellen Parks. But Rector Leighton Parks did not approve of Stokowski for one thing, and by 1906 the young organist was involved with pianist Olga Samaroff.[23]

On the musical side, Stokowski's organ performances were brilliant and so virile and colorful that the normally drab position of church organist was transformed by Stokowski into a musical satrapy with himself as its handsome young prince.[24] He accepted the adoration of his hearers as due him without sign of either delight or surprise, a habit he carried over into the salons of wealthy parishioners who invited the young musician into their homes. The one qualifier was that some people, including fathers and husbands in the congregation, disliked and mistrusted Stokowski's golden appeal. And it was not simply Stokowski's erotic presence that troubled them. There was an aura about him, a personal energy that when combined with his single-minded identification with music, turned away some parishioners as if from a musical Dr. Mesmer, even as others reacted to him as a new musical great—a division prefiguring similar attitudes toward the later conductor.[25]

Subsequently known for his orchestral transcriptions of Bach organ works, the young Stokowski feverishly broadened his organ repertoire for special St. Bartholomew's concerts as well as guest performances all over the city by transcribing choral and symphonic works for the king of instruments, on which he was master romantic performer. With these unique offerings, he was able to draw the cultured and the well-to-do all over the city of New York. But home base remained his Sunday 5:00 P.M. organ recitals at St. Bartholomew's. Here New York society would congregate to both hear the organist and admire the handsome young Stokowski. After a brilliant performance of Beethoven, Wagner, and Chopin works transcribed by himself, with the inevitable Bach as centerpiece, he would remain motionless at the keyboard, eyes raised on high, profile aquiline perfect, contemplating some cosmic mystery of music and the divine while his admirers went wild in their enthusiasm.[26]

To pianist Olga Samaroff, née Lucie Hickenlooper, whom Stokowski met in 1906 and married in 1911, the young organist seemed predestined for a great career because he combined intelligence, sensuality, musicality, and a driving ambition, which he shared with her.[27] With only minimal conducting experience, Stokowski, teamed with Olga Samaroff since 1906, worked toward the badly wanted goal of an orchestra conductorship. By 1909 the matched pair had gotten Stokowski his first orchestra, the Cincinnati Symphony Orchestra. While Olga Samaroff worked behind the scenes to convince Mrs. Christian Holmes, née Fleischman, president of the Cincinnati Orchestra Association, to give Stokowski the vacant conductorship of the orchestra, Stokowski himself conducted a European audition concert to convince Cincinnati music critic J. Herman Thuman and the board that he was the young man for the job. At the age of twenty-seven, the organist had become the conductor, his keyboard an orchestra and his magic wand a baton.[28]

Consolidating the position, Stokowski proved himself to be a first-rate conductor with the orchestra he revitalized between 1909 and 1912. In 1911, before the next move up the musical ladder to Philadelphia, Stokowski and Olga were married. One of Madam Samaroff's assessments of Stokowski as conductor was, if partial, close to the mark psychologically when she described him as a musician with the ecstatic appeal and intensity that hypnotize concertgoers.[29]

The next step to Philadelphia in 1912 would, years later, be indirectly and drolly described by Stokowski to a group of young and aspiring conductors-to-be. With young Andre Previn taking notes in the audience, Stokowski finished a three hour seminar fielding questions from the hopefuls. One such tyro asked how a young conductor just getting started should go about getting his or her own orchestra. Stokowski, quieting the laughter from others in the group, said that the question was a reasonable one and deserved a thoughtful answer. Then, with no mention of his own experience in moving to Philadelphia to lead its orchestra in 1912 at the expense of Karl Pohlig, the orchestra's conductor for six previous seasons and scheduled for a seventh, Stokowski continued by outlining a strategy for the ambitious young conductor. As the conductor described it, the youthful beginner should balance his or her goals between ambition and reality. The first necessity must be to find an orchestra suitable to early career needs, preferably a second-tier orchestra with a shorter season that could be managed, yet a season long enough to allow the beginner to study and play several new works.

In methodically choosing such an orchestra, consideration of its players is important, added Stokowski. They should be good enough to handle the pieces chosen, but not good enough to intimidate the tyro when he works with them. If one can find such an ensemble meeting these requirements, the tyro still cannot claim it until he first arranges to have its current conductor "fired" and himself hired.[30]

* * *

Much of the material touched on so far has the quality of raw material for a Dickens novel—youthful dreaming, luck, struggle, scheming, pathos, and worldly success coupled with elements of the romance and mystery that graced many a Stokowski performance and recording. A hypothesis to explain those contradictions and complexities cited by Mr. Gomberg in 1978 as keys to unlock the man Stokowski enjoins the historian to be realistic about material that is romantic and at the same to be sensitive to the realms of the imagination and to psychological need where their boundaries and Stokowski's career impinge on one another. To reach that hypothesis consider the following.

What do we know of Stokowski so far? We know that he was inordinately good looking. We know that he was an intuitive romantic who could also be realistic and pragmatic about the world around him, even as he spun verbally accented fantasies about his background. He was self-confident about his gifts, although he felt vulnerable about his background. He was egoistic in his identification with music and personally very ambitious, accepting no obstacles as permanently barring his rise to his own destiny. His sense of his own gifts was accepted by many who came in contact with him. Their deference to him transcended their respect for his musical gifts and, by the time he was well established in Philadelphia, approached an adulation that was usually reserved for legendary creators and performers—the like of Bernhardt, Lind, and Richter, who were all romantics and all larger than life. Their own mythic archetypes were to be found in the legends and fairy tales of Western culture. Aphrodite, Golden Apollo, Adonis, Dionysus, Orpheus, Cinderella, and her Prince Charming—all represented idealized heroes and heroines out of the Western store of pagan and mythic romance. And it was within this romantic context that Stokowski achieved his early success.[31] There was the radiant pagan appeal of the young prince to his growing number of followers. There was also the countering mistrust of the young magician, a Cagliostro come from nowhere to seduce audiences with sonic tricks rather than win them with traditional music making. For sober rationalists, particularly among music critics, the image of Stokowski would become that of the charlatan using his looks, his showmanship, and his undeniable gifts for self-serving purposes beneath the dignity of traditional musicianship.

We know that Stokowski was a first-rate musician from a very modest family background. We know that the young Stokowski learned early of his power to gain potential supporters, among both musicians and nonmusicians. He capitalized on his looks and his ability to get where he believed he belonged in a way that was in keeping with the limited possibilities open to one of his great ambition and modest background. As for hostile critics? He seemed to ignore them.[32]

The personal counterweight to this heady mixture of public acclaim and growing mistrust lay in Stokowski himself, in the one area of personal insecurity where he was—to himself—most vulnerable, that is, in his own origins. As an adult, Stokowski's background and parents failed to provide him with real-life origins matching his romantic conception of himself and the roots of his music making. The young prince had been born of lower-middle-class parents, and to make matters worse, his low childhood estate had little of romance about it. There was nothing of the young heir to the throne become foundling, or cast adrift, or raised by gypsies, only to reclaim his rightful place in the kingdom when a comely young man. Analogically, Stokowski's true early story came closer to the Horatio Alger prototype of *Ragged Dick the Matchboy*, a protagonist who by pluck, luck, ability, and marriage to the boss's daughter would finally establish himself as a success. As a basis for explaining his origins and rise, nothing smacking of the Alger model would do for Stokowski. Temperamentally, this accommodation to the reality of his past was difficult to impossible for Stokowski. Yet the problem of origins remained for the adult Stokowski, notably so when he was forced to talk about them!

It is clear from our knowledge of his childhood that while he loved his family, he could not identify with and accept the working world of his mother and father, nor adapt to it as his brother Percy John did. What he did carry over from the family, whether culturally or genetically, were traits that would help Stokowski escape from his own origins. These included a willingness to work hard for what he wanted and an ability to seize opportunity when it appeared or to create it when it did not, coupled with the daring to capitalize on opportunities of both sorts to move toward what his intuition told him was his special destiny.[33]

It was music as Stokowski's destiny that gave biographical cutting edge and identity to his personal quadrivium of romanticism, imagination, comeliness, and the toughness necessary for upward mobility. Naturally musical in early childhood, Stokowski would say of his seized opportunity to conduct at the age of twelve that only then did he discover his artistic identity, which was his true identity. The potential power to command an orchestra and entrance an audience was now added to those characteristics of personality already separating him from his family.

Stokowski moved in a different direction from that of his family when he went to the Royal College of Music at thirteen. It was different not because the London artisan classes were beyond the reach of music's magic—the rich tradition of London's music halls denies that—but it was because the *kind* of music Stokowski was drawn to in the 1890s belonged to that world of belles lettres, drama, and serious music that was subsidized, patronized, and ruled by the wealthy, and there lay the gulf between a boy of Stokowski's background and family on the one hand and his hopes for a future in the field of symphonic music on the other.[34] The class lines of English society, while not absolutely inflexible, were quite as clearly marked in the world of music as they were in the fields of politics and society. To join that world of concerts and applause meant leaving the world of family and small trade.

Many novels, stories, plays, and historical works have been written centering on the torments of the young and gifted artist faced with the painful choice between the world of family and an ambition to be fed; a destiny to be reached only by breaking with the past. Stokowski faced two problems shared by many before him and many after him. First, he loved his family, but he had to leave it physically and psychologically in order to join that alternative world of art and music where he believed he belonged. Such a move inevitably courts guilt and creates in the subject the further need to deal with it somehow unless, of course, the subject is willing to accept the break as final and complete, to walk away, pay the price, and never look back. This, as we shall see, Stokowski was neither willing nor able to do since his affection for his kin, if nothing else, would not permit him to do so. And even after emigrating to the United States, the conductor paid yearly visits to his English family.

The young Stokowski's second problem centered on the future. It concerned his need for legitimacy in the world of serious music toward which he was headed. Logically, Stokowski's past and his future could have been linked through the use of a classic model: that of the poor but talented and ambitious youngster who not only does not hide his past, but glories in it as a sign of his ability to rise above humble origins as an upwardly mobile artist with a mission to perform. Arturo Toscanini, the son of an obscure Italian tailor, is a good case in point, since he was proud of his heritage as the poor boy who made good. But Stokowski's temperament and psychological need were as unlike those of Toscanini as their music making would eventually be, and so the classic common sense model could not be used.

Stokowski's aristocratic sense of his own worth, his "uncommon sense" as he called it, and his psychological need for romantic trappings all dictated against the solid but prosaic model that had admirably suited Toscanini. Stokowski as a young man needed the internal assurance necessary to project that princely artistic aura that came so naturally to him. Others might be artistically legitimate by birth, by training, or by simply rising through their own efforts, but the evidence indicates that Stokowski required an internalized sense of legitimacy wedded to his musical ability and to that peculiarly romantic and aristocratic role in music that the prince was wont to fashion for himself. Alas, such a model was threatened by the reality that his background was not continental but English, and nondescript in addition.

While his name was continental European, his accent marked him as English, and "non-U" English at that. To make matters worse, his new world of music shared the same city—London—as his old childhood world. Even when graduated from the Royal College of Music and choir master and organist of St. Mary's Church in Charing Cross Road, Stokowski could be shamed to tears by the behavior of his mother when she appeared at St. Mary's. In the presence of the rector and the choir, Mrs. Annie Marion Moore Stokowski, in her son's eyes at least, made a spectacle of herself by vulgarly asserting that the position was beneath her son's abilities. Learning to fit the model of style, manners, and speech necessary for a young musician on the rise, the last thing Stokowski wanted or needed was a defense of his abilities put forward out of the past that he must leave. This was true for Stokowski no matter how much he loved his mother and family. Legitimacy of image was impossible when his childhood world intruded so rudely into the world he aspired to. But as long as he was in London, it was likely that this same sort of thing would happen again.[35]

Having already moved out of his parents' home and into an apartment of his own at eighteen, it was Stokowski's luck at this crucial juncture to be offered the position of organist at New York's prestigious St. Bartholomew's Church. In 1905 the Reverend Leighton Parks, rector of the church, had come to the Royal College of Music seeking a choir director and organist for St. Barts. Stokowski was recommended by his teachers, and after hearing him perform, Parks offered him the appointment.[36] Stokowski's acceptance gained him physical escape from London and his past as well as the chance to prove who he *really* was on the figurative frontier of musical New York and, after that, in Cincinnati and Philadelphia.

How did he relate to his family in England following his emigration to America? Publicly he made nothing of their existence, but privately he, and then he and his wife Olga Samaroff Stokowski, visited them nearly every year until 1923, when he was divorced from Madam Samaroff.

The divorce, whose causes included Stokowski's infidelity, caused a bitter row within the family and led to an estrangement between the maestro and his blood kin, an estrangement in which they, not he, had taken the lead. After 1923, while he visited his mother at intervals—his father died in 1924—he had no further contact with his brother Percy John Stock for fifty years, until 1974. Later contacted by Oliver Daniel, who was working on his biography of Stokowski, Stock wrote Daniel that he believed his brother had finally sought him out because of shame over his treatment of the family and made contact by way of amends. Even so, Stock recalled for Daniel, during their childhood the family sacrifices were always for "Leo" and his music, and there was nothing left for either himself or Lydia.[37]

Stokowski's second wife, Evangeline Johnson, recalled for Oliver Daniel that at the time of their marriage in 1926, Stokowski denied that he had any family at all in England, and only by accident did the second Mrs. Stokowski later learn about the conductor's mother and brother. Why did he keep them a secret? She ventured the possibility that he was ashamed of them. That she did learn of them was due to Sonya Stokowski. Even following her divorce from Stokowski, Olga Samaroff and daughter Sonya had kept in touch regularly with Stokowski's mother—Sonya's grandmother—and some years later when Evangeline and the maestro took Sonya to England with them, Sonya telephoned her grandmother in Evangeline's presence. This was how Evangeline Stokowski first learned the truth. As for Sonya Thorbecke née Stokowski's own recollection, she told Oliver Daniel that it was amazing to her that Evangeline could have been married to her father all that time and not know, but added by way of explanation that her father had a way of employing fantasy on his own family background, in keeping with his temperamental and psychological style as what she called the "complete romantic." In another conversation with biographer Daniel,

Mrs. Thorbecke reported that she felt her father would really have liked a more romantic fairy-tale-like background, one in which he was washed ashore in a strange country, seemingly a simple castaway, but in reality a "prince."[38]

Even stranger was Gloria Vanderbilt's experience with the fantasy of Stokowski's English family. During their whirlwind 1945 courtship, Stokowski told Vanderbilt that both his parents had been Polish born as he was, but that his mother, Maria, had died while he was still a baby. As a tragic result of her death, he continued, he was sent to England where he had to live with "strangers," finding affection and understanding from only one person, the nursemaid who took care of him. Stokowski's account ended there. He would say no more and Vanderbilt was left with the reaction that his childhood was so traumatic that he couldn't share more of it with her then, but that with growing trust between them, Stokowski would be able to tell her the whole story. A year or so later, according to her account in *Black Knight, White Knight*, Stokowski, in a meditative mood, spoke to her about sharing his secret, swearing her to secrecy. Fervently promising to keep his secret (she would later remember that they were truly close to each other in that moment) she was shut out as soon as she had made her promise. She immediately felt Stokowski pulling away. The passage ends with the young wife intuitively linking Stokowski's reticence about his past with fear of betrayal should he tell her the mystery of himself. She follows this insight with a declaration that the strength of her love would ultimately break through his defenses and make him truly hers.[39]

Once more in her book, twenty pages and five years later, she directly recounts her experience with the mystery of Stokowski's origins. With Gloria Vanderbilt Stokowski by his side, the maestro had in 1951 returned to conduct in England for the first time since 1912. In this setting of triumphant return in London, after a successful concert with the Royal Philharmonic Orchestra, Stokowski could bring himself to invite Vanderbilt to meet someone important to him—someone in Bournemouth. As to the person's identity, Stokowski would give no answer at all until the next day on the train. Even then, she writes, he answered her query about whom they were going to see indirectly in fantasy language from that core of his being she had never been able to enter. After a long silence, looking out the train window rather than at Vanderbilt, Stokowski said that the person they were going to visit was the English nurse who had cared for him when he was small, after his Polish mother died, adding that she now lived in a nursing home. Vanderbilt responded by asking her name. Stokowski's answer was dead silence.[40]

The person was, of course, Stokowski's mother, but Vanderbilt did not know that then and refused to go to the nursing home with him, angry at his secrecy, his indirectness, and his lack of trust. So the one chance Stokowski had of bringing his personal family fantasy and objective reality together in a meeting of his mother and his wife was lost, as was his chance of sharing the reality of his origins with Vanderbilt.

She would write later that she wished she'd behaved differently, thinking that perhaps it was some peculiar test of Stokowski's to see if she were really worthy of his trust. But how could she have behaved differently facing Stokowski's psychological inability to forsake his fantasy, let himself go, and let his beloved learn the reality of his past. Vanderbilt later felt she had let him down in not meeting his test. It is clear that at the time Stokowski believed very much the same thing, albeit from a strange and psychologically unusual vantage point. Their dilemma was summed up by total silence during the ride back to London—a silence that would grow over the next four years into separation and divorce. Yet Vanderbilt later wrote that she still loved him and knew that he had loved her, that the tragedy was that Stokowski was truly unable to open himself up, to share and to trust when it came to consideration of his background and of his innermost thoughts and feelings.[41]

In tones ranging from humor to anger to the poignancy of Gloria Vanderbilt's statement, Stokowski's immediate family members and wives, then, report on his psychologically strange relationship to his English blood kin. Alienation, shame, guilt, fantasy, romanticism, and loss—they are all there to such an extent that past explanations of Stokowski's fantasizing as mere whimsical mischief pale when justaposed to Stokowski's fantasy memory of growing up with "strangers."

But what about the New World–developed accents—Stokowski spoke standard English when he arrived in 1905—and their relationship to those mythical stories, "Personal truths" he would later call them, of a childhood that didn't exist? Early beginnings of the Stokowski Polish connection came with Madam Samaroff, whose own career as a concert pianist was aided by her name change from Lucie Hickenlooper to Olga Samaroff. In helping Stokowski prepare press material on himself during their early years together, no name change was necessary, but what she did stress was emphasis on his Polish heritage as an assist to his career. Following their marriage in 1911 and leading up to his assumption of the Philadelphia conductorship in 1912, Madam Samaroff effectively helped Stokowski use the press to establish the budding maestro as a Pole, albeit one who spoke perfect English.[42]

With Stokowski safely at the helm of the Philadelphia Orchestra and with his great talent to speak for him, there was no further need for the squibs that had paved his way. Madam Samaroff's Polish press campaign had done its job and, as in the cases of scores of musicians, actors, and writers over the years, the early publicity hype could be left behind to be joked about, even as Olga Samaroff openly and with considerable humor was able to talk about the reasons for her name change.

While it would be impossible for professional reasons for one practicing medicine ever to admit he or she had no M.D. or for the professor to admit to having no Ph.D., the actor, entertainer, or musician altering his or her name or background to break into the world of art or entertainment can later admit that alteration and joke about it, as did Jack Benny (Benny Kabelsky) or John Garfield (Jules Garfinkle). The sophisticated and glamorous actor Cary Grant could admit his humble English origins as Archie Leach and be none the worse for it. The same would have been possible for Stokowski, had he psychologically been able to accept that option.

There are those who argue that Stokowski was ensnared into life-long fibbing to match the press releases of 1911 and 1912. But these people, who point to examples of others who must keep lying life-long in order to cover M.D.'s not earned or college degrees not received as analogous to Stokowski's situation, fail to understand the difference between psychological need and economic greed, between the imperative of psychic self-assurance and the fear of criminal prosecution or job loss due to false professional claims.

Stokowski did not joke about his earlier Polish transformation and reject it. But he was not trapped by it; he wanted and needed it. Why? Because it provided him with a psychologically satisfying, if objectively bizarre, solution to the problem of his own background. This growing psychological set provided him with both a protective wall around his own sense of insecurity and continental European trappings that symbiotically meshed with Stokowski's own romantic sense of who he really was.

What Madam Samaroff began for publicity purposes was, over time, accepted by Stokowski as part of his identity and then broadened and elaborated by him for very personal reasons. As time passed the accents came more frequently and more heavily during the Philadelphia years, according to his personal secretary, Ruth O'Neill.[43] The stories of the mythical childhood and ancestry, going back to General Stokowski, the village of Stokki, his grandfather the freedom fighter, the death of Mother Maria, and Stokowski's exile among "strangers"—all of these fantasies multiplied even as Stokowski coined any number of words that phonetically satisfied this self-created central European, although they rang peculiarly in the ears of both Stokowski's friends and enemies: words phonetically sounding like *blooz* for blouse, *Eedaho* for Idaho, *Cadiyac* for Cadillac, *geerahf* for giraffe, *meestah* for mister, *Fantaseeah* for Fantasia, *archeev* for archive, and *meekraphone*, and *seekological*, and *Hoostohn* and on and on and on.

An apocryphal legend about the maestro, one that circulated for many years, particularly among Stokowski bashers, was that as a child his real name was Leo Stokes and that he later changed it to Stokowski. The core of truth to this story is far more delicious and ironic in view of Stokowski's re-Policization of himself. For it was doubtless Stokowski's mother who fit the boy with that name as a child as part of her campaign at de-Policization of the family. When Stokowski was nine or ten years old, he was known as Leo Stokes to young Sam Grimson and his brothers. He was a boy musician they considered a "sissy" and so was unworthy of inclusion in their childhood games. As mother Stokowski needed to stress the Englishness of her brood, thus escaping ethnic taint for practical reasons, so her son "Leo" would, years later, recapture a Polish heritage for needed artistic and psychological reasons,[44] even as his brother, Percy John, accepted the Anglicized bent of the family by using Stock as his last name because it was good for business.

What it meant for Stokowski was the re-creation of his own childhood in a romantic mold true to his own conception of himself and his identity. While such a re-creation came to provide psychological safety for the young musician, it came at a high price. What Stokowski called the "personal truths" about his past put him at the mercy of objective reality, and many chose to challenge his fantasy account of his antecedents. Further, such a romantic reconstruction replaced factual consistency with an autobiographical treatment that, on the face of it, was historically inconsistent to even the most casual student of dates and places. Stokowski's personal need for such a background was clearly greater for him than the objective dangers posed by his fantasies. The circumstantial evidence, then, indicates not a cunning and rational attempt to con the critics, but a romantic and emotionally needful effort on Stokowski's part to psychologically protect himself from his own real past even at the risk of censure, or worse, laughter from those who knew better. One might describe these stories and the skepticism with which they were met as the price Stokowski paid for following his star in the way he had to follow it!

What I am proposing is that the young Stokowski re-created his past in his own romantic image, while—as the evidence indicates—never losing memories of his real past and antecedents. Based on the evidence, I would judge that he believed these stories at the time of telling as naturally as he accepted his multiple accents as part of himself. In a 1968 Chicago radio interview, Stokowski was confronted with the documented biographical fact that his mother was English. He responded that it was easier for people to get information from encyclopedias than to get to the "*real truth*" (italics mine).[45]

I asked Abram Chasins if he believed that Stokowski self-consciously fabricated these stories or if he felt that Stokowski believed them in the telling? Without hesitation Mr. Chasins answered that on the basis of his experience with the maestro, he felt that Stokowski really did believe his fantasies when he recounted them.[46]

Turning for a moment to a more traditional explanation of these eccentricities, why couldn't one assume—as many critics have—that such attributes were the calculated poses of the charlatan or the tricks of the poseur?[47] I believe that no real confidence man would tell the story of Sonya's doll or of his grandfather in the context that Stokowski did, since he would be—and in Stokowski's case was—found out and made to seem ludicrous or would be patronized as a buffoon, no matter how able he was. If there is one thing the confidence man and the phony share beyond seeming to be what they aren't, it is their great concern that their claims *not* seem to be contradictory to the facts. So far afield was Stokowski from successful flimflam that he gave hostile critics their very best arguments against him through behavior and stories of this kind. Critics of the conductor needed never to come to grips with the music and musicianship of Stokowski; they had only to make him out to be a charlatan and then, by association, make similar claims about his career and music. And, of course, this was often done, creating a stereotypical image of an extraordinary and complex artist that has lasted for better than fifty years. Furthermore, there is not one piece of historical or psychological evidence to indicate that Stokowski might have neurotically courted such ridicule. Nothing in his career or in his person indicates a compulsion to be laughed at or patronized. He took himself seriously and courted a public opinion that would evaluate his career in the same way.

The multiple accents, often succeeding each other in a single conversation, are the worst proof possible of charlatanry, since on the face of it, consistency of pose—including assumed speech patterns—is imperative for the poseur.

One need not be a clinical analyst to begin making sense of Stokowski's seeming contradictions while questioning current cliché stereotypes of the conductor. Historical common sense coupled with psychological good sense will do for a start at least. But in using interdisciplinary sense to reject now very traditional explanations of Stokowski's fantasizing, one is yet left with the need to put an alternative explanation into a credible framework.

Is there such a well-known and accepted historical-psychological context in Western culture within which an alternative Stokowski hypothesis could be seen as realistic, likely, and understandable? There is.[48] In history and folklore it is commonly referred to as the *changeling* concept or motif. It is as common in Western history as is the legend of Faust and his bargain with the devil. It is as old as the prehistorical myths of our culture and as recent as Maurice Sendak's provocative children's book *Outside Over There*. It is as symbolic in meaning as the fairy tales of goblins stealing human beings for their own wicked purposes while leaving identical substitutes, that is, changelings, in their places. At the same time the motif is as psychologically real and modern as the new mother who is so sure that she has been given the wrong baby at the hospital that no one can talk her out of it; likewise, the child who is sure that he or she is really adopted because of some deep-rooted estrangement, some sense of basic difference between that child and his or her parents. Central European, Western European, and Scandinavian folklore abound with accounts of changelings. In one classic variant it is the real son or daughter who has been stolen, with a double left in its place. In the other major variant, it is the family that is believed by a child to have been switched, and it is the child who must suffer unless and until action is taken to restore his or her rightful family and heritage. Even the wicked stepmother so prominent in Western fairy tales is related to the changeling in that the theme shares the poignance of the child bereft of one or both of his *real* parents.[49]

As with all the motifs of myth, legend, and fairy tale, the changeling had its roots in human need and reality. Its substance and trappings became the stuff of legend because the human reality on which it was based was widespread over a long period of time and because it was poignant enough to warrant symbolic treatment in the lore of a people.[50] In short, the reality of the changeling was a part of human life and identity long before the creation of modern psychology.

The changeling, rich with historical and emotional freight, yet ambiguous in analytical terms, would first be accepted for modern clinical study and be given a psychological cutting edge by Sigmund Freud in his essay "Family Romances." Since then and up to this generation, other analysts have extended and refined the concept of the "family romance" to explain not only much in childhood behavior but much in the behavior of romantic and highly creative people who show a high incidence of creating family romances together with dual identities. The so-called normal identity allows the romancer to identify with family and the realities of every day life; the artistic identity is based on a self-protective rearrangement of that reality for psychological purposes. (Please see the appendix for a more detailed discussion of both the concept up-dated by recent analytic work and its relationship to Stokowski's behavior and art. I have placed this material in an appendix because it relates to materials in other chapters as well as this one.)

The contemporary child psychologist Dr. Bruno Bettelheim describes the family romance as a "rearranged reality" necessary for the psychological protection of some people. Out of shame, guilt, fear, or differentness an individual constructs a family romance centered on the idea that the subject is living or has lived in a family that is not his or her own. The individual believes that in reality he or she is the progeny of a more important or more notable person or family, but that negative circumstances have separated the subject from that real heritage and forced him or her to live with persons only claiming to be family. It is common for such a subject to recognize and proclaim this family romance as truth under psychological pressure to do so and as fantasy when no psychological threat is posed by the objective truth of family reality.[51]

Germane to my purposes are both the reality and the fantasy of an artistic young Englishman, a prince transplanted to America's shore, creating his own family romance because of just such psychological pressure. Affection for his real family notwithstanding, Stokowski's sense of his own differentness from that family, his shame at what he believed to be his shabby background—even his guilt at such feelings—coupled with his own burning ambition, became the *reality* of his creative life. His own princely conception of himself mirrored by many around him and his romantic creation of a mythologized family, that is, a family romance, became the *fantasy*. The connecting link between the two, the emotional motive leading from reality to family romance, lay in Stokowski's dualistic relationship to his English kin. On what could be described as the normal human level of identity, Stokowski felt and showed filial affection for his family, but as the family romancer, with a self-created sense of artistic identity, Stokowski could reject his real family as truly his—substituting a romanticized, a rearranged reality of kinship for his genuine English family. The psychological basis for this second identity, with its mother Maria, loving grandfather, and so on, lay in Stokowski's need for family that matched his artistic identity, since his real family members did not meet his artistic and emotional needs nor live up to his own high expectations of what they should be in order to *live up to him!* These characteristics are quite typical of the creative family romancer (see Appendix).

Could a person of Stokowski's temperament, with his gift for fantasy, both know and function on the objective truth of his background and yet on occasion present the alternative "personal truths" of a family romance, believed by the teller in the telling, but at wide variance with reality? Further, could such a person as Stokowski maintain the desired personal truths of the past parallel with the past of reality and do so without serious interference in his successful functioning as a responsible professional? The answer is yes, given what we know about the psychoanalytic framework of the family romance itself and given what we know about Stokowski and the circumstantial evidence of his life and career.[52] Then there is negative evidence indicating that Stokowski, throughout his long career, would have been much less exposed to both hostile criticism and laughter because of his accents and stories of childhood if he had avoided these creations. That he did not do so, but instead unintentionally courted ridicule by his continued reliance upon them through a long and creative career, indicates five elements of a practical hypothesis to the historian: (1) that recreation of his family and background in a family romance was imperatively needed by Stokowski; (2) that the accents and family stories were at the time of telling and use real to Stokowski; (3) that Stokowski's continued reliance on his family romance is evidence of a vivid romanticism wedded to fantasy, but not of charlatanry; (4) that he was not creatively incapacitated by his psychological eccentricities nor by his romanticism; and (5) that his later romantically personalized and often unique readings of symphonic works were related to the same roots as his romantically personalized conception of his own past and identity (a subject I have touched on in the Appendix and in the Discography).

By the time Stokowski had proven himself in Cincinnati and had moved on to Philadelphia, he could look at his life so far as artistically successful. But with this success came regular contact with the wealthy leaders of the American urban social world, with European born musicians whose roots lay in the class structure, the culture, and the musical training of continental Europe, and with largely European born and trained soloists whose lineage and sophistication dwarfed his own.[53] In this milieu, however strange one might objectively find Stokowski's romances and accents, they proved psychologically valuable to the transplanted Englishman of modest origins now in regular contact with the cultural crème de la crème.

Stokowski could and did prove himself professionally in Cincinnati and Philadelphia. His daring led him early to innovative programming and to championing American music and musicians in an America still dominated by central European—particularly German—music and musicians. Indeed, the young Stokowski by example and deed helped break the hold of German trained musicians—Stock, Van Der Stucken, Henschel, Gericke, Paur, Muck, Damrosch, Seidl, Mahler, and Weingartner—on conducting in the United States. Years after their divorce, Olga Samaroff Stokowski would look back on her ex-husband's performance as a turning point in American symphonic music. No longer would the importation of middle-aged European conductors be the seeming imperative it had been prior to Stokowski's arrival as an American conductor.[54] However, Stokowski's sense of his own musical accomplishment was still compromised by his personal past, no matter what he achieved in music. More musical accomplishment was insufficient to overcome this peculiar insecurity.

How different Stokowski was from his first wife Olga Samaroff, the Texas born Lucie Hickenlooper. Madam Samaroff could admit that she had adopted her concert name because, as a woman and as an American pianist, the name Hickenlooper did not provide entrée to the world's concert halls as did the impressive pseudonym she adopted for herself. While she humorously admitted the truth about her origins, the Stokowski of the early Philadelphia period was beginning to exhibit those personal truths about *his* origins. And even though some would glimpse that underlying level of insecurity, that sense of inferiority papered over by his family romance, the conductor could hopefully and gamely believe he was all of a piece—past, present, and future.[55]

It was no charlatan nor poseur who joined the musical greats of Europe for intimate 1916, 1917, and 1918 summer vacations at Bar Harbor, Maine, with the likes of pianists Joseph Hoffman, Ossip Gabrilowitsch, Harold Bauer,and Leopold Godowsky, conductors Karl Muck, Frank Damrosch, and Bruno Walter, dancer Vaslay Nijinsky, violinist Fritz Kreisler, harpist Carlos Salzedo, and cellist Hans Kindler. With the exception of Harold Bauer, who was London born, all of the others had roots in continental European music and tradition.[56] Into this milieu a thirty-four-year-old Stokowski moved in 1916, confident of his ability to hold his own. For he naturally had intelligence and musical skills to match the best of this assemblage and was in the process of creating a continental background to match. If there were those in this distinguished company who had their doubts about Stokowski's background, the young conductor could now hope to ignore such skepticism. He had begun the creation of his true identity at twelve. It was in the process of completion by age thirty-four. It pleased and satisfied the only person Stokowski answered to throughout his long life—himself.

The preceding paragraph, however much it looks like the natural ending to this chapter, is really a penultimate conclusion, for there is that reality parallel to Stokowski's buoyancy to be recorded, a reality that he would carry with him as long as he used those accents and family fantasies to fend it off. It is fitting, I think, to end this section with that parallel shadow side, as described by someone who knew Stokowski in the twenties and recognized the maestro's psychological fragility.

In 1924, Louisa Miller née Knowlton was a young student of cello in the first class of the newly formed Curtis Institute of Music in Philadelphia. The school was closely related to the Philadelphia Orchestra and, until Artur Rodzinski joined the staff to train the Curtis orchestra, Stokowski doubled as conductor of the institute orchestra as well as the Philadelphia Orchestra. Mrs. Miller was able to observe Stokowski in that capacity. Furthermore, as the protégée and companion of Michel Penha, first cellist of the Philadelphia Orchestra, she observed Stokowski off-duty at parties and social events. During our first interview, Mrs. Miller dealt mainly with Stokowski as conductor. At our second session, when I raised the charges made about Stokowski over the years—that he was a phony and a charlatan—and asked Mrs. Miller to comment, she was very clear in saying those labels didn't describe what she saw in Stokowski. He was a "showman" all right. He was always "on," but not as one attempting to convince people of musical gifts that he didn't have. Musical genius and imagination he had in full measure plus the confidence to use them.

However, it was as though these gifts weren't ever enough, and for some reason Stokowski had to prove himself 150 percent all of the time to cover some sense of personal inadequacy that he alone felt real. His stories, accents, and aristocratic airs seemed to Mrs. Miller not the pose of the phony, but the need of a gifted but insecure human being. "You accepted the airs and the accents as part of his style. That was Stoki."[57]

Stokowski's second wife, Evangeline, was more blunt in making the same point in conversation with Abram Chasins, describing Stokowski's sense of insecurity as inconceivable.[58]

2
The Eyes and Ears Have It

In the eyes and ears of Hector Berlioz, his ideal—and huge—symphony orchestra in performance would not be the sum of its orchestral parts nor of its individual instrumentalists, no matter how gifted. It would transcend such pluralism to become, itself, an instrument of such power, range, and color that within its music making,

> would dwell a wealth of harmonies, a variety of tone qualities . . . which can be compared to nothing hitherto achieved in Art. Its repose . . . majestic as the slumber of ocean . . . it's agitations would recall the tempests of the tropics; it's explosions the outbursts of volcanoes; therein would be found the plaints, the murmurs, the mysterious sounds of primeval forests; the clamors, the prayers, the songs of triumph or of mourning of a people with expansive soul, ardent heart, and fiery passions; . . . its crescendo spread roaringly—like a stupendous conflagration. . . . In the thousand combinations practicable with . . . the orchestra we have just described would dwell a wealth of harmony, a variety of qualities in tone . . . beside the radiant colors which this myriad of different qualities in tone would give at every moment.[1]

The colors, voices, and emotions shared by this orchestra are to be found, writes Berlioz, by experimenting with combinations of instruments—large and small—within the orchestra. The exuberant Berlioz then proceeds to demonstrate with eight such groupings to illustrate the following: melancholy, gloom, religious mourning, calm gravity, shrillness, pomposity, brilliance and voluptuousness, joy, menace, and the sinister, but ends noting it as impossible to enumerate the myriad sound combinations possible—exclamation point.[2]

The variables of performance involved, writes Berlioz, include as well the acoustics of the hall, its size and shape, for ". . . it is impossible to indicate arbitrarily the best method of grouping the

. . . performers" except in relationship to the place of performance and to its peculiar sound properties.[3]

Berlioz, arch-romantic and musical innovator, indirectly raised certain questions in his vivid description of the dream orchestra. What effect on performance had the seating arrangement of players and the size and shape of the concert hall? How could the myriad pluralisms of so many orchestra members be transcended and transformed into the monistic glory of the orchestra-as-instrument he described? How could those musicians, as one, encompass the range of orchestra colors, emotions, and dynamics, and beyond these the pictorial expressiveness demanded by Berlioz, particularly when the emotional expressivity demanded by the musical score could only be approximated by performance indicators in the score? Analogically similar is the problem of the play director, faced with the playwright's directions for performance, yet often convinced to go beyond them interpretively in order to make the play *play*.

Berlioz's tropical tempest and his volcanic eruption would musically have to approximate the unexpected surge of hurricane winds and rain in the one case and, in the other, that combination of natural grandeur and destruction that is spontaneously produced by volcanic eruption. In terms of life and nature, a racing heart and pumping adrenaline would seem closer to the mark than the orderly measure of the musical score no matter how spirited and well marked. The same is essentially true of Berlioz's nonpictorial demands on his orchestra. The "prayers and mourning" and the "triumph and fiery passion" demanded by the composer are either emotional states in and of themselves or related states induced by intense personal feeling. As such they require, respectively, a musical translation of personal communion with God, the strangled and jagged cry of grief, and the ecstasy of sexual union, which has its own physical tempo of passion, lust, and climax at once ecstatic and savage. As to the plaintive or melancholy side of mourning, how are more than a hundred instrumentalists to play beyond themselves and their own experience in order to capture that sense of loss and of the lost that is the gray heart of what might have been? A broken heart with all of its physical and emotional signs is an exquisitely painful and difficult physical state to reproduce musically by even the best of players.

The spontaneity, the feeling, the free use of sound-as-color-as-emotion-as-life required by Berlioz's demands of the orchestra certainly go beyond the limitations of the score markings of even so great a piece as the *Symphonie Fantastique*, no matter how carefully marked. But one can be sure that Berlioz was aware of that in writing his description of the dream orchestra, just as he knew that in touching up his own scores for performance and in exhorting his players for yet closer approximations of human grief or ardor, he was reaching for the romantic ultimate. Quite clearly the issues he raised called for innovation, daring, and imagination as great in orchestral playing as he had shown in his most inspired compositions.

Not everyone then or now would accept Berlioz's romantic orchestral ideals, centering as they do on the emotional, the coloristic, and the sensual side of music rather than on its tradition, order, and architecture, nor on his technical concerns with acoustics and orchestral seating. Even Berlioz's life style, his loves, and his music inspired a love-hate relationship between himself and his countrymen that echoes today. But for those tuned to the Berlioz paragon of orchestral possibility in sound and emotion, how clear is the link between his conception of orchestral performance, the questions it raises, and that most romantic of modern conductors, Leopold Stokowski. In both his writings and his music making the maestro paralleled Berlioz's romantic musical concerns. Not only did Stokowski share many of Berlioz's orchestral ideas, but he attempted to put a number into practice. The degree of the conductor's success as orchestral innovator not only created a modern love-hate relationship for Stokowski in the twentieth-century musical world, but forced the asking of several questions about Stokowski's style—love it or hate it—that paraphrased Berlioz's orchestral concerns of long ago.

How did Stokowski succeed in making orchestral players and even soloists play beyond their measured abilities? How was he able to form several orchestras, each in a short period of time, that played with the color, flexibility, precision, and passion associated with the Philadelphia Orchestra of the twenties and thirties? Further, how could he, as visiting conductor with long-established orchestras, change their sound and expressivity almost immediately with few or no words volunteered as to what he wanted? Then, too, why was Stokowski so willful in both the performance and recording of traditional standards? His willfulness included not only considerable score alteration, but idiosyncratic interpretations that varied from all others and indeed from Stokowski performance to Stokowski performance.

And that leads to a further question. How was he able to get a hundred-piece orchestra, rehearsed to perform a piece one way, to "follow conductor" in another direction at performance time and to do so flawlessly?

These questions, it seems to me, are interrelated to each other and to Stokowski's strange sense of his own identity and his conception of music and of orchestral performance generally. On this latter point, Stokowski could be as romantically larger-than-life as Berlioz. In his book *Music for All of Us*, Stokowski describes what the orchestra must be able to do in a chapter called "The Heart of Music." Musical expression must range from "the most subtle and tender to the most white-hot intensity." It must express "burning passion," "exalted love . . . free from passion," "humor," "sunny gaiety," the "elegiac," "dreamlike ecstasy," "masculine vigor," "screaming black fury," "morbid despair," "elemental vitality," and "melancholy." "All of this is only an infinitesimal fraction of the emotions that come from the heart of music . . . from true inner feeling. . . . Music must have true and deep feeling to make it spontaneous and eloquent. Only then will it reach the heart of those who are listening to it."[4]

While there are no tempests or volcanoes here, the emotional and intuitive sentiment is analogous to that of Berlioz. "Intellectual mastery" and "technique," as in Berlioz, are included, but assumed as technical means to sounding emotional ends. Accomplishing these ends is the job of the conductor and orchestra, reaching the "true inner feeling" of the composer through their own feelings. But the key job of re-creating the work lies with the conductor since he or she must infuse the orchestra with that intent and make one hundred performers act as one in projecting it—an interpretation of purpose closer to the mainstream tradition of drama than of music.

It would seem then that the first question to approach is, Who was Stokowski as a musician? Is there some unifying theme to his professional life, some key to his personality that can move us beyond the enigma he has so often been called? In his fine book *Leopold Stokowski: A Profile*, Abram Chasins uses paradox as the major theme of his work with the enigmatic Stokowski seen over and over again as a creature of contrasts and contradictory opposites. Oliver Daniel's thousand-page treasure chest, *Stokowski: A Counterpoint of View*, does not develop this theme as such, nor does the author attempt to analyze Stokowski, but in its immense range of new data on the conductor his work presents the same kinds of contradictions and paradoxes noted by

Chasins and increases them five fold. In his laudatory review of Daniel's book, *New York Times* critic Richard Dyer called attention to this fact, ending his review by pointing out that with all the information provided by Daniel on the maestro, Stokowski remained an inexplicable entity, a mysterious "X" for the undetermined.[5]

The dilemma posed by Stokowski for the biographer is quite clearly explained by yet a third writer working on a biographical study of the maestro. Mr. William Trotter notes first that there is still much factual information about the maestro that is lacking, but more important, we cannot get to the heart, "the essence," of the man because, writes Mr. Trotter,

> there is no essence . . . and the more I attempt to penetrate the enigmas and contradictions, the ambiguities and paradoxes, the more certain I become that there is no central nucleus whose discovery . . . will serve to pull the paradoxes together. . . . [There is] rather an assortment . . . a kaleidoscope . . . of psychic . . . elements . . . held together in the matrix of force that was Stokowski's will.[6]

The dilemma then is real for Chasins, Daniel, Trotter, and others. It has certainly been real for me as well, but my point of concentration on Stokowski has been narrower than that of his biographers. My job has been less arduous since I was not writing a biography, but attempting to explore and explain some of Stokowski's mysteries, often subjecting biographical information already presented to analysis so as to determine what it meant in the pattern of Stokowski's career.

Notice that Mr. Trotter, even while denying some central theme or focus to Stokowski's life, does write that the kaleidoscope of elements in Stokowski's career was held by the grip of his will even as the kaleidoscopic picture changed. Thirty-five years ago one of the shrewdest of Stokowski watchers, Mr. Charles O'Connell, phrased much the same thing in describing the conductor as the classic egocentric or egoist, a person who could be decent, understanding, tolerant, loving, and kind in all things that did not interfere with his main concerns. However, in reaching his core goals the maestro had no sympathy with what he considered weaknesses or flaws in either himself or others. He was, wrote O'Connell, quite capable of using any tactic and all of those around him to achieve his ends and to discard people and tactics when their usefulness ended.[7]

In 1976, a ninety-four-year-old Stokowski, delighted with his new Columbia recording contract—a contract that would carry him to his hundredth birthday—was feted in his London hotel suite by his friends Natalie Bender and Oliver Daniel. Over a bottle of sherry the three friends talked of the contract, of new music, and of future recordings. At one point, recounts Daniel, "I made some rather elaborate but sincere comments about his genius as a conductor. He stopped me with a wave of his hand . . . and said, 'No, no Oliver. You must remember that I am a very modest man.' At this there was a ripple of laughter. . . ." Daniel responded, "You are not modest Leopold. You are egocentric and have been all your life." At that [Stokowski] said, "Then I probably should say I'm egocentric."[8]

Several months later Stokowski was filmed in the last public interview he was ever to give. Recorded by CBS television with Dan Rather as interviewer, one of the several surprises of the show was Stokowski's frank admission that he was "egocentric." Rather lamely responded that everybody had a degree of that but rallied as interviewer to ask the maestro if egocentrism was the force that had kept his ambitions so prominent over a long life? "No," responded the conductor, adding that he had tried the reverse and been bored by it.[9]

In this repartee we get a startling—and I think true—admission of Stokowski's lifelong egoism, almost immediately shielded from Rather's follow-up probe by a typical bit of Stokowskian legerdemain.

It seems to me that Stokowski dodged Rather's question linking his egoism to his musical aspirations precisely because it was so close to the mark, and Stokowski at that point intended no more personal admissions on top of what he had volunteered, a habit of long standing.

It is enough, anyway, for if we measure his admission together with the shrewd insights of Stokowski watchers over the years and add the myriad clues provided by his private life and his professional career, we have at least one solid theme or lifelong Stokowskian "essence" not subject to paradox, contradiction, or ambiguity. And we are dealing with egoism, not with egotism, although Stokowski could match egos with anyone. In the most strict and clinical definition egoism and its linguistic twin, egocentrism, refer to one's habitual practice of placing key personal interests above recognition of the values, interests, or attitudes of others. Egotism defines an excessive reference always to oneself. It is acted out with boastfulness, self conceit, and constant references to me! me! me!

In the preceding chapter and in the Appendix of this book we see Stokowski's psychologically reordered sense of origins and identity firmly based on the strength of his romantic will, in spite of the derision these traits evoked in the music community. One further step and we find the romantic egoist yoked in tandem to his lifelong love of music and to his sense of mission in music making. Stokowski's friend and colleague Sylvan Levin recalls that Stokowski was unique in pursuing his musical goals and ideals in that he was "fearless" in pursuit, whether the goal was performing the music he wanted to perform in Philadelphia, forming a new youth orchestra, or radically altering performance tradition. No matter how difficult the goal or seemingly unattainable the ideal, the maestro was not to be deterred or sidetracked into compromise. Even if temporarily beaten, he merely bided his time until he could resume pursuit of the whole loaf. Mr. Levin quite rightly, I think, notes the heroic in this trait.[10] In my own search for Stokowski's essence or core, I find that this iron-hard determination coupled always with music is also egoism wedded to the musical center of Stokowski's life, which was his core.

Over and over again throughout his life Stokowski referred to music's power and meaning as all-important and uniquely "mysterious" to him. "Music," he wrote, "is the voice of the All," a 1943 quotation he later made his epitaph in stone.[11] Of his own genesis he said that he had been a musician from birth, a fact he couldn't explain, but which had been apparent in him since earliest childhood. Of his ambition at the age of eighty-one he said that it was to improve his music making.[12] Of music as a companion to the ninety-two-year-old Stokowski he said that he heard music in his head constantly.[13] For *Time* magazine an ebullient Stokowski could report that at seventy-five he found music still mysterious in its restorative powers; the art gave more than it took from the artist; the art restored strength. To illustrate its pervasiveness, Stokowski continued that after a concert the music followed him home and into his bed, where he heard it as he waited for sleep. To Reginald Jacques of the BBC Stokowski could say that making music was a constant source of delight, that the word *work* had no relationship to it.[14] Nancy Shear, who was Stokowski's music librarian and confidante during the sixties and seventies, recalled his immersion in music as unique and based on a constantly fresh and childlike sort of pleasure, which after fifty years of music making had not slackened. Any mention of a work he felt close to would immediately alter him in mood and feeling. Oliver Daniel reported Stokowski as saying that his fantasy wish was for an eternal life devoted to playing music forever. Stokowski's friend and neighbor, conductor Andre Kostelanetz, recalled that the maestro at home was always preoccupied with music. When not concertizing, he could most often be found exploring scores old and new for their secrets. Even casual conversation would eventually lead to thoughts and talk of music. It was music that was the core of his life, and his response to it was always direct and childlike.[15]

For the close observer it is as though Stokowski were fueled and fed by music. His very pulse and body rhythms interchangeably commingled with the time and the rhythms of his latest concert piece, creating a very likely explanation for the idiosyncratic phrasing that marked many of his performances—most notably of Tchaikovsky. It would seem that music in his life—to use his own favorite word—was for "mysterious" purposes beyond his own rational cognition, but not beyond his intuitive perception. For those musical rationalists who are tempted to think this last sentence is gush and that what Stokowski said about the mystery of music was humbug, there is abundant evidence to the contrary; this evidence links Stokowski's major musical concerns to those of Berlioz a hundred years earlier, and provides some answers to questions about Stokowski's way with music and music making.

The least mysterious and most explicable concern of Stokowski, shared by the earlier Berlioz, bore directly on the sound of the orchestra as related to a concert hall's acoustics and to the seating arrangement of the orchestra in that hall. This triad was further complicated by the fact that, like finger prints, each hall was distinct in its acoustical character. Adding further sonic challenges to the maestro were the myriad sound characteristics that marked the great variety of pieces played and recorded by him over the years, which might require Stokowski to reseat an orchestra already reseated out of a traditional arrangement some two hundred years old.

The suggestion here is that Stokowski's unique way with orchestral sound was most easily approached in terms of the triple relationship of instrumental sound to seating to acoustics. Yet what seems clear cut is complicated by the varied characteristics of differing concert halls that the maestro conducted in, by his penchant to reseat the orchestra not only in tune with the auditorium's characteristics, but also, on occasion, with the sonic needs of particular compositions played. Further complications at Stokowski recording sessions had to do with adding and balancing into the mix decisions concerning the number of microphones to be used, microphone placement, the number of recording channels to be employed, sound levels to be used, sound takes to be chosen, and the eventual sound mixing to be done. Indeed, all of the technical matters affecting recorded sound concerned the maestro. In short, the permutations of performance and recorded sound were more than numerous and not easily approached at all.

However, while Stokowski regularly reseated orchestras he guest conducted, he did not reseat his own orchestra—be it Philadelphia, Houston, or the American Symphony Orchestra—for each concert.

Instead he evolved basic seating plans for his orchestras over the years, changed them over time and when very special concert fare called for special seating. In this way the many variables were made manageable. At the same time, Stokowski never stopped experimenting and evolving his own understanding of just how important instrumental seating was for performance and recorded sound.

His late career seating arrangement for the American Symphony Orchestra's performances in Carnegie Hall during the 1971–72 season varied from those of earlier seasons and varied even more from his Philadelphia Orchestra seating arrangements of the thirties. In 1971 Stokowski placed the brass at center stage in the extreme rear, with french horns in a row immediately in front of them. Percussion and tympani were placed at the right rear. To the conductor's far left along the wall ranged the basses in a line from stage front to stage rear. In front of the basses, running from stage front to abut against the horns, were the cellos. First and second violins were grouped to the conductor's immediate left, with the violas to his front and right in a row running as far back as the horns. Next on the conductor's right were the woodwinds in two ranks, running from stage front back to the tympani and percussion section in the right rear. Along the right stage wall were harp, celesta, one assumes the piano as needed, and more exotic instruments when called for.[16]

Even seating within the orchestra sections was given special attention by Stokowski, with his ear tuned to the results. A case in point is Elizabeth Neuburg, violinist, who played in the American Symphony Orchestra during its initial 1962–63 and 1963–64 seasons. Her eventual place in the orchestra's seating arrangement began with her initial audition for the maestro.

Ms. Neuburg described her audition with Stokowski as unusual because he was as much, if not more, impressed by her violin than by the violinist herself. Her instrument, a Guadagnini, was immediately recognized by Stokowski for its peculiar beauty of tone, over which he rhapsodized.

Once engaged for the orchestra, her place in the ensemble—her actual place in the seating arrangement—was determined by the way the Guadagnini sound would add to the overall sound of the orchestra when issuing from that particular point.

In his first season auditions, the conductor found one additional Guadagnini player and partnered him with Neuburg. Concluded Neuburg, "That's the way Stokowski was. He had a gift for linking instrumentalists and the sounds of their instruments to their physical placement within the orchestra. He did it to create beautiful sound combinations and it worked."[17]

As he treated the seating of orchestra members, so he treated matters acoustical. Stokowski was not willing to accept each concert hall he conducted in regularly as it stood. He made changes wherever he could to improve acoustical characteristics in matters of sound reflection, absorption, echo, and reverberation with a variety of baffles, acoustical panels, resonators, and reflectors.[18]

Concert halls so altered by Stokowski's acoustical additions included Philadelphia's Academy of Music, NBC's Studio 8-H—much to the chagrin of coconductor Arturo Toscanini—the Mecca Temple in New York City, Houston's concert hall, and New York City's Felt Forum.

One of the maestro's most interesting acoustical creations was the portable music reflector that he designed for use by his All American Youth Orchestra for their transcontinental American tour in 1941. As described and pictured in 1941, the reflector had three sides—right, left, and rear—made of plywood panels with a canvas top. The sides and top fanned up and out toward the audience, with internal support provided by four slender wooden pillars that vertically joined light horizontal wooden braces supporting the canvas top and the wiring for the reflector's internal lighting system. A narrow fencelike lattice work ran decoratively across the front and top of the reflector to break its severe outline. The whole affair was painted blue and subject to assembly and disassembly on notice.

Did it work? According to concert reviews in city after city where the orchestra played in civic auditoriums, outdoor arenas, and stadiums, the reflector worked very well. In Louisville, Kentucky, where Stokowski and company played in the State Fair

Pavilion, the *Louisville Courier Journal* reviewer reported a "tapestry" of exquisite music that carried throughout the pavilion, and added how struck he was by Stokowski's peculiar seating of his musicians within the reflector. With his strings located on risers at the back of the shell, Stokowski had brought his woodwinds and brasses to the front on either side of him. This was for a concert of Novacek, Tchaikovsky, Creston, and Wagner. The audience, invited by the maestro, joined in singing the *Star Spangled Banner* as an encore.[19]

This seating arrangement of 1941 was a variant on his 1939 "upside down" seating of Philadelphia Orchestra members in the Academy of Music. With woodwinds to center stage front—flutes and clarinets on the conductor's left; oboes, English horn, and bassoons on his right—Stokowski arranged his first and second violins, violas, and cellos in a semicircular tier behind the woodwinds, flanked by the trumpets on left stage front and the french horns on right stage front. On center stage rear were the double basses on risers, flanked, respectively, by the harps, tuba and trombones along the left stage wall from the rear to far left stage front. Along the far right wall ranged percussion and tympani from far right stage front back to the double basses.[20]

Coupled with the unusual player arrangement was an equally unusual stage setting in the form of an acoustical plywood reflector constructed around the sides and back of the academy's stage and flaring out to stage front like the mouth of a huge flower or the bell of a mighty horn. The reflector was designed by Stokowski to provide amplification for the string section, which he seated at the rear of the stage. The reflector contributed to the blending of string sound, but also projected it out into the hall. In this arrangement percussion, horns, trumpets, and trombones were given direct, unamplified playing access to the hall while the singing voices of the higher strings and the organlike sonorities of the double basses were boosted and projected to match and blend with the sharper voices of the winds and the more strident voices of the brass section. Shrewdly Stokowski chose his own transcription of the Bach Passacaglia and Fugue in C Minor as one of the pieces played within the reflector, since its voices were ideally suited to both the reflector's main strengths and the seating arrangement of the orchestra.[21]

Although this particular experiment of 1939 was ended by the return of Eugene Ormandy to the podium, one should remember that at least part of the beauty characterizing Stokowski's Philadelphia recordings of the thirties lay in his use of an acoustic resonator of his own design in the Academy of Music for recording purposes, as attested to by RCA chief engineer for those recordings, Charles O'Connell.[22]

Nor were Stokowski's experiments with seating and acoustic devices whimsical, as some have claimed. The basic ideas justifying such experiments can be found in his 1943 book, *Music for All of Us,* most poignantly described in Stokowski's frustration at a tradition of convenience and habit in orchestral seating, which, according to the maestro, had no sonic logic to it and actually violated the ways in which music was produced and projected by the several instruments. He pointed out that the french horn's sound was projected down and to the right of the player, while the tuba's sound was usually projected left and up. Violin tone rose from the f-holes, so if first and second violins faced each other with the conductor between the sections, as in traditional seating, the sound of the first violins would be projected toward the audience while the reverse would happen with the second violins, even as the light sound of the flute rose toward the ceiling. Continuing, the maestro wrote that all of the instruments produced different quantities and qualities of sound, from the delicate and retiring tone of the flute to the warriorlike blast of the trombone. Given these facts, concluded Stokowski, experimentation in seating the several instrumentalists and in achieving tonal balance was not only necessary but imperative. Immediately following this passage is his chapter on the need for acoustical reflectors![23]

While knowledge of acoustics and seating contributed to Stokowski's way with musical sound, his often idiosyncratic musical phrasing and his sense of color as color, and color in instrumental sound, represented the third element of a triad that was turned toward dramatic and musically story-telling ends.

In his only book, the maestro devoted a chapter to the relationship of "Music and Color," describing not only that tie but the story-telling link between color and particular pieces by Beethoven and Scriabin. Extending the connection to describe Tchaikovsky and Van Gogh as sharing like color characteristics and an "almost pathological intensity of emotional expression," In this same passage Stokowski indirectly described his own unique approach to musical interpretation. He was a conductor who controversially phrased music on the basis of feeling and who could recognize and superbly use orchestral color to realize dramatic and emotional musical ends.[24]

Pianist Oscar Levant once analogized Arturo Toscanini's way

with the music of Debussy and Richard Strauss to the use of the X ray. He wrote that the Italian conductor's literal concern with the distinctness of musical statement, with sounding each section in the orchestra at any given moment so that it could be clearly heard, provided a model of unparalleled musical transparency, but at the cost of orchestral color and music's "story telling element."[25]

Toscanini's polar opposite, Leopold Stokowski, just as clearly demonstrated his own analogical links, but at the expense of Toscanini's literalism and transparency. Stokowski's nonmusical ties to music making lay in his gift for fantasy and in his way with the drama of story telling. The artistic bridge between these gifts and actual music making was created by Stokowski's painterly use of color in musical story telling, enhanced, at least in his own mind, by the brush work of his phrasing of the score—idiosyncratic phrasing that often drove critics to distraction!

Again and again he cited the painter as his model in making music. It was a model whose closest links to music lay in the use of color, the brush strokes used in applying that color, and the sense of perspective used by the painter to tell his or her story. The painter focused on the subject here, provided background or relief there, and created dramatic tension with painterly counterpoint as the subject was engaged by other thematic material used to help tell the painting's story.[26]

The maestro extended the analogy when an interviewer asked him about his friendship with architect Frank Lloyd Wright. Stokowski enthusiastically described the water color design sketches of Wright as akin to the music of Debussy, for, as he put it, there were poetry and "dreams" alive in his work as well as architectural function. He was an "artist" as well as an architect.[27]

In a variety of ways the conductor's use of orchestral color and its role in musical story telling echoed not only Berlioz, but Stokowski's own conception of the musician as an artist with a dramatic story to tell.

On the practical performing level his coloristic vision related musically to both the sound of the whole orchestra in performance and the key roles played by instrumentalists with important solo or obbligato roles—Tabuteau, Phillips, Kincaid, Caston, and Schoenbach, among others.

Philadelphia first bassoonist Sol Schoenbach, in recalling his solo during the opening bars of Stokowski's symphonic synthesis of *Boris Godunov,* stressed Stokowski's twin senses of musical drama and instrumental color in asking from him just the right sound of desolation, just the right color, "drab and desolate," to set the stage for the ambitious usurper's tragic story. At Stokowski's insistence, Schoenbach tried reed after reed to catch the color of *Boris* in sound. Stokowski continued to respond, "No that's not the color." Many reeds and much time later the conductor stopped him, exclaiming that Schoenbach had found it—the perfect color in sound to open the story line of *Boris!* Schoenbach's comment was that other conductors he had worked with asked for more or less volume, or a sharper or flatter tone, but never the color deemed essential to the poetry and drama of a musical story. Schoenbach reported the same thing of the eerie bassoon solo that he played opening the Stravinsky *Rite of Spring* episode in *Fantasia*. He played the passage some forty times before Stokowski was satisfied with his phantasmal reading of it as well as with the sound track recording that had to pick up the bassoon's color just so.[28]

In the same vein, Philadelphia Orchestra violinist Sol Ruden remembered Stokowski's intense dislike for literalism in performance as a mechanical rehashing of notes on paper. Instead he strove for a spontaneous sound picture of the music as he imagined it and often described it to orchestra members. Recalled Ruden, he had great respect for the abilities of his players and empowered them with full freedom to bow or blow in their own way as long as they infused the music with the life necessary to create that sound picture.[29]

Edna Phillips, the distinguished harpist of the Philadelphia Orchestra during Stokowski's tenure, remembered the maestro's keen understanding of her instrument and its unique possibilities. Technically Stokowski considered the middle register of the harp nearly ideal with rich tone and warm color, but he was dissatisfied with the near inaudibility of the lower register and the lack of "resonant duration" in the high register. It was with these characteristics in mind that the maestro sent Ms. Phillips to the Philco Laboratories to work on improvements in the harp.[30]

Stokowski's technical interest in the harp was not an end in itself. As with acoustics, orchestral seating, and electronics, his technical interest in individual instruments was a means to a sounding end. He *heard* the harp as an emotional catalyst in the orchestra; its spirals and cascades of sound created warmth, color, and feeling unique in the ensemble, catalytically affecting and ennobling the other instrumentalists in their music making.

It was because of this sense of the harp's romantic color and its importance on joining orchestral elements together that Stokowski hoped to extend its range. As it was, he ingeniously used the instrument in his music making—listen to the emotionally powerful and hypnotic "Berceuse" by Sibelius (RCA LM 1238)—and asked much of the harpist in performance.

In a first rehearsal of one of his transcriptions, Phillips recalled, Stokowski asked her to produce a harmonic on her instrument that she believed was too high to reach. He answered, "Try it," and she retorted that it was not possible. Describing the incident later, Ms. Phillips said that the note requested shouldn't have sounded, but on trying over and over again at Stokowski's insistence, there it was. From her vantage point Ms. Phillips could remember Stokowski for challenging her to take nothing for granted in music, to question and try.[31]

Stokowski's admonitions to his players to be flexible, to feel free when playing, to combine color and feeling with their playing while avoiding the literal, the regimented, and the mechanical in performance are cited a number of times in this book. But particular attention should be paid to perhaps the best known expression of that philosophy as exhibited in Stokowski's approach to "free bowing" and "free breathing" as antidotes for what the maestro was wont to call "mee-kan-ical" playing.

Stokowski's practice of free bowing for his string players was introduced while he was still in Philadelphia, as were those breathing techniques for brass and woodwind players that provided a "seamless sound" for the maestro. The elimination of uniform bowing and breathing was for Stokowski a victory of orchestral color and musical vitality over the "standardization, regimentation . . . and all other conventions which tend to make an orchestra sound mechanical."[32]

By tradition uniform bowing was universal before Stokowski. It was a collective rule in which everyone in a particular string section bowed up and down in unison and in synchronization with their section leader, regardless of differences in hand size and strength, differences in training, and differences in their respective string instruments and in the bows used on them. Stokowski accepted the reality of these differences as primal and therefore empowered the string players to put their own individual primacy of value on string tone, color, and the intensity of their playing. Their individual right and left hand techniques were thus freed from traditional uniformity to better contribute—ironically—to ensemble, the artistically unified playing of the entire section. For Stokowski diversity produced unity while sectional uniformity of playing produced mechanical uniformity of sound—a musical dead end.

This player's up-bow became his or her neighbor's down-bow. The Stokowski idea was that a player, knowing and trying to convey the conductor's wishes, should use his or her own bowing technique to produce the phrasing that matched the spirit of the music rather than the sometimes hobbled sounds that resulted from up and down uniformity set by the section leader. Stokowski's paradoxical position on bowing and phrasing was that fine phrasing produced the necessary bowing, not the reverse and customary notion that uniform bowing gave birth to proper phrasing.[33]

Violinist—later conductor—David Measham, who played the violin with Stokowski and the London Symphony Orchestra for seven and a half years, granted that the uniform bowing required by the gifted George Szell would work beautifully in a Haydn or Mozart work; but if one were playing the romantics—pieces by Brahms, Tchaikovsky, or Wagner for example—Stokowski's free bowing worked superbly because it removed the sound and phrasing limitations necessarily required by uniform bowing. This was particularly true for one who was at the end of his bow in the middle of a phrase, but wanted to maintain the intensity impossible under the yoke of ordered bowing. At least part of the "Stokowski Sound" was based on the player's knowledge that he or she had no need to husband string intensity and volume. With Stokowski leading a free-bowing orchestra, string players could avoid running out of bow should the maestro request greater volume of sound or alter the tempo for poetic effect. The player simply reached the end of the bow and started again the other way, moving at an individual pace and concentrating on what phrasing Stokowski communicated. And Stokowski was free to ask what he wished for in color, intensity, phrasing and volume without the constraints posed by tradition.[34]

The best contemporary test for Stokowski's ideas about free bowing and the response of his string players is to listen to some of his recordings of music for string orchestra: Barber's Adagio for Strings (1956), Schoenberg's *Transfigured Night* (1957), Dvorak's Serenade for Strings in E Major (1975), or Tchaikovsky's Serenade for Strings in C Major (1975), all of which are listed in the Discography.

Whatever one's thoughts or feelings about Stokowski's ways with the orchestra and the creation of a Stokowski orchestral sound, certain innovations and characteristics of Stokowski's music are generally agreed upon as contributing to his approach to sound—such as his matchup of a concert hall's acoustics to the seating arrangement of his orchestra, whether for concert purposes or for recording. Stokowski researched sound and its relationship to electronics and to acoustics, both independently and in conjunction with the University of Pennsylvania, the Bell Telephone Laboratories, Philco Corporation, and the recording companies. This also contributed to his orchestral approach to sound and music. There is factual agreement that he experimented with and used a variety of sound reflectors, baffles, and resonators to improve orchestral sound for concert and recording purposes. There is ample evidence, too, of the effect that free bowing and blowing had on his orchestral sound. And this does not include the myriad lesser sound enhancements and instrument modifications that were a part of the Stokowski color-sound palette. I would hope that most observers might now consider Stokowski a dramatist, a colorist, a story teller in music whose interpretations—however far from the traditional norm—were never without their own dramatic and musical logic.

But many musicians and some music lovers and critics during Stokowski's long career believed that there were yet more esoteric means used by the maestro in his strikingly singular way of making music.

The same Sol Schoenbach who described Stokowski painstakingly searching for just the right bassoon color to open the *Boris Godunov* synthesis—with the bassoonist's emphasis on the empirical search and the trial and error process necessary to find the right reed—the same musician during the same interview could describe playing with Stokowski in radically different terms, carrying the discussion from the empirical and the experimental to the mysterious and the rhapsodic. As he described playing with the maestro, matters acoustical and empirical were balanced by something else, something unique about Stokowski's actual conducting that was freeing to his players. It was something that made you play as though "you could do anything you wanted [to do]." So strong was this sense of playing beyond oneself that it almost seemed to Schoenbach as if Stokowski were there to accompany him.[35]

Similarly, violinist George Zazofsky, who had played in Stokowski's All American Youth Orchestra, could remember the conductor's two oft-repeated admonitions that they should play *bogen frei* and *noten frei*. *Bogen frei* harked to Stokowski's empirical concern with the importance of free bowing. But the concept of *noten frei* (free of the notes), moved Zazofsky then, and the reader now, into a more controversial and esoteric world of Stokowskiana. As Zazofsky put it to biographer Oliver Daniel, *noten frei* did not mean memorizing your part in everything you played with Stokowski, since that was neither Stokowski's intention nor physically possible. It did mean he needed eye contact with the player, and through that eye contact the performer negotiated key portions of the score without reference to the notes.[36]

There seems then to be evidence of other concerns and of other "mysterious" ways in which Stokowski, in his age, sought much the same musical goals that Hector Berlioz had sought a hundred years earlier, which brings me back to fundamental questions raised by Berlioz about the nature of music. Even more important, it brings me back to those questions raised earlier in this chapter about *how* Stokowski was able to do what he did with orchestral players and with orchestras—both his own and those he conducted as a musical visitor.

As far as I know, no other conductor of the twentieth century has been consistently referred to as "sorcerer," "magician," "Merlin," and "wizard" of the orchestra. That being the case, the evidence in explanation of such terms is itself likely to be unusual. But then the historian takes his or her evidence and asks only if it is true and, if coupled with other evidence, if the whole will show some realistic—not necessarily rationalistic—pattern or outline. If the evidence is unusual and the pattern out-of-the-ordinary, so be it. That does not invalidate the evidence nor discredit the pattern, for variety and uniqueness are as much a part of human life and history as is conformity to the norm. No more convincing proof of this thesis exists in our culture than the musical deeds—or misdeeds if you prefer—of Leopold Stokowski.

My first witness is violinist Carl Flesch,[37] and my first question is whether Stokowski was able to get players to perform beyond their normal abilities, and, if so, how was he able to do it? As violin teacher at Curtis Institute during the midtwenties when Stokowski was conducting the student orchestra, as well as the Philadelphia Orchestra, Flesch was in an ideal position to observe both his students at work under Stokowski and the maestro himself. To Flesch, Stokowski was "Faustian," restless, and searching, always musically questioning, delighted by the modern. He was "Promethean," bringing his message of musical fire from heaven to ignite Philadelphia orchestra players to perform with a brilliance previously unknown. Their concerts were not only the glory of Philadelphia, but were the best attended in the New York season as well. But, continues Flesch, Stokowski was not an unselfish servant of music. As musical Prometheus he actively intruded himself into the music played. His "egoistic" nature obtruded even into the composer's role as claimed cocreator. Always reaching for the musical heavens, for towering sound, it was as though the orchestral performance itself, not the composer's score, were of primary importance. Of his Curtis violin students, who graduated to play under Stokowski in the Philadelphia Orchestra, Flesch noted in wonderment that only one had shown more than middling ability, yet these players, when concertizing with the maestro, were transformed into violinists capable of astounding performance.[38]

Flesch quite shrewdly caught Stokowski's egoistically Promethean sense of mission and his romantic sense of orchestral performance, analogically adding the restlessnss and daring of Faust to the mixture. But how did he get the Philadelphians to play like that? Since this ability to get musicians to play beyond their limits lasted far beyond the Philadelphia years to Stokowski's achievements with the New York City Symphony, the Houston Symphony, the London Symphony, and the American Symphony Orchestra, the question deals with that consistent nonparadoxical core or essence of Stokowski's being as a musician.

Morton Gould, composer, pianist, and conductor, rhetorically asked the same question in the 1970s, noting that he had watched Stokowski work with an orchestra and, as a trained musician and conductor himself, could analyze what went on. But he could not explain the beauty and power of performance on the basis of Stokowski's conducting style or of personnel or rehearsal ingredients. He ascribed it to the "magic" of an imperative vitality that he couldn't further describe.[39] After attending a 1965 performance by Stokowski's last youth orchestra, the American Symphony Orchestra, Eric Salzman of the *New York Herald Tribune* wonderingly described the conductor in action in terms of wizardry and the magical.[40] And finally turning to a thoughtful 1963 appraisal by the *New Yorker*'s Winthrop Sargeant of an American Symphony Orchestra concert under Stokowski, one is again struck by familiar themes reiterated by the music critic. The orchestral playing was extraordinary noted Sargeant and characterized by instant phrasing reaction to the conductor's wishes. Then too wrote Sargeant, the orchestra's sound was characteristic of each of Stokowski's orchestras over the years, and all of this from an eighty-two-year-old whose way with the orchestra was unique.[41]

In the above mentioned cases, Stokowski had the advantage of working with an orchestra that was his and that he regularly conducted; but what of equally "magic" performances as a visitor with an orchestra regularly led by another world-class conductor? For me no better nor more clear-cut example exists than Stokowski's guest appearances with the Cleveland Orchestra, from his first appearances with George Szell's orchestra in December of 1951 to his last in 1971. For here was one of the world's great orchestras, made such by the tenure of conductor Szell,[42] who was then and is considered today one of the twentieth century's leading conductors. Not only was Szell a great orchestra builder and director, but in musical interpretation he was the antithesis of Stokowskian romanticism—a strict disciplinarian, opposed to romantic liberties in music making, and a literalist in interpretation. Szell's approach to music was close to that of Toscanini, who had been an influential model for him.[43]

No wonder then that Joseph Wechsberg's 1970 *New Yorker* Profile "Orchestra," centering as it did on Szell and his orchestra, should offer for flavor a vivid account of Stokowski's very different way with the orchestra, if only because Szell had so clearly shaped the orchestra and its performing style in his own image for a generation. Wechsberg quotes Louis Lane, then associate conductor under Szell, who was there for Stokowski's rehearsals.

Lane noted that Stokowski first reseated the orchestra to match the acoustics of Severance Hall. But the miracle of performance change came within a very short time after Stokowski's down beat at the first rehearsal and with nothing yet said by the maestro to the orchestra except for the name of the piece he wished to rehearse.

What he saw, heard, and recorded was that Szell's characteristic sound and attack disappeared as the voice of the orchestra became warmer and more sensual, with dark juicy color appearing almost instantly. Although a seasoned musician himself, Lane used the word "*incredible*" to describe what he had seen and heard; but he couldn't reasonably explain it, beyond writing that the players must have given Stokowski what he wanted by instinct and without the need for verbal direction.[44] F. R. Dixon, Cleveland concert goer and friend of several members of the orchestra, gathered them together for drinks after a stirring sixties performance of *Scheherazade* with Stokowski conducting. Once the group was seated he described their playing as the finest *Scheherazade* he had ever heard, but couldn't understand the Cleveland Orchestra producing the Stokowski sound so wholeheartedly. He asked if they recognized the differences in color and phrasing? They had, and were themselves surprised at what they had done. As to how they had done it, they were mystified.[45]

Free bowing, free breathing, orchestra reseating, and the like were certainly important to the Stokowski method of getting what he wanted from an orchestra. But it is hard to imagine that these technical changes could not only alter the basic sound of an orchestra and its range of tonal color, but also empower it to follow those peculiarly Stokowskian changes of musical tempo and pulse as well. Such changes, often spontaneous and unrehearsed, have always been marked as real by both the maestro's admirers and his detractors. By those—I think musically romantic—admirers of Stokowski, his way with the musical phrase has most often been described as poetry. To those often choleric critics of the Stokowski style—I think most likely rationalist and literalist in their musical outlook—his idiosyncratic approach to phrasing, his concern for spontaneity and story telling in music, was, at the least, simply eccentric, and at worst, travestry. Even Stokowski could be called to witness since he typically defended his kaleidoscopic approaches to the same work by saying that he played a work as he felt it at the time he was playing it.

But the *point is* that all Stokowski watchers, friend or foe, were aware of the skipper's unique ability to nudge the orchestral ship's tiller, to alter its speed and direction as he wished, while the ship was under way. The *question is*, How did he do it?

While there are authenticated accounts of Stokowski's ability to direct changes of playing style and of the quality of playing with numerous orchestras,[46] there are far fewer attempts to explain *how* he did it, and that is the more important question. But there are clues even in mystification, such as the power of Stokowski's will, his acceptance of music's cosmic relationship to himself (see Appendix), his egoistic concentration of energy toward the project or concert at hand, his ability to draw from performers what he wanted qualitatively and coloristically with little or nothing said to them, and over and over again the word "magic" used to describe what the "sorcerer" of the orchestra did.

Critics, careful to avoid being considered romantic, or worse yet delusional, have skirted the edges of explanation, but at least one came very close to letting Mesmer out of the bag. Winthrop Sargeant, describing the second concert given by the youthful American Symphony Orchestra in 1962, was bowled over by the brilliance of performance and interpretation. Focusing on Stokowski as the cause of this effect, he reminded his readers that critics had for years explained the Stokowski style and sound as truly the product of the Philadelphia Orchestra; but, continued Sargeant, the maestro had left Philadelphia twenty years before and had since conducted orchestras, some far less virtuosic than the Philadelphia, with the same beautiful sound and vitality that were his during the Philadelphia years. Therefore, mused the critic, it would seem that his unique way with music and concertizing exists autonomously in himself, separate from whatever orchestra he is conducting at the moment.

Sargeant then narrowed his focus to the American Symphony Orchestra and to the brilliant concert he had heard it play. He offered his own explanation of Stokowski's unusual abilities by describing the maestro's projection of some sort of powerful vitality and influence that he was somehow able to share with the musicians so that they were moved to play music in ways not ordinarily thought possible. It may be, ended Sargeant, that Stokowski's "secret" was based on a kind of hypnosis.[47]

And there in rough and brief outline are twin hints toward the further explanation of Stokowski's ability to lift players beyond their limits and to get those orchestral phrasings, colors, explosions, murmurings, and cries that Berlioz yearned for so long ago, even from an orchestra trained for far different music making. The force of his will, commitment to the concert in hand, an unusual "life energy level," as John Diamond, M.D., calls it, plus something else (as we shall see) created and projected a positive energy level so great in the conductor that when shared with his players, as Mr. Sargeant surmised, it swept the orchestra into doing things otherwise impossible. But the "something else" was not the hypnosis Sargeant alluded to; it wasn't that. It was Stokowski's gift to both generate and project an energy flow to his musicians and to communicate with players nonverbally.

Such an energy transfer and such nonverbal communication represent two of the several paranormal gifts grouped for study under the headings of parapsychology and psychic research. While recognized by some as real for hundreds of years, such gifts traditionally have provoked hostile jeers from many, including nineteenth-century scientists and rationalists. This repudiation was not based on insensitivity so much as on the appealing mystique of the natural sciences and their law givers that pulled one ever more strongly toward what seemed to be the sensible mechanistic world. In such a world psychic phenomena seemed to be discontinuities, without context; they were incoherent, actually violations of the new religion of science and common sense, and as such were to be punished or ignored. Those open only to the sensible world view were instinctively repelled by psychic phenomena, including those for which there was considerable factual evidence. Such acceptance or even serious consideration would attempt the impossible mix of "oil and water," that is, the mix of psychic exceptions to the new mechanistic scientific rules, which often passed for law. More recently the paranormal has seemed to many to threaten the now traditional scientific world, as science, once a revolutionary force, has become a secular religion, dominating western culture. As such it now represents a conservative part of the status quo—an added reason to censure or to ignore psychic reality and research.[48]

Troubles no less serious for the acceptance of psychic research and researchers have been created by fraudulent mediums, clairvoyants, and telepaths. For as long as there have been genuine paranormal experiences and adepts gifted with such abilities, there have been con-men and women trading on the weaknesses of the gullible, the miserable, and the just plain stupid in the area of psychic experience. Separating the false from the genuine on the basis of evidence has been a major job, a time-consuming effort performed not only by the traditional scientific community, but by psychic researchers themselves, since all evidences of fraud and trickery in the field have tended to discredit both genuine paranormal experience and the researchers investigating it.

As a result of these several obstacles, psychic phenomena and research, the study of the paranormal, and groups like the American Society for Psychical Research and the Parapsychological Association have had a rather hard time of it in the nineteenth and the twentieth centuries. Yet persistence, hard work, and the growing body of evidence in support of the existence of the paranormal have given such researchers hope and even the new respectability of affiliation with the American Association for the Advancement of Science. Affiliation was given in 1969—after three earlier refusals—on the basis of mounting evidence for the seemingly strange, mysterious, and unexpected—evidence that was simply too important to be ignored any longer.[49] This scientific validation was thus indirectly given to the classic parapsychological fields of psychokinesis, telepathy, clairvoyance, and precognition.

That branch of psychokinesis bearing most directly on my analysis is concerned with paranormal human energy generation and transfer in one form or another. The energy itself is variously called bioenergy, life energy, and psychic energy, depending upon the authority consulted. For present purposes it will be called psychic energy.

As to the likely Stokowskian variant on this phenomenon, it has a history going back much earlier than our own century. It has been known longest under the historically sanctioned and theologically tinged name, *charisma*. It is not the TV politician's smile nor the sex goddess's aura that modern hucksters and PR men describe with the word charisma, thus cheapening it, but an older meaning in which an individual so gifted exercises influence and authority over people out of his or her very being through the commitment and energy charge radiated from that being, sometimes even projecting a visible aura—the halo of religious traditon.[50]

Charismatic power has been reported over a long period of time for a wide range of individuals, including prophets, political leaders, healers, and artists. The best known modern field for the proven release of charismatic energy is in the healing arts. Here the gift of psychic healing is now accepted by a considerable number of doctors and therapists. Kirlian photography, first developed in 1939 in the Soviet Union, has even documented the aura of energy emanating from the practitioner's hands when he or she exerts the concentration and psychic energy force necessary for one kind of healing session. In the United States, the Kirlian photographic experiments of UCLA professor Thelma Moss, of the Neuropsychiatric Institute of Los Angeles, are well known.[51]

Closer to home, let me state that I have not only heard and met Olga Worrall, the first Western healer documented both by therapeutic results and by the Kirlian photographic process, but was for several years the beneficiary of psychic healing as practiced by a dear friend who practiced professionally as well.

There are those, still thinking of science and parapsychology as oil and water, who believe the whole idea to be esoteric mumbo jumbo. But the basic concept is sensible, simple, and based on the thesis that energy is the life force for humankind. Any blockage or diminution of a person's bodily energy through bodily hurt or psychological trauma is debilitating, or worse, life-threatening. Psychic healing is literally the transfer or gift of energy from the high-energy-level practitioner to the patient to either unblock the stoppage or focus additional energy on the point of hurt to promote healing. It is a vitalist and organic concept rather than a mechanistic one; it recognizes the major differences in energy levels possessed by different human beings. The body is not seen as a machine, but as a living organism whose life-force must be maintained by the necessary level and balance and movement of energy through the body, a fact of life for those who are weary in the evening and rise refreshed in the morning after a good night's sleep.

Indeed it is this concept on which the success of acupuncture is based. This ancient Eastern medical treatment postulates twelve body pathways through which psychic energy flows to all parts of the body. Blockage of any pathway results in loss of vitality and oncoming sickness. The acupuncture treatments are no more than a means of unblocking these pathways and allowing the body to repair itself. While more and more Western doctors admit that acupuncture works, they still deny that its success has to do with energy flow in the body, and they admit they don't know why it works.[52]

In dealing with an abnormal blockage of energy in the human body there are two basic Western paranormal methods of transferring energy from practitioner to patient. The first and better known—if only because it has received considerable attention by the media and has occurred in at least one motion picture—is often called "healing-by-touch." In this method the practitioner, by concentration, focuses psychic energy to the hands and from the hands into the patient's body, producing measurable and proven temperature increases in the practitioner's hands from a normal 98.6°F to 120°F or more, while the patient feels this energy as a warm tingling or as similar to the warmth of diathermic treatment.[53]

As an aftermath the practitioner is temporarily drained of energy—literally—but is capable of recharging the body's battery in a matter of hours with the proper rest. The patient often shows a much more rapid recovery period and a remarkable increase in vitality.

The second method of psychic healing is similar to the first in that the practitioner shares energy with another and at the end of the process requires time for recuperation. But the process of sharing energy and the method by which this is done are different as shown in the following example drawn from the experience of an adept.

In order, the process begins with the practitioner's sincere commitment to the project at hand and his or her concern for the patient. Meditation is necessary to clear away the concerns and stresses of the everyday world while opening up to the alternative world of the "All" or the Divine through an altered state of consciousness. In this psychic change the practitioner figuratively leaves the sensate world to achieve spiritual unity with the patient and with that parallel world variously named as the "All," the "Universal," and the Divine. In achieving this state, the practitioner is able to share in or tap into the paranormal harmony and energy thus made available and to create the bridge or psychic connection between the patient, the practitioner, and the All.

In this approach to psychic healing there is no sense of the practitioner *doing something to the patient* as in healing-by-touch or in hypnosis. Rather, there is a concentration of purpose toward psychically merging with the patient so that he or she is free—free to be able to reach out of self, beyond self, to claim that psychic energy and sense of harmony now made available for self-help recovery. It is, then, a freeing and free will offering of the means for healing and/or restoring vitality drawn from the uniting of the practitioner, the patient, and the All.[54]

The process is similar to—some might say synonymous with—orthodox religious experiences of the most transcendant kind. Hence the above, while seeming strange to the dweller in a strictly mechanistic, sensible world, will not be strange to readers of William James's great book *The Varieties of Religious Experience;* nor will it be strange to spiritually adept Christian sects and many Far Eastern devotees of transcendant faiths wherein that cosmic world energized by the All or by God is understood metaphysically to be related to humankind—and more intimate yet—to be available to those who call for help—the most profound meaning of prayer. East and West, although separated by a variety of creeds, holy writings, beliefs, and purposes imputed to the Divine, share an understanding that establishing the rules governing the sensible world does not explain all that is truly real, beneficial, and powerful.

As for the paranormal healing model described above and for the purposes of this chapter, one should seriously register the key components of psychic healing: commitment to it by the practitioner; the meditation necessary to make it possible and to open the way; the juncture where practitioner, patient, and the All meet; the free will offering of harmony and energy to the patient as engendered by the practitioner; the patient's free receipt of the same, necessary for his or her own revitalization; and, finally, the concluding weariness of the practitioner, his or her energy spent by the revitalization process.

This brief account of paranormal healing has been offered as a frame of reference or a paradigm to be considered when one reads the accounts of musicians who played with Stokowski. Similarities in their accounts of Stokowski's variously named "occult" or "mesmerizing" or "hypnotic" influence on them in performance are, I think, suggestive of the paranormal healer's approach translated into the musical world. Pointing similarly to this approach are their descriptions of feeling energized, of playing beyond themselves, of feeling at one with the other musicians and the conductor, yet conversely of feeling free to do anything they wanted to do.

I do not claim the two situations are analogous, but I do believe that there are suggestive similarities well worth considering.

We are aware that Stokowski thought and felt in cosmically metaphysical terms (see Appendix) and often described music in the same way. We know that during the Philadelphia years he meditated before performance, carrying his trancelike state from dressing room to podium in seconds, where he began to conduct immediately. As Sylvan Levin described it to me, "Stokowski was already conducting on his way to the podium."[55] He conducted without a score in order to maintain eye contact with his players during performance, and when that performance ended, preferred leaving the concert arena—due to weariness I would think—to exchanging pleasantries in the Green Room. As to how he got such remarkable results from his players, his reponse was apt to be that it was a "secret" or that it was a matter of acoustical knowledge, the seating of the orchestra, and the free bowing and breathing techniques used by his orchestra, which of course it was *in part*. In anecdote and remembrance however, those who worked with him have recounted remarkably similar stories about Stokowski's secret.

As to the significance of energy in Stokowski's performance, a startling example of its effectiveness is to be found in volume one of the Bell Laboratories' experimental recordings of Stokowski and the Philadelphia Orchestra during the 1931–32 concert season. The Bell engineers asked Stokowski to perform a piece of his choice that would test the maximum frequency and volume limits of their equipment. Stokowski's choice was Berlioz's *Roman Carnival Overture,* not scheduled for concert performance, but providing what the Bell people were looking for. For me that performance is the greatest live or recorded treatment of the score I have ever heard. Across fifty years and even through the electronic intermediaries of the recording process, glitches included, the musical energy level established between conductor and players is astonishing and communicates itself quite clearly to the listener, both aurally and physically. Of this recording the Bell engineer in charge reported that while the playing time was only ten minutes, Stokowski left the podium totally spent; he was so drained of energy that he could barely speak. The reason was that he had put so much of himself into the performance. It was, said the engineer, "unbelievable."[56]

For evidence of the musical translation of energy generation and transference as illustrated above, but in normally empirical terms rather than in paranormal terms, let me direct the reader to John Diamond, M.D., *The Life Energy in Music,* and to his experiments in behavioral kinesiological testing, that is, testing for the evidences of "life energy" in performance. Using a testing device based on the research work of George Goodheart in the field of behavioral kinesiology, Diamond has tested several thousand individuals, both lay persons and musicians, to gather evidence on the importance of energy itself in the world of music and musical performance. A key theme of his book is that beyond skill and training there is the matter of life energy in music as a galvanic force that lifts performers and listeners into a realm beyond correct performance. It is thus that music performs its therapeutic and ennobling magic. From Diamond's perspective music is both a healing and a life-enhancing art. Furthermore, his findings are that life energy in musical performance is measurable. On the basis of twenty-five years of testing, Diamond offers the following insights into the importance of energy in music from his own experience.

> Every musical combination, from duet to full symphony orchestra, will have its energy level set by one member of the group who is the leader, whether appointed or not. It is his energy level that determines the transmission of the pulse by the group.
>
> In an orchestra this level is invariably set by the conductor and thus we find the same orchestra may test at many energy levels depending on that of the particular conductor. . . . Thus it is that many high energy orchestral players tell me how tired and dispirited they feel after playing under certain conductors. We always find on

> test that these conductors are low energy conductors. And of course the conductors under whom the orchestral players tell us that they have played beyond their limits test as high energy conductors. . . .
>
> A conductor must have [an] infectious love of music. . . . He must test strong when he says "I love music" and he must rekindle this love in the players who are . . . bored with playing the same work yet again [otherwise the performance is routine].
>
> Great music is created not in the mind of the composer but in his heart. It transcends all questions of method and formulae and laws. . . . Unlike the prayers of Jesus or St. Francis . . . music comes to life only when it is re-created by the performer. This is his holy function, to take the inert prayer of the composer and bring it to life. . . .
>
> It is essential that the conductor be unstressed during performance. . . . If he is . . . then all those under him, even if they are usually stressed by the act of performing, will rise above this in response to the pulse that he transmits to them. . . .
>
> Imagine an orchestra in which not only did the conductor have a high life energy, but all the performers as well. . . . Then we should really know the glory of music as we have never experienced it.[57]

While Dr. Diamond never tested Stokowski's energy level, his comments match rather remarkably what eye witnesses recounted of the maestro in performance and what Stokowski himself described as the essentials of performance. In earlier pages I have described testimony of Stokowski's ability to lift performers above their normal stress and competency levels through powers of his own. Further, there is clinical evidence that such powers are not occult—a word often used by performers playing with Stokowski to describe the maestro—but paranormal, that is, beyond what is considered the normal level of human ability, but not supernatural as that word is customarily understood.

A telling account of such a phenomenon was shared by Abram Chasins in his biography of the maestro. After describing Stokowski in performance with Philadelphia Orchestra players, Chasins went on to describe an exchange with Stokowski centering on just what he gave or shared with his players that produced such remarkable results. Chasins reported that Stokowski told him of what seemed to him in performance as a mysterious force encompassing himself and his players with monumental "energy." And it was this force that was shared by conductor and orchestra with its effects further transferred to an energized audience. Describing its effect on himself, he told Chasins that it was at such times that he was able to reach the universal, union with everyone and everything.[58]

It is one thing to wax ecstatic after a brilliant artistic performance and, out of the enthusiasm of the moment, to use an old figure of speech to laud the performer as a magician. It is quite another thing to take that magic seriously and document its consistency over a long span of years, translating it into a rare combination of physiological and psychological gifts driven by artistic commitment. It is this second course I must adopt if I am to explain what in Stokowski's case was reported over and over again, but has often been accepted only as the enthusiastic lip service of the moment following a concert.

In his biography of the maestro, Chasins does seriously mention this second course of evaluation. However, it is but one of scores of themes that crowd the pages of his book and so it is liable to be lost in the sheer volume of Stokowskiana; but it is there. Of soloists working with Stokowski, writes Chasins, Barry Tuckwell, Mitchell Miller, Sergei Rachmaninoff, Joseph Hofmann, Fritz Kreisler, Laurence Tibbet, Helen Traubel, Jan Peerce, and Emanuel Fuermann all reported performing beyond themselves because of the maestro's unique gifts exercised during performance.[59]

Armed with this reference I asked Mr. Chasins about his own experience with Stokowski since he had premiered his Second Piano Concerto with him in Philadelphia in 1933 and had written glowingly of Stokowski's ability to bring out the composer's meaning by clarifying the score here and there—all with Chasins's permission.[60]

Of his experience as pianist in the concert's premiere, Chasins described it as unique in his career and attributable to Stokowski's "mesmerizing" power. In his performance he felt none of his usual stage fright. Instead there was the positive sense that he was free of all restraints, free to play into the heart of his music. There was no consciousness of the audience, nothing but an unusual concentration of will and energy on the art of that moment. As Chasins described the experience, he said he instinctively knew at the time that his own feeling was being shared by the conductor and the orchestra players as well. The source of this power, said Chasins, was Stokowski.[61] Note the suggestive correlation of Mr. Chasins's personal experience to Lawrence Leshan's account of paranormal healing, Dr. Diamond's empirical findings, and Stokowski's own description of performing.

Much the same thing was told me by Sylvan Levin, who had played solo piano with the maestro and the Philadelphia Orchestra in a number of concerts and on recordings. He particularly recalled performing and recording Scriabin's *Prometheus: Poem of Fire* in 1931, where the composer's mysticism and the music's content were particularly close to the maestro's own feelings. Mr. Levin recalled that he, too, was literally mesmerized in performance. He recalled the strange sense of unity he felt with the conductor and the orchestra as though they were one, but in a creatively freeing way, not as though Stokowski were controlling musical puppets.[62]

Continuing our talk, I brought up the subject of Stokowski's batonless conducting, noting that a variety of explanations had been given—including contradictory explanations by the maestro himself—as to why he abandoned the stick in the twenties. Bursitis, egotism, and accidents had all been cited, but, I asked Mr. Levin, what about the conductor's eyes? If it were true as reported that Stokowski could communicate and transmit with his eyes, what would be more natural than to abandon the baton in order to move the performers' attention away from the tip of the stick and closer, via his hands, to the conductor's eyes?

Levin said that the argument that it was bursitis or egotism about his hands that had led the maestro to cease using the baton was nonsense; his batonless style of conducting did indeed draw attention to the hand and arm arc of activity centering on his face and eyes. Levin concluded that "Stokowski practically conducted with his eyes." It was, thought Levin, perfectly in keeping with the maestro's penchant for secrecy that he would support erroneous theories about his batonless conducting in order to obscure the real reason.[63]

If Stokowski had such abilities, there is no statement from him as to how early he realized his gifts and worked to strengthen them in performance; but there is an interesting description of Stokowski's first concert with the London Symphony Orchestra in 1912 from no less a musician than Joseph Szigeti. Szigeti would recall that the Stokowski sound was already there, as was the plasticity of orchestral phrasing. It was for Szigeti, a memorable concert that galvanized the London audience.[64]

An episode of 1923 illustrates well the confusion that could be generated by Stokowski's peculiar gifts utilized in the premiere of a new work. In his autobiography, composer Daniel Gregory Mason contrasted his first happy contact with the maestro in 1916 to his second contact in 1923. In the latter year Stokowski was to perform Mason's Prelude and Fugue for the first time and asked the composer to stand by him on the podium to offer criticism or suggestions on interpretation. At the first rehearsal

Mason asked Stokowski for a particular approach to a specific phrase in the score. Stokowski turned to the orchestra. Down came the conductor's arm. And to Mason's amazement the phrase was played exactly as he wished it. But how was it done? he asked the maestro. Tartly Stokowski replied that it was his business. Laughing, Mason then commented, so it's a "secret" then? To which Stokowski answered that there was nothing secret about his method, that anybody could "see" how he did it.[65]

To Mr. Mason Stokowski's curt response was proof that he had been made insensitive by his success in Philadelphia. To me it indicates Stokowski's wariness, his need to obscure just how he did get that phrase right even while slyly admitting the method by saying that it could be seen by anybody.[66]

Philadelphia first desk men William Kincaid, Marcel Tabuteau, and Saul Caston each told Abram Chasins that Stokowski's psychical ability to draw paranormal playing abilities from his musicians showed itself to each of them in turn at their first rehearsals with the maestro.[67] Michel Penha, first cellist with the orchestra during the midtwenties, described it this way to his young protégée Louisa Knowlton: "I don't even like the Bach-Stokowski transcriptions, but caught up in performance with the maestro they truly become the most important music in the world."[68] Describing his experiences with Stokowski in the late fifties as something of a "mystery," as mesmerizing, Gunther Schuller, who often played with the conductor, described him as doing nothing out of the ordinary, simply announcing the piece to be rehearsed and conducting it, but within "three minutes" of the downbeat, the orchestral sound of "any orchestra" became Stokowski's sound.[69] José Serebrier, associate conductor of the American Symphony Orchestra in the sixties, testified that Stokowski had a "hypnotic effect" on his players and, by way of illustration, mentioned Stokowski's first performance of his own *Elegy for Strings*. Others had performed it. Serebrier himself had conducted the *Elegy* with the Minneapolis Orchestra. But, as Serebrier put it, it was at Stokowski's concert performance that he had really heard the piece as he had intended it. Stokowski, continued Serebrier, had cut to the emotional-musical inner meaning of the piece and at concert time—rehearsals had shown none of this—had wordlessly communicated this meaning to the musicians, who faithfully translated it to the audience in the hall.[70]

Stokowski verbally admitted none of this until his late eighties and nineties, calling it his "secret." Considering the earlier fate of others so gifted, he was wise in his silence. But Robert Gomberg recalls that point in Stokowski's 1977 CBS interview when the maestro was asked how he got what he wanted from an orchestra and Stokowski said quite simply that he conducted with his eyes in communicating his wishes to orchestra members. Gomberg writes that he roared with laughter at that for it was exactly what he remembered from his days as a performer with the maestro.[71]

Four years earlier Stokowski had been asked approximately the same question by music critic Edward Greenfield, and his answer was a variation on the same theme. Stokowski described looking at a player and wanting a particular kind of "phrasing or tone"—very often quite different from the traditionally expected—and getting it. Stokowski told Greenfield that he couldn't explain how it was done but that it happened consistently.[72]

In 1982 New York Philharmonic associate principal cellist, Nathan Stutch, described the receiving end of this nonverbal communication in a one hundredth birthday tribute to the late maestro, writing that Stokowski was unique in interfacing with each performer during performance so that it seemed he was conducting only you, and you in turn were playing only for him. It was very private music making and, Stutch believed, the chief reason for the Stokowski sound and the fact that the maestro was able to re-create that sound with any orchestra he conducted.[73]

While Stokowski only spoke of his parapsychological gift late in life, quite likely when failing health and eyesight diminished or precluded its use, he did write about it much earlier in his 1943 book, *Music for All of Us*.

> Conducting is little understood and greatly misunderstood. . . . The . . . visual part is essential for the players to be able to see clearly the notes they are reading, and at the same time to be able to see the conductor's eyes so there can be understanding . . . among all those in the orchestra. . . .
>
> Conducting is only to a small extent the beating of time—it is done far more through the eyes—still more it is done through a kind of inner communication between players and conductor.[74]

With such evidence as the foregoing in mind, I presented a paper including this theme at the national conference of the Sonneck Society for American Music in Tallahassee, Florida, in March 1985. The audience—largely made up of musicians—was supportive and at the end of the presentation, during the ten minute break between papers, several people came to the podium to talk about their recollections of playing with Stokowski, putting much emphasis on his eyes and his gift for just such inner communication. The group included a gentleman who described himself as a former Houston player, who flatly stated that the orchestra did not play as well before nor after the maestro's tenure in the late fifties. The reason, he said, was Stokowski's "hypnotic" power in obtaining performances beyond the usual abilities of the players, and he began citing Houston recordings made with Stokowski as proof. However, at that point the next paper was announced for presentation in an adjoining hall, and I lost my informants and my chance to make notes on what else they might have said.[75]

Dominique-Rene de Lerma is now a professor of music, but his experience of playing with Stokowski came not in a top tier orchestra such as Chicago or Philadelphia, nor in a second-rank orchestra like Houston, but when Stokowski served as guest conductor of the University of Miami Symphony Orchestra in 1955—the same Miami visit that generated the abortive Stokowski radio incident cited earlier. For him it was a most unusual kind of music experience, but he was either unwilling or unable to clearly identify how this music was made. The following report concerns his mystification about how Stokowski got from the university orchestra the sound and phrasing he wanted for the Bach-Stokowski Toccata and Fugue in D.

The scene as described by de Lerma was the first rehearsal, and the piece to be played was the Bach-Stokowski transcription. De Lerma was already aware of the Stokowski sound from recordings and from his training time at Curtis Institute, where he had studied oboe with Marcel Tabuteau. But what was Stokowski going to do with the Miami Orchestra, wondered de Lerma? Not only was the orchestra far below the caliber of the Philadelphia Orchestra, but the opening piece was one whose fluidity of phrasing might defy the orchestra's ability to follow Stokowski.

The rehearsal began, and with the downbeat the "mystery" increased, according to de Lerma. The orchestra followed Stokowski's phrasing naturally, and equally surprising, it did not produce its usual collegiate sound. Instead, almost immediately, it became a Stokowski orchestra with the maestro's sound and color.

The rehearsal itself left the young oboeist with additional questions. While Stokowski's conducting gestures were clear enough, they couldn't explain the orchestra's ability to follow his idiosyncratic phrasing and certainly couldn't account for the transformation of the orchestra's sound.

As de Lerma explained it, Stokowski was accomplishing something unusual that changed the players' performance abilities, but with the hindsight of a number of years de Lerma would write that he didn't know in 1955 what that something was, and he still didn't know at the time of writing his recollections in 1979.[76]

It is evident that some players like Nathan Stutch accepted as fact that Stokowski had paranormal powers, while others like de Lerma recognized the phenomenon even if they couldn't or wouldn't name it. My own question is this: If he had no such paranormal gifts, how was he able to convince knowledgeable critics and trained musicians of his abilities, variously described as "magic," "occult," "hypnotic," and "mesmerizing?" Figures such as Sol Schoenbach, Morton Gould, Abram Chasins, Winthrop Sargeant, Gunther Schuller, Nathan Stutch, Oscar Shumsky, José Serebrier, and others who *were* convinced. Certainly until someone makes a realistic case against the evidence of Stokowski's unusual abilities and explains away that evidence, one has every reason to believe that Stokowski combined great musical gifts with esoteric psychic abilities of the most unusual kind.

Let me carry this theme one step further. Stokowski's gifts were freely given; so if they were accepted by musicians, they had to be freely accepted, and there were musicians unwilling to join Stokowski in this partnership (see Jerome Toobin's *Agitato*, 47–49, for a Stokowski conflict with an unlikely partnership candidate).

I think it likely that this is one of the reasons why Stokowski had such fantastic success in Philadelphia, where he rebuilt the orchestra player by player, looking for musicianship and for players who could share his vision of flexibility and spontaneity in performance; they became true partners in the creation of the Stokowski Sound. Further, I think it likely that this is one of the reasons why Stokowski so much enjoyed working with young musicians at the Curtis Institute, in the All American Youth Orchestra, and in the American Symphony Orchestra. Their prejudices were less strong, cynicism had not set in, and their openness to the joy of music and to its feeling element made them ideal partners in the creation of that personal and spontaneous kind of music making so dear to the maestro.

Since Stokowski was increasingly frail during the last three or four years of his life, say from 1973 to his death at age ninety-five in 1977, I would venture the guess that his power to infuse performances with his own energy and to communicate with players declined or was ended. It would circumstantially help explain why he stopped conducting in public and why his last recordings, although showing great musicianship, show less personal poetry—or eccentricity if you prefer—in interpretation and more reliance on the literal printed score than earlier. That is, he *had* to rely more on "the black marks on white paper," which he had always disparaged as only the beginning of music making. Ironically, there are reviews of some of his late recordings that are favorable in part because Stokowski had mended his ways—supposedly—and now conducted exactly what the score dictated, without Stokowskian retouching. Violist William Primrose also expressed this view in his memoirs, *Walk on the North Side* (p. 157).

However, none of this shows in his performances up to extreme old age. As witness to what he could do with his players until near the end, we again turn to Sol Schoenbach for testimony on what was most controversial about the conductor's way of "co-creating" music, that is, his habit of experimenting, not only with personalized phrasings and sonorities, but with orchestration as well.

Stokowski as musician not only felt color and sound to be emotionally-artistically related, but as earlier described, likened the conductor's art to that of a painter. In illustrating his penchant for painting in sound, Philadelphia Orchestra bassoonist Sol Schoenbach told biographer Oliver Daniel that without prearrangement, Stokowski might simply point at the bassoon section to play at a certain passage during performance, even though there was no part for the bassoons at that point in the score. "He was just like a painter who decides he wants to put a little red here, a little blue there and he would do things right on the spot."[77]

With his delight in experiment, in playing with orchestral combinations, in sound colors and sonorities, I wonder what Berlioz would have thought of Stokowski's touching up the *Symphonie Fantastique* with a "little red here, a little blue there?" Would he have shared the horror of those twentieth-century critics for whom Stokowski could do no right? Or would he have accepted experimenter Stokowski, on balance, as bringing yet more musical possibilities to birth for the possible delight of humankind? In romantic parlance, would he have considered the maestro a kindred promethean or would he have seen him as a musical Dr. Frankenstein.

In his essay "The Orchestral Conductor," Berlioz notes that the orchestral composer, alone of "producing artists," depends upon so many intermediaries for the breath of life that will take his music from the page to the stage and so to reality. And here the key figure, writes Berlioz, is the conductor because of his power over the orchestra. There are bad conductors who reign "with all the calm of a bad conscience in . . . baseness and inefficiency," "malevolent" in their effect. There are conductors "full of good will, but incapable," representing "innumerable mediocrities . . . who, fancying they are able to conduct, innocently injure the best scores."

The good conductor's job "is a complicated one." It goes beyond being a mere "beater of time." He must "conduct in the spirit of the author's intentions . . . must see and hear . . . be active and vigorous . . . know the composition, the nature and compass of the instruments [employed]." But beyond these are

> other almost indefinable gifts without which an invisible link cannot establish itself between him and those he directs; *the faculty of transmitting to them his feeling is denied him* and thence power, empire and guiding influence completely fail him. [In lieu of such communication] . . . *they should feel* that he feels, comprehends, and is moved; then his feeling, his emotion communicate themselves to those whom he directs, his inward fire warms them, his electric glow electrifies them, his force of impulse excites them, he throws around him [self] the vital irradiations of Musical Art.[78] [italics mine]

Note Berlioz's wistful emphasis on the ideal conductor, on a leader able to soundlessly communicate energy, emotion, and meaning to his players during performance, which he, Berlioz, immediately then denies is possible. In its place he puts the normally possible outward show of feeling and commitment on the part of the conductor, adding that the orchestra members will "feel that he feels" and therefore will commit themselves too, providing that they believe he is trying to reach them.

What composer Berlioz might have thought of conductor Stokowski is subject to debate, but in terms of a romantic and emotional approach to music, the two musicians speak to each other antiphonally over the years. In answer to Lyman Bryson's question as to the mystery of how a conductor actually achieves a fine orchestral performance, Stokowski's response in the sixties was to reply that he personally knew of no more important "mystery." Speaking for himself and his way, the conductor said that the process began with the way he felt the music. Then he communicated that to his players, not vocally, but nonverbally, through his eyes. The players responded with the tone, the feeling, and phrasing he asked of them. Stokowski could not technically explain that kind of communication, but "communication" it certainly was.[79]

While rationalist critics would claim that Stokowski's approach to music was too romantic, larger than life, too filled with color and emotion, it is doubtful whether the maestro could have approached the romantic ideal of music without that set of character traits and psychological gifts that made him unique among performers. "Volcanoes, tempests, murmurs, prayers, passions . . ." wrote Berlioz; a conductor and an orchestra that can translate such scenes and feelings into sound "can be compared to nothing hitherto achieved in Art."

What I have tried to establish so far is that this was the direction in which Stokowski moved and from early years. His zeal and sense of mission—"Promethean," Carl Flesch called it—wedded to an egoistic passion for music and the romantic ideal, were at the core or essence of Stokowski the musician.

To Stokowski's formidable knowledge of electronics, sound, acoustics, the peculiar characteristics of the instruments in his orchestra, and of countless music scores, we can add his psychic gifts, which lifted himself, his soloists, and the orchestra players out of musical routine and into a transcendent realm. There, as violinist Oscar Shumsky put it, Stokowski and the soloist were joined as one, their separateness voided, while they were almost metaphysically liberated to play with complete freedom, yet paradoxically with a unity that was "predestined."[80]

3
Stokowski in Philadelphia

In 1979 conductor Michael Gielen discussed both his hopes and his concerns in assuming the leadership of the Cincinnati Symphony Orchestra in 1982. This he did with Nancy Malitz of *Musical America*. Maestro Gielen shared with Ms. Malitz his hope of bringing more contemporary music to Cincinnati audiences, in the tradition of Reiner and Stokowski. But there were potential pitfalls in both the reaction of the audience, which expected beloved chestnuts, and in the historical paucity of well known conductors who had been successful in performing contemporary repertoire. There were only a few conductors, continued Gielen, who had braved the irritation of concertgoers in the comfortable tradition by substituting innovation for musical safety. And of these the most notable was Stokowski. Praising Stokowski for the enlightened programming of modern works, including many American compositions, Gielen next explained Stokowski as a special case. Since his ties with the Philadelphia audience were so close, explained Gielen, he could brave popular reaction without risk.[1]

While conductor Gielen was right about the dominance of that gemütlich tradition of programming for America's concert halls then and now, he assumed as a given the close relationship of Stokowski to his Philadelphia audience from the beginning of Stokowski's tenure. In 1912, when Stokowski first took over the Philadelphia Orchestra, there was no such relationship, nor was there a tradition of balancing Philadelphia Orchestra programs between classic and romantic works on the one hand and modern works on the other. When the Stokowskis first came to Philadelphia, they found a match between the city and the orchestra. The community was a musical suburb of both New York and Boston, whose citizens viewed Philadelphia with condescension as a musically insignificant city with a third-rate orchestra. Only twelve years old, the orchestra had little support among Philadelphia's classes and none among its masses relative to New York and Boston. Season tickets were underpledged and concerts in the three-thousand-seat Academy of Music often drew as few as six hundred ticket holders.[2]

Long before the relationship between Stokowski and the Philadelphia audience could be taken for granted, a multifold job had to be done. With his own sense of identity established to his satisfaction, those Stokowski gifts and characteristics already discussed were brought into play to create a great symphony orchestra supported by an entire city. Stokowski's egoism as centralness of purpose, his energy and enthusiasm, his ability to mesmerize potential backers as well as musicians, and his capacity for hard work in what he believed, coupled with great organizing skill, were employed to the full before the orchestra became Stokowski's orchestra and the Stokowski sound became the Philadelphia sound. Nor should one forget the role of Olga Samaroff Stokowski, who worked as hard as her husband, but whose portion ten years later would be divorce, not glory.

Central to the efforts of the Stokowskis for ten years from 1912 forward were a series of interrelated activities, each linked to the others, in a beneficent upward spiral of mutual reinforcement. Basic to performance were the players in the orchestra. By his own account, Stokowski found the playing of what he called the "German" orchestra of 1912 inflexible and without feeling. Many of its players performed, at best, in a mechanical way, at least for the needs of the romantically expressive young conductor. As we have seen, Stokowski, in the tradition of Berlioz, stressed the need for more emotionally telling readings of symphonic scores; in his description, the performance of music needed drama, color, and spontaneity in order to live. During his first few years in Philadelphia he set about finding performers and soloists of top flight ability who could accept his kind of musical partnership and share his kind of flexibility; many of them were young and many of them were American. As a result, by 1921 only five players remained of the original Philadelphia Orchestra; Stokowski had added twenty-one new players during that year alone.[3]

Players alone were not enough, however. Money must be found to pay for them, and a Philadelphia audience must be created and educated to come and hear them at the Academy of Music. Further, Stokowski as master organizer—for such he was—realized that some striking musical event—an event that would tap the energies and pride of Philadelphians—was needed to make the city as musically conscious as Boston and New York City.

Barely 2½ years into his career in Philadelphia, the makings of that event found their way into Stokowski's hands when the maestro, with American performance rights secured, was able to bring the score of Mahler's *Symphony of a Thousand* out of Germany at the beginning of the First World War. Stokowski had attended and been deeply moved by the world premiere of the work in 1910 with Mahler conducting. His idea of galvanizing Philadelphia musical life was to stage the American premiere of this monumental work in Philadelphia. With Stokowski carrying the huge score under his arm, the couple barely escaped internment in Munich, Germany, in August 1914, since the English-born Stokowski was an enemy alien.

Safely back in Philadelphia, Stokowski went to work convincing the orchestra's board of directors that a premiere performance of the Mahler work was a must. Since such a premiere involving over a thousand performers and thousands of dollars expended was unheard of in Philadelphia, the initial negative vote of the board was understandable. The Stokowskis refused to take the board's opposition as final and continued to make the seemingly impossible not only possible, but the means of putting Philadelphia on the musical map. While Stokowski continued to lobby the board and speak to civic groups, Madam and Maestro Stokowski as a team turned their residence at 2117 Locust Street into a key social center of the city as they informally lobbied for the Mahler premiere and for a brilliant musical future for their adopted city. Olga Samaroff Stokowski, who has never received her due in Philadelphia's musical transformation, later stated that in addition to dinners and parties, she received or returned more than seven hundred social calls during the Philadelphia years. In her autobiography, *An American Musician's Story*, she wrote that her husband became a civic personage as a necessity in building the orchestra and a musical consciousness in the city. Not even a musician with the ability and reputation of Arturo Toscanini could have ignored the social politicking necessary to do what was done in Philadelphia. Both the orchestra and that consciousness were possible, but it seemed necessary for the Stokowskis to be everywhere at once.[4]

With Stokowski alternately pleading, politicking, cajoling, and demanding the premiere, one year in the face of this whirlwind was enough to convince board members that their initial financial worries about what they felt was an unworkable venture should give way to Stokowski's will, his confidence, and Philadelphia's need to move forward musically. In 1915 the board voted to support production of the huge choral work for presentation in March of 1916.[5]

As chief publicist for the premiere, conductor Stokowski doubled as promoter Stokowski generating Philadelphia enthusiasm for the project, which in turn generated the funds for the undertaking. In addition to his regular weekly conducting duties with the Philadelphia Orchestra, he auditioned and trained the extra musicians needed for Mahler. Stokowski also created and trained the 400-voice Philadelphia Orchestra chorus. From the city's schools he drew and shaped a children's chorus of 150. While giving the credit to their leaders, Stokowski gave new professional standing and pride to three amateur choral groups; the Philadelphia Choral Society, the Mendelssohn Club, and the Fortnightly Club, whose totalled numbers added up to another 400 performers for Mahler's mighty choruses.

At 7:45 P.M. on the night of 2 March 1916, showman Stokowski signaled for the horn fanfare in the foyer of the Academy of Music as prelude to performance. Earlier in the day hundreds had stood in the rain for hours to get general admission tickets, while scalpers were receiving a hundred dollars apiece for reserved seats.

At 8:00 P.M. the maestro fronted 8 soloists, 950 singers, and the *new* Philadelphia Orchestra of 110 pieces. By 10:30 P.M. musical history had been made. To the original three Philadelphia performances six more were added—all sold out. Philadelphians who had never been to a concert in their lives clamored for tickets while talking about the Mahler performance as enthusiastically as though it were a World Series win by the Phillies. Clearly Stokowski had engaged the imagination and the enthusiasm of the people of Philadelphia. Representatives from New York's Society of the Friends of Music who attended Philadelphia performances were so excited by the experience that New York backers were found to underwrite the cost of transporting the one thousand Philadelphians to New York for performances there—a further boost for musically second-rate Philadelphia. The New York reviews matched the public's enthusiasm and the new pride of Philadelphians in themselves and their accomplishment.[6]

The impressive success of the Mahler concerts in Philadelphia and New York had several interrelated results. With the maestro shrewdly giving major credit to them for the project's success, the members of the special committee, once dedicated solely to bringing about the Mahler premiere, were now enthusiastic backers of the orchestra and of its conductor. They stayed on the job working to generate enthusiasm, ticket sales, new programs, and funding for their orchestra's future. Led by board member Edward Bok—whom Stokowski would single out years later as his first real supporter on the Philadelphia board and a battler for musical ideals—Stokowski won over Bok's wife, the Curtis publications' heiress, Mary Louise Curtis Bok, and influential board members Frances Anne Wister and Alexander Van Rensselaer. The rest of the board enthusiastically followed their lead. In presenting Stokowski with a bronze laurel wreath after the Mahler premiere, Van Rensselaer summed up the new feelings of the board about their conductor and Philadelphia's musical future by describing his accomplishment as not only a major musical feat, but one that benefitted the whole community.[7]

Leopold Stokowski graciously—and shrewdly—returned the compliment; he repeated privately and publicly that the Philadelphia musical renaissance was due to the people of Philadelphia, to civic leaders like Bok, Van Rensselaer, and Wister, to chorus director Henry Gordon Thunder and his associates, and to all of the hard working committee members who had now made music and music making the cultural cornerstone of Philadelphia's future. Stokowski described their efforts as an "inspiration" to him.[8] It was also a typical Stokowskian subordination of egotism to the driving force of egoism.

Now the stage was set for more ambitious musical endeavors, more and better musicians in the orchestra playing better instruments, more adventurous programming with more premieres, more series of concerts, and the consequent increase in Philadelphia's musical pride in itself. This in turn resulted in more ambitious fund raising attempts to create a permanent endowment with which to cover the increased operating costs necessitated by such ambitious projects. With Edward Bok anonymously offering a $500,000 matching grant in May of 1916 if and when the people of Philadelphia could come up with a like sum, a second stage in Philadelphia's músical growth was initiated. The orchestra's four women's committees were joined by seventy-nine other groups, including new youth committees, who threw themselves into the effort as though they were saving the city itself. Indeed, they raised money under the logo, "Save the Orchestra." Stokowski's omnipresence drove home two visions of Philadelphia's possible musical future: the disaster of failing to fund for the future, and a glorious musical future in which each season would lead to a new musical plateau and to greater musical possibilities; this was providing, of course, that adequate funding was found. Between Stokowski's near religious proselytizing, the tempting anonymous matching grant as a carrot, and the growing musical pride of Philadelphia, the $500,000 fund was subscribed by November of 1916.[9]

One of the stipulations of Edward Bok's gift was that conductor Stokowski be given a five-year contract as proof of Philadelphia's support of his program and ideas, and that his imagination and ability to get things done be given freer rein. Bok's generous support was symptomatic of the increased trust in Stokowski's leadership shown by the older social leaders of Philadelphia's mainline and by the newer money-men attracted by Stokowski's blend of romantic idealism and hard-headed realism. Here was a musician who understood a balance sheet as well as a score. He knew how to get things done, and if he was sometimes brash and more than a little arrogant, these were traits not uncongenial to the businessman's measure of success. No less important, he was a cultural leader who had about him the aura of frontier American adventure and achievement even as he created new prestige—or "advertising" as one business-oriented money raiser put it—for the city of Philadelphia.[10]

The climax of this era of cultural organizing and psychological consciousness raising began in 1920 when Stokowski was awarded an honorary doctorate of music by the University of Pennsylvania. But the signal event came in Stokowski's tenth year with the orchestra. It was the bestowal of the first Philadelphia Award to Stokowski in 1922. The award was Edward Bok's brainchild with Leopold Stokowski in mind as the first recipient. The gala dinner and presentation ceremony included Stokowski, the members of the orchestra and of the orchestra's board of directors, the governor of Pennsylvania, the mayor of Philadelphia, a United States senator, and other luminaries. The award itself consisted of an illuminated vellum scroll that recounted Stokowski's achievements in the city. The scroll itself, together with a gold medal, rested in a hand-crafted ivory and copper casket—all of it the work of Pennsylvania artist Violet Oakley. In addition, a check for $10,000 was given to the maestro with praise for the "divine music" he had given to Philadelphia and for his unselfish service to the community.[11]

With the Philadelphia Award and the 1921–22 Philadelphia Orchestra season, I have arrived at that point assumed by conductor Michael Gielen for Stokowski's beginnings in Philadelphia. By 1921–22, Stokowski was able to fully exercise his support for new music, but to do so with an orchestra the like of which had not been seen anywhere before and with remarkable civic support. Stokowski treated his subscribers during the 1921–22 season to the American premieres of de Falla's "Suite" from *El Amor Brujo*, Stravinsky's *Le Sacre du Printemps*, Sibelius's Fifth Symphony, Satie's *Gymnopedies*, the Sibelius Violin Concerto, Alfredo Casella's *Pages of War*, Ernest Bloch's Suite for Viola and Orchestra, Walter Braunfel's *Fantastic Variations on a Theme of Berlioz*, Schoenberg's Five pieces for Orchestra, Mahler songs from *The Youth's Magic Horn*, with Elena Gerhardt as soloist, John Alden Carpenter's *A Pilgrim Vision* and yet more contemporary pieces by twentieth-century composers. And we shouldn't forget a piece that was first performed in Philadelphia on 10 February 1922, next carried to Massey Hall in Toronto for a Canadian tryout on February 22, introduced to a Carnegie Hall audience on February 28, and finally repeated in Philadelphia by popular demand, as the last work on the last concert of the 1921–22 season. The work was Stokowski's orchestral transcription of the Bach Passacaglia and Fugue in C Minor.[12]

While the Bach-Stokowski transcription was immediately a Philadelphia favorite, how was Stokowski able to program so much new, often dissonant and controversial music for the Philadelphia audience and not only get away with it, but actually increase his musical standing in the city—a mystery of sorts? It was not simply his hard won support based on past performance, nor yet the psychologically apt scolding of his audiences if they left or hissed performances of new works, in spite of his pleas for Philadelphia patrons to give such works a chance. More fundamental, it was his skill and imagination in programming. Typically, rather than programming whole concerts of crowd pleasers, thus lulling audiences into the complaisance and generally bovine musical enjoyment still common today, Stokowski kept his audiences on edge, generated tension and excitement by balancing romantic and classic, often ancient and very modern works, with works he knew his audience would love—their musical dessert after a dinner of often prickly fare. On 3 March 1922, the *Rite of Spring* was balanced by excerpts from Wagner's *Ring*. On 25 November 1921, Schoenberg's Five Orchestral Pieces, the spinach of the concert you might say, was surrounded *before* by Beethoven's *Coriolan* Overture and Schubert's Symphony no. 8 and *after* by a gut-churning favorite of Philadelphians, Sibelius's *Finlandia*, which certainly relaxed the tension and strain of Schoenberg with its whistleable tunes and patriotic fervor.

It has only been recently with Brian Plumb's systematic year-by-year listing of the Stokowski-Philadelphia programs in *Toccata*, the journal of the London-based Stokowski Society, that many of us have been able to appreciate the brilliance and range of Stokowski's programming. Stokowski possessed an amazing psychological awareness of the audience and directed his thrust toward shaking them, while educating them, while delighting them—a combination traditionally as rare in the concert hall as in the classroom, but just as needed.

Think of Stokowski's unorthodox musicianship, his family romancing, his parapsychological skills in communicating with and energizing his players, coupled to major abilities as organizer of both an orchestra and the musical life of a major city; then add his futurist role as musical innovator and acoustician. Is it any wonder that the critics covering his Philadelphia years found it difficult to analyze and evaluate who he was and what he was doing? To make matters more complicated Stokowski was morally, religiously, and sexually unconventional, which contributed to making him as unique and unusual a great musician as America has ever seen (See Appendix).[13]

Any revisionist study of Stokowski dealing with who he was and what he did—oh how simple that sounds—must, I think, deal with just how different Stokowski was when compared with his critics and with his peers in the conducting world. His penchant for innovation, together with a lack of concern for tradition, his peculiarly intuitive approach to music, and his disdain for the critics, all of these characteristics—whatever their intrinsic merit—made Stokowski a dangerous enigma to those critics and commentators who do much to shape our views of music and musicians. He was dangerous because he often ignored their norms, substituting his own goals for those traditionally expected. He was enigmatic because he ran outside the range of their experience and was impossible to measure, categorize, and compare in the usual way. They ignored the mysteries of Stokowski and concentrated on those foibles of the man that, when properly shaped became the stereotypical Stokowski, a grotesque of the real person.

For critics who wanted their conductors seemingly unworldly and guileless, there could appear a very worldly Stokowski. Through the twenties and up to the end of his life he was shrewd in money and contract matters. He was at his ease in the company of moneymen. He frankly enjoyed the entrepreneurial role of money maker and further relished the role of money raiser and booster for causes he believed worth pursuing. He did not share the common artistic antipathy toward science and technology that marked so many of his colleagues. Instead, he respected the skills of scientists and technicians in his and in allied fields. He carried on a lifelong love affair with the technical aspects of acoustics, concert hall design, and the making and reproduction of music. Without the faintest hint of apology, he also opted for the role of popularizer of symphonic music for the masses. He stressed the need to nationalize music, to move beyond eastern urban centers to find musicians, and to make music everywhere in America. All of these characteristics added up to the kind of musician that many influential critics—with their own ideas of how a conductor dedicated to serious music should act, look, and perform—would fear and detest at the same time.[14]

And here it would seem is the heart, the core, of much negative critical sentiment toward Stokowski over the years. Stokowski's lifestyle, his own conception of music and of dedication to music, ran, by turns, playfully, exuberantly, and arrogantly counter to the serious sense of mission shared by critics, who believed that there was a code of conduct and of performance standards that Stokowski brazenly violated.

The thoughtful concert goer can recognize the critical intellectual credo of the concert hall while groping to describe it. Such a credo has about it a certain high solemnity; a concern for matters of form that befit high culture. It leans toward humorlessness and tends to be extremely conventional in upholding standards that are already well established. It makes its own allowances for genius and excess in the cause of art, but within critically prescribed limits of interpretation and personal conduct. Within terms of this code, genius lies in the selfless search for purity of musical interpretation and the ability to get the orchestra to go along. Acceptable excess equates to the nervous irritability, high-strung demeanor, and temper—even tantrums—allowed to one felt to be engaged in the near religious search for musical perfection. There is an ecclesiastical quality that is at the center of this critical composite of values, and the conductor is supposed to be both priest for and the servant of the composer whose music he is playing.[15]

Acceptance of this gospel would make fair appraisal of Stokowski's gifts very difficult since so much in his musical style and accomplishment and in his complicated personality, even in his admitted excesses, ran counter to the social and musical conventions of his time.

Stokowski was neither a servant nor a priest in the House of Music. He was a Dionysian experimenter in music; he was sorcerer rather than priest, sensualist rather than servant. He was a playful pagan in a musical world dominated by serious-minded priests, scribes, and disciples. He was playful in the sense that unregimented youth is playful, that is, curious, delighting in the new and the experimental, and seeing old things with new eyes and hearing with new ears—always his own. His goal was always the innovation of tomorrow rather than the tradition of yesterday.

Those seemingly eccentric Stokowski touches—the hands sculpting the air in conducting; the halo of hair; the accents; the dark shirts and light ties; the love affair with recording dials (and with younger women), not to leave out his orchestral transcriptions and often idiosyncratic musical interpretations—all of these were of a piece with what Stokowski was, not with what he ought to have been to live up to critical expectation. And here, I think, is what is wrongheaded in much of the past writing about Stokowski. He has been appraised *in the light of what he wasn't* rather than in the context of what he was and what he achieved. With that in mind let me turn back to who and what the maestro was in the musical life of Philadelphia in the twenties and thirties.

By the midtwenties, with the founding of Philadelphia's Curtis Music Institute by Mary Louise Curtis Bok, again with Stokowski as a driving force, the maestro had rounded out what could in itself be considered a full and fruitful career. Until the press of other commitments drew him away, Stokowski taught conducting at Curtis and came into professional contact with gifted young conductors, instrumentalists, composers, and singers.[16] Here in the midtwenties, with enough accomplishments for more than one career completed, and surrounded by the ferment of Curtis, Stokowski now moved in another direction; he innovated in a new way that tapped into or built upon previous accomplishments and experience while transcending them. Stokowski, now in his midforties, was most likely undergoing the challenge of midlife and the need to change and to grow. When it came it was a daring and fateful move not only for the conductor, but for the arts in America, as Stokowski moved into the multimedia world of music-as-dance-as-drama-as-theater, with the special production needs—lighting, staging, costumes, and choreography—of such a world thrown in as well. Note, too, that as his working and personal relationships would be immensely broadened by cooperative work with skilled professionals outside the world of the concert hall, so his musical vision was propelled even more into tomorrow.[17]

The first step toward this career change came in 1927 when Stokowski, now forty-five, was introduced to Clair Reis of the League of Composers through their mutual friend, Wanda Landowska. The league was America's foremost producer of avant-garde staged musical productions. Ms. Reis wanted to enlist Stokowski's support and skills for league performances. At this and subsequent meetings, the maestro was intrigued and challenged by the idea of linking music and the stage in performance of new works. In 1928 he accepted from Ms. Reis the assignment of directing the dancers and pantomime, while conducting the singers and instrumentalists, in a league-sponsored U.S. premiere of Igor Stravinsky's *Les Noces*. In accepting, he explained to her that one of his reasons was that he knew musicians and singers but had never met theater people.[18]

By the time *Les Noces* triumphantly premiered at a packed New York Metropolitan Opera House later in the year, Stokowski had formed a firm friendship with Robert Edmond Jones, America's foremost director of stage lighting and design, who, like Stokowski, had volunteered to work on the production. Together they created a synthesis of design and lighting geared to the music's development. This was accomplished at the cost of Stokowski's battling with Serge Soudeikine, who wanted the lighting used primarily to show the cast's costumes—his costumes—to best advantage. Stokowski won. Soudeikine lost.[19] The premiere was an unqualified success, and Stokowski, immensely buoyed by the enterprise, pushed forward into this new and pioneering stage in much the same way that he ventured in 1912 when he had first come to Philadelphia at the age of thirty.

He did not relinquish his post as director of the Philadelphia Orchestra, and he continued, indeed stepped up, his ventures into unfamiliar repertoire in the concert hall, premiering the twenty-two-year-old Dmitri Shostakovich's First Symphony and making superb new electrical recordings for RCA.[20] But he entered a related yet new career and turned an important corner in his life. Greater than the change that came between 1936 and 1941 when he left the Philadelphia Orchestra for good were the changes of 1928, 1929, and 1930 that outlined his new stage of development and growth. Contrary to the easy and negative assumptions made by critics about Stokowski's motives for changes (which by the late thirties would lead to the world of film), the facts indicate a man and musician of preeminent ability and imagination bored by the triumphs of the past, capable of growth, and most important of all, possessing the egoistic drive and courage needed to make such a break with his own past while pursuing musical goals both realistic and pioneering.

In short order, following *Les Noces*, Stokowski decided to stage a concert version of the original Mussorgsky score of *Boris Godunov*, which, up to this time, had been performed in the United States only in Rimsky-Korsakov's prettified version of the opera. Traveling to the Soviet Union in 1929 for a copy of the original score, Stravinsky and his wife, Evangeline Johnson, were treated to a Moscow performance of *Boris* bowdlerized by the Soviet authorities into a propaganda vehicle for the communist regime. At a reception with Soviet musical greats following the performance, Stokowski was asked to speak. Angrily he denounced the production as a violation of great music, noting that his hosts' generosity toward him did not equal their prostitution of Mussorgsky's great opera for political purposes. With a photocopied score in hand, Stokowski and his wife hastily left a now hostile Moscow atmosphere and traveled to the more congenial company of young composer, Dmitri Shostakovich, and his circle in Leningrad.[21]

Back in Philadelphia and with the invaluable assistance of the young Sylvan Levin, Stokowski performed the opera in the original during that same year, utilizing the talent of the Curtis Institute and of the Philadelphia Orchestra in performance. Not until forty years later would the Metropolitan Opera Company perform *Boris* in the original.

Again during 1929, Stokowski inaugurated the first American commercial radio broadcasts of symphonic music with an initial program of the Philadelphia Orchestra playing Mozart's Symphony no. 40, followed in innovative Stokowski fashion by Stravinsky's controversial *Le Sacre du Printemps* during the second week's broadcast.

Stokowski now accepted an offer from the League of Composers to serve as musical director for perhaps the greatest premiere in American musical history.

The 1929 offer was to direct twin premieres, in one evening, of major works by Arnold Schoenberg and Igor Stravinsky. Surely, one of the great moments in American music, theater, and dance occurred when Musical Director Leopold Stokowski conducted the Philadelphia Orchestra in the League of Composers' premiere productions of Schoenberg's musical pantomime, *Die Glückliche Hand*, and Stravinsky's fully staged ballet, *Le Sacre du*

Printemps, on the same evening. Stokowski, having accepted the volunteer assignment in 1929, now had to find the funds necessary to pay for it. The 1930 productions were necessarily preceded by a 1929 battle between Stokowski and Philadelphia Orchestra manager, Arthur Judson, over whether the Philadelphia Orchestra Association would underwrite the heavy costs of production for the league. Stokowski's plan called for three performances in Philadelphia and two at the Metropolitan Opera House in New York. Judson vowed that such works could not fill the house and charged that they would be economically disastrous whatever their supposed merit might be. Stokowski countered with arguments centering on the board's duty to new music, on the need for just such a venture at this time (the time of the 1929 crash) and pragmatically sweetened the gamble with the promise of a Philadelphia Orchestra benefit concert to guarantee costs of the league production. Stokowski won.[22]

Apparent in this particular victory was Stokowski's extraordinary singleness of purpose and his lifelong tendency to refuse compromise in musical concerns that were, for him, of first-rate importance. Once he had made up his mind on what should be done, he bent his whole effort toward accomplishing his purpose by making that purpose *seem* and *be* possible, rather than by negotiating down toward the hallowed half-loaf. For many, his positive accomplishments in using this method were negatively outweighed by his rigidity and arrogance. Certainly Arthur Judson never forgot Stokowski's intransigence.[23]

Finances were guaranteed, and Stokowski was set as music director of the double production by late 1929. Doris Humphrey, America's number two dancer after Martha Graham, was enlisted to dance-pantomime the Schoenberg piece, while Martha Graham herself was persuaded to dance the sacrificial maiden in Stravinsky's ballet. Nicholas Roerich, to whom Stravinsky had dedicated the *Sacre*, agreed to repeat his 1918 role in the Paris premiere by designing costumes and scenery for the league production. Léonide Massine choreographed the ballet. Robert Edmond Jones created his own revolution in lighting for both productions, advancing the cause of proper theater lighting to match the contributions of Reis and Stokowski. Rouben Mamoulian—director of the later *Porgy and Bess*—took over the arduous job of stage directing *Die Glückliche Hand*, whose singing cast of three and chorus were coupled with the story-telling light and shadow of Humphrey's pantomime into a new kind of art form.[24]

The Philadelphia and New York performances took place in April of 1930 to sold-out houses. The artistic gamble was won. Popular audience reaction was enthusiastic. The principals were proud of their creation. But Clair Reis retrospectively probed the one painful spot in the whole affair, which was the response of music reviewers who did not, from past experience, understand nor appreciate what had been done in the productions directed by Stokowski. As traditionalists, the critics seemed unaware of the new linking of drama to music, the new lighting techniques, and the adventurous stage direction.[25]

At the very least, she argued, drama critics should be assigned to such productions to balance the limitations and traditionalist skew of establishment music scribes. Olin Downes, music critic of the *New York Times* and dean of the city's brotherhood, set the tone for reviews of the twin performances. He described Stokowski as the right conductor for this sort of thing, then spent the bulk of his review on the tastelessness and decadence of the subject matter. His heading for the twin review telegraphed the account, for in its bold print he found the Schoenberg piece to be "decadent" and the *Sacre* better without the ballet—this with Martha Graham dancing! The review's themes amounted to a string of negatives and bottomed out as Downes found the affair un-American, even though there were points of interest in the twin productions, including the "primitive" energy of the *Sacre*.[26]

Earlier I mentioned the critics' difficulty in dealing overall with Stokowski the man and what he was to American music rather than what he wasn't according to the canon, credo, gentleman's agreement—call it what you will—of the American musical establishment. With the efforts of America's number one and number two dancers, aided by the genius of Mamoulian, Jones, and Roerich and the playing of the Philadelphia Orchestra, those 1930 performances marked Stokowski's newest push into the future. All of this indicates the provincial limitations of critical judgment in America in 1930, but specifically, in reference to Stokowski, it signals the contemporary and, I believe, later failure of critics to recognize a special and unique force in American music. Stokowski's pushing toward the future went on even as Arturo Toscanini was touring Europe with a New York Philharmonic Orchestra that played twenty-three concerts in fifteen cities and nine countries without once playing a piece by an American composer. This fact was noted by American composer Roy Harris, who sadly wrote that such musical behavior was perfectly acceptable to American music critics. At that, he was kinder than Edgard Varèse, who blanketed Toscanini as the arch opponent of all contemporary music.[27]

As for Stokowski's herculean labors in introducing Americans to new and unfamiliar European works at the time, he had gone too far and too fast, and Olin Downes, bewildered by his evening at the Met, could only view the event as un-American, which meant simply that it was outside his range of experience and insight as indeed Stokowski was as well.

A forty-eight-year-old Stokowski's reaction to all of this was to redouble his efforts in this new direction by following the Stravinsky-Schoenberg double bill with a Philadelphia depression premiere of Alban Berg's *Wozzeck* the following year. Again utilizing the talent of the Curtis Institute, the Philadelphia Grand Opera Company, and the Philadelphia Orchestra, this monumental first was staged at the Academy of Music under Stokowski's direction and without League of Composers sponsorship. The project was underwritten by Mary Bok and required 148 rehearsals of the difficult and culturally unfamiliar score. As at the earlier Stravinsky-Schoenberg premiere, the audience was ecstatic, but this time even the critics acknowledged *Wozzeck* to be a work of genius, beautifully performed by Stokowski's combination of student and professional forces.[28]

Strengthening the likelihood that Stokowski's artistic explosion of the late twenties and early thirties was a life stage change of direction was the fact that he seriously considered forming an opera company following *Wozzeck's* success. But the realities of the depression convinced even Stokowski that this sort of a new career venture was not possible.[29]

Instead of pioneering in one such unified area of endeavor, the conductor directed his energies into three channels that were diverse, yet were linked to Stokowski's need to grow and to his fascination with America's musical future. He retained the directorship of the Philadelphia Orchestra under contractual terms that gave him full decision-making power over program, soloist, and guest conductor choices. His programs continued to emphasize new music, balanced by older and little-played music, with popular concert items included to sweeten this sophisticated diet. At the same time he followed up the successes of *Les Noces*, *Le Sacre du Printemps*, *Boris Godunov*, and *Wozzeck* with premieres of new and challenging stage works whenever the opportunity appeared or Stokowski could create the opportunity.

Third, the maestro broadened and deepened his early interest in the acoustics and technology of music played and recorded.

He had been the first conductor in America to acoustically record symphonic music (1917) and the first to electrically record an entire symphony (1925).[30] As the thirties opened Stokowski's interest in new recording technology provided him with a third avenue in which to express his creative curiosity and his tendency to experiment with tomorrow. He made eighteen 33⅓ RPM recordings for RCA Victor before a depression-borne decline in sales forced Victor to cancel the program.[31]

Of more lasting interest than the abortive long plays was Stokowski's work on frequency modulation (F.M.) and stereophonic reproduction at the University of Pennsylvania that culminated in a cooperative venture with Bell telephone Laboratories on America's first symphonic stereo recordings. During the concert season of 1931–32, Stokowski and the Philadelphia Orchestra made one hundred experimental recordings utilizing equipment set up in the Academy of Music by Bell Laboratories.[32]

In the fifties Stokowski and his friend, Fritz Reiner, made the first commercial symphonic stereo recordings (1954), and in the sixties Stokowski made the first symphonic recording utilizing London Records' twenty-channel Phase 4 system (1964). But the 1931–32 Philadelphia recordings are more important because they allow us to hear in rich—occasionally stereo—sound the results of one of the great musical partnerships at its peak.[33] Stokowski, who had already become the most sophisticated acoustician among the world's conductors, became the first electronically knowledgeable conductor as a result of his work at the University of Pennsylvania and with the Bell engineers. Stokowski was everywhere, notebook in hand, questioning the technicians, experimenting with stereo sound levels and the placement of orchestral choirs and soloists, and mastering the relationship between the music played and the electronic equipment needed to translate that music onto record. Out of this work—in Stokowski's case I am tempted to write *play*—grew the world's greatest recording conductor. By that I mean the most knowledgeable in all phases of the interrelated playing and recording of symphonic music and the most skilled in translating that knowledge into recordings of the richest sound possible. Charles O'Connell, then artistic director of RCA Victor's Red Seal Division and supervisor of many Philadelphia Orchestra recordings sessions with Stokowski, described the conductor of the thirties as unique in his ability to blend artistic performance and technical knowledge in recordings that were at the time the most beautiful sounding and most technically advanced performances ever committed to disc.[34]

Most of these recordings from the thirties were, for financial reasons, of standard concert fare at the expense of the new or controversial works that the maestro so faithfully championed on stage or in the concert hall. But in 1932, even as he inaugurated a new series of radio concerts on NBC, Stokowski combined his penchants for recording and for performing controversial works with a live performance recording of Arnold Schoenberg's mammoth *Gurrelieder* at Philadelphia's Metropolitan Opera House. Five soloists, three choruses, a narrator, and an agumented orchestra of 122 players—a total of 537 performers—played and recorded the work in April 1932. So great was the public response that the production was repeated in New York to sell-out attendance.[35]

Radio and public concerts, technical research into sound reproduction, and recording activity did not keep Stokowski from continuing his interest in musical theater. In 1931 and 1932 Stokowski conducted and directed no less than four additional premieres of major works for stage and orchestra, incidentally furthering his rightful position as a dramatist in music.

His continuing association with the League of Composers led him into three of these. Again working with theater people, including the gifted Robert Edmond Jones, Stokowski directed New York productions of Prokofiev's *Pas d'Acier* and Stravinsky's *Oedipus Rex* in 1931, and of a truly startling production of Schoenberg's *Pierrot Lunaire* in 1932. With the stage dark and the instrumental ensemble's music photostated by Stokowski onto black paper with notes in white, the light needed by the musicians to play was reduced to next to nothing. Even their white collars were shrouded by Stokowski in black cloth against the darkened stage. Mina Hager, as Pierrot, was caught by a baby spot light to become the center of audience attention. However, Stokowski's hands were also lighted to cue Pierrot and the musicians.

Coincidentally with these New York performances, Stokowski premiered Carlos Chavez's ballet, *H.P.* (for horsepower), in a 1932 Philadelphia production. The young Mexican composer's balletic theme was the contrast between the traditional slow-moving agrarian life of the tropics and the incursion of a dynamic industrial progress into this world. With choreography by Catherine Littlefield, the production dazzled the eye with costumes and sets designed by Diego Rivera. Of lesser musical interest than the productions of Prokofiev, Schoenberg, Stravinsky, and Chavez, but with a poignancy all its own, was the Stokowski U.S. premiere of Kurt Weill's cantata, *Lindbergh's Flight*, with libretto by Bertolt Brecht. This was the first American work that Weill composed in fleeing Hitler's Germany.[36]

Given Stokowski's unprecedented work load and accomplishments from 1928 to 1933, one is almost tempted to sympathize with those critics who, facing this protean force, continued to comment on his lifestyle rather than to seriously deal with his exuberant conception of music and music making.

Since Stokowski was a futurist, far ahead of his time, even the health regimen, begun by him in the twenties and maintained for many years, became a part of the caricature rather than a tribute to his insight and an explanation of his ability to carry a workload and maintain an innovative schedule that would have overwhelmed any three other men or women. Deep breathing exercises, meditation, yoga, a diet light on meat with an emphasis on grains and vegetables, little tobacco, alcohol in very sparing amounts—these nutritional and emotional health practices were, I believe, inextricably linked with his self-created family romance, his cosmic sense of music's meaning, psychic powered performances, and the ability to relax completely at will. So armored, the fifty-year-old Stokowski was able to handle the schedule of the late twenties and early thirties with twelve-hour workdays and six hours of sleep a night without so much as a cold, let alone serious illness.[37]

Since millions of Americans now subscribe to one or more of the above mentioned practices proven scientifically and statistically to be the preventive key to good health, is it not fair to describe Stokowski, once caricatured as a "food faddist," to be a prophet in this area as in so many others?

As Stokowski rounded out those five creative years of change, from 1928 to 1933, neither his capacity for hard work nor his innovative skills made him immune to the influences of the Great Depression and to the increasing demand of his ego for change.

By 1933 the financial reality of depression, Stokowski's new stage and electronic interests, his uncompromising position on the need to play contemporary music for Philadelphia Orchestra audiences, and the understandable concern of the orchestra's board of directors over loss of revenue added up to a rupture between Stokowski and management. A board demand that he stop playing too much new music too soon infuriated the maestro. As early as 1931, Stokowski, well into his new enthusiasm for the theater and for opera, had defied the board when, without his knowledge, its members had informed subscribers that until better times returned, the orchestra would not be playing avant-garde works and added that Stokowski was in accord with this policy. This was in violation of Stokowski's contract, which gave him sole right to determine programs for the season. In defense of board action, it should be noted that the preceding season had shown a deficit, its first in more than ten years. Stokowski's response when told of the board's action by his chief backer among board members, Alexander Van Rensselaer, was an angry one-two verbal punch to the effect that he didn't need instruction in programming and would play what he wanted to play.[38]

Stokowski, supported by the subscribers, did exactly that for the next two seasons, but by the concert season of 1933–34, the rupture came. Only phenomenal support by subscribers kept him in Philadelphia at all after that. As it turned out, he was subsequently away more and conducting in Philadelphia less each year until he left for good after the 1940–41 season. The interim period marked Stokowski's emotional and professional break with Philadelphia. With a triumphant Philadelphia Orchestra national tour in 1936 to sweeten the parting, Stokowski found himself in Los Angeles for the final concerts of the tour at Shrine Auditorium. Prior to concert time, Stokowski called the musicians together to ask for all that they had to give since their finale was to be their best. A young Robert Shaw, who was in the audience for his first orchestral concert and who was bowled over by the performance, later told Abram Chasins that that concert had changed his life.[39]

Within a year, the man who had once wanted to meet theater people would be hobnobbing with motion picture people and would be in the thick of yet another innovative challenge at the age of fifty-five.

For many critics it meant that Stokowski had sold out. Even harsher was the judgment of Arturo Toscanini, who referred to Stokowski as a "prostitute."[40] For millions of Americans who had never been to a symphony concert, particularly young Americans in small towns, Stokowski's decision would shortly introduce them to the concert world by way of film, acquainting them with great symphonic music. In this case it was magnificently played by the Philadelphia Orchestra and presented on a multi-channel, 35 mm tape as the soundtrack to *Fantasia*—eight years after Stokowski's pioneering stereo work and nearly fifteen years before stereo became a part of the recording industry.[41]

In the fifties, long after *Fantasia* had been made and even longer since Martha Graham had made history in *La Sacre du Printemps*, Lincoln Kirstein paid tribute to the League of Composers team saying that their work in the late twenties and early thirties to bring music, dance, and theater together had directly paved the way for the idea and the creation of the New York City Centre for Music and Drama.[42] Stokowski had not only paved the way in the early thirties, but was actually there in New York in 1944 at Mayor Fiorello La Guardia's request to spur the project on by creating the New York Symphony Orchestra as the resident ensemble of the New York Centre. Serving as creator and conductor of the orchestra without fee, Stokowski arranged for recordings,[43] planned the concerts, and designed the acoustical shell for the Mecca Temple concert hall. In addition, he arranged for printing and publicity as well as footing the bill for a 1944 Christmas pageant. He stayed but one hard-working and formative season, leaving the orchestra in 1945 to his long time associate, Sylvan Levin, and to the twenty-five-year-old conductor, Leonard Bernstein, once a student at Curtis Institute.[44]

It is now more than a generation since Lincoln Kirstein's tribute in the fifties. From our contemporary vantage point, it is clear that the later Lincoln Center in New York, the Kennedy Center in Washington, and the Music Center for the Performing Arts in Los Angeles are also as directly in that line of descent, as we are in debt to the pioneering Stokowski of the twenties, thirties, and forties for his work on behalf of multi-media art in an appropriate setting.

As for Stokowski's later career, after the experiments of the twenties, thirties, and forties and his wandering years during the fifties, there would be two more clear-cut stages of artistic growth. The first, centering on the creation and flowering of the American Symphony Orchestra, was highlighted by Stokowski's championship of another musical maverick, Charles Ives. Stokowski's last life stage began at age ninety with his move to England and a last five year period devoted, from late 1975 to 1977, exclusively to recording. The life of maverick Stokowski, like the life of maverick Charles Ives, could be summed up by yet a third maverick, Henry David Thoreau:

> A man's life should be a stately march and when to his fellows it shall seem irregular and inharmonious, he will only be stepping to a

livelier measure, or his nicer ear hurry him into a thousand symphonies and concordant variations. There will be no halt ever . . . or such pause as is richer than any sound, when the melody runs into such depth and wildness as to be no longer heard, but simplicity consented to with the whole life and being . . . for then the music will not fail to swell into greater sweetness and volume, and itself rule the movement it inspired.[45]

Stokowski (seated on podium) with choral director, soloists, the Mendelssohn Choir, and the Philadelphia Orchestra in Toronto's Massey Hall. The picture most likely commemorated the orchestra's 1922 four concert appearances in Toronto, during which a complete performance of the Berlioz *Damnation of Faust* was given at the 21 February concert. Courtesy of Paul Hoeffler.

This signed Stokowski photograph of the conductor in action out of doors was made for Miss Sarah Thompson prior to 1926. Note the twig baton. Courtesy of Dr. Edwin Heilakka, Curtis Institute of Music, Philadelphia.

This sketch of Stokowski both conducting the Philadelphia Orchestra and consoling his daughter, Sonya, was made in 1925 by concertgoer Margaret G. Kairer who explained it as follows: "A Saturday afternoon youth concert at the Academy of Music with the Philadelphia Orchestra, Leopold Stokowski conducting. Among a group of very young dancers was Stokowski's daughter, Sonya. During the performance Sonya tripped and fell. She picked herself up and went crying to her father at the podium and he comforted her without pause in the program." Courtesy of Dr. Edwin Heilakka, Curtis Institute of Music, Philadelphia.

Stokowski in Havana's La Florida Bar, 1934. Courtesy of Sylvan Levin.

White plaster plaque of Stokowski done by Charlotte Mercer Jones about 1935 and donated to Curtis Institute of Music by Miss Jones's nephew Franklyn Wynne Paris. Courtesy of Dr. Edwin Heilakka, Curtis Institute of Music.

Stokowski in Vanguard Records control room with Seymour Solomon, producer of the 1967 baroque set *Jesu, Joy of Man's Desiring*. Courtesy of Igor Kipnis.

Stokowski shaking hands with cellist Charles McCracken at the Vanguard Records recording session of 21 April 1967. Courtesy of Igor Kipnis.

Stokowski in 1969, New York City, © Paul Hoeffler.

Informal 1969 portrait photograph of Stokowski, © Paul Hoeffler.

Stokowski with American Symphony Orchestra tympanist Elayne Jones, Central Park, 1969, © Paul Hoeffler.

Stokowski discussing the 1970 premiere of Andrzej Panufnik's *Universal Prayer* with Thomas Grady, organist of the Cathedral of St. John the Divine, New York City, © Paul Hoeffler.

February, 1971 Stokowski rehearsal of the American Symphony Orchestra, Carnegie Hall, New York City, © Paul Hoeffler.

April, 1971 Stokowski rehearsal of the American Symphony Orchestra, Philharmonic Hall, Lincoln Center, New York City, © Paul Hoeffler.

American Symphony Orchestra players, Personnel Manager Arthur Arron (in white shirt) and Stokowski at an orchestra softball game, 1971, Central Park, New York City, © Paul Hoeffler.

Stokowski waiting for the throw, American Symphony Orchestra softball game, 1971, Central Park, New York City, © Paul Hoeffler.

Stokowski with American Symphony Orchestra softball players, 1971, Central Park, New York City, © Paul Hoeffler.

Stokowski talking things over with a teenager, 1971, Central Park, New York City, © Paul Hoeffler.

Stokowski with Urania Giordano, 1971, New York City, © Paul Hoeffler.

Stokowski in his Fifth Avenue apartment, 1971, New York City,

Stokowski at his work table, 1971, New York City,

Stokowski at his work table, 1971, New York City, © Paul Hoeffler

Stokowski with right-hand man and confidant Jack Baumgarten, April 1971, New York City, © Paul Hoeffler.

4
Leopold Stokowski: A Reevaluation

In his delightful 1958 book, *The Musical Life,* critic Irving Kolodin, drawing on an essay originally written for the *Saturday Review,* deliberately torpedoed the clichés of many of his colleagues in describing conductor Leopold Stokowski. He told no stories about the "glamour boy" of conducting, his womanizing, or his Hollywood adventures. Instead, with only the slightest of needles to Stokowski, Kolodin offered several insights about the musician and asked a couple of thoughtful questions, doing so with something like awe of the seventy-year-old conductor. Kolodin remarked that Stokowski was unique among conductors and was difficult to fathom because he combined a boy's sense of wide-eyed wonder with a mature musical sophistication of the highest order, the whole governed by a deep intuitive grasp of things rather than by rational judgment and pragmatic logic.

Describing Stokowski's performances as memorable, but often mystifying, Kolodin wrote that he would gladly go to any New York concert that Stokowski gave, aware in advance that performance traditions would not be observed by the conductor. Quite unlike, yet fully the equal of, traditionalist Toscanini, Stokowski seemed to draw his interpretive power and his strength of command from within rather than from musical tradition and accepted concert norms. Like a volcano, continued Kolodin, he tapped his reserve out of some fundamental energy source deep in his nature. His performances were musically engrossing and exciting even when they seemed to be wrongheaded, but, mused Kolodin as though contemplating some mystery of nature, how could a gifted musician with two generations of experience in the concert hall remain so contrary, so highly charged, in a traditionally regulated art form so clear cut in its basic outline and rules? And with the acknowledgment that Stokowski was and had ever been outside the established order of the concert world, Mr. Kolodin moved on to other musical matters.[1]

In preceding material and in the Appendix I have explored the reasons for some of what Mr. Kolodin wondered at, finding fantasy, romantic musicianship, egoism, unusual psychic gifts, and a cosmic identification with music at the elemental level of Stokowski's approach to *Euterpe*. Nor was this music making a profession or a job in the normal sense. Music was the muse-mistress to be constantly pursued and wooed in vibrant sensual sound. As to his willfulness in performance, it proceeded from the performer's belief that the truest sort of music was generated by the emotional-musical communion of the conductor with the work of the composer, or as he sometimes put it, with what was in the composer's heart. He did not mean it in the traditionalist sense of strict and unvaried adherence to the printed score; for a score—as Stokowski was wont to remind us—often included misprints and copyist's errors, while leaving out the composer's revisionist markings for actual performance. The maestro's sense of communion was based on attempting a living and spontaneous performance, described by Stokowski as sometimes in accord with his own feeling for the work and hopefully in accord with the spirit of the composer. To the question, What makes you certain that what you're doing with a piece of music matches the composer's intent? Stokowski replied, at age ninety-two, that he couldn't be certain but hoped that it matched. A year earlier Stokowski had answered critic Edward Greenfield's question about interpreting Beethoven in a similar vein, saying that he tried to ask help of the immortal, so that in conducting a Beethoven work he wouldn't ruin it. At first reading this kind of response seems unlike the maestro of the Philadelphia thirties who as Sylvan Levin recalls, threw a score to the floor then stamped on it with the observation that notes on paper weren't music, that what you did with those notes—and did "from the heart"—separated routine mechanical performances from the attempt to realize the life and spirit of music.[2]

Yet the feisty Stokowski of the thirties and the aged maestro of the seventies both believed that there was a music, a beauty, an emotional truth that lay beneath the notes and in the composer's heart; this truth could only be expressed by actual performance—or recording—in which the re-creator of the music tried to realize the creator's intent, transmitting it to his players and presenting it to the public as a spontaneous and living work of art. His or her next performance might well play differently, but the attempt at the emotional-musical essence would remain the same.

This performance approach of Stokowski's seems to have remained much the same for more than sixty years, causing considerable controversy, because to re-create music in this fashion was, in effect, to cocreate it, an obligation and an honor that Stokowski on occasion claimed as his.[3] Had his field been drama, there would have been little or no outcry since the fashion in drama has been to accept a variety of approaches to playing both contemporary works and classics. Beyond the basic stage directions and attributes described for the characters and provided by the author, there have been tens, scores, hundreds of nuance variations available to directors and actors, which change the performance of a play or even its basic themes. Imagine prescribing the *only*, the *correct* way to do Shakespeare, Euripedes, or Ibsen. Yet that is exactly what one finds in the tradition of commentary on symphonic music. To the musical purists Stokowski's sin was not only experimentation with symphonic fare in the matter of nuance, color, and interpretation as such, but as well his delight in transcribing nonorchestral works for orchestra and in arranging symphonic syntheses of operatic works such as *Parsifal, Tristan and Isolde*, and *Boris Godunov* for symphonic performance. There you have it: purity versus curiosity; traditionalism versus experiment; literalism versus spontaneity; in these two sharply divided codes of creativity and performance, the drama consensus has come down on one side and the musical consensus on the other.

Through all of the controversy over his maverick approach to the muse of music, musical dramatist Stokowski went his way transcribing, cocreating, and experimenting, as in his fourth guest appearance with the Boston Symphony Orchestra in 1968. In addition to Mozart, Beethoven, and Tchaikovsky, the maestro included his symphonic synthesis of *Boris Godunov* on the program. In advance of his arrival, Stokowski's own edition of the score arrived so much added to, deleted from, and generally amended as to be difficult to decipher. However, even the latest corrections failed to predict what would occur during Stokowski's several performances of the work with the Boston Symphony Orchestra. Each performance of *Boris* was noticeably different from the others, sometimes veering completely away from Stokowski's own markings in the score. When the orchestra's librarian asked the conductor about these variant interpretations, Stokowski responded disingenuously that he was still experimenting with the piece and as yet had no single satisfactory approach to it. One should note that as of 1968 the work was more than thirty years old and had been twice recorded by the maestro in equally varied interpretations (see Discography). Across the Atlantic, London Symphony Orchestra flutist Gerald Jackson would write in that same year of 1968 a most succinct explanation of this phenomenon as he had experienced it. Those dog-eared parts that were constantly being changed were only a secondary means for achieving spontaneity. Essentially, wrote Jackson, Stokowski's goal was to achieve a fresh approach to the work each time he played it,[4] a rare tribute to both his musical skills and his unusual interpretive power with the performers.

Perhaps no musician understood so well nor responded more favorably to what Stokowski was doing than did the late Glenn Gould. A fiercely independent and cocreative force in his own right, Gould recalled in the late seventies what the conductor had meant to him as a young music student in the forties and fifties. He noted that to admire Stokowski within the musical walls of academe was not done. Musical academics described him as a "sell-out" who had given up serious music. They contrasted him to their own hero, Arturo Toscanini, whose devotion to music was pure, whose authentic orchestral interpretations were a weekly guarantee of traditional musicianship on NBC. As Gould remembered his own academic experience, he cited one of his teachers who couldn't believe that the young Gould could appreciate Bach, play Bach on the organ, and yet respect Stokowski.

Gould used such judgments as the negative basis for a most vigorous and succinct counterattack in support of Stokowski and his accomplishments. And he did so by listing a few things he believed that Stokowski had done during his career. Hadn't he positively changed the direction of symphonic music in the United States by his accomplishments with the Philadelphia Orchestra? Hadn't he created in that orchestra a model of playing excellence for the world? Hadn't he, time after time, performed new music against the wishes of the traditionalists and by so doing risked conducting positions and his relative standing in the world of music? And why as it, queried Gould, that the sound of his numerous recordings stood the test of time so well when compared with those of his peers?

All of this was true, wrote Gould, yet it was as though it didn't count since Stokowski wasn't a *proper* musician and as the consensus had it, was a "sell out." In short, as Gould presented his case, a discussion of Stokowski with proper musical authorities began and ended, in circular fashion, with the same conclusion.

Yet as the older Glenn Gould remembered his own youthful

reaction to Stokowski when he, Gould, was a student, it was antithetical to that proper consensus view. Gould summed it up by recalling that radio and record performances by Stokowski left him feeling consistently energized and ennobled. For the young soloist-to-be, Stokowski created a model of what the performer could and should dare in musical performance.[5]

Not until 1957 did Gould meet Stokowski. Not until the sixties did they work together. It was in New York where the patriarch—how he would hate that word—of American conductors was working with his American Symphony Orchestra that Stokowski came into close working contact with the brilliant young Canadian pianist. Gould, as we've seen, was much taken with Stokowski's musicianship and with his courage as innovator and interpreter. Out of this came a most unorthodox recording of Beethoven's *Emperor Concerto*[6] as well as a published conversation with the maestro and a radio portrait of him for the Canadian Broadcasting Corporation.

Gould's greatest admiration for Stokowski was reserved for that spontaneous and improvisatory style of performance that had characterized the Stokowski interpretation for so long. Gould used the word "ecstatic" to describe the phenomenon. While in preparation for a concert or recording, Stokowski intellectually studied and emotionally felt his way through the work to be performed, and he shared the fruits of that process with his musicians; however, at concert time he would throw caution to the winds. Immediately before a concert, Stokowski would meditate alone in his dressing room, removing mind and energy from the planning and interpretive concerns of preparing for the concert so as to focus his energy for actual performance. His practice was to move from trance to podium to down beat in seconds, and, with distractions left in the wings, he would command the performance on the basis of his feeling for the composer and the work at the moment. It was then that he released all of the communicative energy at his command, drawing on that elemental and internal force described by Irving Kolodin and explored in chapter 2. This spontaneous approach often provided the unexpected—indeed often interpretively unrehearsed—performance of Tchaikovsky or Brahms. Gould saw in this artistic gamble the intuitive key to the excitement generated by Stokowski's conducting since his performances would succeed or fail on the basis of his ability to imbue the orchestra, in performance, with his own feeling and interpretive voice.[7]

Stokowski allowed—no—empowered in himself and his players the freedom to react with the music on a psychological, intuitive, and emotional level. Such an approach allows for no paradigm of planning the perfect performance, rehearsed for a note-perfect reading and executed with perfectly calibrated tempi, phrasing, and dynamics. The *ecstatic* Stokowski, in Gould's sense of the word, threw the performance into peril by attempting at concert time to find the blood and heart of the work and to project its emotional life in the here and now. A note-perfect performance is repeatable, adds Gould. An ecstatic performance cannot be duplicated since it comes from the performer's very being and his or her feeling for the work being performed at the time of performance.[8]

In the late forties Mr. Charles O'Connell described much the same phenomenon, although from a different perspective. O'Connell had served as classical music director for RCA Victor and for Columbia Masterworks, and as chief engineer for many Stokowski recordings during the thirties and forties. He, too, noted the marked break between careful and planned preparation for a concert and the performance itself. O'Connell remembered that Stokowski invariably arrived for rehearsal after intensive study of the score, knowing what he wanted from the musicians and what he believed to be the interpretive heart of the work he wished to project in performance. He rehearsed on the basis of that interpretation, enlisting his players' aid in realizing his vision. Stokowski's effect on the orchestra in actual performance, remembered O'Connell, was quite different in several ways. The orchestra's range of expressivity was markedly greater, and the performance generated an almost painfully intense level of playing that had not been heard in rehearsal. It was as though the orchestra, in a musical sense, became a part of the maestro; this characteristic was most clear-cut when Stokowski altered orchestral phrasing previously rehearsed and did so with a single look toward the section concerned. It was only at concert time, recalled O'Connell, that Stokowski drew out of the players everything they had to give and more.[9]

In harmony with O'Connell's understanding of the difference between Stokowski's rehearsals and concerts were Edna Phillips's memories of working with the maestro. As harpist with the Philadelphia Orchestra during the thirties, she had been through scores of rehearsals and concerts with Stokowski. In her address at the 1982 Stokowski Centennial celebration at Curtis Institute she recalled that rehearsals, which were models of order and regularity, did not telegraph what would happen at performance time, when the beauty and power of the orchestra could transcend normal limits and reach the "stars"—an image Ms. Phillips attributed to oboeist Marcel Tabuteau.[10]

Even earlier than O'Connell and Phillips, H. L. Mencken caught something of the same thing when Band Master Leopold Stokowski led Philadelphia's 1925 Band of Gold—145 strong—through his own transcriptions of Strauss, Sibelius, Sousa, Wagner, and Bach. Here the musical theme lay in the contrast between the martial manliness so much associated with band music and what the maestro served up in addition. There was, wrote Mencken, unending and varied color, shading and sound volume that could be reduced to the softest of pianissimos, splendid phrasing, and playing that held the concert goers rapt, with neither cough nor whisper to break their attention. And, wonder of wonders, there was Bach for band that was "*kolossal*."[11]

From the twenties into the seventies come reliable reports of the intuitive unorthodoxy and orchestral magic practiced by Stokowski. Like Chaplin, Stokowski could be the master showman, could innovate, could present to the world a classic artistic success story; yet, again like Chaplin, he could remain in touch with the secret of his success, that is, his experience, his deepest feelings, and his fantasy life. Just as Chaplin could excite an audience with his daring and break its heart with the pathos of his tramp, so Stokowski could pierce the heart of his audience with the drama, majesty, sensuality, and, above all, the pathos of music in which he had found the link to his own being through that of the composer.[12]

However, to offset all of those who were in varying ways delighted by the conductor and who forgave his sometimes failed sound experiments and his sometimes oversexed or overindulgent musical offerings, there were other judgments of Stokowski much harsher in tone. There were criticisms that Stokowski's so-called magic and sorcery were nothing of the kind. Rather than sorcery, Stokowski's way with an orchestra—however he did it—was sound seduction at best, and at worst it was a travesty of musical values, tradition, and concert hall style. Sensitive critics with their own deeply held traditional approach to music could find Stokowski's way inexplicable and awful in what they believed to be its excesses. For such critics the most galling factor of all was his ability to communicate with his musicians and with countless audiences over nearly three generations—an ability that led to packed houses and millions of record sales. Stokowski's unorthodox psychological-aesthetic approach to music remained unimpaired for sixty years in spite of exceptionally harsh, sometimes choleric, criticism. For six decades a good many musical authorities accused him of playing for the crowd, of injecting himself into the composer's role, and of emotionally rather than intellectually playing music that was close to him; which of course he did. He was alternately—and in contradiction—accused of playing and recording too many chestnuts loved by his audiences and too much new music, too many premieres in disregard of the public's wishes.

Stokowski's emotional and musical affinity for Mussorgsky's music is well known. Yet the late B. H. Haggin, in reviewing a 1943 performance of *Pictures at an Exhibition* that Stokowski had transcribed for orchestra, could write that Stokowski's approach to the work was to be compared with a vandal defacing a great painting in a museum as Stokowski hacked, tore, and luridly daubed over a great masterwork in his vulgarity of approach.[13] Mr. Haggin was clearly and savagely out of sympathy with Stokowski's general approach to music in 1943 as he had been before and would remain.

What fascinates me in my own attempt to come to grips with the mystery of Stokowski is not the savagery of Haggin's attack—which simply meant he was tuned to a very different symphonic approach and approached his job as critic seriously—but Haggin's 1943 "nonreview" of Stokowski's only book about what the conductor held most dear in his approach to music. *Music For All of Us* (1943) has been described critically as platitudinous and as gagging to intellectuals in the music community.[14] Haggin went one better with a statement to the effect that after twenty-five years of watching and listening to Stokowski, he could not bring himself to read whatever Stokowski had written, let alone review it; that was in itself a damning review, by contempt and in absentia.[15]

The late Mr. Haggin's criticism, which I have read and enjoyed over the years in the *Nation*, the *New Republic*, the *Yale Review*, and in anthology, has always been noteworthy for its precise, serious, and cerebral discussion of things musical. He could write enthusiastically, most notably about conductor Arturo Toscanini and pianist Artur Schnabel, whose marked similarity lay in their painstaking study—note by note—of a limited number of works and their near priestlike dedication to performing those works in a manner dictated by such dedication. About Toscanini's performances of the Beethoven Symphonies and

Schnabel's Beethoven Sonatas, Haggin could rhapsodize, albeit in a most intellectual way. In his writing at its most enthusiastic, the head was always clearly in charge of the heart.

What I cannot imagine is that Haggin and other influential members of the intellectual musical community would be able to read Stokowski's book as the author had written and intended it, because it is so simply direct, so unabashedly emotional, and so linked to the triangular communion between the realities of sound, one's experience and feeling, and the place of music in this process. Admittedly it shows no writing style. It is a "gee-whiz" book of the most sincere and childlike kind. Even the chapters on musical technology and sound reproduction—wherein Stokowski was the most technically expert conductor of *several* generations—even these chapters, while mediocre prose, show knowledge and insight, even as they exude wonder, anticipation of the future, and enthusiasm of a most youthful sort. Groping for an analogy of critical reaction to Stokowski's writing, I am reminded of the critical literary reaction to Ray Bradbury's far superior prose when it first appeared. Bradbury, emotional, imaginative, lyrical, and as fine a story teller as we have ever had, was found by many critics to write with too little concern for structure, too little subtlety, and too much "gee-whiz" exuberance. In short, he wrote for himself and for his audience, not for critics. In the same way Stokowski's chapters, like his recordings, were intended for music lovers but not for musical mandarins. The chapters on the science of sound and the technology of music reproduction were clearly intended to share knowledge about these subjects with readers who were not already expert, and Stokowski did a good and enthusiastic job of it. As for the chapters "All Sound Can Be Music," "Music and Young Children," "Music and Color," and "Music and the Dance," they were accurate, straightforward, and informative as well as exuberant. But more than that there were 1943 insights based on Stokowski's values, experience, and intuition that antedate and preview the findings of contemporary humanistic psychology by forty years. Stokowski's generalizations dovetail nicely with the insights of Fritz Perls, George B. Leonard, and Erik Erikson into the need for human expression of organic authenticity as contrasted to formalized and mechanical conformity to proper intellectual standards imposed from the academy or by tradition. Stokowski simply set such a theme into a musical framework for his book.

Since *Music for All of Us* was read and reviewed—or not read but reviewed in Mr. Haggin's case—by many who summed it up as gush or humbug, I conclude that they missed or chose to ignore a good many interesting themes in the text. Missed as well, I think, were tip-offs in Stokowski's own words about the whys, the hows, and the whats of his approach to music. I have found these admissions by the conductor valuable when corroborated by other sources.

In "All Sound Can be Music," Stokowski described the openness of people to sounds around them as related to their "varying ranges of consciousness." For some, only "formal music" properly played could pass the test of musicality, which is like conferring personhood only to those of the proper color or with the proper manners or class affiliations. As with Charles Ives, Stokowski noted that for others, musical consciousness and emotional range were much greater; new levels were continually discovered through life experience, with one's musical range widened and deepened by each new or recurring experience. The complexity and rhythm of everyday "street sounds" matched for Stokowski the "mysterious and complex" music he encountered in a Tibetan monastery. The sound of the soft beating of a huge drum before the altar was crossed midtemple by the chanting of the monks in enclosures on either side of the temple. "Each one was chanting in a different key and singing a different chant, but they were all singing with deep voice and extremely softly"; an "agitated murmur" of music filled the chamber as the differing rhythms and keys crossed each other in a unique and new tapestry of sound never before encountered by the conductor.[16]

As Stokowski was philosophically and emotionally open to sound as music, how much more keenly was he emotionally tuned to the message of musical change and of composition outside the traditional concertgoing canon. This is practically attested to by his lifelong championship of new or unplayed works. While Stokowski's list of world and national premieres (near two thousand) is probably longer than that of any other conductor in history, there is an important episode from late in Stokowski's career that illustrates his tenacity in the cause of new music better than any other single event in his long and eventful career. Then, too, it sets into relief his unique philosophical and musical values, not in the words of Kolodin, Mencken, O'Connell, or Gould, but in Stokowski's own action for a cause and a composer he believed in. The preface to this story also illustrates Stokowski's role as teacher and sponsor of young American musicians. Perhaps his story belongs as much to the young musicians of the American Symphony Orchestra during the sixties as it does to Stokowski and to Charles Ives.

In 1961, after five seasons as music director of the Houston Orchestra, the seventy-nine-year-old maestro decided to found another youth orchestra. He had created the All American Youth Orchestra in 1940 after leaving Philadelphia. He had tried and failed at founding the "Collegiate" Orchestra in the fifties. As he turned eighty he was again auditioning young performers, planning programs, booking Carnegie Hall, and making up out of his own pocket a portion of the first of the consecutive yearly deficits that would appear during each of the years he served as music director of the new American Symphony Orchestra. As with his earlier youth orchestra, so now with the American Symphony, Stokowski served without pay.

New and unheard older music would be heard regularly with standard repertoire. Young musicians, particularly women and minorities, would get a chance to play and to conduct with a first rate orchestra and a master teacher-conductor. In preparation Stokowski conducted all of the auditions—a minimum of twenty-five a week—himself. In answer to Henry Swoboda's later question as to what Stokowski had learned in putting the orchestra together, Stokowski answered that it was in the number of musically talented young Americans generally, particularly the number of women.[17] Training both orchestral performers and young conductors, Stokowski empirically learned that his youngsters were in demand by older and established orchestras when once trained. There was a large yearly turnover of personnel because training with Stokowski and the American Symphony opened doors to other orchestras.[18] Stokowski's new group was the best and most important single orchestral training ground for young musicians during the sixties, particularly for minority men and for all women as the age of equal rights opened.

At the age of eighty Stokowski conducted the first concert of the American Symphony Orchestra in November 1962. The same sonority, responsiveness, and expressivity associated with Stokowski performances for forty years was present in opening night performances of Gabrieli, Bach, Beethoven, and Shostakovich, and in later recordings made by Stokowski with the orchestra.[19]

One might imagine that the creation of the orchestra from first audition to first performance in under two years would have been enough. It wasn't and that brings us to the Ives story, which tells us so much about maestro Stokowski. During this same fall of 1962 Stokowski confided to his twenty-five-year-old associate conductor, José Serebrier, that he was going to give the world premiere of Charles Ives's most ambitious work, the Fourth Symphony, with the American Symphony Orchestra. He had wanted to perform the symphony in Houston during the fifties, but the complete score had not yet been available.[20]

Ives considered this piece his finest work (critic Harold Schonberg would later call it a masterpiece), but it is also one of the most complicated symphonic scores ever created by an American composer. The piece calls for augmented symphony orchestra, chorus, and three conductors to keep as many as seventeen different overlaid rhythms going at once.[21] To further complicate matters, while Ives had included his own transcendentalist philosophy in the work, he had included only the sketchiest of traditional musical markings to indicate how the music was to be played. Ives did, however, indicate in his *Memos* that the orchestra members should not be positioned in their customary places on stage, but grouped into smaller ensembles at varying distances from the audience so that the sounds made by each group traveled greater or lesser distances before reaching the ears of the listeners. It would create a spatial sonic effect he considered important, particularly in the second and fourth movements of the symphony. Ives followed this passage with a discussion of sound waves, music, and space that was very similar to Stokowski's concerns discussed in *Music for All of Us*.[22] For Stokowski to play the Ives Fourth Symphony meant a job of near complete interpretation philosophically and musically. Secondly, it meant interpreting the overlays of sound and rhythm as sound-waves blending together as near to Ives's ideal as possible. To these tasks was then added the traditional conductor's task of mastering the score once conceived and marked, preparing two associate conductors, David Katz and José Serebrier, and then rehearsing with chorus and orchestra.[23] At that, Stokowski was lucky to have the whole of the manuscript. Only ten years before had crucial missing pages of Ives's last movement to the Fourth Symphony been turned up in his papers during a search by Henry Cowell and John Kirkpatrick following the composer's death. With the manuscript of the work finally as complete as it would ever be, the maestro determined to give the work its world premiere.[24]

Until 1962 Stokowski had been unable to command the backing and the musical forces necessary to prepare and to play the work. Serebrier (later to provide another first-rate recording of the symphony)[25] recalled that during their more than two years work toward performance of the piece, he learned a lot about Ives but never gained the empathy for the man, his philosophy, and music that Stokowski intuitively commanded. Stokowski was taken not only with the music, but also with Ives's personal courage and independence and daring shown in his work. At the same time Stokowski was seriously concerned at the challenge of doing justice to Ives's symphony. Serebrier recalled his own amazement at the conductor's audacity. Here he was over eighty and surely eligible to coast on standard repertoire, yet he was concerned enough that the Fourth should be played that he accepted the work load and the headaches that went with first performance.[26]

Stokowski was eighty years old when he told his associate he would premiere the Ives with the American Symphony Orchestra no matter what the obstacles were. He was eighty-three when he triumphantly did so in 1965 at a packed Carnegie Hall concert that was beamed around the world by satellite. Between those dates Stokowski had also had to raise special funding from the Rockefeller Foundation to allow for the two months of rehearsal time necessary on the exceptionally difficult score—the longest rehearsal time ever devoted to a piece of American symphonic music.[27] The concert created an even greater stir than Leonard Bernstein's noteworthy premiere of the Ives Second Symphony during the fifties.

Serebrier, who, along with David Katz, coconducted that night, remembered that even with the successful premiere, Columbia Records refused to put up the backing for a recording of the symphony by the same artists. In fairness to Columbia, it should be noted that they had recorded and released John Kirkpatrick's historic performance of Ives's *Concord* Piano Sonata years before, and had recorded and released Bernstein's performance of the Ives Second Symphony after its premiere. However, the recording costs for this complex symphonic work were much greater. So while Ives's name was somewhat better known in the American musical world than it had been in the forties, Columbia refused to gamble its money on a first recording of his most complicated symphony.[28]

Determined now to record the Fourth, Stokowski again repeated his earlier search for foundation backing, this time to record the work. He got that funding from the Samuel Rubin

Foundation, recorded the work on the Columbia label and achieved a major Ives breakthrough with a classical bestseller. By the late seventies, when Serebrier provided his account, more than thirty-eight thousand copies of the record had been sold, which for a difficult, modern, American work was a remarkable achievement.[29]

Stokowski's interest in Ives, his capacity for hard work, his musicianship, and perhaps most of all his canny sense of timing opened up Columbia and other recording companies to make a number of Ives symphonic premiere recordings, with Leonard Bernstein sharing honors with Stokowski for several of the firsts. The Ives boom had now begun both in concert halls and on recordings. Its beneficiaries? All Americans and music lovers everywhere.

Two years after recording Ives's Fourth Symphony and the *Robert Browning* Overture, again with grant money, Stokowski led his American Symphony Orchestra, the Greg Smith Singers, and the Ithaca College Choir in first recordings of four Ives works for the then upcoming Ives centenary.[30]

A favorite Ives orchestral recording, and another of the Stokowski gifts to us from his last years, is the Orchestral Set no. 2, recorded for English Decca (London Records) in 1970.[31]

In an attempt of this sort to put Stokowski into perspective, I should make it clear that the Orchestral Set no. 2 has special meaning in the way it highlights Ives's audacious gifts as a composer and their affinity to the unique gifts of Stokowski as conductor and interpreter. The piece was scored for large orchestra with accordion, organ, multiple percussion, piano, choir, and separate distant orchestra. The three tone pictures of the piece represent Ives's emotional-musical re-creation of the religion of his boyhood, the transcendental America of the nineteenth century, and, finally, the everyday city music of New York City in 1915 juxtaposed to and countered spiritually by the impact on these New Yorkers of the news that the Lusitania had been sunk. The musical gifts of Ives, with his reliance on layers of sound, on sound far and near, and on the counterpoint of rhythms and melodies, creatively illustrates in this work many of the ideas that Stokowski as conductor had acted upon in interpreting music during his long career. Indeed, much in this music and in Ives's attitudes and writing creatively parallels the values and beliefs Stokowski had lived by and had included in *Music for All of Us*.[32] In love with sound as music and with music as a deep emotional power to communicate on a profound nonverbal level, and unwilling to accept domination by the musical interpretive canons of the past, Stokowski once again partnered Ives. One of America's greatest composers, who was also America's most imaginative insurance man, once more was marvelously interpreted by one of America's greatest conductors, a man whose values, eccentricities, and extra-musical abilities had, like those of Ives, made ambiguous his true place in music even while he courted the world as assiduously as Ives shunned it. One might describe them as extrovert and introvert transcendentalists in a world of musical rationalists and utilitarians.

This last Ives recording, made in 1970 with the London Symphony Orchestra and, alas, now out of circulation, was shortly followed by Stokowski's farewell to the American Symphony Orchestra and his return to England for the last phase of his career. From 1962 until 1971 he had directed the New York orchestra while providing personal funding to cover a portion of its deficit each season. Paul Robinson, author of a recent book on Stokowski, remembered those concerts as developing new and younger concertgoers delighted by Stokowski's varied programming and the orchestra's performance even as they had been "turned off" by better known orchestras whose style ran to stuffy programming in a traditionally elitist environment.[33]

Stokowski left a healthy and vibrant ensemble, telling his players to govern themselves. He intuitively turned toward his own earliest roots by returning to England in 1972, thus rounding out a life cycle that had begun there in the 1880s.

In England he was honored at a Stokowski Gala celebrating his ninetieth birthday and the sixtieth anniversary of his first concert with the London Symphony back in 1912. Stokowski repeated and recorded live the same 1912 program for English Decca (London Records).[34]

During 1972 and 1973 Stokowski continued to conduct in the United Kingdom and on the Continent. He made recordings with several orchestras on the English Decca label that were released in the United States as London Records. In 1975 Stokowski left the concert stage and ceased writing and giving interviews except for that last puckish appearance on CBS. He had renewed his recording ties with RCA in 1973 and with Columbia in 1976 while continuing to record for lesser known labels when he could not record what he wanted to record with a major company. Up to the time of his death in September of 1977 he was as active in the recording studio as his health would allow, and on the morning of his death he was scheduled to begin work on a recording of the Rachmaninoff Second Symphony for Columbia Records.[35]

Surely Leopold Stokowski was the greatest recording conductor ever, and his late recordings represent his important last gift to us. However, in a paradoxical way we may have missed the larger gifts he gave us over a near seventy-year career because along with the recordings there were so many other gifts, and because he was so prodigal in his giving for such a long period of time that we took him for granted. It may be that only now after his death, with the fading of controversies stirred up by the maestro for nearly three generations, can we begin to assess his contribution to our culture and his unique approach to music and to life. If this is so, I would hope for a renaissance of interest in the man and his contribution to all of us.

More than seventy years ago a thirty-four-year-old amazed the American musical world by directing Philadelphia and New York premiere performances of Mahler's *Symphony of a Thousand* with a Philadelphia Orchestra, 110 players strong, 8 soloists, and a chorus of 958 singers. The fanfare from the foyer heralding those performances announced a great twentieth-century symphony orchestra and our most audacious and daring symphonic musician. The Bandmaster of Philadelphia's Band of Gold in the midtwenties, alias symphony conductor Stokowski, was on his way toward introducing more new music than any other conductor in history. From his first victrola recording in 1917, through his 1924 premiere electrical recording, through his 1926 and 1929 premiere radio broadcasts with, respectively, the Curtis Institute Orchestra and the Philadelphia Orchestra, through his 1931 introduction of 33⅓ RPM long play records for RCA, his experimental stereo recordings with the Bell Telephone Laboratories and in *Fantasia*—his simultaneous introduction of both 35 MM multichannel tape recording and the power of symphonic music in film—through all of these activities he experimented with acoustics, with orchestral seating arrangements, with instrumental design, and with concert hall design itself. It was Stokowski who introduced free bowing to his strings and new breathing and playing techniques to his brasses, who directed America's first light show to the music of Rimsky-Korsakov's *Scheherazade* in the twenties, who first introduced "youth concerts" with eighteen- to twenty-five-year-olds helping him create the programs, and who topped that with free Philadelphia Orchestra concerts until he was halted by the depression. In 1954 it was Stokowski, along with Fritz Reiner, who made the first commercial stereo recordings of symphonic music—in Stokowski's case with excerpts from Prokofiev's *Romeo and Juliet.* In 1907 it was a twenty-five-year-old Stokowski who predicted the coming of electronic music in the technical journal, *Electrical World.* It was a seventy-year-old Stokowski who presented America's first public electronic music concert at the museum of Modern Art in 1952. In the sixties Stokowski was the first symphonic conductor to record in English Decca's new multichannel stereo process, Phase 4, while introducing the Dolby noise reduction system in symphonic recording.

In the twenties, thirties, and forties, Stokowski pioneered the linking together of theater, music, dance, and drama with lighting and design worthy of this new multimedia approach. From then until the seventies he expended thousands of hours and dollars in the creation of nonsexist, nonracist orchestras that provided first class music for concertgoers and record buyers. He trained hundreds of young musicians and several budding conductors, who, after a season or two with Stokowski, were hired by orchestras eager to have able young performers trained in the Stokowski school.

By his own accomplishment and by model, Stokowski did more to improve orchestral quality in the United States than did any other twentieth-century musician. In so doing he provided us with memorable concert performances and recordings. Through all of the controversy over his transcriptions and his often idiosyncratic interpretations of symphonic fare, he gave us marvelous readings of Russian and French music, of contemporary American and European music, and model readings of Wagner, Strauss, Debussy, Ravel, and Sibelius. By example and by artistic contact with the public, Stokowski gifted all of us lavishly through a better than seventy year career. He conducted seven thousand live concerts before ten million concertgoers, with hundreds of radio and television concerts reaching untold millions. Throughout, he fought consistently for new music, for artistic innovation, and for the right of the individual to fulfill him- or her-self. He opposed regimentation in all of its forms.

In a time such as ours, with the greyness of conformity, decision by committee, passivity, and fear threatening our right to be ourselves and to act creatively for ourselves, the example of Stokowski—a last gift—is as meaningful in human and in moral terms as it is to our musical history. Just as our sometimes seeming lack of concern for future generations can be countered by the example of the future-oriented Stokowski, so we, more fearful of the dangers around us than of the creative forces of life and freedom within us, have in Stokowski's example and music what he believed to be the nurturing power of music for all of us:

> We are conscious of two opposing forces in the world—one destroys, the other creates. Music is one expression of the creative force. It has scarcely any material existence, but is almost completely an expression of spirit, emotion, and the powers of evolution within us.[36]

Appendix: Stokowski and the Family Romance

To use a psychoanalytic model in the consideration of historical figures, including artists such as Wordsworth, Shelley, Beethoven, Lewis Carroll, and Jonathan Swift, is a means of further understanding the ways in which they expressed their art, as related to their lives as lived. Second, it is a method of getting closer to the combined gift and burden of their creativity as they had to cope with it, doing the best they could in a world where few might at first recognize such creativity and even fewer would be able to understand the effects of such talent on their behavior, which moved them a little, or largely, away from what society calls normality.

In the same way, Erik Erikson's studies of the creative outlets of Mohandas Gandhi and Martin Luther related the burden/gift of their creativity to the shaping life experiences of the two and to their coping skills as they both wrestled with gifts they had not asked for but must express.

It is pretty clear, then, that the use of the psychoanalytic model to try to more fully understand a subject does not mean that the subject is either neurotic or psychotic, that is, unable to successfully function as a human being. But it does suggest that the subject is complicated. He or she shares a common humanity, norms, and sense of family with the rest of us but often functions creatively in ways that seem strange and unusual to those of us not so gifted. Such a person often compromises what we believe is possible, such as in the artist's need to create two or more identities to accommodate the self.

It is in this spirit that the psychoanalytic model can be used to analyze the gifted. It is a tool to explore the gift of creativity and its cost rather than—as most of us are conditioned to think of it—simply a technique for exposing the pathological.

Particularly fruitful in this exploration has been that psychoanalytic model for what is known as the "family romance," a name taken directly from Sigmund Freud's 1908 essay "Family Romances."

Freud's initial essay was the seminal piece in a field denoted later as the study of the "family romance." Freud's short analysis centered on how some children become so estranged from their parents that, under psychological pressure to do so, they created a substitute parentage, ergo a family romance. As he had done with the truths of other mythic and religious themes, so Freud had done with the *changeling* motif; he translated its historic reality and its contemporary meaning into a useful psychological tool. While the estrangement itself lay at the core of Freud's original conception, he noted that the accompanying creation of the family romance required unusual imagination, and from the evidence of his own time and experience, he created a dual classification of such romancers. On the one hand were certain genuine neurotics, but in a second category were particularly creative individuals whose imaginations roamed free in the world of day dreaming or fantasy; they carried this trait from childhood through puberty and beyond. As Freud explained it, the family romance was a product of this fund of fantasy and served the creative dreamer as a way to fulfill his or her wishes and to correct the mistakes of reality. The chief correction, wrote Freud, was the job of freeing oneself from family whose values and ideals were far from those of the subject, and of replacing them with other fantasy kin whose status and values were in keeping with the subject's sense of who he was and who he should have had as family in order to match his gifts and his aspirations. Freud wrote that the kind of fantasy family so created would depend upon the kind of material the subject had to work with and on the subject's ingenuity and imagination.[1]

Freud, early in this century pursuing a number of themes that would provide the basis for psychoanalysis, wrote no more on the subject of the family romance after his initial essay, but his work on this theme was later followed up by others in the growing field. In modern psychoanalysis a major figure in pursuing the theme of the family romance has been Phyllis Greenacre, M.D. She chose as a special field the study of creative and artistic people in their high incidence of such romancing, noting the trials and triumphs that marked their divergence from normality.

Considering Freud's and Greenacre's work, as their analytic model relates to Stokowski and his unusual psychological traits, one is struck first with how close in real life Stokowski was to Freud's initial model.

I have already, in chapter one, discussed Stokowski's ingenuity in defying the realities of his own past and of European social structure by creating an aristocratic great grandfather who marched on Moscow as a general in Napoleon's army, and a beloved grandfather, Leopold, who in fantasy was a symbol of patriotic Polish yeoman values—the best of the European folk tradition—and a music lover as well. Once a dweller in the family village of Stokki, it would be grandfather, run off the family property by Czarist police, who would lead the family to England and become in Stokowski's telling the kindly father and mentor figure with whom Little Leopold could identify in fantasy. Grandfather would intuit little Leopold's innate musicality, and when asked—in a gathering place of continental European émigrés—for a violin by a small boy overcome by the music and the emotionality of these expatriates and their culture, grandfather would agree.

What one has here is an idealized fantasy background for the maestro that includes not only a point of origin, Poland, but links to the Continental aristocracy through great grandfather (the general), and to the folk tradition through the fantasized yeoman grandfather. Never mind that the realities of European class structure were defied in Stokowski's fantasy. It was enough that the fantasy gave Stokowski links to both the continental European aristocracy and to the peasant folk tradition. What was important was that a fantasized Poland took the place of grimy London and a mythical grandfather became a mentor and father figure to the maestro. As to his own father, Joseph Boleslaw Kopernik Stokowski, although we know he was a skilled craftsman in wood working (because of a handsome profile portrait he did of Leopold when he was eighteen, and because of a beautifully worked jewel box sent to Leopold and Olga upon their marriage in 1911), we have little or nothing in Stokowski's own words or memories to link the maestro to his father, and certainly the position of father figure and mentor was played out by the fantasized grandfather.

As to his mother, Annie Marion Moore Stokowski, while the conductor in real life loved her and would regularly visit her until her death at ninety-two, her fate in Stokowski's fantasy is not an enviable one. As I noted in chapter one, her very existence was for a while unknown to Stokowski's second wife, Evangeline, who learned about her only by accident. Stokowski's third wife, Gloria Vanderbilt, heard yet another part of the fantasy—the mother fantasy—out of Stokowski's family romance. In this portion of the romance, Stokowski's mother, Maria, had died after Stokowski's birth on Polish soil and the infant or child, Leopold, was sent to England to live with "strangers." As Stokowski described it to her, while living in this land of strangers, the only person to give him love was his nursemaid. In real life this nanny was his mother; but so real was the family romance version of his family and origins to Stokowski, that he seriously damaged his own relationship with Vanderbilt in order to maintain the fantasy against any real meeting between his wife and his mother, and thus between real life and the life created by his fantasy.

It is Vanderbilt who describes Stokowski protecting his secret, shutting her out of the dual identity that was his, and of the dual reality created by his family romance. Just how serious this secrecy was can be measured by Vanderbilt's conclusion that Stokowski's failure to share his inner life with her was a major part of their breakup, a breakup between two people who genuinely loved each other.

The early Freudian model of the family romance, then, certainly holds true for Stokowski's fantasy with, overall, an estrangement from London and its world of small trade. No matter how much Stokowski loved his kin in real life, his real father gives way to the fantasy grandfather and his real mother is only grudgingly admitted to the family romance in the guise of the English nurse. As to his idealized fantasy mother Maria, she supposedly died when Stokowski was very young. Thus, within the artistic identity of Stokowski as romancer and in the language of his family romance, the mother who *would have* understood him, who *would have* shared his sense of ties to things Polish who *would have* lauded his unusual gifts and shared his romantic way of seeing music and culture through continental European eyes, *this mother had not been there for him.* Instead there was an Englishwomen, a nurse, in a land of strangers, who couldn't understand him but at least gave him love.

Turning from the romance itself and the sense of estrangement on which it was based, one asks how it could have come about? In answer we must turn to the work of the modern analyst Phyllis Greenacre.

Dr. Greenacre writes that not all artistic prodigies are born and nurtured in a family environment in which their differentness and their precocity can be accepted and shared by their parents. Even if their talent is recognized and furthered, it may be done in the furtherance of the ambitions and goals of the parents and understood within their own frame of reference, not that of the youngster, as artist in the making. If the child appears with a wholly unexpected and spontaneous artistic gift that demands expression, and does so within a family whose interests and values provide little means for coping with this loved but rather alien youngster, even their best intentions and concern cannot narrow the gap between themselves and their prodigy. He or she remains something of a stranger to them and they, to him or her.

In this situation such gifted children are bound to feel their differentness painfully and to feel lonely even when loved. They realize their difference from their kin and feel themselves both isolated and inferior in relationship to those around them who share common bonds. When they do come to understand their peculiar gifts, they are not less isolated, but can turn to fantasy for comfort until the time when, with greater maturity, their gifts can be realized in some definite expression, of which they are the master. This early fantasy stage is the first formative stage in the development of the family romance.[2]

Remember Stokowski's recollections that he was a musician from birth, that as soon as he was able to think, he knew music was his destiny, and that he found his artistic identity only when he first stood before an orchestra at the age of twelve. Then, too, there were those hours on end when Stokowski as child played the piano by himself and, as he described the experience in *Music for All of Us*, gained the "vision of an ideal world of beauty . . . as surely as [he] learned to know the material world of school and play." It became for him an invaluable part of what he called his "inner life," even as the boy musician could be considered strange or a sissy by others his own age.[3]

The inner life, the vision, the aloneness, the early discovery of a real identity and destiny in music—all of these, set against the work-a-day world and values of his family, seem to me to be evidences in Stokowski's childhood of the psychoanalytic model for the creation of the family romance.

Where is the role model for such a child, writes the analyst, the adult figure who in a normal family situation could provide understanding and a model of style, behavior, and values for the young Stokowski? Dr. Greenacre points out that the prodigy is lucky if his own father can live up to the exceptional role model needed by such a gifted offspring, and it is quite possible that there will be no one to play this all-important role. If not, writes the analyst, the gifted child as romancer in the making is likely to create and carry an idealized vision of such a father figure with him as though it were real. In this situation the idealized vision can later crystallize as the father-figure role model within the imagined reality of the family romance itself.[4]

In Stokowski's case the evidence indicates that childhood fantasy and his own search for just such an idealized father figure gave birth to the grandfather Stokowski of the conductor's family romance.

Ideally, the artist as child would have around him or her not only a suitable role model, but other family and peer group members whose relationships with the subject would make easier the artistic gift/burden he or she bears. However, it is likely that even with the best intentions in the world those coming into contact with the subject will reinforce his or her sense of differentness and further the subject's sense of alienation. Given this increasing pressure on the subject's sense of self or identity, it is not only possible, but likely, that the potential family romancer is emotionally pushed toward a split in his or her sense of identity. From such beginnings the pressure toward such a split grows until it does indeed occur with the creation of two or more identities.

For the burgeoning artist as romancer the most typical split is between the more acceptable identity of the normal family and community member—a sharer of common bonds, obligations, norms, and affections—and the other identity of the artist, for which no real model nor understanding can be found, but which demands room for expression. These identities may at times exist harmonically together in the subject, with each showing its face to the world, or there may be warfare between the two. In this kind of situation the psychological push toward the creation of the family romance becomes a means of achieving a sort of harmony within the self because it provides a real, if fantasy, framework for the functioning of the creative self. At the same time the identity of the conventional self pays the socially expected and personally felt dues to the obligations of filial love and to conventional social norms. One should remember that this process occurs over time, carrying the subject from childhood to adulthood as he or she copes with conflicting psychic obligations and attempts to reconcile them, not in one identity as has been proven impossible to the subject, but in two or more identities.[5]

How like Stokowski's ambivalence toward his English family, to alternate affection and loving visits with denial of that family's existence. At the same time the elements of Stokowski's family romance take shape over a considerable period, stimulated, ironically, by Olga Samaroff's attempts to make a Pole of the maestro for external and quite different purposes; this impetus Stokowski used during the Philadelphia years to shape and to express his artistic identity, revealed in tip-off accents not heard earlier. The full-blown romance has about it fantasy elements aplenty. It includes Polish family members, a Polish birth for Stokowski, claims (sometimes hints) of wonderful links to continental European culture, and Stokowski's delight in being called Prince, as his daughter Sonya would remember her father wishing, fairy-tale-like, that he actually had been a prince in disguise, washed up on the shores of America, there to claim his rightful inheritance. The maestro's kaleidoscope of verbal accents and conversational topics also compliments the image of the family romancer. Appropriately enough, this constellation of expressive characteristics, family romance and all, find their way into Stokowski's dramatic and superbly imaginative way with music making. His idiosyncratic style was constantly at odds with traditionalism and literalism, but he knew the beauty of great performance and delighted millions with his own inherent romantic logic through a career seven decades long and more.

However, the appearance of such elements as these does not end the creative process that includes the family romance in the analyst's model, nor does it end the parallel between that model and Stokowski's real life story.

For the psychoanalyst, the creative artist in whatever field is not such simply as a result of his or her professional training, hard work, and dedication, which are traditional elements in the making of a skilled professional. Beyond these is a necessary artistic capacity for imagination, for seminal and fresh thought, and for seeing with new eyes and hearing with new ears. Out of this combination is born new art and the voyage of discovery, whether in painting, music, sculpture, or writing.[6]

Using this description as a bench mark, consider Stokowski's varied and creative contributions to the world of music, dance, drama, theater, acoustics, electronics, and motion pictures for which the maestro was responsible. When I think of Stokowski's conducting peers during the Philadelphia years, I think of Koussevitsky as a fine conductor and supporter of new music. I think of Sir Thomas Beecham as wit and bon vivant in addition to being a gifted conductor. To Toscanini's great skills as musician and conductor I might add the designations Italian patriot and antifascist. The great German conductor Furtwängler is remembered as well for his tragic position, caught betwen his own humanistic gifts and the scourge that overtook his society. But to describe the protean interests and creations of Stokowski beyond being a musician, transcriber, teacher, and conductor would require a separate appendix to the appendix. Let the text in which many of these creative achievements are mentioned stand in place of such a listing.

The psychoanalytic model of artistic creativity carries with it a correlatively high incidence of the family romance in the lives of the creative, as contrasted to those who through learning, practice, and professionally defined orientation toward artistic goals, make solid workmanlike contributions to art and to society. Not only is the family romance with its multifaceted identity/identities characteristic of the enthusiastic and creative artist, but such people in their differentness often show another trait. They carry the family romance to a higher stage in which the inner and the outer worlds of the artist show less identification with real people and real things, but an intensified identification with transcendent figures—either real or mythical—and with ideals and emotions that can only be described as "cosmic."[7]

When Greenacre publicly presented her research on "The Family Romance of the Artist," she was joined by M.D.s and fellow analysts, Drs. Leo Stone, David Beres, and Robert Bak, as commentators in exploring this transcendant variant on the family romance. Through their findings one can describe this state with sequential logic as to the steps involved in its creation by the artist.

The aloneness of such persons and their perception of their differentness, based on realization of their gifts, leads to both the creation of the family romance for protection and the multifaces of their identity/identities, and to more as well. Through all of this such persons also need and seek relationships that will join them to others. If denied these among family members and peer groups because of the romancers' differences, they reach out with both their gifts and their needs to find substitutes for the personal relationships denied them. Through their imaginations they create or seek out ready-made entities to relate to. Such entities are then felt by the subjects to be intimately connected to themselves, both personally and symbolically. It is, I think, worth noting that in commentary on Greenacre's work, poet Shelley's perception of and sensed kinship with Prometheus, poet Wordsworth's intensely personal and mystical relationship to nature, and the mystic longings of painter Vincent Van Gogh were brought up respectively by Stone, Beres, and Bak to round out and support Greenacre's thesis.[8]

A subject deeply feeling and acting on this unusual although sophisticated set of concepts creates ideals and emotional relationships that are cosmic in nature as an emotional extension of the family romance and as a substitute for family and friends. The artist here substitutes idealized images, personages, and abstractions for parents and for other personal relationships. Such cosmic relationships are not limited by space nor by time, and the very differentness of the subject here shows in the romancer's sense of fusing with the universal. It allows him or her to establish such cosmic linkage to, for example, nature, mythic beings, heroes of the past, composers, thinkers and philosophers, the muses, as in "Music, the voice of the All," God, nature as God, or the "Other."[9]

Again, do we have evidence that Stokowski created and believed in such cosmic relationships? We do, in the conductor's own words describing music and its "cosmic" relationship to himself:

> . . . The soul of music is the most difficult to describe with words. . . . Certain kinds of music seem to be a direct message from the divine soul to the soul of man. . . .
>
> All sound can be music to some. . . . It is like a varying range of consciousness. Some are to a degree conscious of the whole *cosmos*, including *cosmic thought and feeling* [italics mine].
>
> The sphere of the purely musical is a world apart . . . we cannot put it into words—because where the words end music goes on. All those deep and subtle reactions within us are personal and sacred.[10]

This was, of course, what Stokowski often referred to as his "inner life," but was this cosmic vision not only a part of Stokowski's extension of the family romance, but also the essence of his religious sense—itself a topic of debate and dispute over the years?

Stokowski was baptized an Anglican, but during his long life he claimed, on occasion, to be a Catholic, a Theosophist, an agnostic, a Buddhist, and—perhaps by free association of his fantasy of a Polish mother Maria, who loved and understood him—a worshipper of a mother goddess as described to Gloria Vanderbilt; the specific term, the *Divine Mother*, was first used by him to describe music in his book, *Music for All of Us*. Such claims were made, I would think, through free association and/or as his sense of fantasy suggested at a given time. Closer to the mark were the ideals of a creed shared by Stokowski with Evangeline Johnson shortly after their marriage in the twenties. In it Stokowski pledged his aspiration toward reaching a higher stage of "inner life" and linking that pledge to entities that were cosmic and pantheistic by orthodox Western standards, and included "beauty, strength, nature, love [and the] sun." The "inner life," the real life, was described by Stokowski in 1943 as capable of connecting one to the "universal," the "divine," and the "cosmic." As religion, this seems to me a rare and unusual mix, somewhat like crossing pagan pantheism with Eastern mysticism.

Charles O'Connell wrote that if Stokowski worshipped anything, it was nature. I would go a bit further and suggest that, accepting science and nature as worthy of commitment, the maestro went a step beyond in his unique religiosity to embrace what his personal gifts told him was out there in terms of the cosmic force that most of us accept in our orthodoxy as an anthropomorphic God. In this I believe he linked his musicianship, personal values, sense of fantasy, and paranormal gifts to a unique sense of oneness with the universal.[11]

Whether considered to be religious or not in Stokowski's case, the cosmic extension of the family romance in its psychoanalytic model next follows the relationship of the cosmic to the artist-as-romancer into the artist's sense of his or her unique role as a connecting link between the cosmic, the All, and humankind. As Promethean link, writes the analyst, the artist is poignantly sanctified in his creativity, be it drama painting, prose, poetry, or music. His art becomes a conduit between the cosmic message and the waiting audience. His gifts, be believes, are meant to be, and in exercising them, even against opposition, the artist is figuratively blessed by the gods and becomes a Promethean figure interacting and sharing the creative experience with his audience through performance; but the price is high.[12]

Replicating this model almost perfectly in real life, Stokowski writes:

> A true musician concentrates so intensely on these [referring to the previous paragraph] . . . places in our deepest consciousness of understanding, vision, illumination . . . that he loses himself in music. . . . He becomes a medium of forces infinitely greater than any of the talents that Nature may have given him. . . . He must be a *channel through which these freely stream*" [italics mine].[13]

In conversation with Glenn Gould, whom he trusted, Stokowski described such creativity and originality together with the price paid for it by citing the example of Dmitri Shostakovich, who was blessed with true creativity and originality, but at the same time cursed by being misunderstood for his very gifts by those around him. That, noted Stokowski, is the cost paid by the creative, whether they are in the arts, the sciences, or philosophy. Revealingly, given the context of his saying it, Stokowski also declared that it takes "originality" to be able to recognize the same in others.[14]

For more normal relationships the artist-as-romancer has then substituted the mysterious cosmic link between the Other and himself, with himself as artistic conduit to the audience. In the case of Stokowski, whose conductorial art was re-creative, and in his mind cocreative in bringing life and spontaneity to the spirit of the composer as expressed in "black marks on white paper," Stokowski writes:

> The conductor takes the score—studies every note of it—and gradually . . . tries to penetrate so deeply into the thought and feeling of the score that when he later conducts it he will feel as if he were spontaneously re-creating [cocreating] it at the moment.[15]

While Stokowski pays tribute to the composer as creator—divinely inspired in putting his feelings on paper—the music remains inert until brought to life in performance by a messenger (cocreator) also sanctioned by the divine. In Stokowski's philosophy, composer and performer are treated essentially as equals in the process of music making. "Music the voice of the All" is dually the responsibility of composer and musician, who act as conduits for this divine voice. Such a philosophy corresponds rather well to the analyst's description of the romancer substituting the cosmic for the human in describing artistic creativity and identity. It also relates to Stokowski's more earthbound description of the cocreative role and helps explain why critics understandably found the conductor so arrogant in his equation of the composer as creator and himself as cocreator, a kind of musical Prometheus bringing the Creator's musical fire to man. To critics it was egotism. To Stokowski it was the direct application of his own romancer's philosophy wedded to his cosmic sense of music's mission and to the paranormal powers given him for its accomplishment.

The ethical problem of claimed cocreation is neatly sidestepped as this sense of input from the Other, from the cosmic, is expressed, in Stokowski's case, by his answer to BBC commentator John Bowen's question as to where his own ethical sense came from. Stokowski's divergence from the customary Judeo-Christian tradition and his peculiar link to the cosmic is, I think, well illustrated by his answer. Translating Bowen's question about *ethics* into an answer about *creativity*, Stokowski described the source of creativity as a "mystery," but a mystery out of which instinctually came great literature, painting, and music. Implicit in this answer, if not directly stated, is his own place in the creation (cocreation) of great music.[16]

We now have some sense of the romancer as artist in both the psychoanalytic model and in the corresponding individual case of Stokowski as musician, but what of the human price paid for such cosmic identification? According to the psychoanalytic model, the more fully blown and intense the subject's pattern is of substituting the cosmic for the human, the more difficult it will be for him or her to establish and maintain personal relationships of an intimate kind with flesh and blood human beings. The pattern in such cases is for the artist-romancer's difficulty to become disappointment as such attempts fail. Failure and disappointment will give rise to greater and greater efforts by the subject for self-realization through creative artistic endeavors rather than through friendship, love, and family ties. As this pattern deepens, the artist becomes afraid that such relationships, together with home and hearth, actually have a negative effect on his or her artistic creativity. In place of a well-rooted personal life, artistic romancers substitute a kind of restlessness, a search for the novel and the new. Their responsiveness to the new and the unusual becomes a striking trait as does their identification with the world, rather than with some permanent and beloved home site, as their home. In their evaluations of the world around them, they show clear-cut streaks of innocence and naiveté along with sharply contrasting blends of world-born shrewdness and sophistication, which seem to the observer quite paradoxical. With unsuccessful long-term love relationships a kind of rule for them, such artists substitute any number of short-term affairs, which may be serious but are not permanent. Even their choice of temporary love partners is striking, because of the number and sheer variety of types so chosen.

With their primal commitment to life focused through their art rather than through devotion to home, family, and friends, their private lives tend to be chaotic as personal interests collide with their self-created cosmic relationships. This collision of the real, the imperfect, and the earthbound with the fantasy of the perfect and the universal is strong enough so that it creates psychic and emotional confusion for the romancer as he or she identifies an earthly love interest with the cosmic muse. Great expectations and yearning are then dashed to the ground as the beloved—once again—turns out to be merely mortal.[17] Not only is he or she not the perfect mate predestined above, but also one with whom the secrets of the romancer lover's *true identity*, the artistic identity, cannot be shared.

Again Stokowski's own life follows the configurations of the analyst's model. After the failures of his marriages to Olga Samaroff and to Evangeline Johnson, basically because of his infidelity, Stokowski had sworn he would never marry again. Yet he did, at age sixty-three, marry the twenty-one-year-old Gloria Vanderbilt; it was a third try based on a mutual attraction so great that Vanderbilt would recall it forty-two years later as the great passion of her life. In 1945 she wrote that her whole existence centered on her love for Stokowski. She was possessed by it. So, following their marriage, off they went on a gypsy honeymoon in an auto and trailer, he and his love setting out to find the utopia matching their commitment to each other. In Taos, New Mexico, they were lionized by Freida Lawrence, Mabel Dodge McLuhan, and Dorothy, Lady Brett, as though Leopold were the reincarnation of D. H. Lawrence. Lady Brett, flirting outrageously, dubbed Stokowski "Prince" once again. To his Prince, Vanderbilt played "Scheherazade," as he called her.[18]

It was lovely while it lasted and totally in keeping with the pair's shared romanticism, but it very shortly gave way to Stokowski's "inner life" and call to make music, to travel what seemed to Vanderbilt to be roads without end. In contrast, Vanderbilt wanted children, a home with her husband, and some sense of rootedness. She described Stokowski's rootlessness and his rovings in service to the muse as a kind of treadmill, which for her, never got them anywhere.[19]

Truly the world, not one place, was home to Stokowski, and over the years his restlessness, his unrootedness, his ultimate passion for music, and his secretiveness about those things deepest within him were to erode their marriage.[20]

There was also what Stokowski derisively believed was Vanderbilt's overconcern with the outer world. This simply amounted to Vanderbilt's desire to mingle with friends, to meet people, and to find her own creative outlet in the arts, in short, to have normal relationships of her own. For Stokowski this could not be. Metaphorically put, Scheherazade was the beloved of the Prince and so should be reclusively on call for him when he returned from his triumphs and artistic travels. Her place was at home, not in the marketplace. In fairness it should be noted that Vanderbilt describes Stokowski as building up her sense of self-worth and her inner security in her own abilities and encouraging her in her painting and writing—both solitary pursuits—but he was openly hostile when it came to her acting and socializing with her friends.[21] It would seem that the romancer's ideal beloved had shown herself to be all too normal, yet another disappointment for the romancer.

In all, Stokowski's fantasylike treatment of the very real love and passion he and Vanderbilt shared would, in the end, help destroy their relationship even as his own family romance lived on. Again, Stokowski proves himself a near perfect example of the analyst's clinical description of the inconstancy of the romancer-as-artist-as-lover.

As a human counterweight to this kind of failure and personal pain, the analyst poses several positive traits most likely to be shown by such creative artists—traits that are not only conducive to creativity, but that help alleviate the emotional pain felt by the romancer. Such persons are likely to be mischievous with a childlike sense of play. Their freedom in fantasy and playfulness creatively substitutes for the more common norm of the work ethic in giving birth to art. Their commitment to free play and childlike wonder leads them to the diverse and the original in art, to new connections between fields not seen or sensed by others.[22]

Nancy Shear, Stokowski's music librarian and confidante during the sixties and seventies described Stokowski for me as being, on occasion, "childlike" or "childish." In this same context Marguerite Friedeberg's memories of Stokowski from 1937 to 1939 are germane. She described Stokowski to me as a delightful fantasist who often "acted like a kid" and was given to the whimsical "play acting" of fantasy; reminding her of "Charlie Chaplin's gift for story telling." London born like Chaplin, Stokowski in private and at his most natural had a soft accent, recalled Friedeberg, which sounded to her like "cockney" as softened by thirty years in the United States.[23]

In this light we recall Stokowski's delight in the company of children, in playing with children, and his interest in their intuitive insight into things as well as their capacity for joy in play. We remember the fairy-tale quality of Stokowski's thought and feeling that his daughter Sonya recollected as the key to her romantic father's character. We recall Stokowski as an old man saying that music making wasn't work, that it should have another name. We call to mind Stokowski's sense of mischief in making pronouncements shocking to many in the world of music. Nor do we forget the delicious fantasy of Stokowski's children's concerts and of a delight on his part as great in creating them as that of the small fry for whom the concerts were intended. Children, Stokowski believed, truly loved music. They didn't analyze it, nor critically agonize over it in an intellectual way. They felt it physically and emotionally and responded in the same way. Stokowski enjoyed hearing children talk about music they had heard, because, as he put it, not only were they honest and open in their feelings, but unlike their elders, they still had and could use their imaginations creatively.[24]

Translating the playfulness and imagination of the child into the creative endeavor of the artist, who, more than maestro Stokowski, saw interconnections between music, drama, dance, and electronics and then acted as prophet in interlinking the latest in modern technology with them? Who, more than Stokowski, saw in his mind's eye and then built the superb modern symphony orchestra as we know it and did so using Philadelphia, which was a musically second-rate backwater when he arrived in 1912.

Again, using the analyst's model as our bench mark, note that Stokowski put in his seventy-year career, with his twelve-hour days, yet created a varied legacy not as though he were working, but as though he were enthusiastically at play in the garden of possibility. He remained playful although surrounded by the dutiful. He remained a pagan although surrounded by the orthodox. These are characteristics that Stokowski maintained through his eighties and that, I believe, his life amply proves.

But what, in turn, is the further cost of such unorthodox and such romantic cosmic conceptions as we have charted so far?

Turning again and for the last time to psychoanalysis for a diagnosis of what underlies the pathos and triumph of the creative artist, we come to a painful reckoning. According to the analyst, such commitment to fantasy, free play, and wonder becomes the stuff of the new and the original in art, but it comes at a great price. Ultimately and on balance, the exercise of such creative gifts can give delight to and make progress for humankind, but its cost in misunderstanding and personal pain for the romancer is great. Even the artist's sense of accomplishment brings with it agony in the Promethean sense,[25] since historically, progress and new ideas have never been welcomed by the orthodox and have always been first created and welcomed by a small minority, which over time only swells to a majority when what was once new and progressive has itself now become orthodox and in need of updating (see *Fantasia* entry in the Discography).

How much more intense is this experience for the creative artist if along the way his natural talent and his romance are joined by realization that he has been given paranormal powers not shared or at least not developed by most of those around him? In what is admittedly conjecture, one imagines a likely sequence of reactions on the part of musician Stokowski.

> Where has this power come from? I don't know. It's a mystery. Why have I been chosen to get it? Again it's a mystery, but, I do know that I was born a musician and can only assume that some transcendent agency has chosen me to exercise my gift for music in conjunction with my gifts for inner communication and energizing musical performance. While still mysterious in point of origin and in intended purpose, what evidence I have leads me to believe that it is intended that such gifts should be used creatively for the expression of Music, the voice of the All.

Through much of Stokowski's long professional career, there were self-defensive episodes in which Stokowski obscured such likely realities about himself that might have led the hearer or the reader to learn too much about the maestro for his, Stokowski's own good. A number of these episodes are included herein and mostly deal either with the "secret," as he called it, of his use of paranormal powers in music making, or with the "secret" of his artistic identity and with those "personal truths" beyond the range of birth certificates, encyclopedias, and the like. Only in his book and in a few interviews late in life did the maestro admit his secrets, but even there the admissions were not taken seriously, given the aura of obfuscation Stokowski himself had created through most of his career. Admirers have always been inclined to sum up Stokowski's claimed secrets as simply mischievous behavior on his part, and since mischief was a part of his temperament, the explanation has been accepted as a plausible one, particularly since all else seemed to be inexplicable paradox. His detractors preferred to see his secrets and his late life admissions as the continuing pose of a musical phony. His book, *Music for All of Us*, was likewise written off as romantic gush and humbug.

Stokowski's real legacy of accomplishment exists uncomfortably, I think, with such apologies and such negative charges. But if the reader considers the above too speculative or historically too highfalutin, let me end by simply summing up what we know of Stokowski, the romancer as artist. I began with the gifted but lonely child and young man of chapter one chasing his destiny through a family romance and creating that veritable assemblage of accents and conflicting facets of identity even as admirers dubbed him the new Richter and detractors likened him to Cagliastro. The magician, sorcerer, and Merlin of chapter two, a musical pagan in a concert-hall world of the orthodox, whom Carl Flesch would dub Faustian and Promethean in his musical search, was the singly minded egoist who, like Berlioz, would attempt to find the ultimate in orchestral color and musical expressivity not only with the natural gift of his musicianship, but with the addition of parapsychological powers. The Philadelphia Stokowski of chapter three organized a city to "Save the Orchestra" even as his first marriage collapsed under the weight of his own creative needs and that hungry and unstable eroticism of the artist that Sylvan Levin summed up for me as need. "He needed them all, from shop girls to world class beauties."[26] And while still with the Philadelphia Orchestra, this eroticism would cost him his second marriage. Yet his creative activity innovatively burst into fields unmatched by any other American musician, even as the shambles of his personal life would lead Elizabeth DeYoung Levin to describe the Stokowski of this period as "one of the loneliest people I have ever met."[27]

However this same Stokowski of the thirties could mischievously describe his succession of love partners as "nurses," as "angels of mercy," whose ministrations led to rejuvenation. In a humorous ship-board note of the period to Sylvan Levin in Philadelphia, Stokowski would slyly tease his friend with a reference to "nurses" that Stokowski facetiously suggested were after him (Levin), ending with the observation that those old Biblical prophets were certainly right; "My rod and my staff, they comfort me." Alternately, a younger Stokowski still in his twenties once described sexual love as an unappeasable appetite, an attempt to gain love that only ends in sexual sensation, and is destined to be repeated for a lifetime.[28] What one has here are the painful and the playful sides of the artist, constantly in alternation, thus creating some strange kind of equilibrium in lieu of the balance ordinarily associated with normality.

Finally, there is the "ecstatic" of chapter four, cocreating with the composer and answerable only to music and to himself. Once in his eighties, he became the grand old man of American music, continuing his artistic love affair with young people and with new music in one final public stage of his career, this time as mentor to the American Symphony Orchestra and amanuensis to a strangely kindred yet unlike soul, Charles Ives. This was followed by and ended in the full circle return to the England of his childhood, not as the poor but ambitious young artist who had left sixty-five years earlier, but now returned as a musical lion who could plan his own epitaph on the basis of his commitment to unique gifts and to a romance that had served him strangely, painfully, but well. As he phrased it:

> . . . There is a power which is like electricity, only far more subtle and penetrating. This power is all-pervading. . . . If we understood this power we would know the secret of the magical influence of music . . . why this invisible intangible power can so . . . influence our inner life. For some of us this inner life . . . is the real life—the life we touch intimately. The outer life seems definite—hard . . . the less real life. This outer life sometimes delights and thrills us—but . . . it is fleeting—superficial. . . . The inner life never disappoints us—it is eternal.
>
> Through music we see a vision, and something within us responds with intense longing . . . for the ideal. . . . When we reach its ultimate source, music is the voice of the All—the divine melody—the cosmic rhythm—the universal harmony.[29]

Leopold Stokowski: A Discography Chronologically Arranged by Set

Introduction

Leopold Stokowski began recording in 1917 and as of the early morning of his death on 13 September 1977 was scheduled for a recording session of Rachmaninoff's Symphony no. 2 the same day, with another five years of recordings contracted for by Columbia Records. Between his first recordings and his last—a period of sixty years—he recorded extensively with many orchestras, including his own pickup group, and on a number of labels.

In contrast to other Stokowski discographies, the purpose of this compilation is to list chronologically his recordings by set and by year to illustrate the cyclical nature in which he returned again and again to rerecord some favorite pieces—three long-play *Firebird* Suite recordings, for example—while venturing into new repertoire throughout his life. This kind of discography is an indicator of his musical interest and direction in recording over the years, that is, providing one is aware of the constraints placed upon him by recording companies whose directors seriously curtailed his recordings of the twentieth-century composers he championed so faithfully in the concert hall. One amendment to the foregoing; I have also included live recordings, not commercially recorded at the outset, but later commercially released, and both commemorative recordings and those released by the English and the American Stokowski Societies on long-play.

This discography includes all of those Stokowski recordings currently available at the time of writing. It also includes releases from the twenties through the seventies not currently listed in the Schwan catalog, but available on the collectors' market or through society offerings. Since the biographies of Stokowski by Preben Opperby and Oliver Daniel already list the older 78 RPM recordings never transferred to long-play, I have not duplicated their listings, preferring to list playable recordings, that is, LPs and compact discs chronologically listed, noting the pieces coupled on those discs over the years where known. For the record hunter, the most peculiar of these recordings are those on the RCA Camden label, on which Stokowski is not identified as conductor, and the Philadelphia Orchestra is called the Warwick Symphony Orchestra, the Hollywood Bowl Symphony Orchestra becomes the Star Symphony Orchestra, and the New York City Symphony Orchestra becomes the Sutton Symphony Orchestra. The correct attributions are made herein.

The listings included are then intended to outline the recording phase of Stokowski's professional career during the long-play era and to further our knowledge of it while indicating 78 RPM transfers to LP as well. I have ventured an indication of historical interest or of superior readings with an asterisk (*) and of truly classic performances with the double asterisk (**). Since

Stokowski's recordings, in terms of sonics and engineering, were for the most part models of their time, there are performances dating back twenty, thirty, and a few even fifty and sixty years ago worth finding today on the collector's market. Luckily, a number of these recordings have already been rereleased by the companies who made them originally, often in a budget series. Others have been reissued on new labels, such as Stokowski Decca Gold Label recordings later released on Varèse-Sarabande, or the classic 1927 RCA performance of Beethoven's Symphony no. 7 on Parnassus and then on the English Stokowski Society's label. One can also find memorable rereleases on the English labels, dell' Arte, Cameo, and Nimbus, and on the labels of the English and the American Stokowski Societies. Most recently, live concert recordings by Stokowski have appeared on the Melodram, Accord, Poco, Movimento Musica, and Grandi Concerti labels from Europe. Complicating matters are the remastered rereleases of earlier recordings and the transfers of recordings to compact disc. All of these I have tried to include when known.

As to the annotation, I have followed a practice customary with historians writing annotated bibliographies, but not, I think customary in musical discographies. On some of the entries I have written comments or miniessays on the events surrounding a particular recording or on what the recording represented in terms of Stokowski's career or style of music making. With some of the recordings I have ventured opinions as to their worth or cited the comments of professional critics.

In all, I have been guided by the need to explore those interesting turns and accomplishments of a great recording artist's career as close to the actual recordings as possible and linked to his treatment in the text. In this regard I have occasionally indicated this link "see chapter," "see Appendix," and the like. It is my hope that this discography will be read as integrally related to the text and Appendix that precede it.

I have also followed the bibliographical essay custom of avoiding full footnotes to the text where possible. Where it seemed needed I have included references to individuals, to reviews of recordings, or to source works in the text itself or in parenthesis. Often in citing a work I have used the shortest possible reference. For example, Oliver Daniel, *Stokowski: A Counterpoint of View* (New York: Dodd Mead & Co., 1982) becomes Daniel, *Stokowski.* Full publication data can be found in the textual notes and in the Selected Sources.

More than any other American recording conductor, Stokowski loved to record cameos, smaller pieces of singular intensity, mood, or color—often in transcription—many of which, in the days of 78 RPM records, fit on one side of a ten- or twelve-inch disc. With the advent of long-playing records, Stokowski continued to record these miniatures—many of them exquisite—with record companies, coupling and often recoupling them in more than one record set.

The musical delight inherent in this practice can be heard by any listener, but it poses a problem in this kind of listing. In rereleases of older cameo pieces, as on Camden CAL-120, which contains seven such short selections, the original recording dates range from 1927 to 1939. Rather than make endlessly long entries with full titles and recording dates for each piece, where known, I have in a number of entries used inclusively dated entries indicating the composers represented on multiple title albums. Where fewer works are included in an album, composer and title entries are complete. In the RCA recordings of the twenties through the fifties and in the Angel Seraphim (EMI-Capitol) and the London (English Decca) recordings of the fifties through the seventies, recoupling became so common that seemingly *new* albums were released out of recordings made only a short while before and coupled differently for their initial appearance. Where this is apparent, I have tried to avoid duplicate listings just as I have avoided such duplicate recordings in my own Stokowski collection.

A common judgment repeated until it has become cliché holds that Stokowski's *major* work in performance and recording, as in orchestra building, took place with the Philadelphia Orchestra in the twenties and thirties. Without detracting at all from the importance of the Philadelphia era, a reconsideration of his later career seems warranted. Creation of the All American Youth Orchestra in 1940 and creation of the New York City Symphony in 1944 generated recordings and a new generation of players trained by Stokowski. Stokowski's work with the NBC Orchestra in the forties and fifties and his subsequent revitalization of the Houston Orchestra were crowned in 1962 by his creation of New York's American Symphony Orchestra—another youth organization—and the 1965 premiere, and premiere recording of Charles Ives's Symphony no. 4 with that orchestra. A pioneer still, the seventy- then eighty-year-old Stokowski continued to premiere new music while recording standard fare in performances often equaling and sometimes surpassing the best of the Philadelphia days. Furthermore, the years from 1962 to 1972 with the American Symphony Orchestra provided for that time the best single—and the only nonracist, nonsexist—orchestral training ground for yet another generation of orchestra players, and for conductors like Joseph Eger, José Serebrier, David Katz, Ainsley Cox, Judith Somogyi, and Matthias Bamert.

At ninety, Stokowski ended his association with the American Symphony Orchestra and returned to England for a last five-year career stage in which he concentrated in the main on recording. In terms of creativity, this late harvest of recordings produced some sterling performances, such as that live performance of Elgar's *Enigma* Variations with the Czech Philharmonic Orchestra, recorded by English Decca in 1972. For all of these reasons, it seems to me, Stokowski's post-Philadelphia achievements deserve more attention than they have gotten up to now.

In a record compilation of this sort one is faced with the choice of spelling the names of composers and of compositions uniformly according to the fashion of today, or of listing their sometimes variant spellings as they appeared on recordings made over a number of years and in several countries. I have opted for the flavor of variant spelling related to the time and place of recordings issued or reissued. Thus the Italian release of a live 1962 Stokowski-Philadelphia Orchestra performance of Tchaikovsky's *Romeo and Juliet* is listed as Ciaikovsky, *Romeo e Giulietta*, while its discmate the Suite from *Petrouchka* is listed as *Petruska*. I am sure that no one reading this book will have trouble identifying any of the recordings listed.

Discography

1917–24: Leopold Stokowski: The Early Years, including Brahms, "*Hungarian Dances*" nos. 5 and 6 (1917); Gluck, *Orfeo and Euridice:* "Dance of the Blessed Spirits" (1917); Mozart, Symphony no. 40 in G Minor: Minuet (1919); Beethoven, Symphony No. 8: Allegretto (1920); Wagner, *Tannhäuser:* Overture (1921); Stravinsky, "Fireworks" (1922); Rimsky-Korsakov, *The Snow Maiden:* "Dance of the Tumblers" (1923); Wagner, *Tannhäuser:* "Fest March" (1923);

Liadov, "Dance of the Amazons" (1924). Philadelphia Orchesra. Leopold Stokowski Society LS 3.

This set represents much effort by members of the English society who sponsored it, designed the record jacket, and wrote the notes. H. Ward Marston IV made the transfers from shellac to tape. The set includes Stokowski's, and America's, first symphonic recordings in the Brahms "Hungarian Dances" nos. 5 and 6, both recorded on single-sided shellac discs on 24 October 1917.

Stokowski and the Philadelphians cut 450 sides for Victor from 1917 to 1924, of which only 66 were approved by the conductor for release. From those approved, the performances on this set are drawn. Of these the most interesting are the Beethoven and the Mozart selections because Stokowski never did a complete commercial recording of either symphony.

1927: Dvorak, Symphony no. 9 in E Minor. Philadelphia Orchestra. RCA CRL 2-0334 (two records).

RCA Victor's M-1 set in 1927. The recording rereleased in the 70s has until recently been available in long-play coupled with Stokowski's 1973 recording of the same symphony for RCA. (See entry on the 1973 performance for a comparison of the two.)

1927: Beethoven, Symphony no. 7 in A, and Schubert, Symphony no. 8 in B Minor. Philadelphia Orchestra. Parnassus 5.

This set was earlier released on LP as RCA Camden CAL-212.

***1927–31: Stokowski Conducts Beethoven,* including Symphony no. 7 in A (1927) and Symphony no. 5 in C Minor (1931). Philadelphia Orchestra. Leopold Stokowski Society LS 13.

This recording of the Beethoven Seventh is the same as that in the preceding entry on the Parnassus label, but what a positive difference in sound between the two; the result of H. Ward Marston's transfer from disc to tape and the subsequent direct metal mastering. The recording was legendary as a 78 RPM set, but with this disc we are much closer to the actual sound of performance; a "reincarnation" that "is nothing less than perfect" according to critic Robert M. Connelly, *American Record Guide* 52 (May–June, 1989), 2.

As for the Beethoven Fifth, it was originally cut as the first of Victor's few experimental 33⅓ RPM sets in the thirties, a project doomed by the depression. There it languished until it was included in the limited edition set of orchestral classics by Nieman-Marcus some years ago. As with the Seventh, the transfer to tape of the Fifth was done by Marston.

**1927–37: Leopold Stokowski and the Philadelphia Orchestra Play French Music,* including Franck, Symphony in D Minor (1927); Bizet, *Carmen* Suite (1927); Franck, "Panis Angelicus" (1936, and orch. Stokowski) and Andante from *Grand Piece Symphonique* (1937, and orch. Charles O'Connell); Satie, "Gymnopedies" nos. 1 and 2 (1937, and orch. Debussy). Leopold Stokowski Society of America, LSSA-3.

The disc to tape transfers for this 72-plus-minute set were made by Marston.

Reviewer Robert M. Connelly of the *American Record Guide* described the set as a "joy," basing his judgment on the record's performances, sound, and surfaces (American Record Guide, 51 July–August 1988, 74–75).

Included as well is one of Stokowski's "Outline of Themes" talks on the Franck Symphony, with Artur Rodzinski, no less, at the piano, illustrating the themes described by the maestro. While the talk is stilted and wooden,

Stokowski's assessment of the music is fascinating because he refers to it in terms of that private world explored in the Appendix, "Stokowski and the Family Romance." He describes the work overall as belonging to the world of dreams and mysticism, as an artistic work created out of organist Franck's contemplation of the cosmic.

Whatever, if anything, this description had to do with Franck, it was certainly a classic instance of Stokowski's expression of his own artistic identity and represents evidence of the romancer as artist and of Stokowski's motivation as co-creator. The commitment and intensity of such an identification is carried over to the performance.

**1927–40:* Mussorgsky-Stokowski, *Khovantshina:* Entracte to Act 4 (1927), *Boris Godunov:* Symphonic Synthesis (1936), *Pictures at an Exhibition* (1939), and "Night on Bald Mountain" (1940). Philadelphia Orchestra. Leopold Stokowski Society LS 14.

In this set the English Stokowski Society has made available all of Stokowski's Mussorgsky recordings performed with the Philadelphia Orchestra in fine transfers to long play by Ward Marston (see discography note to the RCA Camden release of the 1936 *Boris Godunov:* Symphonic Synthesis).

**1927–40:* Wagner, *Die Meistersinger:* Prelude to Act 1 (1936), *Lohengrin:* Prelude to Act 1 (1927), Prelude to Act 3 (1940), *Tristan and Isolde:* Prelude to Act 1 (1937), "Liebesnacht" (1935, and freely transcribed by Stokowski), and "Liebestod" (1939). Philadelphia Orchestra. Leopold Stokowski Society of America, LSSA P 1986.

This third release of the Leopold Stokowski Society of America was a stunning set of Wagner excerpts by Stokowski and the Philadelphians. The disc to tape transfer by Marston is first rate, revealing in modern sound what was there, but muffled by shellac, in my old RCA Victor album, M508.

Using Stokowski's own conducting score and orchestral parts marked by him, maestro Mehli Mehta recorded the "Liebesnacht" and the "Liebestod" from *Tristan and Isolde* with his Los Angeles–based American Youth Symphony Orchestra in 1983. This attractive recording is to be found on Protone Records PR 159, coupled with Strauss, Suite from *Der Rosenkavalier.*

**1927–29: Leopold Stokowski plays Bach*, including *Brandenburg* Concerto no. 2, Chorale Prelude: "Wir glauben all' an einen Gott," Prelude in B Minor from Book 1 of the *Well-Tempered Clavier,* Chorale Prelude: "Aus der Tiefe ruf' ich," Toccata and Fugue in D Minor, Prelude in E Flat Minor from Book 1 of the *Well-Tempered Clavier,* Chorale Prelude: "Ich ruf' zu dir, Herr Jesu Christ," and the Passacaglia and Fugue in C Minor. Philadelphia Orchestra. dell'Arte Records DA 9001, under sponsorship of the Leopold Stokowski Society.

Controversial works in their own right, the Bach-Stokowski transcriptions authorship was for years subject to additional debate. Here they are as originally recorded by the Philadelphia Orchestra.

When a very young organist, Stokowski transcribed many orchestral works for organ. Once a conductor, he began transcribing songs and organ and piano pieces for orchestra. The maestro's own scores for the transcriptions, overlayed with later Stokowski notations and paste-on score changes, are now housed in the Stokowski Collection of the Curtis Institute of Music, Philadelphia. However these scores are not at rest there since musicologists probe them for their secrets, and conductors like Eric Kunzel, Robert Pikler, Zubin Mehta, and Michael Tilson Thomas borrow copies of them for performance or recording.

This album represents a fine transfer of those historic 78 RPM recordings to modern long-play and a worthy acquisition for any music lover. While this set differs interpretively from Stokowski's last Bach set of 1975 in that the performances of the twenties are lean, muscular, and intense where the valedictory set tends to more spacious pacing and the introspection of summing up—listen carefully to the "Kom Süsser Tod" of 1975—the two sets have one thing in common. Neither shows those overly mannered to theatrical touches that would mar some of the Bach-Stokowski recordings of the forties and fifties.

A curious feature of the early Philadelphia recordings linked, I think, to Stokowski as a Bach performer, is the fact that the *Brandenburg* Concerto performance is the weakest on the set. Governed by Bach's own orchestration, Stokowski's gifts for illuminating what he felt was the spirit of the music by transcription seem lost and with them much of his magic at capturing mood, message, and emotion in sound. The same thing is apparent in his 1960 Philadelphia Bach album, where the *Brandenburg* no. 5 is interpetively weaker than the chorale preludes transcribed by Stokowski for orchestra.

While the very young Stokowski gloried in freely transcribing orchestral works for organ, the later counterpart to this trait was conductor Stokowski's delight in translating the genius of Bach's organ works into romantic orchestral color. Ironically, where Bach orchestrated his own works, as in the *Brandenburg* Concerto, Stokowski's performance becomes stolid, as though Bach's eighteenth-century form dampered Stokowski's cocreative zest at projecting what he conceived of as Bach's romantic essence with the full range of the twentieth century's orchestral resources. Even romancer Stokowski grew cautious at tampering with the fully formed orchestration of the *Brandenburgs*, but, accepting the governance of an eighteenth-century form, became pale in presenting it.

***1927–37:** *Centennial Celebration: Leopold Stokowski-Igor Stravinsky*, including Stravinsky, *Firebird* Suite (1927), *Le Sacre du Printemps* (1929), and *Petrushka* (1937). Philadelphia Orchestra limited edition record set. RCA Special Products DPM 2 0534 (two records), from WFLN/Philadelphia Orchestra Marathon VI, 1982.

The 1927 *Firebird* Suite and the 1929 *Sacre*, complete on a single disc, are available from dell' Arte on DA 9005.

Of the *Sacre* rerelease, *Stereo Review*'s critic praised the recording (April 1983), commenting on the intense energy of the performance, its bristling rhythms, and orchestral color, the whole of which was governed by a strong sense of the work's structure.

It was Stokowski with the Philadelphia Orchestra who gave this work its American debut in the fully staged ballet version starring Martha Graham (1930), its first American concert performance (1922), and its first radio broadcast (1929) as well as this, its first American recording. Although Stokowski's personal relationship with Stravinsky was, by his own admission and Stravinsky's, prickly, both his feeling for Stravinsky's music and his abilities as interpreter were great. Asked by Ainsley Cox in the sixties whose music of twentieth-century composers he felt closest to, Stokowski named Stravinsky along with Schoenberg, Richard Strauss, Sibelius, and Rachmaninoff. That Victor agreed to record the controversial work in 1929 was a tribute to Stokowski's championship of the composer.

**1927–40: Stokowski–The Philadelphia Orchestra: Favorite Showpieces*, commemorating the sixtieth anniversary of Stokowski's Philadelphia Orchestra debut, including Bach-Stokowski, Toccata and Fugue in D Minor (1927) and

Passacaglia and Fugue in C Minor (1929); Sibelius, "Swan of Tuonela" (1929) and "Finlandia" (1930); Saint-Saëns, "Danse Macabre" (1936) and *Samson and Delilah:* "Bacchanale" (1927); Wagner, *Die Götterdämmerung:* "Closing Scene" (1927) and *Die Walküre:* "Magic Fire Music" (1939); Mussorgsky, "Night on Bald Mountain" (1940); Glière, *Red Poppy:* "Russian Sailors' Dance" (1934); Rimsky-Korsakov, *Russian Easter* Overture (1929); Ippolitov-Ivanov, *Caucasian Sketches:* "Procession of the Sardar" (1927); Liszt, "Hungarian Rhapsody" no. 2 (1926–27); and Berlioz, *Damnation of Faust:* "Rakoczy March" (1927). RCA VCM-7101 (two records).

This 1972 release of "showpieces" earlier recorded by Stokowski and the Philadelphia Orchestra is a collection of rousers for the most part, all of which, from the twenties through at least the fifties, were associated in the record-buying public's mind with maestro Stokowski. But they represent only one facet of Stokowski's art and programming. Recalling her girlhood years at symphony with Stokowski and the Philadelphians, Marcia Davenport remembers, in *Too Strong for Fantasy* (1967), that each concert ended with "a Big Noise." It might be Wagner, a Bach transcription, or a Russian staple that would send audiences home whistling. In Davenport's terms, then, this is essentially a "Big Noise" commemorative and as such fails to indicate Stokowski's range as a musician and performer.

For his study of the Philadelphia Orchestra from the 1920s to the 1960s, *Bach, Beethoven, and Bureaucracy* (1971), Edward Arian notes that a study of Stokowski's programs during the twenties and thirties revealed program originality and imagination. His concern with broadening the taste of his audiences was readily apparent in his anything-but-routine programming. If, as Davenport suggests, Philadelphia concerts ended with musical dessert, one could be sure that the audiences had eaten their salad and broccoli as well. In *Worlds of Music* (1952) Cecil Smith described Stokowski's Philadelphia Orchestra programming as the most innovative in American orchestral history, an adventure that ended in Philadelphia when he left the orchestra.

However, the Stokowski style in programming did not end with the Philadelphia years. He carried it through his years with the NBC Orchestra, the Houston Orchestra, and the ten golden years (1962–72) with the American Symphony Orchestra. Of those years Edmund Haines wrote (*High Fidelity—Musical America*, February 1968) that the maestro's adventurous programming was ever balanced between the old and the new and between schools of music. As such Stokowski remained on the cutting edge with continually fresh and thoughtful programs.

This rare ability, carried from the Cincinnati years to the end of his career—a span of more than sixty years—cannot be explained by musicianship and daring alone. I think Stokowski's unique and psychological understanding of music and of his listeners is the key. There are pieces that an audience will predictably love, and others, chiefly avant-garde, that they will intensely dislike. Programming with a further admixture of good soloists, beloved symphonic works, ethnic spice, and the like, plus at least one rouser or "Big Noise" piece, keeps an audience unsettled, expectant, and emotionally attentive because its planes of feeling and understanding are challenged by variety. There is no room for smugness and Kultur with a capital *K*, that is, boredom, to set in. And of course it was this kind of emotional range that Stokowski built into his concerts. In interview sessions over the years Stokowski was on record about the importance of emotional range as a key part of the musical process. He told

William Malloch in the early sixties that the worst audience reaction to a concert was no reaction at all; better hisses than calm. Cerebral calm, analysis, and decorum were not what music was all about. Listeners should not analyze music as an intellectual exercise, but open their hearts and minds to it freely. Preferably they could simply accept it for what it was worth to them in terms of interest, beauty, and emotion.

And so I am back to the sixtieth anniversary commemorative. As good as the set is it represents only the most saleable aspect of Stokowski's art, not the range of it. Would that Victor had allowed that artistic range in the recording studio as often as it showed up in the concert hall.

1927–40: Concert Gems, short selections by Brahms, Sibelius, Schubert, Novacek, Debussy, Weber, and Ippolitov-Ivanov. Philadelphia Orchestra. RCA Camden CAL-123.

1927–39: Concert Classics, selections by Bach-Stokowski, Boccherini, Handel, Haydn, Sibelius, and Wagner. Philadelphia Orchestra. RCA Camden CAL-120.

While both Camden 120 and 123 contain encores and shorter pieces in the standard Stokowski repertoire, one piece in Camden CAL 120 deserves special mention. The set contains the only recording made of Stokowski's transcription of the Bach Fugue in C Minor from Book 1 of the *Well-Tempered Clavier* (1934).

**1928:* Brahms, Symphony no. 3 in F. Philadelphia Orchestra. RCA Camden CAL-164.

This is a better and more vigorous performance than his 1959 recording for Everest. Particularly noteworthy is the barely restrained energy level of the first movement always threatening to burst out of the form containing it. The whole performance illustrates Stokowski's avoidance of the bland in favor of muscularity and vigor in interpreting Brahms.

***1929:* Rachmaninoff, Piano Concerto no. 2 in C Minor, with soloist Sergei Rachmaninoff. Philadelphia Orchestra. RCA ARM 3-0296, from *The Complete Rachmaninoff,* vol. 5 (three records).

When the concerto was recorded in 1929 the Rachmaninoff-Stokowski collaboration was nearly twenty years old. They had performed this concerto with the Cincinnati Symphony Orchestra in 1910. During the twenties and thirties Rachmaninoff made frequent appearances as pianist and conductor with the Philadelphia Orchestra, which he considered the world's greatest. Premieres of Rachmaninoff's *The Bells* (1920), *Three Russian Songs* (1927), dedicated to Stokowski, the Fourth Piano Concerto (1927), the Rhapsody on a Theme of Paganini (1934), and the Symphony no. 3 (1936) were all made with the Stokowski led Philadelphia Orchestra. In each of the premiered piano works Rachmaninoff was soloist.

Not only is this recording a fine performance, but it is one of the most creatively symbiotic examples of soloist, orchestra, and conductor as one that I have ever heard. Its beauty and power are not dimmed by 1929 sound. It is well worth hearing each time a new and predictably "spectacular" recording is made of this work. This recording has now been transferred to RCA compact disc 5997-2-RC coupled with the Third Piano Concerto recording of 1939–40 under Ormandy.

**1929–40:* Bloch, *Schelomo* (1940), with cellist Emmanuel Feuermann; Saint-Saëns, "Danse Macabre" (1936); and Strauss, *Salome:* "Dance of the Seven Veils" (1929). Philadelphia Orchestra. RCA Camden CAL-254.

A strange and unfitting coupling of the great 1939 Bloch recording with the Strauss and Saint-Saëns pieces. Yet the Danse and the Dance *are* performed brilliantly. As to the Bloch, it is one of the great cello recordings of all time—I have seen it described as the greatest—and it can also be found on the collectors market in a ten-inch RCA LCT 14 long-play "Immortal Performance," which it certainly is.

The Schelomo was rereleased in 1985 on long-play by the Smithsonian Institution as one side in its seven-record set of great performances entitled *Virtuosi*. R 032 LGR-9265.

1929–36: Music for Easter, including Rimsky-Korsakov, *Russian Easter* Overture (1929), and Wagner, *Parsifal:* Prelude and "Good Friday Spell" (1936). Philadelphia Orchestra. RCA Camden CAL-163.

But for the Philadelphia Orchestra's 1936 transcontinental tour, the *Parsifal* recording of that year might have been a complete opera recording. In 1934 Stokowski, assisted by Sylvan Levin, had conducted a concert version of the opera presented in three segments over four days, with two Philco Radio Hour broadcasts of portions of the production (see Daniel, Stokowski, 273–76).

The success of that production, plus Stokowski's 1931–32 sound experiments with Harvey Fletcher and the technicians of the Bell Telephone Laboratories (see note on *Early Hi-Fi: Wide Range and Stereo Recordings Made by the Bell Laboratories, 1931–1932*. vol. 2) fired Stokowski's imagination as to the possibility of a new, revolutionary production of *Parsifal*. The team of Stokowski and Fletcher had in 1933 demonstrated what newly developed and experimental sound equipment could do with the transmission of an orchestra concert. With assistant conductor Alexander Smallens leading the Philadelphia Orchestra in its home city, and with Stokowski at the control panel in Washington D.C., Bell technicians and equipment had carried a live concert from Philadelphia to Constitution Hall in Washington D.C., where an invited audience of influential scientists, engineers, government officials, and business leaders was treated to a unique event: live orchestral and vocal sound in a bare concert hall! Bach, Wagner, and Debussy, from one hundred miles away, were as live as that heard in the orchestra seats of the Academy of Music. The concert was a huge success. Audience reaction was ecstatic, and Stokowski was moved to consider the possibilities of such electronic magic in terms of opera production, with *Parsifal* in mind.

Among other things it meant that a staged opera could be produced with just the right actors and actresses miming key characters on stage to get the drama right, while orchestra and singers performed back stage, their music electronically projected into the hall. No longer would a middle-aged tenor have to publicly attempt to act the role of the youthful and heroic Parsifal. Nor would the delicious seductress Kundry have to appear in the person of a hefty and matronly soprano. With fine singers behind the scenes and first-rate dramatic performers on stage, all the drama, eroticism, and spiritual power of *Parsifal* could be felt and seen by the audience. Furthermore with modern technology linked to free artistic association, scenery, lighting, and special effects could enhance both the music and stage action toward a union of the musical, the artistic, and the dramatic into a transcendant whole, as Stokowski put it.

That dream opera was not to be—yet. For when Harvey Fletcher contacted Stokowski to pledge his and Bell Labs' support for the 1936 *Parsifal*, the maestro was in the midst of preparations for the Philadelphia Orchestra tour and postponed the opera project indefinitely. 1936 brought forth not the opera, but only a new recording of the Prelude and "Good Friday Spell," while any future plans for electronic opera were later swallowed up by Stokowski's work on *Fantasia*. However, even in *Fantasia* the hand of Harvey Fletcher could be felt, for it was the physicist who devised the process for recording on film, described it to the maestro in 1938, and saw it incorporated in recording the score of *Fantasia*. (For a full discussion of Stokowski's work with Fletcher and the Bell Laboratories, including the aborted *Parsifal*, see McGinn, "Stokowski and the Bell Telephone Laboratories," 38–75.

As for the dream of an evocative *Parsifal* employing all of the advances in electronics and media, it came true forty-six years later in 1982, when a German film director and romantic, Hans Juergen Syberberg, came uncannily close to creating Stokowski's vision of the opera—not on stage, but on film (see Kevin Thomas, "Parsifal," *Los Angeles Times*, 20 July 1983, part 6, 3).

1929–30: Brahms, Symphony no. 2. Philadelphia Orchestra. Leopold Stokowski Society LS 11.

Originally released as RCA Victor set M82, the four movements were recorded at three sessions in 1929 and 1930.

**1921–32: Early Hi-Fi: Wide Range and Stereo Recordings Made by Bell Telephone Laboratories in the 1930s, Leopold Stokowski Conducting the Philadelphia Orchestra, 1931–1932*, vol. 1, including all, or portions of, Berlioz, "Roman Carnival" Overture; Weber, "Invitation to the Dance"; Mendelssohn, *Midsummer Night's Dream:* Scherzo; Wagner, *Tristan and Isolde:* "Liebestod"; Scriabin, *Prometheus;* and Mussorgsky-Ravel, *Pictures at an Exhibition*. Released in 1979 by Bell Telephone Laboratories Inc.

This is an extraordinary recording in all respects. Bell Laboratories pioneered both 33⅓ RPM recordings and stereophonic recording in the twenties and thirties. At the same time the pioneering Stokowski, who made eighteen 33⅓ recordings for RCA in the early thirties, was studying the potential of frequency modulation and stereophonic reproduction. In a great orchestral collaboration, conductor Stokowski and the Philadelphia Orchestra at the height of their combined powers are now made available to us, at times in stereo, through the 1979 release of these fifty-year-old recordings created from another collaboration—that of Bell's engineers with Stokowski and the orchestra in rehearsal and in live performance.

While all of the recordings are of historical interest (e.g., Stokowski playing Maurice Ravel's transcription of *Pictures* rather than his own), four of the pieces are musically worth searching out fifty years after performance: The Berlioz, with its razor sharp attacks, power, and dazzling virtuosity; the Mendelssohn, never commercially recorded by Stokowski and quite lovely; the *Prometheus: Poem of Fire* with Sylvan Levin as piano soloist, which was separately recorded by RCA as M125 during the same season; and finally Wagner's "Liebestod" from *Tristan and Isolde*, as erotically fervent a performance as this great orchestra was ever likely to give. The sound does vary because of the experimental nature of the recordings, and the splices are sometimes apparent, but no matter. The experiment was and is a sonic success.

**1931–32: Early Hi-Fi: Wide Range and Stereo Recordings Made by Bell Telephone Laboratories in the 1930s, Leopold Stokowski Conducting the Philadelphia Orchestra, 1931–1932*, vol. 2, including all or portions of Wagner, *Die Walküre:* "Ride of the Valkyries," "Wotan's Farewell," and "Magic Fire Music," *Siegfried:* "Forest Murmurs," and *Die Götterdämmerung:* "Siegfried's Funeral

Music" and "Brunnhilde's Immolation," and concluding with Stokowski's end-of-the-season talk to the audience (29–30 April 1932). Master tape and notes prepared by Marston. Released in 1981 by Bell Telephone Laboratories Inc.

The Bell Laboratories recordings provide us with stunning evidence of not only the beauty, power, and precision of the orchestra under Stokowski, but also the importance of the collaboration of Stokowski with Bell's scientists and engineers, particularly Harvey Fletcher.

The maestro had been most dissatisfied with the sound equipment—more precisely the sound—provided by RCA for the Philadelphia radio broadcasts during the 1930–31 season. Since Stokowski turned to the Bell labs only three days after the last RCA/NBC broadcast of 5 April 1931, the circumstantial evidence indicates that his concern for good broadcast sound motivated him to volunteer himself and his orchestra for experiments to improve orchestral sound in transmission and recording. After all, it was the Western Electric Company of the Bell system that had developed American electrical recording in 1925 and had licensed the system to Victor that same year. Stokowski was the first conductor to record with this vastly improved system. The maestro then visited the Bell Labs in 1930, meeting Harold Arnold, a fifteen year veteran with Bell, and the brilliant physicist Harvey Fletcher. By late 1931 they were working together. More than one hundred experimental recordings were made during the 1931–32 season. With the equipment in the basement of the Academy of Music, microphones moved from place to place in the auditorium during the season the foyer was turned into a giant sound room for testing the recorded results.

Out of these experiments grew symbiotic benefits for both the worlds of art and of technology. In the words of Harold Arnold of Bell, Stokowski was an inspiration to the technologists, for he could turn their inartistic science into radiant sound and "living" art; in short, it was the wedding of technology to the aims of art. Nor was it true that the conductor knew nothing about the science and technology of electronic recording and reproduction. He was versed in this field at the beginning of the experiment and expertly versed at its conclusion. More important, noted the scientists and engineers he worked with, was that his effort at mastering the field was a way station toward the expression of artistic "daring and imagination."

As for the Bell Laboratories' engineers, they had achieved the first binaural or stereo sound with the Philadelphia Orchestra utilizing new recording equipment and their latest sound gear. The best portions of these recordings equalled commercial recordings that wouldn't appear until the 1950s. The implications of the tests were equally great for performance, for radio transmission, and for recording. The first fruits were produced in new electrical transcription discs—fifteen minutes per side—whose fine sound was better than the live pickups of the 1930s. The new transcription process was introduced almost immediately.

Taken as a whole, these experiments with their immediate and long range results, represent an important musical and electronic collaboration in the history of recording and of broadcasting (see McGinn, "Stokowski," 38–75).

**1932:* Schoenberg, *Gurrelieder*, with soloists Jeannette Vreeland, soprano, Rose Bampton, mezzo-soprano, Paul Althouse and Robert Betts, tenors, Abrasha Robofsky, bass, and Benjamin de Loache, narrator. Princeton Glee Club and Choruses of the Fortnightly Club and the Mendelssohn Club, and the Philadelphia Orchestra. RCA AVM 2-2017 (live, two records)

Leopold Stokowski premiered six major works by Arnold Schoenberg, including *Gurrelieder.* He gave early performances of many others and became, for the beleaguered Schoenberg, his major American champion. A grateful Schoenberg described Stokowski as a real individualist willing to take his chances with audience disapproval in the performance of his (Schoenberg's) works. From Schoenberg's perspective, Stokowski was a true friend in the arts (see Stein, "Stokowski," *Journal of the Arnold Schoenberg Institute* 3 [October 1979]: 219–22).

Stokowski returned Schoenberg's respect and named him one of the five living composers he felt closest to, but, according to Abram Chasins, the only two Schoenberg pieces that Stokowski was personally fond of were the youthful and romantic *Verklärte Nacht* and *Gurrelieder,* which were also those that he recorded. His feeling for Schoenberg then, was in the main admiration and respect for a pioneering composer working against great odds to compose what he believed in regardless of public antipathy and neglect; this was an empathy he also felt for Varèse, Ives, and others.

That Stokowski performed so much of Schoenberg's astringent twelve-toned music was admirable; that he did so at great professional cost to himself is, I think, unusual in American music. It indebted innovator Schoenberg to innovator Stokowski. An instance of the price the conductor paid lay in his loss of the coconductorship of the NBC Symphony Orchestra in the forties. Already playing too many modern works to suit the network, Stokowski's chief crime was to premiere the Schoenberg Piano Concerto during the 1943–44 season. His judges were the wrathful traditionalist, Arturo Toscanini, and sponsor, the General Motors Corporation. Between them, Toscanini and a culturally deprived GM blocked the renewal of Stokowski's NBC contract for 1944–45, which was a discreditable action all around (see Daniel, *Stokowski,* 466–69, for the best single account of the affair).

As to the 1932 live recording of *Gurrelieder;* there were no splices and no chances for corrections on any of the fourteen 78 RPM records that made up the 1932 set. It was up to that time the largest and most musically awesome piece ever recorded: it included an augmented Philadelphia Orchestra of 122 pieces, three choruses, five soloists, and a narrator—532 performers in all. The whole giant cantata was a late romantic tour de force, wrote admiring critic Paul Rosenfeld.

We know that the Stokowski of the 1960s wanted to commercially rerecord *Gurrelieder.* He didn't get the chance, but it is quite likely that live recordings were made of his 1960 performance with the Philadelphia Orchestra and of his 1961 Edinburgh Festival performance with the London Symphony Orchestra. Either performance might prove suitable for rerelease on compact disc.

**1932:* Sibelius, Symphony no. 4 in A Minor, included in *The Philadelphia Story* with other recordings conducted by Eugene Ormandy and Sergei Rachmaninoff and featuring Fritz Kreisler and Emmanuel Feuermann as soloists. Philadelphia Orchestra. RCA SRS 3001 (three records).

A poetically sure interpretation of this sombre score marks the recording. It was the premiere American recording of the symphony. Darkly lyric and spare, it was beautifully played by the Philadelphia Orchestra.

1934–39: Saint-Saëns, *Carnival of the Animals* (1939), with duo pianists Sylvan Levin and Jeanne Behrend; and Tchaikovsky, *Nutcracker* Suite (1934). Philadelphia Orchestra. RCA Camden CAL-100.

The *Carnival of the Animals* was a staple of the Childrens' Concert series in Philadelphia. An extremely popular series with children and adults, these concerts were full of surprises. An elephant appeared on stage during a concert performance of the *Carnival of the Animals*. At another childrens' concert, a fully uniformed motorcycle policeman walked on stage during the concert and prepared to hand Maestro Stokowski a speeding ticket for his pell-mell reading of Mozart's Overture to *The Marriage of Figaro*. With the whole routine prearranged, Stokowski now talked his way out of the ticket by letting the officer, an expert xylophonist, perform *Flight of the Bumblebee* with the orchestra. Children and adults loved it (see Kupferberg, *Fabulous Philadelphians*, 91–93).

**1934*: Rachmaninoff, Rhapsody on a Theme of Paganini, with soloist Sergei Rachmaninoff. Philadelphia Orchestra. RCA ARM 3-0296. from *The Complete Rachmaninoff*, vol. 5 (three records).

While the orchestral sound is somewhat muffled, the piano sound is true. Rachmaninoff's interpretation is ruminative and poetic rather than showy; it is as fine a recording as the 1929 recording of the Second Piano Concerto with the same pianist, conductor, and orchestra. The Rhapsody has been transferred to RCA compact disc 6659-2-RC along with the First and Fourth Piano Concertos conducted by Ormandy with Rachmaninoff as soloist.

1934: Dvorak, Symphony no. 9 (listed as no. 5). Philadelphia Orchestra. RCA Camden CAL-104.

This is one of six Stokowski recordings of the work; the first dating from 1925, the last from 1973. This piece whose color and musical-emotional range were well suited to Stokowski's gifts illustrates the conductor's habit of re-recording a favorite work periodically in order to keep a current version available. Not only was the maestro fond of the work, but he shrewdly recognized that the record-buying public was as well; a trait he showed in recording other popular concert pieces.

1934: Tchaikovsky, Symphony no. 5 in E Minor. Philadelphia Orchestra. RCA Camden CAL-201

This work was one of those symphonic standards with which Stokowski could enchant not only Philadelphia audiences but New York audiences at Carnegie Hall as well. As noted by Irving Kolodin, Stokowski filled a musical void in New York during the 1920s. His programs were exciting. Russian, French, and native American music balanced Germanic offerings. Avant-garde works by Schoenberg and Varèse with their strange (at the time) dissonances and peculiar orchestral color and effects would give way to the Latin exoticism of Villa-Lobos and hence to the beauties and "Big Noise" of Tchaikovsky.

New Yorkers loved it. The regular Philadelphia visits, first begun in 1918, were uniformly sold out, while New Yorkers lined up at concert time hoping for returned tickets. Not until Toscanini's era with the New York Philharmonic began in 1929 did Stokowski have a rival for the musical affection of New Yorkers. And rivalry it was through the 1930s. That Stokowski remained a New York favorite until he left the Philadelphia Orchestra in 1941 was a tribute to his musical ability and to his programming imagination. As Howard Shanet has pointed out in *Philharmonic* (1975), Toscanini was limited by a repertoire that in eleven seasons with the Philharmonic saw Beethoven, Brahms, and Wagner make up fully 40 percent of his programming, to which were added overlarge portions of Italian music, some good, much mediocre. At the same time he played very little modern music in general and only five pieces by American composers. Against this conservative record one can understand the delight of New Yorkers in the variety and range of Stokowski's offerings.

One can get a solid sense of that programming adventure and of the maestro's New York appeal in Richard Schickel's *The World of Carnegie Hall*, (1960) and in Brian Plumb's serialized record of Stokowski's Philadelphia and New York programs, which can be found in *Toccata*, the journal of the English Leopold Stokowski Society.

1934–40: Dukas, "Sorcercer's Apprentice" (1937); Mussorgsky, "Night on Bare Mountain" (1940); and Ravel, *Rapsodie Espagnole* (1934). Philadelphia Orchestra. RCA Camden CAL-118.

These three were Stokowski specialties, two of which are indelibly associated with the motion picture *Fantasia*.

**1935–41:* Shostakovich, Symphony no. 5 (1939), Prelude in E Flat (1935, orch. Stokowski), with the Philadelphia Orchestra, and Prokofiev, *Love For Three Oranges:* "Infernal Scene," "March," and "The Prince and the Princess" (1941), with the NBC Symphony Orchestra. Leopold Stokowski Society of America, LSSA 4.

These were orginally RCA recordings, which appeared to good reviews on their initial releases from 1935 to 1941.

Stokowski was an early champion of both composers with American premieres of three major works by Prokofiev and five by Shostakovich. More than that he regularly performed their works over the years—cold war or no—and recorded them when he could.

1935: MacDonald, Symphony no. 2: "Rhumba." Philadelphia Orchestra. Included in RCA Camden CAL-238.

1935: Brahms, Symphony no. 1. Philadelphia Orchestra. RCA Camden CAL-105.

***1936–39:* Mussorgsky-Stokowski, *Boris Godunov:* Symphonic Synthesis (1936), and Debussy, *Nocturnes:* "Nuages," "Fêtes," and "Sirèns" (1937–39). Philadelphia Orchestra and Chorus, RCA Camden CAL-140.

Both of these recordings are among the truly classic Stokowski-Philadelphia collaborations. Their poetry, power, and color are undimmed by the intervening years. It is hard to believe this kind of orchestral sound was commmitted to shellac fifty years ago.

Stokowski had given the American premiere of Mussorgsky's original *Boris* in 1929. Indeed it was the sensation of the Philadelphia musical season. Seven years later Stokowski introduced his "symphonic synthesis" of the work at Philadelphia's Academy of Music. This masterful transcription—composer Lou Harrison described it to Oliver Daniel as among the finest jobs of transcription he'd ever encountered (Daniel, *Stokowski*, 221)—drew music from the opera's Introduction, Pilgrim's Chorus, Coronation Scene, Varlaam's Song, Revolutionary Scene, Simpleton's Song and the Death of Boris. Vocal leads were given to orchestral instruments and so sensitively was the transcription done that the synthesis stands by the opera as a near independent work of art, by turns joyous, majestic, foreboding, savage, and tragic. The power of the music and the recording are enhanced by Stokowski's use of a whole battery of oriental gongs used at key dramatic moments. The gongs were, in the main, Stokowski's own, from a collection he had gathered over the years and used earlier in the 1929 *Boris* premiere.

Sylvan Levin was in charge of gong-percussion for the *Boris* premiere and recalled for me that Stokowski requisitioned the box seats nearest the stage and to his line of sight so as to avoid crowding the stage or the pit with his amazing array and to sonically provide an offstage percussive counterpoint adding to the drama of the music onstage. Mr. Levin described the premiere as one of the most exciting and exacting nights of his musical carer. That excitement carries over to the synthesis recording.

The remake of the synthesis, a 1968 recording made in Phase 4 stereo sound simply doesn't have the savage power and beauty of the 1936 original with the Philadelphia Orchestra.

In a completely different context, that of the impressionistic and ethereal world of Debussy's *Nocturnes*, the magic is also there. As recalled by conductor Andre Previn in Edward Johnson's *Stokowski: Essays in Analysis of his Art* (1973), Previn's first record at the age of six was Stokowski's earlier 1927 recording of "Fêtes," which in his delight he eventually wore out. After replacing it with another copy, he discovered the later Stokowski recording of the three *Nocturnes* and trebled his musical experience. Concluding his essay on Stokowski, Previn described the maestro as the most beneficent living force (as of 1973) in American orchestral music and, quite possibly, in the orchestral music of the world. Certainly the two performances on this record could be cited as historical evidence to back up Previn's conclusion.

1937: Borodin, *Prince Igor:* "Dances of the Polovetzki Maidens" (arr. Stokowski), and Stravinsky, *Petrouchka*. RCA Camden CAL-203.

**1939:* *Walt Disney's Fantasia*, including Bach-Stokowski, *Toccata and Fugue in D Minor;* Tchaikovsky, *Nutcracker* Suite; Dukas, "Sorcerer's Apprentice" (arr. Stokowski and recorded in Hollywood with the Disney Studio Orchestra); Stravinsky, *Rite of Spring* (arr. Stokowski); Beethoven, *Pastoral* Symphony (arr. Stokowski); Ponchielli, "Dance of the Hours;" Mussorgsky, "Night on Bald Mountain" (arr. Rimsky-Korsakov and Stokowski); and Schubert, "Ave Maria," with Juliet Novis, soprano. Philadelphia Orchestra. Buena Vista STER 101.

This is an unparalleled achievement in linking film to symphonic music and in advancing recording technology through the use of tape and multichannel techniques in recording.

I recently saw the film again—a motion picture that had delighted, frightened, and moved me as a child. What struck me about the film this time was how much of Stokowski's playful paganism and nature worship were included. Even the final "Ave Maria," meant, in part, to dilute the diabolism of the preceding "Night on Bald Mountain" sequence, doesn't play fair with Christian orthodoxy. After all that pious singing and marching to get to the cathedral entry, what opens up as church to the viewer? Another sylvan scene. In *Fantasia*, Stokowski's God, like Jefferson's, was "nature's god." Pagan gods, centaurs, and nymphs—more properly nymphets—coupled with the evolutionist message of the *Rite of Spring* all smack of Stokowski's philosophical influence on the film (see Appendix).

Stokowski purists—irony intended—have expressed outrage at the 1982 Disney Studio's rerecording of the *Fantasia* sound track by film conductor Irwin Kostal and a 127-piece studio orchestra (Buena Vista, 104). The decision was technically sound and intended to bring the score into the digital and dolby capabilities of the eighties. A la Stokowski himself, Kostal is quoted as saying that he changed the Bach and the Mussorgsky arrangements in order to take advantage of improvements in sound technology, that is, to make them sound (*Los Angeles Times* Calendar, 14 March 1982). Musically working from Stokowski's own marked score and bound by the limits of synchronizing that score to film, Kostal has provided a good and workmanlike interpretation, but one which is bland where the original was spicy, deliberate where Stokowski was daring and seemingly spontaneous. Compare the two and the differences are clearly apparent. However the sound *is* upgraded and, Stokowski purists aside, one can imagine the maestro himself enjoying the delicious irony of his once ultramodern sound being termed outmoded. And we can imagine Stokowski, from a perspective of more-than sixty years of work as a futurist, accepting his *own* dicta in application to his *own* work with a knowing "I told you so."

Now, however, the irony of Kostal's rerecording of *Fantasia* may be undone. Disney officials have announced (*Los Angeles Times*, 26 Dec. 1988) that a test to digitally remaster the original Stokowski recording has been successful and that the studio plans to have the complete Stokowski sound track digitally remastered for the 1990 reissue of the film on the fiftieth anniversary of *Fantasia's* release.

1940: Glière, *Ilia Mourmetz:* Symphony no. 3 in B Minor. Philadelphia Orchestra. RCA LCT 1106.

This recording of a Stokowski speciality was transferred from 78 RPM discs to RCA's "Immortal Performances" series on long-play. It was one of Stokowski's valedictory recordings with the orchestra during their last year together. The orchestral playing and Stokowski's interpretive control of the ensemble are first-rate, although the 1940 recorded sound is dull. In terms of comparison though, his 1956 stereo recording of this work with the Houston Symphony not only has much better sound but the orchestra, revitalized by Stokowski's tenure in Houston, plays beautifully as well. Finally, Stokowski's realization of the work's drama is masterful and more dramatically straightforward than that of the 1940 recording. There are arbitrary and lurid touches to the 1940 performance that actually interfere with the unfolding of Ilia's heroic Russian melodrama. William Trotter, writing in *Toccata* (Winter 1982–83), ascribes such touches to a series of Stokowski Philadelphia performances during his last two years with the orchestra and believes they were attributable to his never-ending battles with the board of directors of the orchestra and to his boredom with things as they were. As Mr. Trotter remembers Stokowski during that time, he inclined to self-indulgence and to creating theatrical effects in performance rather than realizing the poetry and drama inherent in many of the pieces that he played. In short, the 1940 *Ilia* was a sign that it was time for Stokowski to move on.

As to his 1956 performance with the Houston Orchestra, it is a dramatic, succinct, and beautifully shaped poem in sound with anticipated entrances and seamless transitions—a classic example of the themes from chapter 2 concerning the Stokowski sound, the maestro's magic way with the orchestra, and his dramatic gifts as musical story teller.

It was Stokowski who convinced Glière in 1931 that editing was needed to bring the original of *Ilia*—running between seventy and eighty minutes—down to reasonable concert length. Not only would such editing make *Ilia* easier to schedule, but it would enhance the drama and the contrasts of the meandering musical story line. Glière and Stokowski worked together on the original editing job. Comparison of Stokowski's 1940 recording with his 1958 Houston recording shows further skillful editing on his part. Stokowski's Houston recording (38:2) is not only musically and dramatically preferable to the bloated 1975 Melodiya-Columbia recording of the whole work (CBS MG 33832 at

73:11), it is preferable to the 1972 edited version of Eugene Ormandy and the Philadelphia Orchestra (RCA LSC-3246 at 56:46) on both dramatic and musical grounds.

1940: Mozart, Sinfonia Concertante in E Flat, with soloists Marcel Tabuteau, oboe, Bernard Portnoy, clarinet, Sol Schoenbach, bassoon, and Mason Jones, horn, Philadelphia Orchestra. RCA Camden CAL-213.

While the soloists are a delight, the orchestral texture, for me at least, is too thick and sluggish for this music. Stokowski's musical-dramatic flair doesn't live comfortably with the needs of this music.

1941: Prokofiev, *Peter and the Wolf,* with narrator Basil Rathbone. All American Youth Orchestra. Columbia ML 4038.

The only recording made by Stokowski and the All American Youth Orchestra to be transferred to long-play. This recording gives us entrée to the 1940 and 1941 tours made by Stokowski with his youth orchestra of the early forties. The completion of *Fantasia,* a bitter break with the Philadelphia Orchestra management, the romancer's restlessness so characteristic of the maestro, and a chance to dare all with the formation of an orchestra of teenagers and very young adults—all of these things motivated Stokowski to form the All American Youth Orchestra. But perhaps most important of all was the chance to tour Latin America in 1940 with his new orchestra. He had the political but not the financial backing of the government for this "good neighbor" gesture. Even here the "ferocious rivalry," to use critic Roger Dettmer's words, of Toscanini and Stokowski came into play. Toscanini, learning of Stokowski's plans, blocked RCA funding and sponsorship of Stokowski's tour by proposing to RCA a Latin American tour of the NBC Orchestra with himself as conductor immediately before Stokowski's proposed tour—which previously RCA had agreed to fund. RCA backed Toscanini.

In the end Stokowski turned to Columbia records to underwrite the tour, and, in order to win their support, agreed to switch his recording allegiance to Columbia with a series of records to be made by Stokowski and his new youth orchestra. But the time taken by RCA's ultimate refusal and the time needed to win Columbia's support left Stokowski with only four months in the spring and early summer of 1940 to audition players, plan logistics, and to train this new orchestra. While the conductor did not audition all of the fifteen hundred young performers who applied, he did audition over a thousand by June and was able to select ninety players, aged fourteen to twenty-five, for a first rehearsal on 26 June 1940. By late July the orchestra gave its first concert in Atlantic City, to glowing reviews, then went on to Latin America. With a new Bach transcription—the Prelude from the Violin Partita in E Major—prepared on shipboard, the orchestra disembarked in Rio de Janeiro on 7 August 1940, to be met by Heitor Villa-Lobos at the dock. An orchestra of 108 players, of whom 15 were women, gave twenty-seven concerts in six Latin nations before returning in the fall. In addition they added thirteen recordings to the Columbia Masterworks label.

Rave reviews had marked the trip. Rave reviews greeted welcome-home concerts in New York, Philadelphia, Washington, and Baltimore. So enthused was Stokowski that he announced early on a 1941 summer tour for his new orchestra, this time a tour of the United States in which each concert would include a piece by a modern American composer.

On both tours Stokowski had salted his youthful orchestra with experienced players from the Philadelphia Orchestra. In 1940 there were eighteen. By 1941

Stokowski was so sure of his youthful musicians, and so short of funding, that he took only ten members of the Philadelphia Orchestra as section leaders. Again there were fifteen women in the orchestra—a musical heresy in the forties—as well as eighty-four men.

During twelve weeks beginning in April of 1941, they played in fifty-six cities across the country. Carrying a portable plywood sound reflector or acoustical shell of Stokowski's design, they played and were heard in civic auditoriums, state fair pavilions, colosseums, baseball parks, and stadiums as well as in concert halls.

One of those young players, Gustav Janossy, who played bass viol in the orchestra, sent me his seventy-four page account of that trip. Made up of clippings from the newspapers of towns and cities where the orchestra played, it is a vital record of the interest and enthusiasm generated by the second tour, and I am deeply grateful to Mr. Janossy for sharing it with me.

For instance the 16 June concert in Kansas City, Missouri, was held in the arena of the Municipal Auditorium to accommodate eight thousand ticket holders. The normally poor acoustics of the cavernous hall were countered by a special seating arrangement for the players and by Stokowski's use of the acoustical shell within which his orchestra played. According to the *Kansas City Times* (17 June 1941) the huge audience arrived in city clothes, country clothes, sportswear, and formals, filling every seat in the arena and the additional seating added to handle standees. The one noticeable characteristic of this truly mixed audience was the "preponderance" of young people attending.

As to the sound of the orchestra, Stokowski's special seating of his players and the benefits of the acoustical shell within which they played provided good sound from "down in front" to the far end of the arena.

The program began with Stokowski's transcription of a Bach Fugue in G Minor (either the "Great" or the "Little"), followed by the Brahms Third Symphony. Prior to intermission Stokowski talked to the audience about music's importance to America and of the wealth of young musical talent all over the United States. Closing the first half he asked the audience to join with the orchestra in singing the "Star Spangled Banner."

After intermission the orchestra played "With Humor" by American composer Paul Creston and closed with the "Liebestod" from *Tristan and Isolde*. Called back again and again, Stokowski and his charges played three encores; another Bach transcription, the Tchaikovsky-Stokowski "Solitude," and a "Big Noise" rouser to close, the Liszt "Hungarian Rhapsody" no. 2.

What did this concert and all of those of the 1940 and 1941 tours accomplish? William Trotter, in "The Conductor as Musical Hobo," suggests this:

> Considering how briefly the ensemble functioned its legacy is phenomenal, for its graduates had broad and lasting impact on the orchestras and music schools of America, . . . This project focused on the untapped ever growing wealth of musical talent to be found in the United States. . . . The mere existence of the [orchestra] inspired many hundreds of musicians . . . both as performers and as teachers of generations not yet born when the orchestra disbanded.

And disband it did at the end of that 1941 tour, with a last concert in Pasadena, California, played for fifteen-thousand concertgoers and the series of Columbia recordings made in Hollywood—of which the *Peter and the Wolf* was one. War time draft needs and lack of funding ended the two-year life of the orchestra, but not before its impact had been absorbed by American culture.

Simply to look over the roster of its players and recognize names well known in the music world during subsequent decades is a measure of that impact: Israel Baker, Paul Shure, Edward Murphy, Dorothy DeLay, Elizabeth Waldo, and Ralph Hollander, violin, Milton Thomas, viola, Joseph Druian, cello, Robert McGiniss and Mitchell Lurie, clarinet, Harold and Ralph Gomberg, oboe, Albert Tipton, flute, and James Chambers and Robert McInnes, horn.

For the most part, the financing of the second tour had been underwritten by Stokowski himself, since Columbia Records had withdrawn its subsidy. Stokowski served without pay as he had on the first tour, but the burden of underwriting the second tour probably cost the maestro anywhere from $75,000 to $100,000, since ticket prices—from 40¢ to $2.25—hardly generated a self-supporting income for the orchestra and its travels.

I cannot imagine another twentieth-century conductor with the daring, the practicality, the imagination, and—yes—the generosity to have carried off the futuristic coup that was the All American Youth Orchestra.

Ironically, the very largess of the achievement—like that of *Fantasia* three years before—worked against Stokowski in the minds of many traditionalist critics. Some simply refused to accept what Stokowski had to say about the orchestra, the tours, and their meaning for the future of music in America, preferring to claim that the whole thing was simply a showman's gimmick, a charlatan's trick that cheapened American music rather than enriching it.

**1941:* Tchaikovsky, Symphony no. 4. NBC Symphony Orchestra. Leopold Stokowski Society of America, second release (no number).

The recording was originally released as RCA DM 880 and marked Stokowski's return to the RCA fold as well as his appearance at the helm of the NBC Symphony Orchestra after Toscanini had left—temporarily—in a huff.

What a turnabout; 1941–42 saw Stokowski playing and recording Tchaikovsky with the NBC Orchestra, while Toscanini was conducting and recording Debussy and Respighi with the Philadelphia Orchestra.

Stokowski's success with the NBC Orchestra was responsible in part for Toscanini's 1942 request to return as head of that orchestra. The result was the uneasy coconductorship of the orchestra by Toscanini and Stokowski until 1944.

It is public record that Toscanini was unhappy with Stokowski's acoustical revamping of NBC's studio 8H, with his reseating the orchestra for his own concerts, with his ideas about free bowing for the strings, and with his choice of broadcast repertoire—too much more modern music. By 1944 Toscanini urged the nonrenewal of Stokowski's contract on the grounds that Stokowski was bad for the orchestra. NBC's acceptance of the dictum prompted critic Virgil Thomson to answer in the *New York Herald Tribune* that Stokowski had never been bad for any orchestra, that the real reason lay in Toscanini's feelings about Stokowski and in his antipathy toward the modern repertoire. (See Daniel, *Stokowski*, 467–69; Sachs, *Toscanini*, 274–80; and Thomson, *Virgil Thomson*, 398–99.)

The recording of the Tchaikovsky Fourth itself is characterized by the passion and intensity of a performance that is idiosyncratic in the extreme. It is one of those interpretations related to Stokowski the romancer with a program known only to him. At any rate it is powerful stuff delivered in a blazing and technically brilliant performance.

**1944:* Richard Strauss, *Death and Transfiguration*. New York City Symphony Orchestra. RCA Camden CAL-189.

A 1982 rerelease in a coupling with Stokowski's 1952 recording of *Parsifal* excerpts was issued to commemorate the one hundredth anniversary of the conductor's birth. Leopold Stokowski Society LS 5.

1945: Beethoven, Symphony no. 6 in F. New York City Symphony Orchestra. RCA Camden CAL-187.

**1945:* Bizet, Music from Carmen. New York City Symphony Orchestra. RCA LM 1069.

Of the three commercial recordings Stokowski made with the New York City Symphony Orchestra, two were among my first 78 RPM symphonic recordings purchased as a teenager. The 1945 *Pastoral* is a fine-sounding orthodox performance of the symphony, although not up to the level the maestro achieved with the NBC Symphony Orchestra in his 1954 recording. The *Death and Transfiguration*, which Stokowski billed in performance as *Death and Illumination*, is even finer in its Stokowski Society transfer to LP than I remembered it in its first life. The program and drama of this work were ideally suited to Stokowski's romantic gifts, and in this, his third and last recording of the work, he wrought a truly fine performance. As for the 1945 *Carmen* excerpts set, which I found only recently, it is an "exciting and beautiful recording," in Paul Robinson's words, of both orchestral and vocal music from the opera, with the arias transcribed by Stokowski for orchestra.

The context in which these recordings were made, which was Stokowski's creation of the orchestra for New York's City Center, is a curious story, both poignant and musically inspiring.

With the wartime end of the All American Youth Orchestra in 1941 and the cancellation of his NBC Symphony Orchestra contract in 1944, Stokowski was at loose ends. Chronologically he was sixty-two, but in terms of his need for challenge both as a musical futurist and as an organizer he might as well have been thirty going on thirty-five. Then, too, he needed something as antidote for NBC's treatment of him.

In this swirl of feeling and frustration Stokowski was contacted by New York Mayor Fiorello La Guardia about the possibility of creating a symphony orchestra for the new arts center, an orchestra for the less affluent music lovers of New York City. On 9 February 1944 they met, and Stokowski enthusiastically accepted. The timing of events helps, I think, to let us understand something of Stokowski's enthusiasm for the project as somehow fated to come about successfully at this time and his lack of any realistic skepticism about the promises of New York politicos.

It was only three days earlier, 6 February, that Stokowski had premiered the Schoenberg Piano Concerto on NBC radio with Edward Steuermann as soloist. He had been forewarned that to do so would destroy his contract renewal for the 1944–45 season, which it did. Furthermore, his last NBC concert of the current season was less than three weeks away, 27 February. In this context it must have seemed providential that the La Guardia offer should come when it did, and with Stokowski's intuitive optimism, it must also have seemed fated that the challenge would lead to high achievement and a permanent position in New York. Certainly in urging his friend Sylvan Levin to pull up stakes and move to New York as associate director of the orchestra, Stokowski was thinking in these terms. Two letters from Stokowski to Mr. Levin illustrated his ebullience and his belief that Mayor La Guardia's vision of music at the center was as great as his own. The first, written on 16 February only a week after Stokowski's first meeting with La Guardia, already deals with the need for "modern and interesting opera" at the center, only allowing that it might take a "little time" before that would happen. The letter ends with the confident valedictory, "I would love to work with you again and have always felt it would happen."

By summer 1944 Stokowski was planning New York City Center premieres of two operas—William Grant Still's *Troubled Island* and Darius Milhaud's *Bolivar*—while writing to Sylvan Levin that he considered his own work in New York to be "permanent" (Stokowski, letter to Levin, 26 August 1944). For public consumption Stokowski described his purpose in New York:

> . . . Symphonic music and opera were mainly heard by a relatively small and privileged class. Though radio and records millions are now interested in music and many of these would also like to hear the actual performance in the concert hall and opera house. One of our chief aims is to make symphonic music and opera available to all of these music lovers at a cost within their reach.

Mayor La Guardia's interest in City Center was no doubt sincere, but the political and financial constraints of his office were as real as Stokowski's dreams of a great performing arts center for music, ballet, opera, and drama. The building itself on West 55th Street had been the Masonic Shriners' Mecca Temple until 1943, when by tax dafault it landed in the lap of the city. Mayor La Guardia, in concert with Newbold Morris, worked out a plan whereby Morris and a group of associates could rent the building and dedicate it to the arts for general civic betterment. In other words, as of 1944–45 the good intentions were there but not the money to make Stokowski's dreams come true.

However, there was a three-thousand seat auditorium in the Mecca Temple. Stokowski did transform the sound of the hall with acoustical additions of his own design. He agreed to serve the first year as conductor without pay and in addition put $20,000 of his own money into the project. More important yet he put together another orchestra from scratch; this was doubly difficult because so many musicians were in the armed forces. To do this he once again recruited very young musicians, showed no prejudice against hiring women musicians, and found New York free-lancers to head the various sections. According to the *City Center of Music and Drama: Personnel of the N.Y. City Symphony*, fully a third of the listed personnel were women—at the time unique in the history of symphonic music! And Stokowski recognized the place and particular problems of women in the orchestra through female representation on the personnel committee (Stokowski, letter to Victor Vanni, Orchestra Personnel Manager, 4 July 1945).

During 1944 and 1945 Stokowski was firmly on record as to what the center should stand for ethically as well as musically. "I am determined to have no racial or any other kind of prejudices there. I had enough of all that in Philadelphia" (Stokowski, letter to Levin, 28 July 1944). Stokowski was opposed to the 1945 increase in ticket prices from their initial range of 60¢ to $1.80 on the grounds that it was "all wrong for City Center" as it would discourage the attendance of less affluent New Yorkers. "When I return to [New York City] I am going to try hard to make the comittee understand my conception and follow it. The old ideas of social prestige are entirely out of place today" (Stokowski, letter to Levin, 4 July 1945). "[They are] the ideas of yesterday, based on social prestige and class distinction" (Stokowski, letter to Levin, 20 July 1945).

Operating within the budgetary constraints of the 1944–45 season, and conducting an orchestra smaller than was desirable, the New York City Symphony under Stokowski gained its audience, achieved good reviews of its concerts, and was successful with its three RCA Victor recordings. On the basis of these uniform successes and executive board promises in the spring of 1945, Stokowski hoped to improve both the orchestra and the concert programs for 1945–46. Instead he ran into summer 1945 budget cuts proposed by Mayor La Guardia and accepted by the executive board while he himself was in California conducting at the Hollywood Bowl. Perhaps worse yet, Stokowski learned of the mayor's offhand remark that sixty-five musicians should be enough for a good orchestra—Stokowski had been aiming at an orchestra of one hundred musicians for 1945–46.

Stokowski's response was resignation, but with a statement to Newbold Morris that indicated his willingness to return if his minimal musical hopes for City Center could be realized. These "essentials," as Stokowski called them, were certainly reasonable in terms of musical need, whatever the budget problems of the city of New York. Stokowski's request was for:

1. A really fine orchestra with larger string section than we had last season, and a good woodwind section with good intonation.
2. A chorus adequate for the compositions of Bach, Mozart, Beethoven, Brahms, Verdi, Mahler, etc.
3. An executive director equally experienced and understanding in music and drama. This person must coordinate all artistic activities.
4. The necessary means of producing each season at least one contemporary opera such as Still's *Troubled Island* or Milhaud's *Bolivar.*
5. The whole conception to be carried out in harmony with world conditions today, and not according to the ideas of the past (Stokowski, letter to Newbold Morris, 14 August 1945).

The failure of his appeal to gain any positive response led to one of the rare moments in his career when he admitted his vulnerability and his hurt—Stokowski was most often silent where criticism or setbacks were personally painful—at what he believed to be the shabby treatment he and his orchestra had received. From his summer 1945 base of operations at Hollywood Bowl he wrote Sylvan Levin, "I have definite and unshakable ideals about music. I had equally definite ideals about City Center. . . ." Then noting the inadequacy of a sixty-five piece orchestra for much of the symphonic repertoire and the imperative need for subsidization of music as for "education, libraries, museums," and the like, Stokowski concluded that "La Guardia's idea that music must pay for itself shows that he is not thinking clearly." As for himself, Stokowski noted, lowering his guard, he had given up an entire season of guest engagements in order to work without compensation for the success of City Center. "As people do not seem to understand my ideas of giving my services for idealistic reasons I am not going to do it any more. People are going to pay me for my services in the future just as Hollywood Bowl is doing at the present" (Stokowski letter to Levin, 4 July 1945 and 20 July 1945).

Seventeen years later Stokowski would again serve without pay and would contribute tens of thousands of dollars of his own money to make the first ten years of New York's American Symphony Orchestra a success.

1945: Hindemith, Concerto for Violin and Orchestra (1939), with soloist Robert Gross. New York City Symphony. Townhall S 32.

This recording was issued in 1982 in commemoration of the maestro's one hundredth birthday. The live performance on this disc was the New York premiere of the work recorded on acetate discs, which accounts for the very poor sound.

1939–46: Symphonic Favorites, including Tchaikovsky, "Marche Slav" (1945), "Humoresque" (1945), and "Solitude" (1945); Wagner, *Siegfried*: "Forest Murmurs" (1946); Offenbach, *Tales of Hoffmann*: "Barcarolle"; Purcell [*sic*] Clarke, "Trumpet Prelude" ("Trumpet Voluntary") (1946); and Strauss, "Tales from the Vienna Woods" (1939). Philadelphia and Hollywood Bowl Orchestras. RCA Camden CAL-153.

This is a potpourri of Stokowski favorites and encore pieces, five of which are in transcriptions or arrangements by the conductor. Although most of these pieces would be recorded again by the maestro, this is his only recording of the "Barcarolle." It is done in Stokowski's own transcription and is quite lovely. The set also includes his only recorded performance of his arrangement of the Strauss Waltz. All of the recordings were made with the Hollywood Bowl Symphony Orchestra in 1945 and 1946 except "Tales from the Vienna Woods," made with the Philadelphia Orchestra in 1939.

1945: Brahms, Symphony no. 1 in C Minor. Hollywood Bowl Symphony Orchestra. RCA LM 1070.

**1945*: Tchaikovsky, Symphony no. 6 in B Minor. Hollywood Bowl Symphony Orchestra. RCA Camden CAL-152. Rereleased by the Leopold Stokowski Society in 1983 on LS 9.

1945: *Percy Grainger Plays Grieg*, Piano Concerto in A Minor. Hollywood Bowl Symphony Orchestra. International Piano Archives IPA 508 (live).

**1946–50*: Falla, *El Amor Brujo* (1946), and Borodin, *Prince Igor*: "Dances of the Polovetzki Maidens" (1950, arr. Stokowski), with Nan Merriman and the Hollywood Bowl Symphony Orchestra performing the Falla and the Leopold Stokowski Symphony Orchestra with women's chorus performing the Borodin. RCA LM 1054.

That Stokowski smarted over this treatment by NBC and New York City officials we know from George Antheil's autobiography, *Bad Boy of Music*. With his new bride Gloria Vanderbilt, Stokowski visited his friend, composer George Antheil, in 1945. In conversation Stokowski said that his efforts for music seemed to him to be consistently misconstrued, leading always to unfair criticism, which, if continued, might drive the Stokowskis to leave America for Europe. Both Antheil and his wife, Boski, sensed that beyond chemistry, the Stokowskis had been brought together by common hurt and were now providing shelter and support for each other in a world they found to be unfeeling, and worse, cruel. Antheil was particularly sensitive to Stokowski's feelings since the conductor had earlier had to battle NBC brass in order to premiere the composer's exuberant Symphony no. 4 with the NBC Symphony Orchestra; that premiere came just one week after Stokowski had enraged NBC and Arturo Toscanini with his premiere of Schoenberg's Piano Concerto in February 1944. To Antheil, Stokowski's very courage in programming his symphony under the circumstances was poignant proof of his commitment to music and evidence of his critics' narrow-mindedness. Wrote Antheil, here he was, one of the greatest conductors in the world, but great beyond that because he had built orchestras, including the pioneering of the youth orchestra. He had through his own efforts lifted radio, the movies, and recording to higher levels while championing countless new composers and compositions. However, to small-minded commentators who either did not know what he had done or did and resented him in the doing, his accomplishments were made to seem tricks or stagy maneuvers, and so they badgered him consistently (see Antheil, *Bad Boy of Music*, 339–42).

However, Stokowski's resiliency stood him in good stead as he began a two-year tenure as music director of Hollywood Bowl, 1945–46, during which he acoustically revamped the bowl's playing shell, mounted a fully staged *Carmen*, complete with horses, and made several fine recordings. Stokowski wrote to Sylvan Levin in 1946 that the orchestra "is just wonderful, so quick so intelligent, friendly and all masters of their instruments. I am enjoying working with them every minute." Not even references to his recordings with the orchestra as "Hollywoodized" and "sunkist" daunted the maestro (Stokowski, letter to Levin, 23 July, 1946).

Of the recordings, the Brahms First is a vigorous and muscular performance, beautifully recorded. The Tchaikovsky Sixth is, I believe, a memorable performance and worth getting in its Stokowski Society rerelease. What can one say of the Falla other than that the Stokowski-Merriman recording in 1945 was as definitive for that generation as his 1960 performance with Shirley Verrett would be for the generation following. Unfortunately, Stokowski's Hollywood Bowl Orchestra recording of Virgil Thomson's *The Plough That Broke the Plains* was not transferred to long-play by RCA. It too was fine and accepted as such by the critics. Fortunately, Stokowski rerecorded this piece along with Thomson's Suite from *The River* in 1961 with the Symphony of the Air for Vanguard.

This recording of the Grieg Concerto is an oddity, a peculiar, driving interpretation by Grainger with lots of clinkers, sympathetically accompanied by the conductor. It has poor sound due to the live noncommercial recording conditions.

1946–60: Rachmaninoff, Symphony no. 2 in E (1946) and Prelude in C-sharp (1960, orch. Stokowski). Hollywood Bowl Symphony Orchestra playing the symphony and the Philadelphia Orchestra playing the prelude. Both performances are live. Discocorp/Leopold Stokowski Society of America LSSA-228.

This was the first release of the Leopold Stokowski Society of America. The sound of the Rachmaninoff recording is mediocre as one might expect with a forty-year-old, live, open-air performance. However, Stokowski's interpretation of this romantically ripe and rambling work is such as to heighten its romantic poetry while tightening its musical structure. The artistic economy of the Stokowski performance led *Fanfare* critic James Miller (January–February 1985) to describe it as the fleetest performance on record. It took less than fifty-one minutes for the uncut version, compared to Rachmaninoff's sixty-five minute premiere and Simon Rattle's sixty-one minute recording with the Los Angeles Philharmonic Orchestra.

The sound of the prelude is much better, and of course this 1960 live recording marked Stokowski's return, after a nineteen year absence, to the great orchestra he had built. The Philadelphians perform brilliantly for him, but nothing helps to make the Stokowski transcription less vulgar than it inherently is.

**1947–50: New York Philharmonic/Leopold Stokowski: In Celebration of the 100th Anniversary of the Conductor's Birth,* including Bach-Stokowski, three Chorale-Preludes (1947–49); Handel, Concerto in B-flat for Harpsichord and Orchestra, with soloist Wanda Landowska (1949); De Falla, *Nights in the Gar-*

dens of Spain, with soloist William Kapell (1949); Prokofiev, Symphony, no. 6 in E-flat Minor (1949); Hupfeld, "When Yuba Plays the Rhumba on the Tuba Down in Cuba," with soloist William Bell and commentary by Leopold Stokowski; Thomson, *The Mother of Us All*: Symphonic Suite. New York Philharmonic Orchestra, recorded live. NYP 821-22 (two records).

This two-record set released in 1982 served the double function of celebrating the conductor's one hundredth birthday and of enticing potential Philharmonic subscribers to sign up for season tickets or to contribute to the orchestra. It is splendid in every way. Its sound—that of Philharmonic radio broadcasts—is acceptable. Soloists Landowska and Kapell give spirited performances, and the repertoire is interesting. While some members of the English Stokowski Society expressed outrage that a children's concert rendition of "When Yuba Plays the Rhumba on the Tuba Down in Cuba" was included in the album, it seems to me altogether fitting since Stokowski's affinity for children and for children's concerts never abated from the Philadelphia years to his last years with the American Symphony Orchestra. Of particular delight are Stokowski's comments to the youthful audience when tuba player William Bell finishes playing "Yuba" with the Philharmonic. Noting the enthusiastic applause for this pop number, Stokowski says Bell has another such that the maestro, in one of his several rich accents, describes as, "When Vehroneeka Plays the Hahrmoneeka on the Piehr at Sahntamahneeka." More applause for the "wahnafool Meestah" Bell.

In all of these pieces there is the essential Stokowski as music maker, from playing with and for the children to eliciting his sound from a very temperamental orchestra. And that is what, among other things, Arthur Judson was looking for in 1946 when he asked Stokowski to coconduct the Philharmonic. So successful was Stokowski with both audiences and critics that he remained for three seasons with the realistic expectation that he would eventually be named music director. After more than one hundred concerts, the Judson-managed Philharmonic board named Dimitri Mitropoulos music director to the surprise of the musical world and the silent chagrin of Stokowski.

Stokowski's lowest years, the wandering years of the early fifties, were to begin, but not without some—too few—commercial recordings being made between 1947 and 1950 with the Philharmonic for Columbia Masterworks and memorable radio performances for those like myself who were still living in small towns far from any concert hall, let alone Carnegie Hall. As for those actually there, let conductor Mehli Mehta—then a young musician from India studying music with Ivan Galamian in New York—sum up the magic of Stokowski regularly conducting a world-class orchestra. It also represents the beginning of an interesting musical relationship between the houses of Mehta and Stokowski. In a letter to his family in Bombay Mehta wrote that he had attended a Stokowski Philharmonic concert, which became in itself a unique event. On the one hand were technical triumphs: the richness of the strings; the orchestral precision; the transparency of sound. But beyond that was the passion and the intensity of the performance. Noting that he felt privileged to have seen the maestro at work, Nehta promised to bring Stokowski recordings back to his family in India so that they could hear this artist at work for themselves.

Fifteen years later it was Stokowski who provided Mehli Mehta's son Zubin his chance for twin conducting premieres in America by arranging for the young Mehta to conduct summer concerts—originally scheduled for Stokowski himself—with Philadelphia's Robin Hood Dell Orchestra and the summer incarnation of the New York Philharmonic, that is, the Stadium Symphony

Orchestra. Then Stokowski gave Mehta additional exposure by inviting him to conduct Stokowski's own American Symphony Orchestra (see Bookspan and Yockey, *Zubin*, 7–8, 71–73, 79–80).

It was New York Philharmonic conductor Zubin Mehta who in 1982 volunteered to conduct Philadelphia's Curtis Institute Orchestra in a one hundredth birthday concert in memory of maestro Stokowski.

***1947–49:* Vaughan Williams, Symphony no. 6 in E Minor (original version), and Messiaen, *L'Ascension:* Four Symphonic Meditations. New York Philharmonic Orchestra. Columbia ML 4214.

This is a beautiful coupling of the Messiaen recorded in 1947 and the Vaughan Williams symphony recorded in 1949. Both works were given their American recording premieres by Stokowski, whose musical-spiritual affinity for each piece is clearly heard in this recording. Vaughan Williams deals with the fear and horror of a world at war except in the concluding "Epilogue," while Messiaen adores and praises God in his own romantic musical language. In addition to their shared contemporaneity, another link between the works lies in the religiosity of the Messiaen piece and the ethereal "Epilogue" of the symphony. Eschewing any emotional-spiritual description of the "Epilogue," the composer deliberately understated the power and beauty of this section by saying that it wasn't subject to analysis. In fact it is a transcendental and deeply religious meditation that reaches the stars as surely as the final coda of Beethoven's Sonata, op. 111.

***1947:* Griffes, "The White Peacock," and Copland, *Billy the Kid:* "Prairie Night" and "Celebration Dance." New York Philharmonic Symphony Orchestra. Columbia ML 2167.

This early ten-inch LP set also includes selections by Morton Gould, conducted by the composer, and by Dimitri Mitropoulos; but the musical treasure of the album is the Griffes tone poem. Griffes's tone picture of the solitary peacock, dreamily master of a moon-drenched landscape, is an impressionistic reverie perfectly tuned to Stokowski's romantic temperament. In a 1958 interview with R. C. Marsh, Stokowski contrasted formally correct and literal playing rooted in proper musical etiquette with heartfelt performance tuned to the warmth and impulsiveness of human feeling. Only the latter could catch the poetry of life and of our dreams. Such is his reading of the Griffes piece with the Philharmonic players, fully within the same spell.

Incidentally, it was Stokowski who gave the world premiere of the orchestrated "White Peacock," along with an additional tone poem from Griffes's *Roman Sketches* called "Clouds" and the Griffes earlier, "Notturno" from his 1915 *Fantasy Pieces*. All three were premiered at Philadelphia Orchestra concerts of 19 and 20 December 1919.

1947: Lalo, *Sinfonie Espagnole* (movements 1, 2, 4, and 5), with soloist Jacques Thibaud. New York Philharmonic Orchestra. Bruno Walter Society, IGI-339 (live).

This off the air recording has very bad sound. It was picked up by the Bruno Walter Society for the artistry of Jacques Thibaud. The concert itself was Stokowski's first under the new agreement with Judson. Stokowski's portion of the concert—exciting and venturesome—included Milhaud's *Saudades du Brazil*, Hindemith's First Symphony, and Stokowski's transcription of a motet by the sixteenth-century polyphonist Thomas Luis de Victoria. And so began three seasons of beautiful and imaginative music with the New York Philharmonic.

**1947:* Wagner, *Rienzi:* Overture and *Die Walküre.* "Wotan's Farewell" and "Magic Fire Music." New York Philharmonic Orchestra. Columbia ML 2153.

Both works received splendid readings by Stokowski and the sound on this early LP recording is exceptionally rich and vibrant. Thirty years after this performance Stokowski once again paired these works together on a fine Wagner set made during his last years (RCA ARS 1-0498).

***1947:* Khachaturian, *Masquerade Suite,* and Tchaikovsky, *Francesca da Rimini.* New York Philharmonic Orchestra. Columbia ML 4071.

It is the *Francesca* that makes this record worth finding. Although controversial because of Stokowski's cuts in the score, it is the finest recorded performance of this music that I know of, and superior to Stokowski's two later recordings of the same piece. Even the 1947 sound is only a minor detraction from his dramatic interpretation of the damned lovers. It was available for a time in Columbia's "Special Products" series as P 14137.

1947: Tchaikovsky, *Sleeping Beauty* Ballet (excerpts). Leopold Stokowski Symphony Orchestra. RCA LM 1010.

This was one of RCA Victor's first long-playing records, and it was generally praised upon its release. Stokowski's sumptuous 1977 recording of the "Aurora's Wedding" portion of the ballet has the advantage of finer sound, but the interpretations—thirty years apart—are much the same, and the playing on both is first rate.

Stokowski's performances of Tchaikovsky ballet music have consistently been more graciously received by critics than have his performances of the symphonies, often dubbed eccentric and willful. Whatever one's feelings about Stokowski's personal way with the symphonies, it seems likely that the romancer's "cocreation" of them was based on a personal and dramatic interpretation of them known only to himself and projected to his players. Such seems not to have been the case with the ballet scores since dramatic and theatrical programs were already assigned to them. In this case it seems likely that the scores as written and programmed were enough in themselves to satisfy Stokowski's need to achieve a personal communion with, and dramatic statement of, the music.

1947: Dvorak, Symphony no. 9 (jacket listing as Symphony no. 5). Leopold Stokowski Symphony Orchestra. RCA LM 1013.

This is the fifth of Stokowski's six recordings of the *New World* Symphony. In interpretation it harks back to the high-speed performance and the razzle-dazzle interpretations of the Dvorak by Stokowski and the Philadelphia Orchestra, rather than pointing toward the spacious and lyrically poignant 1973 recording made by the maestro with the New Philharmonia Orchestra.

1947–49: Liszt, Les Preludes (1947), and Haydn, Symphony no. 53 in D (1949). Leopold Stokowski Symphony Orchestra. RCA LM 1073.

The Liszt and the Haydn are a peculiar pairing and the peculiarity doesn't end there. *Les Preludes* is usually recorded with emphasis on its more bombastic elements, what Liszt in his preface to the work called the "trumpet's loud clamor" calling the hero to arms. Stokowski mutes the bombast and concentrates instead on those quieter passages idealizing the love, calm, and serenity of the the hero between such episodes. It is a convincing interpretation and performance of the score, although the sound is not up to other Stokowski-RCA recordings of the late forties and fifties.

This recording has recently been rereleased by the English Stokowski Society on record LS 8, coupled with Stokowski's reading of the Schumann Symphony no. 2 from 1950.

The Symphony no. 53 was the conductor's only recording of a Haydn symphony and was no doubt prompted by Stokowski's lifelong desire to be first in premiere. In this case it was the recorded premiere of a long lost symphony of Haydn. What fascinates me is the simplicity with which the maestro plays the work. While his performance would not challenge the recorded bounce of Haydn in the hands of Beecham or of Szell, it is charming and graceful. Now, it has been a favorite cliché of critics for fifty years that Stokowski couldn't conduct Mozart and Haydn without intruding wayward romantic elements, that he was incapable of eighteenth-century style. Here is proof that he could, when he chose to. Why then didn't he choose to more often? We know by his own testimony that he loved the music of Haydn and Mozart, but just as he turned down the chance to conduct Gluck's *Alceste* at the Metropolitan, because, while beautiful, it didn't equate with his gift for the dramatic (it was not music for the theater and so wouldn't be right for him), in the same way he tended by choice to avoid fellow eighteenth-century classicists Mozart and Haydn as not native to his conducting gifts. Stokowski's own instinct for the "dramatic dynamic," as he put it (see Daniel, Stokowski, 749–50), most likely made any consistent straining after eighteenth-century niceties of balance and proportion a chore, not a pleasure.

1947–50: Debussy, *Nocturnes:* "Nuages," "Fêtes" and "Sirèns," "Claire de Lune," and "Prelude to the Afternoon of a Faun." Leopold Stokowski Symphony Orchestra with the Robert Shaw Chorale's women's voices. RCA LM 1154.

This set has been rereleased by the Leopold Stokowski Society as LS 6.

1947–50: Bach-Stokowski: The Great Transcriptions. Leopold Stokowski Symphony Orchestra. RCA AGM 1-5280.

These recently rereleased recordings were taken by RCA from three earlier sets, digitally remastered and released in the company's "Legendary Performers" series in 1985.

**1947–50:* Wagner, *Tannhäuser:* Overture and "Venusberg Music," with women's chorus (1950), and *Five Wesendonck Songs*, with soloist Eileen Farrell (1947). Leopold Stokowski Symphony Orchestra. RCA LM 1066.

An ideal coupling: the sensuality of the Tannhäuser excerpts matches the erotic fervor and yearning of Mathilde Wesendonck's poems modelled into song settings by Wagner, who was working on *Tristan and Isolde* at the same time. Stokowski's pickup orchestra plays beautifully and Eileen Farrell sings gloriously.

The *Wesendonck* set has been rereleased by RCA as Victrola AVM 1-1413.

**1947–51:* Stravinsky, *Fire Bird* Suite (1950); Ibert, *Escales* (1951); Berlioz, *Damnation of Faust:* "Dance of the Sylphs" (1951); Sibelius, "Swan of Tuonela" (1947); and Granados, *Goyescas:* Intermezzo (1947). Leopold Stokowski Symphony Orchestra. RCA LM 9029.

In the fifties this set represented a fine buy for the music lover because of the quality of the performances and the number of selections included on one disc. All of these pieces were Stokowski specialties, and, with one exception, all would be rerecorded by Stokowski on records, many of which are still available. The exception is the lovely Granados Intermezzo in Stokowski's only recording of it, which was never rereleased.

1947–55: In the Lighter Vein, including selections by Humperdinck, Tchaikovsky, Johann Strauss, Bach, Mozart, Beethoven, and Rachmaninoff. Leopold Stokowski Symphony Orchestra and the NBC Symphony Orchestra. RCA LM 2042.

Although Stokowski RCA recordings with the Philadelphia, the New York City, and the Hollywood Bowl orchestras were, by 1947, discs of the past, Stokowski continued to record for RCA during the late forties and early fifties with established orchestras such as the NBC Symphony Orchestra (later known as the Symphony of the Air), the Philharmonia, and the San Francisco Symphony Orchestra. In addition, Stokowski recorded for Victor as "Leopold Stokowski and His Symphony Orchestra." This New York pickup group was brought together exclusively for recording purposes. While its personnel varied from session to session, the players, picked in the main from Stokowski's earlier experience with them, were of uniformly high quality, drawn from the New York Philharmonic, the NBC orchestra, and the best of New York's free lancers. According to Oliver Daniel, RCA's cheese-paring ways forced a reduction of orchestral size on Stokowski for a number of these recordings—strings down from sixty-five to twenty—yet Stokowski's electronic and orchestral skills were such that the recorded results were still opulent and full sounding.

The cameos of *In the Lighter Vein* were recorded over a nine year period, some to appear on LP only in this collection. Although the liner notes indicate that all the recordings were made with Stokowski's pickup orchestra, four of the nine, according to Oliver Daniel, were probably made with the NBC Symphony Orchestra.

My own favorites on the set are the perky Mozart "Turkish March" from the Sonata in A, K. 331, the Rachmaninoff, "Vocalise," the "Polonaise" from Tchaikovsky's *Eugen Onegin*, and Stokowski's transcription of the Bach Prelude in B Minor no. 24 from vol. 1 of *The Well-Tempered Clavier*. One could wish that either the English or the American Stokowski Society would rerelease a cameo set of such short works, including as well pieces such as Silvestre Revueltas's *Sensemaya*, which Stokowski recorded as a single in 1947 and which was never included on long-play.

1949–50: Stokowski Conducts Percy Grainger Favorites. Percy Grainger songs (1950), coupled on the second side with Chopin, Preludes in E Minor and D Minor (1950); Sibelius, *The Tempest:* "Berceuse" (1950) and "Valse Triste" (1949); Schubert, *Tyrolean Dances* (1949); and Mozart, German Dance no. 3 (1949). Leopold Stokowski Symphony Orchestra. RCA LM 1238.

With Percy Grainger at the piano, this set of Grainger songs, including "Country Gardens," "Shepherd's Hey," "Mock Morris," "Handel in the Strand," "Irish Tune from County Derry," "Molly on the Shore," and "Early One Morning," was rereleased in 1978 on RCA ARL 1-3059, but has since again disappeared. This is a shame because the arrangements done by Grainger for Stokowski in 1949–50, with Stokowski's help, were more vibrant and colorful than were his earlier orchestrations. Stokowski's verve and sense of style in the recording of 1950 fully projected the colors of this folk material in recorded sound that still holds up today.

Stokowski and Grainger had performed together as early as 1916, when the pianist played the Grieg Concerto with the Philadelphia Orchestra. They concertized over the years, with their common interest in the fields of diet and exercise bringing them closer together than music alone would have. So it was not to a stranger that Stokowski wrote early in 1949 saying that he was interested in recording a set of Grainger's pieces. He noted the strength of the folk element in the composer's songs and said he did not want to record this music with heavy orchestration suitable for a symphony orchestra. Rather, it should carry the feeling of village music and dance.

Grainger was enthusiastic about the idea and agreed to both the reorchestration and a meeting with Stokowski to go over the new scores. The recordings of the new transcriptions in two sessions were made in 1950 and released on long-play in 1951.

As was so often the case with cocreator Stokowski, the conductor had not been chary about suggesting changes in the revised Grainger scoring. Of these, Grainger wrote to Stokowski that the recording itself was testimony to the soundness of the changes. The composer then listed nine such as particularly apt, noting that the whole set was a delight. (See Tall and Bird, "Stokowski and the 1952 Grainger Settings," 12–19).

Of the recordings on the reverse side of this disc there is one, the "Berceuse" from Sibelius's *The Tempest*, that must be singled out. It is beautiful music beautifully played, but beyond that, with the harp part as musical catalyst, it is hypnotic in its power. It is a mesmerizing recording.

1949–50: Debussy, *Children's Corner* Suite (1949), and Tchaikovsky, *Nutcracker* Suite (1950). Leopold Stokowski Symphony Orchestra. RCA LM 9023. This monophonic set was later rereleased in artificial stereo sound as RCA ANL 1-2604 (e).

1949: Poulenc, Concerto Champêtre for Harpsichord and Orchestra, with soloist Wanda Landowska. New York Philharmonic Orchestra. In Desmar IPA 106–107 (two records, live).

This private recording was taped live at Wanda Landowska's last public performance of the Concerto *Champêtre*. The piece was dedicated to her by Francis Poulenc and this graceful performance is a tribute to both soloist and composer. Stokowski provides elegant support.

1949: Vaughan Williams, *Fantasia on Greensleeves*, included in *Honoring the 125th Anniversary of the New York Philharmonic*. New York Philharmonic Orchestra. Columbia BM 13.

1949: Falla, *Nights in the Gardens of Spain*, with soloist William Kapell. New York Philharmonic Orchestra. Opus MLG 71-A (live).

This is the same performance as on the New York Philharmonic Stokowski Hundredth Anniversary set (1947–50), but in dreadful tinny sound.

1949: Wagner, *Die Götterdämmerung*: "Siegfried's Rhine Journey" and "Funeral Music," and Tchaikovsky, *Romeo and Juliet*. New York Philharmonic Orchestra. Columbia ML 4273.

These are fine performances muffled by mediocre sound.

**1949:* Schoenberg, *Gurrelieder*: "Song of the Wood Dove," with soprano Martha Lipton. New York Philharmonic Orchestra. Columbia ML 2140 (ten inch).

When compared to the sumptuous sound of the later Ozawa and Boulez recordings of *Gurrelieder*, the 1949 Columbia excerpt sounds ancient. Yet the performance is haunting as an account of grief and lost love. I have not found another that gives more meaning to the Wood Dove's message, "I flew far, sought for grief, and have found much."

1949: Mozart, Piano Concerto no. 21 in C Major with pianist Dame Myra Hess. New York Philharmonic Orchestra. MJA 1967-1 (live).

1949: Handel, Concerto in B-flat for Harpsichord and Orchestra, with soloist Wanda Landowska. New York Philharmonic Orchestra. In *Landowska Plays Music of the Baroque.* Bruno Walter Society BWS 720 (live).

It was with this piece that Madame Landowska made her American debut during the 1923–24 concert season, playing it with Stokowski and the Philadelphia Orchestra. This Bruno Walter issue is the same performance as that included in the New York Philharmonic's two-record set celebrating the centennial of Stokowski's birth. The Philharmonic release has better sound and surfaces.

1950: The Heart of the Ballet, including selections from Adam, *Giselle;* Weber, *Le Spectre de la Rose;* Chopin, *Les Sylphides;* Delibes, *Sylvia;* and Tchaikovsky, *Swan Lake* and the *Nutcracker.* Leopold Stokowski Symphony Orchestra. RCA LM 1083.

Several of these recordings are also found on the ten-inch disc, *Stokowski Conducts Ballet Music.* RCA LRM 7022.

1950: Sibelius, Symphony no. 1 in E Minor. Leopold Stokowski Symphony Orchestra. RCA LM 1125.

This fine recording is outdistanced by Stokowski's 1976 recorded performance with the National Philharmonic Orchestra on Columbia.

**1950:* Wagner, *Tristan and Isolde:* Prelude, "Liebesnacht," and "Liebestod." Leopold Stokowski Symphony Orchestra. RCA LM 1174.

There is less frenzied abandon but more intimate poetry in this recording than in Stokowski's last recording of excerpts from that opera (1973). The sound is more intimate too—the better to show off the superb playing of a hand-picked orchestra, whose lead instrumentalists are listed.

***1950:* Schumann, Symphony no. 2 in C. Leopold Stokowski Symphony Orchestra. RCA LM 1194.

With the exception of "Traumerie," recorded on a single 78 RPM disc in 1941, this is the only commercial Schumann recording that I know of made by Stokowski and a superb one. The "adagio" particularly is a tour de force of pathos and of sweetly lyrical song. Fortunately, dell' Arte Records, in association with the English Stokowski Society, has rereleased this recording as LS 8, recoupled with the *Les Preludes* recording of 1947.

1950: Stokowski Conducts Bach (vol. 1), including Passacaglia and Fugue in C Minor, Partita no. 2: "Chaconne," Sonata for Clavier and Violin in C Minor: "Siciliano," and "Mein Jesu." Leopold Stokowski Symphony Orchestra. RCA LM 1133.

For those who reject the Bach transcriptions on principle, this recording will have negative value. For the rest of us? Stokowski's performance of his Bach transcriptions varied a great deal over time and by piece. Included here is a florid "Chaconne" but a sensitive and beautifully played performance of the Passacaglia.

Six of the nine Bach-Stokowski transcriptions in RCA's 1985 remastered set, *Bach-Stokowski: The Great Transcriptions,* are from this set and the set included in the following entry.

1950: Stokowski Conducts Bach (vol. 2), including Suite no. 2 in B Minor for flute and Strings, with flutist Julius Baker, "Little" Fugue in G Minor, "Wir glauben All'an Einen Gott," "Komm Süsser Tod", "Jesu, Joy of Man's Desiring," "That Sheep May Safely Graze," and *Easter* Cantata: "Jesus Cristus Gottes Sohn." Leopold Stokowski Symphony Orchestra. RCA LM 1176.

By the late forties and fifties the popularity of the Bach-Stokowski transcriptions was dimming as the tide of literalism and historical authenticity was rising in critical circles. One result was a decline in the sale of the transcription recordings. Yet at that time and since, Stokowski's romantic way with Bach has never been without supporters. Eric Salzman, writing in *Stereo Review* 46 (March 1981), described the transcriptions as the work of a unique musician who would not barter his "soul" for the sake of changing fashion. Winthrop Sargeant, writing in the *New Yorker* (19 October 1963), noted that the transcriptions that in the last few years had earned the scorn of purists actually projected a majesty of the sort that Bach quite likely was trying to achieve.

In my interview with Abram Chasins, I asked him where he was on the subject. Chasins described Stokowski as having large gaps in his musical education. One of these was his lack of training in formal baroque style and usage. Chasins added that during the thirties he had talked to Stokowski about the matter in relationship to the maestro's Bach transcriptions, noting that criticism of Stokowski's romantic approach was bound to come. To this Stokowski answered not a word. He only smiled, reported Chasins. When the criticism did come in the late forties, it was vehement and continued to mount during the fifties and sixties. Yet, as Chasins pointed out, while Stokowski's approach was technically incorrect, he had emotionally and intuitively caught the color and spirit of Bach even though some of his performances live and on record verged into the overdramatic.

1950: Stravinsky, *Petrouchka.* Leopold Stokowski Symphony Orchestra. RCA LM 1175.

**1950–59:* Mahler, Symphony no. 8, *Symphony of a Thousand,* with soloists Frances Yeend, Uta Graff, Camilla Williams, Martha Lipton, Louise Bernhardt, Eugene Conley, Carlos Alexander, and George London, and with the Westminster Choir, Schola Cantorum, and Children's Choir from Manhattan Public School no. 12, with the New York Philharmonic Orchestra; Debussy, *Nocturnes:* "Nuages," "Fêtes," and "Sirèns"; and Ravel, *Rapsodie Espagnole,* with the Leipzig Gewandhaus Orchestra and womens chorus. Music and Arts of America compact disc set 280 (z) (two records, live).

Once available only in the pirated Penzance Records set PR 19, the Mahler *Symphony of a Thousand* in the live performance of 1950 was rereleased with much improved sound on CD in 1988 together with live performances of Debussy and Ravel, conducted by Stokowski in 1959. The CDs were made for Music and Arts by Denon in Japan.

Stokowski conducted the American premiere of this work in 1916 with the Philadelphia Orchestra; he followed it up during the same concert season with the American premiere of *Das Lied von der Erde,* which he had heard at its European premiere under Bruno Walter. In 1917 he programmed one of Mahler's *Ruckert Songs* and the *Kindertotenlieder.* In 1921 he performed both the Symphony no. 2 and songs from *Des Knaben Wunderhorn.* This last song cycle was repeated during the 1927 and 1931 Philadelphia Seasons.

Thirty four years after its premier, Stokowski conducted the mighty Eighth as the last concert item of the 1949–50 season with the New York Philharmonic, either as an ace up his sleeve to win the musical directorship of the Philharmonic, or as a beautiful parting gift at the end of three seasons. There is disagreement on Stokowski's purpose. Stokowski as usual was silent, beyond saying that it was beautiful music and that he wanted to perform it.

At any rate it created the major moment in the musical season with critic Virgil Thomson, in a review of superlatives for the performance, describing his evening as a "glorious" experience and thanking Stokowski and his assembled hundreds of musicians for letting New Yorkers again hear the work (see review of 7 April 1950 in *Virgil Thomson Reader*, 341–42).

Stokowski elsewhere described his own sense of kinship with Mahler as centering on Mahler's *Sehnsucht* (sense of longing), his musical irony, and his unusual ability to turn from loneliness and misery to almost orgiastic joy—all of which show clearly in his music.

As a young man in Munich in 1910, the maestro had been slipped by musician friends into Mahler-led rehearsals for the world premiere of the Eighth, where Stokowski described himself as overcome by the beauty of the music and fascinated by Mahler's style as a conductor and composer. Stokowski's recollection centered on a Mahler who experimented with phrasing and rephrasing passages while on the podium and who made numerous changes in the score, on the spot, as dictated by the sound of the music—a memory which, of course, buttressed Stokowski's own approach to music.

In 1970 Stokowski interviewer Jerry Fox of the Bruckner Society told the maestro that the 1950 production of Mahler's Eighth with the New York Philharmonic had been a major musical experience for him, describing the performance as "magnificent." Fox followed up by asking if Stokowski had consciously attempted to recall the Mahler approach in his own. Stokowski responded laconically that he had learned a lot from Mahler.

Remembering those on-the-spot changes by Mahler back in 1910, changes incorporated into his own score, but not included in the score as printed, the conductor told Mr. Fox that he had written to Mahler's widow in 1949 attempting to borrow that marked score. But like so many things in music that are lost, strayed, or stolen, he didn't get it. (Stokowski interview with Bruck and Fox).

1950–51: The Tone Poem, including Debussy, "Nuages," and Ibert, *Escales*. Leopold Stokowski Symphony Orchestra (also included are tone poems conducted by Arthur Fiedler, Pierre Monteux, Charles Munch, and Fritz Reiner). RCA LM 6129 (three records).

1950–53: Borodin, *Prince Igor:* "Dances of the Polovetzki Maidens," with women's chorus (arr. Stokowski), and *Caucasian Sketches:* "In the Steppes of Central Asia." Leopold Stokowski Symphony Orchestra. RCA LRM 7056 (10 inch).

This is a recoupling of the 1950 *Prince Igor* excerpt to the 1953 recording of "In the Steppes of Central Asia."

**1951:* Tchaikovsky, *Eugen Onegin:* "Tatiana's Letter Scene," and Villa-Lobos, *Bachianas Brasileiras* no. 5, with soloist Licia Albanese. Leopold Stokowski Symphony Orchestra. RCA LM 142 (10 inch).

Like the 1949 "Song of the Wood Dove" this set is a hard-to-find collector's item and is justly prized for fine performances by both soloist and orchestra.

**1951:* Rimsky-Korsakov, *Scheherazade*, Philharmonia Orchestra, RCA LM 1732.

In his book, *Stokowski*, Paul Robinson reminds us that overfamiliar though it is, *Scheherazade* is a work of genius combining a range of sound colors for orchestra in a way unique up to its time of composition. Stokowski's way with phrasing, the work's fairy tale program, and its orchestral color make this set—the first of three Stokowski long-play Scheherazades—a recording to cherish. It was Stokowski, back in 1925, who did the first American light show with this work as a means of relating color as color to color as sound in *Scheherazade*.

This set has been rereleased by the Leopold Stokowski Society as LS 12.

**1952:* Vaughan Williams, Fantasia on a Theme by Thomas Tallis, and Schoenberg, *Transfigured Night*. Leopold Stokowski Symphony Orchestra. RCA LM 1739.

As with Stokowski's personalized feeling for and interpretation of certain pieces by Franck, Elgar, Tchaikovsky, and Sibelius among others, so with *Transfigured Night* and the Vaughan Williams Fantasia we have in Stokowski's own liner notes the romancer's identification with the mystical and the transcendent in these works.

The performances and the variety of string tone and color on this older set are remarkable. Would that it were still generally available.

1950–52: Weber, Symphony on Poems of William Blake (1950) with Warren Galjour, baritone, and the Leopold Stokowski Symphony Orchestra, and Harrison, Suite for Violin, Piano, and Small Orchestra (1952), with Anahid Ajemian, violin, Maro Ajemian, piano, and small ensemble. RCA LM 1785.

The Lou Harrison suite for this set would later be coupled with Stokowski's 1957 recording of Henry Cowell's *Persian Set and released as Composers Recordings Inc. CRI-114.*

1952: Goeb, Symphony no. 3, with the Leopold Stokowski Symphony Orchestra, and Bartok, Sonata for Two Pianos and Percussion, with Gerson Yessin and Raymond Viola, pianists, and Elayne Jones and Alfred Howard, percussion. RCA LM 1727.

The RCA recording of the Goeb Symphony would be recoupled with the 1950 recording of Ben Weber's Symphony on Poems of William Blake and released on Composers Recordings Inc. CRI-120.

The recordings noted in the last two entries, together with their CRI recouplings and rereleases stemmed from one of the several directions taken by Stokowski after losing the conductorship of the New York Philharmonic in 1950. This particular tack was a creative endeavor toward performing and recording more modern American music. In tandem with Oliver Daniel of CBS radio, who was a key figure in the American Composer's Alliance, Stokowski gave his time and reputation toward: (1) the creation of the Contemporary Music Society; (2) conducting a series of historically important concerts and broadcasts of new music from New York's Museum of Modern Art—the most important of which was the first public concert of electronic music in this country—and with the Weber and Goeb recordings of 1950 and 1952 respectively; and (3) the birth of Composer's Recordings Inc. (CRI), now the largest American nonprofit record company with several hundred titles devoted exclusively to modern music (see Daniel, Stokowski, chap. 55, "Plans and Projects," 559–74, for a full account).

In 1906 a twenty-four-year-old Stokowski attended the first public demonstration of Thaddeus Cahill's Dynamophone, a primitive ancestor of the later electronic synthesizer, which he followed by writing an enthusiastic piece for the journal *Electrical World* describing the importance of this kind of electronic approach for the future of music. During the twenties and thirties Stokowski included music for the Theremin and the Ondes Martenot in his concerts. These were precursors of modern electronic instruments, but by 1952 the experiments of Vladimir Ussachevsky and Otto Luening at Bennington College and at Columbia University had led to the experimental production of true electronic music (see Ruscoll, *Liberation of Sound*, 33).

News of their work reached Stokowski and Daniel as they were working on the Musuem of Modern Art concerts. At their behest, Ussachevsky and Luening brought their electronic gear and their compositions for performance at the 28 October 1952 concert. Stokowski conducted the Lou Harrison Suite for Violin, Piano, and Small Orchestra and the Ben Weber Symphony on Poems of William Blake, as well as the premiere of Elliot Carter's Eight Etudes and Fantasy for Woodwind Quartet, during the first half of the concert. At halftime Stokowski described the upcoming electronic portion of the program as illustrative of a new, a more direct, way of composition and performance. Likening electronic composition to painting, the conductor noted that many of tomorrow's composers would compose their music directly in tone itself, superimposing sounds on one another to create new sonorities and a new music.

There followed Ussachevsky's *Sonic Contours* and Luening's *Low Speed Adventure* and *Fantasy in Space*. But beyond the concert were repeats on New York radio, a follow-up demonstration on NBC's *Today* show seen across the country, and articles in the New York Press, in *Down Beat*, *Billboard*, and *Vogue*.

The same program was repeated in 1953 on the *Music in the Making* series at Cooper Union with follow-up demonstrations at Juilliard, Sarah Lawrence, Duke, Eastman-Rochester, Reed College, the University of Oregon, and Capetown University in South Africa.

It was, wrote conductor David Randolph, the start of a new epic in American music making. (See Luening, *The Odyssey of an American Composer*, 509–59. Herbert Russcol, "Music Since Hiroshima" in Gregory Battcock, ed., *Breaking the Sound Barrier*, 203, and Russcol, *Liberation of Sound*, 94–96).

1952: Ciakovsky, Sinfonia no. 5. Symphony Orchestra of the Northwest German Radio. Movimento Musica 01.041 (live).

This recording, released in 1982, was taken from a live concert performance of the Tchaikovsky Fifth, noncommerically recorded in the Hamburg, Germany, concert hall on 7 July 1952. The performance is passionate, intense, and more poetically personal, that is, idiosyncratic, than Stokowski's commerical recording for RCA the following year. The sound is remarkably good given its noncommercial origin.

This is one of several live recordings by Stokowski to appear since the conductor's death, from among English, Japanese, Italian, French, Danish, German, and American sources.

1952: Wagner, *Parsifal:* Prelude to Act I and Music from Act 3, and Schubert, *Rosamunde:* Ballet Suite. Leopold Stokowski Symphony Orchestra. RCA LM 1730.

The *Parsifal* excerpts coupled with Stokowski's 1944 recording of Strauss's *Death and Transfiguration* were rereleased in April 1982 to commemorate the conductor's one hundredth birthday. Leopold Stokowski Society LS 5.

While the RCA set titles list the inclusion of Prelude to Act I of Parsifal, musicologist Edward Johnson notes that the music played is the "Good Friday Music" and has so listed it on LS 5, along with Music from Act 3, which is correctly named on both sets.

1952: Early Italian Music, including Vivaldi, Concerto Grosso in D Minor (arr. Stokowski); Cesti, "Tu Mancavi A Tormentarmi Crudelissima Speranza" (arr. Stokowski); Lully, Nocturne from *Le Triomphe de l'Amour* and Marche from *Thesee;* Frescobaldi, "Gagliarda" (arr. Stokowski); Palestrina, [sic] "Adoramus Te" (arr. Stokowski), *"O Bone Jesu";* and Gabrieli, "Canzon Quarti Toni A 15" and "In Ecclesiis Benedicte Domino." Leopold Stokowski Symphony Orchestra with brass choir, a cappella chorus, and organist Charles Courboin. RCA LM 1721.

This set provides a rather peculiar and poignant twist to the Stokowski story in the fifties, a twist centering upon the time of its appearance, the contents of the album, and the use made of it.

Consider its timing in the context of Stokowski's career. The maestro was eight years past losing his conductorship of the NBC Symphony Orchestra, six years past leaving the New York City Symphony, and three years past losing the directorship of the New York Philharmonic to Dimitri Mitropoulous. RCA was already complaining about Stokowski recording with an "anonymous" orchestra—AKA "Leopold Stokowski and His Symphony Orchestra"—no matter how good the personnel or the performances. It was necessary, argued RCA executives, that Stokowski have his own orchestral base in order to revive lagging record sales. In three more years RCA would end its recording contract with "has been" Stokowski after thirty-eight years together.

Then, too, after a dozen concerts with the San Francisco Symphony Orchestra during the 1951 and 1952 seasons, plus the stunning RCA *Boris Godunov* excerpts set with the orchestra, the San Francisco Opera Chorus, and basso Nicola Rossi-Lemeni, Stokowski would again lose out in contesting for conductorship of a major American symphony orchestra, this time in San Francisco, to Enrique Jorda (see Chasins, *Leopold Stokowski,* 207–8, and Daniel, *Stokowski,* 570).

At this career low point common sense would seem to argue against recording such a set for several reasons. In the early fifties there was little general musical interest in the kind of prebaroque music represented on LM 1721. What interest there was came from specialists, who were at the same time leading the fight against just the kind of transcriptions that had been so much a part of Stokowski's career and art, and that were used in several of the nine selections in this set.

Finally, circumstantial evidence indicates that RCA could not have been particularly interested in recording this set since Stokowski's choice of selections had little sales appeal at the time. His earlier Bach-Stokowski transcriptions sets, *Stokowski Conducts Bach,* vols. 1 and 2 (LM 1133 and LM 1176) of 1950, had been met by a rising critical tide of authenticist disapproval and disappointing sales, and the 1952 Italian set was to be done with the "anonymous" orchestra. There would be no built-in sales base founded on Stokowski's performance with a name orchestra.

How Stokowski persuaded RCA executives to approve this project I do not know, but, in common sense terms, his success in doing so did him little practical good and perhaps did him harm in the judgment of RCA executives since sales were disappointing when the set was released.

A couple of years later RCA came out with LM 1875, a set called *Restful Good Music;* on its cover a pretty blue-eyed reddish blonde young woman reclined in a chair with one breast all but bare. Liner notes by Mr. Edward Benjamin and Mr. Walter Diehl described the set as a serious attempt to cope with the stress of modern urban living through the therapy of listening to restful good music. The notes indicated that Mr. Benjamin had commissioned Mr. Diehl, described as the former head of two classical music stations in New York City, to do an analysis of all of the classical recordings available to him to find the most suitable music in recordings to provide therapy for stress-ridden record buyers, to provide them with an ideal set to listen to at the end of a hard and jarring day.

And, lo, the selections chosen for the set by Mr. Diehl were all RCA recordings, all Stokowski recordings, with two-thirds of the ten cuts from Stokowski's *Early Italian Music* album of 1952 and the two Bach-Stokowski sets of 1950. The remainder of the set included the Adagietto from Stokowski's *L'Arlesienne* Suite no. 1 (1952), the second movement of Beethoven's Sixth Symphony (1954), and the never before released "When I am Laid in Earth" (1950), in Stokowski's own arrangement of Purcell's music.

Whatever the validity of the set as a restful tonic for urban stress, it also gave RCA a second chance to push poorer-selling Stokowski recordings from three earlier sets *a second time* by using the angle of allegedly providing music therapy for the American record buyer and to do so without additional recording costs.

To whatever degree Stokowski was a party to this, it did him a disservice and further added, I would guess, to the downturn of his career during the early- to midfifties.

The irony in all this is that the *Early Italian Music* album did contain beautiful music carefully prepared and presented by Stokowski's hand-picked forces. Much later, during the sixties and seventies, such prebaroque works would earn raves at Stokowski concerts, but even during the early fifties, Stokowski's "uncommon sense" in performing this music in concert and in recording it bore fruit. For example, Pulitzer-Prize-winning poet Richard Howard would remember Stokowski performances of such works during his boyhood, emphasizing two things about those presentations: first, how beautiful and unusual those little-known works were, and second, that Stokowski was the only well-known American conductor with the imagination and the daring to do them at the time. Mr. Howard told me that he would never forget the experience and that he had always believed much of Stokowski's bad press came not from poor musicanship, but from his daring and originality in the world of music (Richard Howard, conversations with the author).

1952: Monteverdi, *Vespro Della Beata Vergine*, excerpts, with soprano Miriam Stewart, contralto Dorothy Clark, tenor William Miller, and baritone Bruce Foote. University of Illinois Symphony Orchestra and the Oratorio Society Chorus conducted by Paul Young. University of Illinois School of Music Custom Recording Series CRS 1.

The recording includes eight of the fourteen sections of the *Vespro*. They are: "Domine Ad Adjuvandum," "Nigra Sum," "Lauda Jerusalem," "Ave Maris Stella," "Dixit Dominus," "Sonato Sopra Sancta Maria," "O Quam Pulchra Est," and "Magnificat."

The performance and recording was part of a larger conception in which Stokowski wanted to organize another youth orchestra—the "Collegiate Orchestra"—drawing on college-age musicians on campuses all over the country for personnel. The conception was grand, the college administrators were timid, and by 1954 the project was dead.

Like his very effective early fifties work for the Contemporary Music Society and the American Composer's Alliance, the idea of the Collegiate Orchestra was another creative tack of a conductor without an orchestra (see, "Stokowski Plans Collegiate Orchestra" *Musical Courier*, 149 1 October 1953, 3).

1952: Ballet and Bizet, including *L'Arlesienne:* Suites 1 and 2, and Symphony no. 1 in C. Leopold Stokowski Symphony Orchestra. RCA LM 1706.

1953: Tchaikovsky, "Aurora's Wedding," from *Sleeping Beauty* Ballet, excerpts arranged as a suite by Serge Diaghileff, and Tchaikovsky-Stokowski, "Humoresque" and "Solitude." Leopold Stokowski Symphony Orchestra. RCA LM 1774.

1953: Tchaikovsky, Symphony no. 5 in E Minor. Leopold Stokowski Symphony Orchestra. RCA LM 1780.

1950–54: Restful Good Music, including selections by Cesti, Frescobaldi, Lully, Purcell, Bach, Beethoven, and Bizet. Leopold Stokowski Symphony Orchestra. RCA LM 1875.

1954: Highlights from Saint-Saëns: Samson and Delilah with soloists Rise Stevens, Jan Peerce, Robert Merrill, and the Robert Shaw Chorale. Members of the NBC Symphony Orchestra. RCA LM 1848.

This is a fine set marred by the sometimes forced vocalizing of Jan Peerce as Samson. Robert Merrill makes a fine high priest and Rise Stevens a luscious Delilah, but the accolades must also be shared by the Robert Shaw Chorale and the NBC Orchestra. Stokowski's orchestral accompaniment to the soloists is good, and never has the "Bacchanale" sounded more orgiastic to me.

***1952:* Mussorgsky, *"Boris Godunov"* Highlights, with soloist Nicola Rossi-Lemeni. San Francisco Opera Chorus and San Francisco Symphony Orchestra. RCA LM 1764.

One wishes Stokowski had recorded the entire opera on the basis of this recording. The San Franciscans sound like full-throated Russians and Rossi-Lemeni makes a fine Boris. This recording has been reissued by dell' Arte Records as DA 9002.

**1953: Night on Bald Mountain: Great Russian Showpieces*, including Mussorgsky-Stokowski, "Night on Bald Mountain," *Khovantchina:* Prelude to Act 1, "Dance of the Persian Slaves," and "Entracte" from Act 4; Glière, *The Red Poppy:* "Russian Sailors' Dance"; Borodin, *Caucasian Sketches:* "In the Steppes of Central Asia"; and Rimsky-Korsakov, *Russian Easter* Overture, with bass soloist Nicolo Moscona. Leopold Stokowski Symphony Orchestra. RCA LM 1816.

This album of romantic Stokowski favorites was rereleased on Quintessence PMC 7026.

**1953–54:* Gould, *Dance Variations,* with duo pianists Whittemore and Lowe and the San Francisco Symphony Orchestra (1953), and Menotti, *Sebastian:* Ballet Suite, with members of the NBC Symphony Orchestra (1954). RCA LM 1858.

As of this writing there is no listing of the Morton Gould *Dance Variations* in the Schwann Guide, which is a pity. This counterpoint of duo pianos and orchestra through ten dance forms is delightfully infectious. Climaxed by a throbbing tango and a delirious tarantella, the variations receive a brilliant performance by Stokowski and his forces in a fine-sounding recording. The Menotti ballet suite on the reverse side, recorded in 1954 in both mono and on stereotape, was rereleased by RCA in stereo in 1978 on RCA ARL 1-2715. There should be a rerelease of the Gould piece; preferably on compact disc.

**1953–55: Rhapsody,* including Enesco, "Roumanian Rhapsodies" 1 and 2 (1953), and Liszt, "Hungarian Rhapsodies" 1, 2, and 3 (1955). Leopold Stokowski Symphony Orchestra and members of the NBC Symphony Orchestra. RCA LM 1878.

This set was rereleased by Quintessence on its "Critics Choice" series as PMC 7023.

Reviewing a Stokowski concert of the late forties, Virgil Thomson praised the sensitive interpretation accorded the New York premiere of Vaughan Williams's Sixth Symphony, but noted that Stokowski closed the program with Liszt's Second Rhapsody, interpreted by the conductor in his "old barnstorming" way, a style of approach that Mr. Thomson thought Stokowski long ago had left behind. He hadn't, as later proven by his 1955 recording with members of the NBC Symphony. It included Gypsy fiddlers, a cimbalon, altered scores, and chutzpah in performance; recordings of the first three rhapsodies are to delight in or to damn, depending upon your point of view. The accompanying Roumanian Rhapsodies are equally colorful, but a little less exuberantly mannered in performance.

When I listen to this set, I believe I can hear echoes from grandfather Stokowski's émigré's club in London, as imagined by the romancer.

**1954:* Beethoven, Symphony no. 6 in F. members of the NBC Symphony Orchestra. RCA LM 1830.

The Stokowski recording has remarkably good sound for 1954, the better to pick up the remarkable color shown both in ensemble playing and by soloists. The pace is leisurely overall and skillfully in tune with the differing needs of each movement, without the benefit of eccentric touches.

The English Stokowski Society has returned this recording to circulation as LS 10.

**1954:* Sibelius, Symphony no. 2 in D. Members of the NBC Symphony. RCA LM 1854.

This recording has been rereleased as dell' Arte 9002. The music is beautifully played and the orchestral color is as vivid as any on record. It was Stokowski's only recording of the work and the program annotation he provided for the RCA original in its romanticism and sense of fantasy provides a clear link between the Stokowski of the Discography and the family romancer of the Appendix. Indeed, Stokowski's own words about Sibelius's innermost world of "feeling" and his visionary "imagination" are apt descriptions of the conductor himself in communion with the music of Sibelius.

***1954–55:* Tchaikovsky, *Swan Lake:* Acts 2 and 3, complete. Members of the NBC Symphony Orchestra. RCA LM 1894.

This set has been reissued in the "Critics' Choice" series on Quintessence PMC 7007. It has stood up beautifully over the years in terms of both sound and performance.

1954: Prokofiev, *Romeo and Juliet:* Ballet Suite, and Menotti, *Sebastian:* Ballet Suite. Members of the NBC Symphony Orchestra. RCA ARL 1-2715.

Recorded also in stereo on tape at the time of their monophonic release in 1954, these performances finally appeared on stereo disc in 1978 after Stokowski's death. It should be noted that Stokowski was, with his friend Fritz Reiner, the first conductor to record in stereo commercially, experimenting with the technique before it was accepted generally. The Prokofiev is a slow-paced, restrained performance of selections from all three of the suites created by Prokofiev from his *Romeo and Juliet* score. Elegance and restraint rather than passion mark the Stokowski performance.

1955: The year 1955 shows a dearth of recording activity by the maestro. On 27 Dec. 1954 Gloria Vanderbilt Stokowski left her husband, taking with her their two sons, Stan and Chris. The new year of 1955 was traumatically rung in for all concerned, a trauma that lasted for several years. Then too his continued lack of an established orchestra of his own had worked against Stokowski in recording for RCA.

Since Stokowski had recorded a series of fine performances—of Saint-Saëns, Beethoven, Sibelius, Tchaikovsky and Prokofiev—with the NBC Symphony Orchestra in 1954 after maestro Toscanini's retirement, it seems logical that RCA could have continued the orchestra's life with Stokowski named as director. After all, Stokowski had begun American symphonic recording on the Victor label in 1917, had sold millions of symphonic recordings for RCA and had earlier been quite successful as the orchestra's codirector.

RCA's answer to this kind of logic was that paring expenses by disbanding the orchestra took precedence. Then, to add the shabby to the cheap, RCA cancelled Stokowski's contract in 1956. This they did even though Stokowski had informed RCA in April of 1955 that he had been appointed conductor of the Houston Orchestra and that he wanted to record with that orchestra for RCA. Not until May of the following year did he receive a definitive answer. When it came it was in the form of a double negative; no recordings for Houston and no contract for Stokowski (see Daniel, *Stokowski,* 570, 622–23).

Clearly RCA believed that Stokowski, age seventy-four, once again amid the wreckage of a marriage—his third—was washed up or at least in precipitous decline.

The bright spot in this dark picture lay in the oil-rich city of Houston, a city that had had an orchestra of sorts since 1913. It was not until the arrival of conductor Efrem Kurtz in 1948 that the process of building a first-rate orchestra began. The conductor's efforts were backed to the full by the doyenne of cultural Houston, Miss Ima Hogg. Heiress to a major oil fortune, Miss Hogg either provided or raised the money needed. Kurtz rebuilt and trained the orchestra.

During these years Stokowski guest conducted during the 1950–51, 1951–52, and 1953–54 seasons, making an excellent impression despite including novelties like Carl Ruggles's *Organum* in his programming.

Kurtz left in 1954. His successor Ferenc Fricsay, was, from the Houston point of view, a poor choice. He failed to finish his first 1954–55 season as director by mutual consent of the conductor and the orchestra's board of directors.

At this point Miss Ima took matters into her own hands and went "hunting" in New York. Her game—a first class conductor who could bring stability and great music to Houston. There Stokowski's manager, Andrew Schulhof, met with Miss Hogg and suggested Stokowski, and within a week the maestro was appointed principal conductor with a three-year contract.

The marriage of Stokowski to Houston, which lasted until 1960, was one of convenience, wrote Houston music critic Hubert Roussel some years later.

Houston thought only of Stokowski's reputation and of his music making skills, without taking into account his penchant for broad programming that featured so much new music. Stokowski for his part fantasized "Hoostohn," as he called it, as a cosmopolitan cultural center surrounded by the wild west of ranches and cowboys. This latter was most important, because he wanted sons Stan and Chris to experience the life of the west.

Long before there had been an oil-rich, twentieth-century boom city, which is what Houston was in 1955, there had been not cowboys and ranching but slaves and cotton plantations since this area of eastern Texas had been the farthest reach west of the old cotton kingdom.

Despite mistaken judgments on both sides, this love affair or marriage of convenience worked well for both parties for several years. Houston got beau-iful music making and the sense of having arrived musically since its orchestra made records and made news.

Roussel noted that Stokowski made only two personnel changes during his entire stay, yet, wrote Roussel, the orchestra was transformed in performance, as if by musical alchemy. Its source was "sorcerer" Stokowski. At his bidding the orchestra played with new intensity and sensitivity. In short, it became a Stokowski orchestra characterized by the Stokowski sound and style of performance. Stokowski's way of accomplishing this transformation was, wrote Roussel, uniquely his own.

Actually part of what Stokowski was able to realize with the orchestra had to do with his technical skills, which were surely allied to his "sorcery" in Houston music making. He showed this skill early on in working with NBC Television to present the final rehearsal of Alan Hovhaness's *Mysterious Mountain*—a world premiere on national television. For this work and for a variety of other pieces by other composers, he reseated the orchestra, not just to fit the hall's acoustics, but sometimes to meet the needs of compositions, which required variant seatings. He created a sound reflector on stage before which the orchestra played, as well as acoustical panels for the concert hall's walls.

Stokowski received initial enthusiasm and affection from Houston. He also had a musical power base; his own orchestra and the combination plus his own innate optimism and buoyancy aided him in bouncing back from the trials of the midfifties. Not only did he negotiate recording contracts with Everest and Capitol-EMI to record with Houston, but during the late fifties and early sixties he would record with several other orchestras on Capitol, Vanguard, Decca, United Artists, Columbia, CRI, Soviet MK and, yes, the RCA label. Not only was he not washed up, but judging by the recordings of the next few years he was a better master of his craft than previously and just as much a showman.

Over the first three seasons, with premiere after premiere of difficult modern works presented by the maestro a growing number of confused or annoyed Houston subscribers, while still respecting him, cooled toward Stokowski, while venting their feelings. One concert goer, after hearing Ernst Krenek's craggy Concerto for Cello, described the piece as a cold draft seeping into the house.

Stokowski in turn grew increasingly distant toward Houston after three seasons; now spending more and more of his time in New York and less in Texas.

Like a love affair of ages and stages, five years together proved enough. Stokowski wanted to move in another direction, and Houston wanted to move back to Beethoven and Brahms, by moving forward with Barbirolli. By mutual agreement, Stokowski's fall concerts in 1960 were the last he would give in the city. But, summed up Houston critic Roussel, if he had irritated Houstonians with his new music, he had delighted them on many occasions and consistently had educated them as well. He had brought musical sophistication to the city, together with a level of performance standards unknown before, and he certainly brought pride in the orchestra's recordings. Stokowski had also provided the driving force for the Houston Contemporary Music Society, whose musicians he conducted without fee (see Hubert Roussel, *The Houston Symphony Orchestra, 1913–1971*, 133–74).

1956. Holst, *The Planets.* Los Angeles Philharmonic Orchestra with the women's chorus of the Roger Wagner Chorale. Capitol SP 8389.

This is the first recording Stokowski made under his new Capitol-EMI contract. It was a steady seller for many years on the EMI rerelease, Seraphim S 60175, on Toshiba-EMI in Japan, and on the Music for Pleasure label in England.

**1956:* *The Orchestra,* including Dukas, Fanfare from *La Peri* (brass); Barber, Adagio for Strings (strings); R. Strauss, Gavotte from Suite in B-flat for Winds (woodwinds); Farberman, Section 1 of *Evolution* (percussion); Vaughan Williams, Scherzo from Symphony no. 8 (brass and woodwinds); Perischetti, March from Divertimento for Band (brass, woodwinds, percussion); Tchaikovsky, Scherzo from Symphony no. 4 (strings, brass, woodwinds, percussion); and Mussorgsky-Ravel, "The Hut on Fowl's Legs" and "The Great Gate of Kiev" from *Pictures at an Exhibition* (the full orchestra). Leopold Stokowski Symphony Orchestra. Capitol SAL 8385.

For this set each piece was chosen to illustrate a section of the orchestra, or sections in combination leading up to the Mussorgsky for full orchestral sound. A good idea made better by Stokowski's sensitive choice of pieces to illustrate orchestral sound.

The whole was recorded in state-of-the-art sound (for 1956), and the set was accompanied by an informative booklet explaining orchestral sound and recording techniques based on the music played.

Philip Geraci, writing in *High Fidelity* (7 Sept. 1957), described the color and sound as truly remarkable, singling out Barber's Adagio for Strings as "breathtaking"; one of the best-sounding string ensemble recordings ever done. The Barber recording has since been rereleased, first on Angel Eminence recording AE-34481 and then on compact disc CDC 7-47521 2.

***1956:* Glière, Symphony no. 3 in B Minor, *Ilya Murometz.* Houston Symphony Orchestra. Capitol SP 8402.

This was Stokowski's first recording with the Houston Orchestra. It has the romantic dash and color to match the mighty deeds of the Russian hero. It also illustrates early on what Roussel described as the transformation of the orchestra when led by the maestro. Stokowski's gifts for the dramatic and for fantasy in sound receive free play in the recording.

1956–58: Leopold Stokowski Conducts, including selections by Bach-Stokowski, Barber, Debussy, Dukas, Gluck, Mussorgsky, J. Strauss, Tchaikovsky, and Turina. Leopold Stokowski Symphony Orchestra. Seraphim SIB 6094 (two records).

These fifteen short selections were originally released in Capitol albums SAL 8385, SP 8399, SP 8415, and SP 8454. Among favorites often recorded by Stokowski over the years is his only recording of the eleven minute "La Oracion del Torero" by Turina; it is a haunting piece beautifully realized. The Turina piece has since (1986) been digitally remastered and included on Angel Eminence AE-34481.

1957–58: Stokowski and Strings, including selections by Bach-Stokowski, Tchaikovsky, Rachmaninoff, Paganini, Boccherini, Borodin, and Gluck. Leopold Stokowski Symphony Orchestra. Seraphim S-60278.

These nine pieces include Stokowski transcriptions. The recording's highlights are a lovely Air for G String and the melancholy "Vocalise" of Rachmaninoff.

Quoting Stokowski's correspondence to Capitol Records at the time, Oliver Daniel notes that Stokowski was eager to record modern repertoire for the label, urging recordings of Blacher, Webern, Jolivet, Riegger, Yardumian, Tippet, Panufnik, Ruggles, Cowell, Hovhaness, Stravinsky, Martin, Martinu, Roy Harris, Villa-Lobos, Mennin, Revueltas, and Ives (see Daniel Stokowski, 676). As one can see from the above *Stokowski and Strings* and *Leopold Stokowski Conducts*, Capitol had other ideas.

1957–58: Stokowski Plays Bach, including ten pieces—eight in Stokowski transcriptions—that were initially included in Capitol-EMI sets SP 8399, 8415, 8449, and 8489, and have now been transferred to this EMI-Angel compact disc. Leopold Stokowski Symphony Orchestra. EMI-Angel, CDM-7 69072 2.

**1957–59:* Schoenberg, *Transfigured Night* (1957), and Loeffler, *A Pagan Poem* (1959). Leopold Stokowski Symphony Orchestra. Capitol SP 8433.

This set was rereleased by EMI as Seraphim S-60080. Of the Schoenberg, Alfred Frankenstein wrote that at all times there should be a current Stokowski recording of *Transfigured Night* in circulation since he drew from it an ardor and beauty that were unmatched (see Frankenstein, *Records in Review* [1960]: 255).

This recording of *Transfigured Night* has since been digitally remastered and put on compact disc, Angel CDC-7 47521 2.

**1957:* Debussy, *Nocturnes:* "Nuages," "Fêtes," and "Sirèns," and Ravel, *Rapsodie Espagnole*. London Symphony Orchestra and the BBC Women's Chorus. Capitol SP 8520.

Later transferred to the Seraphim label as S-60104, this recording was the first of many recordings made by Stokowski with the orchestra he rejuvenated in 1957. He recorded the pieces after live concert performances in the summer of 1957.

Both the Debussy and Ravel pieces have been digitally remastered and included on Angel compact disc CDC-7 47423 2 along with Ravel's *Alborada del Gracioso*, recorded in 1958.

**1957:* Stravinsky, Suites from *Firebird* and *Petrouchka*. Berlin Philharmonic Orchestra. Capitol SP 8407.

This set was later transferred to Seraphim as S-60229. While Stokowski rerecorded the *Firebird* Suite—his best ever—in 1967 with the London Symphony Orchestra, this 1957 recording includes his last commercial *Petrouchka*.

The 1957 *Firebird* Suite and the Suite from *Petrouchka* have been transferred to compact disc, CDM-7 69116 2, accompanied by Stokowski's 1957 "Clair de Lune" and "Prelude to the Afternoon of a Faun."

**1952–57:* Harrison, Suite for Violin, Piano, and Small Orchestra, with violinist Anahid Ajemian and pianist Maro Ajemian (1952), and Cowell, *Persian Set* (1957), with Chamber Orchestra and soloists. CRI SD 114.

The delightful Cowell piece resulted from the composer's visit to Iran in the midfifties and his fascination with its music. Oliver Daniel received the score from him and contacted Stokowski about recording it. Stokowski agreed and the subsequent recording was paired with his 1952 Museum of Modern Art recording of the Harrison Suite, which had been sponsored by the American Composers' Alliance; the two were then released together on CRI with program notes by Daniel.

Most recently the *Persian Set* has been released in CRI's *Anthology* series as one of the pieces delineating the accomplishments of Henry Cowell (see *Fanfare* 8, July–Aug. 1985; 48–49).

****1957:* Bartok, *Music for String Instruments, Percussion, and Celesta,* and Martin, *Petite Symphonie Concertante.* Leopold Stokowski Symphony Orchestra. Capitol SP 8507.

This was Stokowski's first and *only* chance to do contemporary fare for Capitol-EMI. The Frank Martin piece establishes then heightens a sense of brooding anxiety, near unbearable if very hearable. It is one of those "magic" recordings in which Stokowski's young soloists, harpist Gloria Agostini, harpsichordist Albert Fuller, and pianist Mitchell Andrews play as though possessed. Critic Frankenstein described both performances as "magnificent" (see Frankenstein, *Records in Review,* 1960, 31).

The Bartok has since been digitally remastered and included on Angel Eminence black disc AE-34481 and on compact disc CDC-7 47521 8, along with Barber's Adagio for Strings and *Transfigured Night.* Unfortunately, the superb Martin recording has disappeared. It was one of the few Stokowski Capitol-EMI recordings not transferred to Angel-Seraphim and kept in circulation. Certainly the Frank Martin piece should be rereleased, preferably in compact disc.

With renewed confidence, an orchestral base, and recording contracts, the year 1958 was one of major concert activity and furious recording by Stokowski. In New York he recorded with the Symphony of the Air (the old NBC Symphony) for United Artists, with the Stadium Symphony Orchestra (the New York Philharmonic) for Everest, and with his own pickup orchestra for Capitol-EMI. In Houston he made two widely acclaimed recordings for Capitol-EMI, while his tour of the Soviet Union netted a recording on the Russian label, MK.

The influence of his Soviet trip—he was the first American conductor since the beginning of the cold war to be invited by the Russians to conduct Soviet orchestras—can be seen in the number of Russian pieces recorded by Stokowski in 1958 and in the number of modern Russian pieces he programmed for 1958–59.

The year also marked his fiftieth as a conductor. In honor of the occasion, the Contemporary Music Society sponsored a Stokowski concert in Carnegie Hall with the maestro leading a pickup orchestra in Vaughan Williams's Symphony no. 9, Paul Creston's Toccata, Hovhaness's *Mysterious Mountain*—which, like the Vaughan Williams Symphony, Stokowski had premiered—Wallingford Riegger's "New Dance," and Juan Orrego-Salas's "Obertura Festivo."

While speeches were made, an Eisenhower telegram read, and honors given by Mayor Wagner of New York, the concert itself in its freshness and variety best demonstrated the seventy-six-year-old maestro's contribution to music (see Ronald Eyer, "Stokowski 50th Anniversary Concert Offers Modern Music,"

Musical America, 78 October 1958; 7, and Irving Kolodin, "Music to my Ears," *Saturday Review,* 41 11 October 1958; 57).

1958: Saygun, *Yunus Emre,* sponsored by the Turkish Embassy's New York office of tourism and information, with the Crane Choir and the Potsdam State University Choir. Symphony of the Air. RW 3967-8 (live).

Ahmed Adnan Saygun's oratorio in its American premiere was given at the United Nations Building in New York in honor of that organization. Sponsored by the Turkish delegation, it was recorded live on 25 November (see *Musical Courier 160,* January 1959; 11).

This is one of three Stokowski recordings I have been unable to find on the collectors' market and so have never heard it.

* **1958:* Respighi, *Pines of Rome,* and selections by Gabrieli, Cesti, Frescobaldi, and Palestrina. Symphony of the Air. United Artists UAS 8001.

In December of 1958 Stokowski conducted the Symphony of the Air in a Carnegie Hall concert, whose climax was the Respighi *Pines of Rome;* he followed the concert with a midnight recording of the piece. Of the concert performance Irving Kolodin wrote that it's only rival in his memory could be the last Toscanini performance, noting particularly the intensity and majesty of the last movement in Stokowski's interpretation.

R. D. Darrell described the subsequent recording as masterful in its contrasts and glory of sound, poetry, and discrimination in turn. He concluded that Stokowski's recording was definitive even against the competition of Toscanini (see Kolodin, "*Saturday Review,*" 41 27 December 1958; 22, and Darrell, *Records in Review,* 1960, 403).

Largely ignored by the critics the early Italian pieces on the disc's second side represented Stokowski's recording return to Italian prebaroque music for the first time since the illfated *Early Italian Music* set of 1952. He included three pieces recorded in the earlier set. In the 1958 set they are all in his own arrangements as follows: Cesti, "Tu Moncavi A Tormentarmi, Crudelissma Speranza," Frescobaldi, "Gagliarda" and Palestrina, [sic] "Adoramus Te." To these he added Gabrieli's "Sonata Pian e Forte" in a transcription by Fritz Stein.

All are beautifully performed, but the Cesti piece, "You Have Failed to Torture Me, O Most Cruel Hope" is special, described by Stokowski as a "beautiful expression of the most intense passion and despair."

**1958:* Beethoven, Symphony no. 7 in A. Symphony of the Air. United Artists UAS 8003.

In 1980 Quintessence rereleased this set in its "Critic's Choice" series as PMC 7110. As noted by Martin Bookspan in the August 1960 issue of *Stereo Review,* this fine recording is close in spirit and performance to the classic 1927 Philadelphia Orchestra performance. It is superior to Stokowski's 1973 recording of the work with the New Philharmonia Orchestra. As an added bonus two short pieces by Frescobaldi and Palestrina transcribed for orchestra by Stokowski are included as well, both taken from United Artists UAS 8001, *The Pines of Rome.* Alas the Cesti piece is not included.

**1958:* R. Strauss, *Till Eulenspiegel's Merry Pranks, Don Juan,* and *Salome:* "Dance of the Seven Veils". Stadium Symphony Orchestra of New York. Everest SDBR 3023.

These are zesty performances of *Till* and *Don Juan,* with the finest performance reserved for the poisonous but delectable *Salome.* They are well-crafted performances, beautifully recorded. This set, plus Stokowski's 1960 Everest recording of "Wotan's Farewell" and "Magic Fire Music" from *Die Walküre* with the Houston Symphony Orchestra, have been transferred to CD on Price-Less D 1323X.

***1958:** Tchaikovsky, *Francesca da Rimini* and *Hamlet*. Stadium Symphony Orchestra of New York. Everest SDBR 3011.

This pairing has been remastered and rereleased on dell' Arte DA 9006. While the original of this set was powerful and dramatic, the 45 RPM remaster rises above it—most particularly in the *Hamlet*. *Fanfare's* reviewer Howard Kornblum described the rerelease as combining the most estimable characteristics of Stokowski's conducting style: his dramatic bent, his understanding of color in sound, and the intensity and playing brilliance he could wring from his players. These traits are all in evidence in "these marvelous performances" (see Kornblum, "*Fanfare*," 6 March–April 1983, 273).

The remastered dell' Arte set now appears on that company's CD, CDDA 906.

1958: Prokofiev, Symphony no. 5. USSR Radio Symphony Orchestra, MK 1551.

As part of his European spring-summer tour in 1958 Stokowski visited the Soviet Union and conducted ten concerts with three orchestras between 29 May and 1 July. He performed with the Moscow Philharmonic and the orchestras of Leningrad and Kiev.

In addition to standard fare, he included compositions by Paul Creston, Alan Hovhaness, and Samuel Barber while playing the Shostakovich Fifth and Eleventh Symphonies to the applause of the composer—who by the way was most fond of Stokowski's recordings of his music, an affinity dating back to the Philadelphia Orchestra recordings of his Fifth and Sixth Symphonies in 1939 and 1940 respectively.

Stokowski toured; he sketched and painted Moscow scenes. He was treated to a concert given by the State Orchestra of Russian Folk Instruments; in two words it was a *balalaika orchestra*. Stokowski himself took the podium after intermission and did the Schubert Eighth Symphony a la balalaika!

In addition to the crowds, the applause, and the hands-across-the-sea hype, the conductor's most important accomplishments were his meetings with Soviet composers, which later netted modern Russian works for American audiences and this recording. While the set provides a very limited dynamic range and poor surfaces, the Muscovites play with energy and conviction (see Viktor Gorokov, "Leopold Stokowski Appears Before Soviet Audiences," *USSR*, 6 October 1958, 50–51, and "Stokowski, First American to Conduct Soviet Orchestras," *Musical Courier*, 157 June 1958, 4).

**1958:* Shostakovich, Symphony no. 5 in D Major. Stadium Symphony Orchestra of New York. Everest SDBR 3010.

This is classic performance by an eminent interpreter.

**1958:* Shostakovich, Symphony no. 1 in F Major, Prelude in E-flat Minor (arr. Stokowski), and *Lady Macbeth of Mzensk:* Entracte. Symphony of the Air. United Artists UAS 8004.

This is a memorable recorded performance of Shostakovich's most original symphonic score made thirty years after Stokowski premiered the work in Philadelphia. All the youthful and satirical zip is here with marvelous playing by the Symphony of the Air. Added bonuses are the excerpt from the Shostakovich opera, akin in spirit to the First symphony, and Stokowski's orchestrated version of the Prelude in E-flat Minor, this last a poignant three-minute study in pain and resignation as music. Of the older Stokowski recordings that deserve reissue this is, I believe, one of the most meritorious candidates, along with the Frank Martin *Petite Symphonie Concertante*, Morton Gould's *Dance Variations*, and Griffes's *"The White Peacock."*

**1958*: Khachaturian, Symphony no. 2. Symphony of the Air. United Artists UAL 7002.

Critic Alfred Frankenstein was succinct in his review of the Khachaturian in describing it as a boring work, beautifully interpreted and played by Stokowski's forces (see Frankenstein, *Records in Review*, 1960, 167).

Like Vaughan Williams's Sixth Symphony and the Shostakovich Seventh, Khachaturian's Second Symphony was inspired by the suffering and horror of the Second World War. It is dramatic and colorful if also sometimes bombastic in its programmatic handling of the sufferings and final triumph of Mother Russia. Stokowski's performance is masterful with fine playing by the Symphony of the Air.

***1958*: Shostakovich, Symphony no. 11, *1905*, Houston Symphony Orchestra, Capitol SPBR 8448 (two records).

The original release was spread over four sides to capture the dynamic range of the symphony. Some of those dynamics were lost in transfer to the single disc Seraphim release on S-60228. This symphony, like the first, the third, and the sixth and the First Piano Concerto were premiered in America by Stokowski. The performance itself is stunning, with the Houston Orchestra sounding like one of the world's great orchestras even on the cramped single disc.

Fortunately EMI-Angel digitally remastered this recording and released it in 1986 as Eminence AE-34446 on black disc and on a sumptuous sounding compact disc, CDC-7 47419 2.

1958: Shostakovich, Symphony no. 11, *1905*. Houston Symphony Orchestra. Everest SDBR 3310/2 (two records).

To begin with, how and why there are recordings on both Everest and Seraphim—via Capitol—dating from the same time, I don't know, but I would like to.

Through amanuensis Solomon Volkov, Shostakovich has described this work as not only programmatic of the 1905 Russian revolt, but written in the style of the Russian *yurodivye*—that is, one who hides a politically unacceptable message within a work of art acceptable by the state. In this case the hidden meaning is a commentary on the Red czarist cruelty of the soviet regime. Shostakovich told Volkov that his 1957 symphony dealt with modern Russia even though disguised with the title *1905*. The same governmental oppression marked both eras, so the title and program hid its contemporary purpose.

Elsewhere, Shostakovich-Volkov wrote of the influence of the Mussorgsky of *Boris Godunov*—also *yurodivye*—who composed for those with the wits to understand his real message (see Volkov, *Testimony*; xxv, 8, 240).

Stokowski's performance catches and matches the drama and tragedy of the Shostakovich score.

**1958*: Villa-Lobos, *Uirapuru* and *Bachianas Brasileiras no. 1*: "Modinha," and Prokofiev, *Cinderella*: Ballet Suite. Stadium Symphony Orchestra of New York. Everest SDBR-3016.

This LP includes Stokowski's only recording of the *Cinderella*. More interesting to me is the Villa-Lobos tone poem, with its exotic story and score to match. It is sensuous, mysterious, and barbaric. More interesting yet is the pathos of the "Modinha," marked by its melancholy and by the intensity of performance.

The *Cinderella* Suite has been transferred to compact disc on Bescol Compact Classics CD 519, in what is only a mediocre transfer. Would that the Villa-Lobos pairing, a remarkable testament to Stokowski's musicianship and to his gifts as romancer, were picked up for release on CD.

1958: Bach-Stokowski. Leopold Stokowski Symphony Orchestra. Capitol SP 8489.

This set, retitled *Stokowski Plays Bach,* was rereleased on Angel Seraphim as S 60235.

Stokowski's Bach could be languorous, bombastic, treacly sweet, in short, theatrical in several directions. Individual transcriptions varied in quality; even recorded performances of the same transcriptions varied in interpretation over the years. As a case in point, this set includes a sentimentalized "Come Sweet Death," engaging performances of the Little Fugue in G Minor and the "Shepherd's Song" from the *Christmas Oratorio,* and a fine Passacaglia and Fugue in C Minor. Deryck Cooke, writing in *Gramophone* upon the appearance of this set, was more single-minded in his view of the set as "distasteful" overall (see Teal, *Leopold Stokowski Off the Record,* sec. 2. Five selections from this set appear on Angel compact disc CDM-7 69072 2).

1958: The String Orchestra, including selections by Bach, Boccherini, Berger, Gluck, Handel, Purcell, Tchaikovsky, and Turina. Leopold Stokowski Symphony Orchestra. Capitol SP8458.

The literally off-beat gem of this set, listed only as Berger, "Rondino Giocoso," is a grotesque and inventive round threatening to dissolve at any moment; lovely and strange. The *Gramophone* reviewer identified the composer as, most likely, Austrian composer Theodore Berger, noting that the Rondino provided the "happiest moments" on the disc (see Teal, *Leopold Stokowski Off the Record,* sec. 2).

**1958:* Orff, *Carmina Burana,* with soprano Virginia Babikian, baritone Guy Gardner, tenor Clyde Hager, the Houston Chorale, the Houston Symphony Boys Choir, and the Houston Symphony Orchestra. Capitol SPAR 8470.

Stokowski had already done the *Carmina* in November 1954 with the Boston University Symphony Orchestra, chorus, and student soloists a year and a half before assuming the direction of the Houston Symphony Orchestra. He had met with great success in Boston and repeated the concert item in Carnegie Hall later that month.

Thus aware of the impact of a good live performance of the erotic *Carmina,* he shrewdly incorporated it into his first season in Houston, performing the profane cantata to the delight of the Houston audience and performing largely with a Houston cast.

When his love affair with Houston began to flag, he brought the *Carmina* back again near the end of the 1957–58 season—renewal time for subscribers—and again it was a rousing success.

Following that performance it was recorded by Capitol-EMI. Although now quite old and superceded sonically, this recording remains in the catalog as Seraphim S 60236, and continues to sell because of Stokowski's musically interpretive understanding of the beauty and the hurt of these erotic goings-on. His interpretation, from the beauty of Spring, through Eros requited, to the implacable wheel of fate, is truly in keeping with Orff's music and Stokowski's unique combination of philosophy and experience.

1958–59: Prokofiev, *Cinderella:* Ballet Suite (1958) and *The Ugly Duckling,* with soprano Regina Resnik, (1959). Stadium Symphony Orchestra of New York. Everest SDBR 3108.

Cinderella was better paired with the Villa-Lobos pieces listed earlier. *The Ugly Duckling* is an ugly duckling.

The *Ugly Duckling, Cinderella:* Suite, and the 1959 *Peter and the Wolf* have been transferred to CD on Bescol Compact Classics, CD 519.

1959: Bloch, *Schelomo,* with cellist George Niekrug, and Ben Haim, *From Israel.* Symphony of the Air. United Artists UAL 7005.

1959: Leimer, Piano Concerto no. 4, with soloist Kurt Leimer. Symphony of the Air. Electrola C 063-29030.

Kurt Leimer was a friend of the conductor and his Fourth Piano Concerto with the composer as soloist was given its world premiere in Carnegie Hall in the fall of 1956. The pair repeated the work in Vienna in the 1956–57 season.

I have not been able to find this recording on the collector's market and have not heard it.

1959: Debussy, *Children's Corner* Suite: Three Selections. Stadium Symphony Orchestra. Everest 3327.

The Debussy, played beautifully by Stokowski on RCA in his 1949 recording, is very poorly done here, as though underrehearsed and hurriedly recorded.

1959: Prokofiev, *Peter and the Wolf,* with narrator Bob Keeshan (Captain Kangaroo). Stadium Symphony Orchestra. Everest SDBR 3043.

A poor effort on the part of everyone. Avoid this performance with its double-sided versions of the same musical story, badly told.

1959: Brahms, Symphony no. 3 in F Major. Houston Symphony Orchestra. Everest SDBR 3030.

To me this is a sluggish distorted performance of Brahms, albeit well played, by one who could perform Brahms beautifully as he did in his last recordings of the Brahms First and Second Symphonies in the seventites and in his explosive Brahms Third of 1928.

The set has now been transferred to CD on Bescol Compact Classics CD 517.

1959: Wagner, *Parsifal:* "Good Friday Spell" and Symphonic Synthesis of Act 3. Houston Symphony Orchestra. Everest SDBR 3031.

A performance leaning more to the erotic elements of the story and music than to the sacred, with fine playing by the orchestra.

1959: Scriabin, *The Poem of Ecstacy,* and Amirov, *Azerbaijan Mugam.* Houston Symphony Orchestra. Everest SDBR 3032.

The Scriabin, recorded three times by Stokowski, is best played and recorded with the Czech Philharmonic in a 1972 London recording. The Amirov piece sounds much like the Khachaturian of the *Gayne* Ballet. It is based on a series of folk melodies transcribed for full orchestra.

The Houston Symphony recording of *The Poem of Ecstacy* has been transferred to a Pantheon compact disc, D 1032X, with distinct improvement in sound.

1960: Bloch, *America,* with the American Concert Choir and the Symphony of the Air. Vanguard SRV 346 SD.

Winner of the 1928 *Musical America* award for new works, with Stokowski acting as one of the judges, *America* received its premiere recording in this disc only a few months after the composer's death in 1959.

1960: Wagner, *Die Walküre:* "Wotan's Farewell" and "Magic Fire Music"; Chopin, Mazurka in A Minor, Prelude in D Minor, and Waltz in C Sharp Minor; and Canning, *Fantasy on a Hymn Tune of Justin Morgan.* Houston Symphony Orchestra. Everest SDBR-3070.

I am fond of this recording for the Thomas Canning *Fantasy,* which is, as far as I know, the only recording of this piece by the American composer.

The Wagner excerpts have been transferred to Price-Less CD, D 1323X. The remastered Canning has been rereleased by dell' Arte on a 45 RPM long play, DA 9013.

1960: Bartok, Concerto for Orchestra. Houston Symphony Orchestra. Everest SDBR 3069.

From the above two sets made during Stokowski's last year with Houston, dell' Arte in 1983 remastered the Canning *Fantasy* and the Bartok Concerto for Orchestra, coupling them on DA 9013. The sound is superior.

***1960:* Wagner, *Tristan and Isolde:* "Love Music" from Acts 2 and 3 and Falla, *El Amor Brujo,* with soloist Shirley Verrett. Philadelphia Orchestra. Columbia MS 6147.

This is the second of the three long-play excerpts recordings from *Tristan and Isolde* by Stokowski; this one includes his transcription of the "Liebesnacht" from Act 2 and the "Liebestod" from Act 3. The set also contains a near definitive performance of *El Amor Brujo.*

This Columbia set was rereleased as Odyssey Y 32368.

1960: Stokowski Conducts Bach, including *Brandenburg* Concerto no. 5 in D Major and three Chorale Preludes: "Ich Ruf Zu Dir, Herr Jesu Christ," (arr. Stokowski), "Nun Komm Der Heiden Heiland" (arr. Stokowski), and "Wir Glauben All' An Einen Gott" (arr. Stokowski). Philadelphia Orchestra. Columbia MS 6313.

This is the second of the two Columbia recordings made on Stokowski's triumphant return to Philadelphia. To my ears the *Brandenburg* is too lush and too sluggish. As with the dell' Arte LP of Stokowski's 1927–29 Bach recordings, so with the 1960 set: the chorale preludes arranged by Stokowski for orchestra are better and more persuasive performances than those given Bach in the original. This set was later transferred to Odyssey Y 33228.

By 1960 the score and more recordings that Stokowski had made for Everest, Capitol-EMI, and United Artists were history. United Artists ceased making classical discs. Everest turned toward archival digging, and Stokowski and Capitol parted company—although a large number of those releases would remain available on Seraphim and later on remastered black and compact discs.

However, Stokowski had already proven his resilience and Phoenixlike gift during the late fifties and was invited in 1959 to return to Philadelphia for guest appearances in 1960.

In February of 1960 he returned to the Philadelphia podium after nineteen years, playing Mozart's Overture to the *Marriage of Figaro,* Falla's *El Amor Brujo,* with the (then) little-known Shirley Verrett, Shostakovich's Fifth Symphony, and Respighi's *Pines of Rome.*

Emotional, nostalgic, and eminently musical, the reunion brought a standing ovation to end the concert, and as the audience finally quieted down Stokowski spoke to them, getting as far as "As I was saying nineteen years ago . . ." when pandemonium broke loose again.

The following week he returned with three Bach-Stokowski chorale preludes, Brahms's First Symphony, and the maestro's synthesis of the Love Music from *Tristan and Isolde.* Again the magic was there (see Max de Schauensee, "Stokowski Returns After 19 Years," *Musical America,* 80 March 1960: 13).

As in the old days—the twenties and thirties—guest conductor Stokowski and the Philadelphians headed north for an appearance at Carnegie Hall, where Irving Kolodin reported in the March 5 issue of *Saturday Review* that "rapture" was the order of the evening.

What an ideal situation for record making! So believed Schyler Chapin, head of Columbia Masterworks, for whom the orchestra then recorded. However, negotiations with Stokowski were stalled for a time because of a disagreement over Stokowski's royalty fee. As Chapin recalled later, Stokowski had an inflated notion of what he should be paid.

In a take-it-or-leave-it situation the maestro capitulated just days before the recordings were to be made. The recordings—those listed in the two entries above—were drawn from items on his first two programs. At the recording session Stokowski exacted his revenge for what he felt was the earlier monetary slight. Union rules provided for payment of every member of the orchestra for the first two hours of recording. After that, only those actually playing would have to be paid. Since both Wagner—employing the whole orchestra—and Bach—employing a much smaller number of musicians—were on the program for recording, fiscal common sense dictated that they begin with the Wagner, but Stokowski began with Bach, thus leaving the rest of the orchestra sitting around doing nothing.

When Chapin asked why, Stokowski answered that he felt like playing Bach. In the ensuing blow-up Stokowski was ordered to start with Wagner. The Maestro replied that he would walk out if that demand were enforced. In the end Stokowski got his way, costing Columbia a record amount for the session.

Nor was that the end. Stokowski returned some weeks later when the editing and cutting of his tapes was scheduled, announcing that he wanted to oversee the process since he held an ex officio membership for life in the audio engineers' union. Joining his engineer in the booth, he sat down at the controls and took over the job. Getting wind of what was happening, the chief engineer appeared and ordered Stokowski away from the controls, since given the time and place, this was in violation of the engineers' union contract. Reluctantly, Stokowski gave way, and the professional returned to his seat and the controls. Yet Stokowski hovered over him throughout the rest of the process, getting exactly what he wanted in the recording (see Chapin, *Musical Chairs,* 147–50, and Daniel, *Stokowski,* 735–38).

Now here was a conductor who had given of himself freely and *without* fee more frequently than any other major conductor in America. Why did he do what he did in Philadelphia? His egoism was the likely answer. He should receive what he felt he should receive when it came to a major recording company recording with *his* orchestra. Even in seeming to back down, he didn't—to his cost and to ours. Further recordings on Columbia were not to be, if for no other reason than because of Stokowski's behavior over the initial recording.

However, he returned to Philadelphia again and again for guest appearances from 1960 until February of 1969, when he gave his last concert, making a total of fifty concerts in all during that period.

Live recordings of several of these concerts have been released as commercial or society recordings, and I list them below, beginning with 1960 and ending with 1967.

**1960:* Falla, *El Amor Brujo,* with soloist Shirley Verrett. Philadelphia Orchestra. I Grande Concerti GCL 61 (live).

**1949–62:* Wagner, *Rienzi:* Overture, *Tristan and Isolde:* Prelude and "Liebestod" and *Lohengrin:* Prelude to Act 2, with the Philadelphia Orchestra; Birgit Nilsson and George London in arias from Mozart, Borodin, Gounod, Puccini, and Verdi, with the Philadelphia Orchestra; also included is a 1949 concert recording of William Kapell performing the Prokofiev Piano Concerto no. 3 with Stokowski and, I believe, the New York Philharmonic, although the jacket lists the NBC Symphony Orchestra. Melodram 228 (two records, live).

This is a poorly labelled and double-numbered set with no notes. Yet for all of that, beautiful music is the heart of this 1983 release. John Bauman, describing the set in *Fanfare,* 7 (March–April 1984), used superlatives almost exclusively to describe the participants invoking the magical to describe the maestro's part in it. In short, this long-distance coupling from 1949 and from Stokowski's return to Philadelphia in the sixties is well worth finding.

1962: Rimsky-Korsakov, *Scheherazade.* Philadelphia Orchestra. I Grandi Concerti GCL 68 (live).

**1962:* Ciaikovsky, *Romeo e Giulietta,* and Stravinsky, the Suite from *Petruska.* Philadelphia Orchestra. I Grandi Concerti GCL 57 (live).

1967: Mahler, Symphony no. 2 in C Minor, with soprano Veronica Tyler, mezzo soprano Maria Lucia Godoy, and the Singing City Choirs directed by Elaine Brown. Philadelphia Orchestra. Released by the Leopold Stokowski Society on tape cassette only (live).

1960: Dallipiccola, *Il Prigioniero,* with Norman Treigle as the prisoner, Anne McKnight as the mother, and Richard Cassilly as the jailer and the Grand Inquisitor. New York City Opera Orchestra. Private Edition Recording MR 2009 (live).

Another live recording dating from Stokowski's appearance with the New York City Opera Company, this is a unique pairing of one of the oldest operas in the repertory, Monteverdi's *Orfeo,* dating from 1607, with Dallipiccola's *The Prisoner,* completed in the late forties.

Performing at New York's City Center in late September, Stokowski not only conducted both operas, but was also an active participant in planning the staging.

In addition to the performers in *The Prisoner,* those in *Orfeo* included Gerard Souzay as Orfeo and Judith Raskin as Euridice.

Critic Russell Kerr described the twin bill as wholly successful, with generous credit given the maestro for his triple roles, in conducting, in arranging the Monteverdi for stage production, and in providing a strong interpretive thrust in the Dallipiccola opera (see Russell Kerr, "City Center Stages Operas of Monteverdi and Dallipiccola," *Musical Courier,* 162 (November 1960, 14–15).

***1961:* Thomson, *The Plow that Broke the Plains:* A Suite for Orchestra and Suite from *The River.* Symphony of the Air. Vanguard VSD 2095.

Originally written as music to accompany documentary films by Pere Lorentz, the beautiful scores by Virgil Thomson have lived a fruitful life of their own with considerable credit due to Stokowski. He made a prize-winning recording of *The Plow that Broke the Plains* with the Hollywood Bowl Orchestra in 1946 and rerecorded it and *The River* in 1961 to near universal critical acclaim; take for example, Roger Detmer's citation of the recording as a "national treasure" (see *Fanfare*, 7 [November–December 1983], 151).

This set has now been rereleased on a Vanguard compact disc, VBD 385, to the cheers of the critics (see Mark Koldys, *American Record Guide*, 5 (July–August 1988, 63, and Justin Herman, *Fanfare*, 11 May–June 1988, 304).

**1961:* Brahms, Serenade no. 1 in D Major. Symphony of the Air. Varèse Sarabande VC 81050.

Originally released in 1961 as Decca Gold Label DCM 3205 by the Educational Research Division of the company representing "The Age of Romanticism," the Serenade was reissued by Varèse Sarabande a year after Stokowski's death. Playing and sound are spacious and buoyant in this performance. On first appearance the *American Record Guide*, for December, 1961 gave the recording a rave review noting that the maestro's performance represented a first-rate contribution to the art of recorded performance, continuing to describe the performance as vigorous and precise and so clearly defined that it would be hard to imagine a better realization of the score (see C. J. L., *American Record Guide*, December 1961, 284).

***1961: Stokowski Conducts Wagner,* including *Tristan and Isolde:* Prelude to Act 3, *Das Rheingold:* "Entrance of the Gods into Valhalla," *Tannhäuser:* Overture and "Venusberg Music," and *Die Walküre:* "Ride of the Valkyries," with soloists and chorus. Symphony of the Air. RCA LSC 2555. This set was rereleased on RCA Gold Seal in 1976 as AGL 1-1338.

This is one of Stokowski's two finest Wagner sets. It was greeted with critical raves at its initial appearance and again at the time of rerelease. It should appear on compact disc.

With the Brahms and Wagner recordings of 1961 Stokowski ended his conducting and recording activity with the Symphony of the Air (SOA)—which in turn went out of business in 1963. While Stokowski had worked with the orchestra for six years as the SOA, the figure was twenty years, counting back through the NBC Orchestra days. Considering the many fine recordings and performances shared by conductor and orchestra, the feelings of the maestro toward the orchestra and a considerable portion of the orchestra's feelings toward Stokowski were cool at best. Orchestra members who remembered the halcyon days under Toscanini could still remember reports of that conductor's snorted *"Pagliaccio!"*—clown—in describing his rival, Stokowski. Many, during the rocky economic times of the late fifties and early sixties, still saw themselves as upholding the Toscanini tradition. For these musicians, the very fact that they needed Stokowski for his reputation and recording contacts made matters worse.

For his part Stokowski could rightly judge the economically threadbare condition of the SOA, and he felt that many of its players were too old—too old for the kind of orchestral flexibility he had always associated with young and younger players. He was, according to then general manager of the SOA Jerome Toobin, always trying to get younger people into the orchestra while perennially and unhappily facing gray- to white-haired pros who remembered him from the twenties, thirties, and forties.

Toobin recalled a most traumatic incident when these contrary attitudes exploded in an encounter between the maestro and a trumpeter engaged by Toobin for the SOA.

The man had been with Toscanini years before and had a fine reputation. Delighted with his find, Toobin reported his "good news" to Stokowski. Stokowski replied, "That is not good news. He is old." Stokowski was at the time seventy-six. "He played for me in Philadelphia in the 1920s . . . But he is too old . . . That is not good news."

At the first rehearsal subsequent to the hiring, Stokowski went out of his way to consistently rag the player, obviously trying to get on his nerves. Then came the explosion, with the man's shout, "Look, you goddamned has-been, who do you think you are?"

All those present froze.

"This isn't Philadelphia thirty years ago, and you're nobody. You has-been! Wake up; you're nobody."

Stokowski, seated on his high stool, obviously getting what he had been after, made a slow waving motion with his hand in time to "Good aftahnoon suh. Good aftahnoon suh."

As the personnel manager accompanied the trumpeter offstage, Stokowski benignly said, " 'Mista Too-been, can I see you a moment? . . . Can you get that wahn-dah-fool trumpet player who did Wagner with us?' . . . Stoki, sitting placidly on his stool, the only relaxed man on the stage."

So it went in making beautiful music with the Symphony of the Air (see Toobin, *Agitato*, 47–49).

**1961:* Handel, *Water Music* and *Royal Fireworks Music*. RCA Victor Symphony Orchestra. RCA LSC 2612.

First released as RCA Red Seal, this recording was reissued in 1976 on the less expensive Gold Seal series as AGL 1-2704.

Playing with an orchestra of 125 pieces, including twenty-four oboes and twelve bassoons; annotator Charles O'Connell noted that the maestro also added trumpet and horn, snare drum, piccolo, and harpsichord. The set represented a move toward historically Georgian majesty, even as the musical authenticists were calling for and presenting recordings based on eighteenth-century period scoring for far fewer instruments—and instruments characteristic of the period.

As would be expected, Stokowski was generally and roundly trounced by the critics for his travesty of baroque style.

I have the set also on German RCA in its "Master Plays Master" series, where it is coupled with Stokowski's last RCA set of Bach transcriptions in a two-record set, VL 42054. The digitally remastered *Water Music* and *Royal Fireworks Music* have been rereleased (1988) in an RCA Victrola compact disc as 7817-2-RV.

**1961: Stokowski Rhapsodies*, including Liszt, "Hungarian Rhapsody" no. 2; Enesco, "Roumanian Rhapsody" no. 1; and Smetana, "The Moldau" and *The Bartered Bride*: Overture. RCA Victor Symphony Orchestra. RCA LSC-2471.

There is a unity in the recording of these four pieces. Not only are they all concert favorites, but each represents a self-consciously nationalistic glorification of central Europe's culture—Hungarian, Bohemian, and Roumanian. Stokowski, who wrote the program notes for this set, calls attention to this unity in unabashedly emotional prose. Indeed it goes farther than that in the direction of his family romance, since like his fantasy of his grandfather, Stokowski's notes to this set stress Smetana's role as Bohemian freedom fighter, forced to flee his country because of his patriotism. In tune with the conductor's own sense of his artistic identity, he writes of Liszt as an aristocratic artist whose home was the whole world; a man of international cultural standing, yet like both Smetana and Enesco strongly drawn to the folk tradition and spirit of his own ethnic roots. Like Liszt, writes Stokowski, Enesco was always "dreaming" of his homeland no matter where his travels took him, nor what artistic triumphs he achieved. All three, writes the maestro, combined the gift of mining the spiritual riches of their home cultures while expressing those musical riches in a global language readily understood by all—a Stokowski theme of long standing.

For those averse to Stokowski's lyrically dramatic wedding of ethnic fantasy to beautiful music making, this is not a set to look for.

Critic Mortimer H. Frank described the rereleased "Gold Seal" set in 1981 as first-rate evidence of why many in the world of music were contemptuous of the conductor. He magisterially ended his review with the comment that only "blind" Stokowski zealots would find any worth in the set (see Frank, *Fanfare*, 5 September–October 1981, 288).

The set has now been remastered by RCA and included in its "Legendary Performers" series as no. 59, RCA AGL1 5259, for yet another generation of music lovers or "blind" fanatics, depending upon your point of view.

1961: Hallelujah! The World's Great Choruses, including selections by Bach, Humperdinck, Handel, and Wagner. Norman Luboff Choir and the New Symphony of London. RCA LSC 2593.

Originally recorded by RCA, the set was rereleased in 1976 on the Quintessence label as PMC 7019. Of the twelve performances on this set seven are led by Robert Shaw and five by Stokowski, which are: Wagner, *Tannhäuser:* "Pilgrim's Chorus"; Bach, "Jesu, Joy of Man's Desiring" (arr. Luboff) and "That Sheep May Safely Graze"; Humperdinck, *Hansel and Gretel:* "Evening Prayer" (arr. Luboff); and Handel, *Xerxes:* Largo.

1961: Puccini, *Turandot,* with soloists Birgit Nilsson, Franco Corelli, and Anna Moffo. Metropolitan Opera Orchestra and Chorus. Accord, ACC 150038 (live, three records).

The background to this performance recording is harrowing. Dimitri Mitropoulos, who was scheduled to conduct the Metropolitan Opera's *Turandot* in February 1961, suffered a fatal heart attack on 2 November 1960 while rehearsing Mahler in Milan.

Stokowski had never before conducted at the Metropolitan, but the maestro had done *Carmina Burana* and Stravinsky's *Oedipus Rex* for the New York City Opera in the 1959–60 season and Dallapiccola's *The Prisoner* and Monteverdi's *Orfeo* in the fall of 1960—all to very good reviews.

In this time of emergency Rudolph Bing contacted Stokowski about conducting *Turandot,* and the maestro accepted before the end of November. The next trauma occurred when stage director Yoshio Aoyama underwent surgery in Tokyo in December. Then, at the end of the month, the seventy-nine-year-old Stokowski broke his hip playing touch football with his sons.

Not only was he still committed to doing *Turandot* in less than two months, but he was to appear in concerts with the Philadelphia Orchestra at the same time, doing—among other things—Schoenberg's massive *Gurrelieder.*

That he met both responsibilities is history. He gave nine performances of *Turandot* and six performances of *Gurrelieder* within three weeks' time, commuting back and forth from New York to Philadelphia by train and crutch and nursing an artifical hip joint.

Prior to opening *Turandot* he also battled Rudolph Bing over the production, which was hectic. But *Turandot* went on as scheduled to rave reviews and, except for Bing's own account, Stokowski was given major credit for its success.

Robert Sabin, in *Musical America*, described it as a triumph for Stokowski. The *Musical Courier* correspondent wrote that Stokowski's vision of the opera was a potent one, with musical direction to match his convictions.

Irving Kolodin, in his history of the Metropolitan Opera, noted the difference in the sound of the pit orchestra and of the chorus when directed by Stokowski, while the conductor also exerted a beneficent effect on the self-importance of Franco Correlli as the young prince.

Eight performances were given in New York during February and March, with the company giving one at the Philadelphia Academy of Music on 21 March 1961.

As a post script to his account, Kolodin noted that when this production of *Turandot* was brought back in 1961–62, without Stokowski, its structure began to disintegrate.

Quaintance Eaton, in his own Met history, described the 1961–62 return as a production that declined rapidly (see Robert Sabin, "Stokowski Conducts New Turandot," *Musical America*, 81 March 1961, 30–31. Kolodin, *The Metropolitan Opera*, 628, 641–47, 671–72, and Eaton, *The Miracle of the Met*, 322–23).

As an aftermath to *Turandot* Stokowski was interviewed by Frank Merkling a year later as to why the maestro did so little opera. In brief, Stokowski's answer centered on the need for as much attention spent on the dramatic elements of opera production as on the musical. He had done this in the twenties and thirties with skilled directors handling the dramatic side while he, Stokowski, concentrated on the music (see chap. 3); but he had never since found that kind of support nor opera companies willing to allow proper rehearsal time. The finest performances were possible only if the drama and the music were considered coequally important and treated accordingly, said Stokowski. (See Leopold Stokowski-Frank Merkling, "What's Wrong with Opera," 26 *Opera News*, 24 February 1962, 8–13).

This last points again to the fact that Stokowski claimed to be and was a dramatist in music (see chap. 2) and saw things with the eyes of a director as well as those of a musician and conductor. Indeed, that is the greatest strength of this live recording. Its sound is only fair to passable, but the music and theater of *Turandot* are synchronized and given dramatic point.

**1961–67: The Best of Stokowski*, including Mozart, Serenade no. 10 in B-flat for 13 Winds (1966); Bach, "Jesu, Joy of Man's Desiring" and "That Sheep May Safely Graze" (1967); Vivaldi, Concerto Grosso in D Minor (1967); and Stravinsky, *L'Histoire du Soldat* (1966). Leopold Stokowski Symphony Orchestra, the Symphony of the Air, and the American Symphony Orchestra. Vanguard VSD 707/8 (two records).

When Stokowski left the American Symphony Orchestra and America in 1972 to live and work in England, he left a legacy of recordings made for the Vanguard Recording Society from his 1961 recording of *The Plow That Broke the Plains* up to and beyond the baroque set of 1967. From these recordings, made with several ensembles over a fifteen year period, Vanguard assembled this two record-set. Although I have listed these recordings separately within their individual years of issuance, *The Best of Stokowski* is so choice an item that I thought it worth its own entry.

1962: Beethoven, Symphony no. 2 in D Major, and Brahms, Variations on a Theme of Haydn. Chicago Symphony Orchestra. A 1962 telecast performance privately recorded and released by the Leopold Stokowski Society in 1981 as LS4.

According to annotator Stephen G. Smith, this recording of the Beethoven symphony was virtually dictated by the quality of the live performance, but note as well that the sound is very poor.

1963: Dawson, *Negro Folk Symphony.* American Symphony Orchestra. Varèse Sarabande VC 81056.

Composer William Dawson, born into a poor Alabama family, ran away from home at thirteen to get an education at Tuskegee Institute. Early music training at the institute eventually led to a master's degree in music at the American Conservatory of Music in Chicago and a triumphant return to Tuskegee in 1930 as music director. His *Negro Folk Symphony* was begun in the twenties and finished two years after his return to Tuskegee.

Stokowski, impressed by the work and, quite likely, by the determination of Dawson, gave the work its world premiere in 1934 with the Philadelphia Orchestra, against the wishes of the board, which had attempted a moratorium on contemporary works because of the depression (see chap. 3).

Thirty years later Stokowski chose this work as the inaugural recording with his new orchestra, the American Symphony Orchestra. Recorded for Decca Gold Label on DL 10077 in 1963, Dawson's symphony appeared on the centennial anniversary of the emancipation proclamation. Although later dropped from the record catalog, the recording was returned to circulation in 1976 in a remastered set by Varèse Sarabande.

The Dawson symphony recording provides a fitting entrée to the ten rewarding years during which the maestro was music director of the American Symphony Orchestra. With some foundation backing, the generous support of angels such as Sam and Cyma Rubin, and the public subscription of many small donations as well as the thousands of dollars pumped into the organization by Stokowski himself, the orchestra was born and flourished under Stokowski's direction. For his direction and services, the conductor received no fee.

To find musicians Stokowski consulted his little black book for trained professionals in the New York area to act as cadre for youngsters, who would make up the rest of the ensemble. As for the young players themselves, Stokowski gave auditions, some twenty-five hundred, for those who wanted to try out. The results of those auditions, held from three to five on weekday afternoons, were put into his book. He kept up this practice long after the founding of the orchestra in 1962, since the American Symphony was to be a training ground, a school for players who might be with him a year and then be hired by established orchestras. The same went for budding conductors who, remembered Ainslee Cox, received countless hours of Stokowski's time in seminars on conducting—among them Cox himself, Judith Somogyi, José Serebrier and Matthias Bamert.

What Cox, who became assistant and then associate conductor with Stokowski, remembered most vividly from those sessions included Stokowski's disinclination to teach particular interpretive approaches to works being considered. Instead, he described the search for interpretive approach as an aid to self-discovery for each of his very different charges. His most common response to conducting questions was to ask the questioner how he or she thought a particular piece should be done. To Stokowski there was no right way to conduct which could be taught, but he could help along the process of self-discovery, offer pointers, and congratulate the tyro who found his or her way interpretively and in matters of technique.

There would be no clones, no Stokowski school of conducting, but, wrote Cox, there were Stokowskian emphases: on youth, which to the maestro was a state of mind based on commitment and vitality; on individualism, the uniqueness of the personality of each person in making music; and in living in the present, concentrating on today's projects without forebodings about the future and recriminations from the past. To the maestro the past was gone, the present was here, and the future beckoned.

But what about musical tradition as a part of the past?, queried Cox on one occasion. Chuckling, Stokowski answered anecdotally with an apocryphal story about his grandfather's tailor, who had once made clothes for a gentleman who lived in a house next to one once occupied by Beethoven. Therefore, concluded the maestro, the true Beethoven style is mine. Letting that sink in, Stokowski concluded with a chuckle, noting that the score, not tradition, was what one needed to make music.

The nontraditional approach of the maestro ran the gamut from free bowing, free blowing, and the use of experimental percussion, orchestral reseating, and acoustics to experiments with individual instruments such as using the tam-tam triple pianissimo to reinforce a harmony or attaching contact microphones to the basses for increased sonority. Such practices went in tandem with his adventurous programming of the very old with avant-garde music and with inviting guest performers such as the nineteen-year-old Lynn Harrell as cello soloist, the twenty-five-year-old Ruth Laredo as piano soloist, and a twenty-six-year-old Zubin Mehta as guest conductor. Mehta was so little known in 1963 that the *New Yorker*'s Winthrop Sargeant described him as a Hindu as well as a young conductor to watch in the future.

Underpinning the premieres, first appearances, and musical experiments were those Stokowski psychological gifts described in chapter 2. Ainslee Cox would describe Stokowski's ability to make requests of orchestra members and to project his musical wishes with a look. Henry Levinger of *Musical America* would describe as miraculous how Stokowski could make the orchestra sound in his image. Andrew De Rhen, in *High Fidelity-Musical America*, proved torn between the eccentricities of Stokowski's idiosyncratic reading of Schuman's Symphony no. 2 and the beautiful playing he inexplicably evoked from his young charges yet again. How does he do it? asked de Rhen. Whatever his method, no other orchestral leader can duplicate it.

By the late sixties Stokowski, the "has been" of the middle fifties, had made the American Symphony Orchestra, one of America's most stimulating orchestras. So extolled the lead editorial in the December 1967 issue of *High Fidelity*, naming him its musician of the year. In quick succession Stokowski was awarded the Golden Baton Award for 1968 and the first International Montreux Award, the *Diploma d'Honneur* for his contribution to music and to recording. This was granted by eleven critics from eight nations and awarded to Stokowski by another polymorphously gifted artist, Peter Ustinov.

In 1968 the orchestra's activities were outlined for interviewer Martin Bookspan by orchestra manager Stewart Warkow. Just as Stokowski's young musicians from the 1940–41 All American Youth Orchestra were now to be found everywhere in music, so graduates of the American Symphony Orchestra were already playing with the Amsterdam Concertgebouw orchestra, the Netherlands Chamber Orchestra, the Cleveland and Chicago Orchestras, the New York Philharmonic, and many others.

Its mix of ethnic and racial minorities was unique as was the number of women players. In the orchestra could be found father and son, husband and wife, and brother and sister combinations.

While the regular number of subscription concerts had been increased steadily over the years since 1962, the maestro had spurred the development of children's concerts, concerts geared to teenagers and young adults, and concerts for working-class men and women who had never had the chance earlier to hear live symphonic music. The senior citizen series of concerts for those sixty-five and over had been visited and praised by Lady Bird Johnson.

A chamber orchestra jointly organized by the maestro and interested players gave special concerts in New York area veterans' hospitals. This last series, noted Warkow, was not only conducted by Stokowski, but was completely paid for by the maestro.

Caught up in the conductor's enthusiasm and gift for organizing, the players had, on their own, formed a string quartet, a quintet, and a harp duo to give musicales for fund raising purposes and for community education. Furthermore, during the 1966–67 season they had organized for softball in Central Park with the orchestra's men vs. the women, and with maestro Stokowski acting as umpire. American Symphony audiences were invited to the announced games. Warkow noted that the orchestra ball players—men and women united—had issued a challenge to the New York Philharmonic players, but received no answer.

In this fountain of youthful creativity, we can also identify Stokowski's gifts at their clearest as they mirror in real life the clinical discussion of the romancer-as-artist-as-creator in its most playful and creative manifestation. But it had to end, even as the ninety-year-old conductor finally grew tired of the increasing administrative duties carried over a ten year period. Then, too, although Stokowski had made records with his orchestra, from the Dawson Symphony in 1963 to a last controversial and dazzling recording of Tchaikovsky's Fourth Symphony in 1971, recording costs had grown and it became more and more difficult for free-lancer Stokowski to get recording dates in America. However, his European recordings had grown in number and in critical acceptance. For these reasons, and, I think, more personal reasons, he decided to leave the orchestra and return to England, making his announcement in May of 1972:

> Because of the impossibility of recording in the United States it is necessary for me now to record in Europe. For this reason I shall only be able to conduct the first pair of concerts for the '72–'73 season. Since I am leaving next week for Europe, and will return only for those concerts, it is necessary for me to resign as Music Director . . .

He left a vibrant and lively orchestra to govern itself. And although his leaving was traumatic, the orchestra continued, and as I sit at my work table with their recording of Morton Gould's *Burchfield Gallery* on the turn table, the same orchestra remains a part of New York's cultural life. (See Ainslee Cox, "Essay," in *Stokowski: Essays*, ed. Johnson, 18–26. Leopold Stokowski, "What is the American Symphony Orchestra?" in Seltzer, *The Professional Symphony Orchestra*, 67–68. Warkow, interview with Bookspan. *Musical America*, 82 December 1962, 25–28; 83 June 1963, 24; 83 November 1963, 25. *High Fidelity-*

Musical America, 16 July 1966, MA 17; 17 December 1967; MA 7–8; 21 January 1971, MA 12–13. Winthrop Sargeant, "Musical Events," *New Yorker*, 39 6 April 1963, 116–18; 39 19 October 1963, 201–3; 39 23 February 1963, 137–38).

**1964*: Canteloube, *Songs of the Auvergne*; Villa-Lobos, *Bachianas Brasileiras* no. 5; and Rachmaninoff, "Vocalise," with soloist Anna Moffo. American Symphony Orchestra. RCA LSC 2795.

This is a colorful performance of the Canteloube songs matched by the Stokowski-Moffo partnership in Villa-Lobos and Rachmaninoff. The set has been rereleased by RCA on its Gold Seal label, while the "Vocalise" has been released yet again on RCA Gold Seal GL 42923 with Stokowski's 1968 Chicago Symphony Orchestra recordings of Khachaturian's Symphony no. 3 and Rimsky-Korsakov's *Russian Easter* Overture. The latest incarnation of the 1964 set finds the Cantaloube, the Villa-Lobos, and the Rachmaninoff selections all back together again on RCA Gold Seal compact disc, 7831-2-RG, released in 1988.

***1964*: Rimsky-Korsakov, *Scheherazade*. London Symphony Orchestra. London SPC 21005.

This is Stokowski's first Phase 4 recording for London and a classic performance of *Scheherazade*. Producer Marty Wargo, who also wrote liner notes for the set, recalled that Stokowski's understanding of the possibilities of Phase 4's twenty recording channels was immediate. Stokowski's suggestions in the areas of microphone placement, seating, acoustics, and sound levels, indeed in all aspects of the process, from first rehearsal to final editing, were both practical and inventive. The results were an outstanding *Scheherazade*. By turns sensuous, ferocious, and majestic, each phrase shaped in sonority and color makes this a poetic delight. In interpretation it is quite unlike Stokowski's 1975 recording for RCA and those of its chief rivals in 1964, the recordings by Sir Thomas Beecham and Ernest Ansermet. The American Record Guide for March, 1965 rated Stokowski's reading as without question "the best," adding that Stokowski was without peer in understanding the work. Other critics expressed horror at the recording because of its lack of what they called concert hall realism and because of Stokowski's interpretive touches.

From our own vantage point we can understand just how close romancer Stokowski was to this score and why he lavished so much feeling and care in its performance on this recording as well as on the other four recordings he made of it. (see also R. D. Darrell, "Stokowski's Scheherazade from All of Phase 4's Twenty Channels," *High Fidelity*, 15 March 1965, 87–88).

This set, coupled with the 1969 "Polovtsian Dances" from Borodin's *Prince Igor* and the 1973 *Capriccio Espagnole* by Rimsky-Korsakov, has been transferred to compact disc as London 417 753-2.

***1965*: Ives, Symphony no. 4. American Symphony Orchestra. Columbia ML 6175.

This set was rereleased in 1983 in the Masterworks Portrait series and coupled with the *Robert Browning* Overture.

Not only was this a landmark recording, but Stokowski's twin entrepreneurial efforts, first to raise the money to rehearse and premiere the work and then to raise additional funding to pay for its recording by Columbia—since Columbia was too timid to venture its own capital—were remarkable. Such feats by an eighty-five-year-old with a young symphony orchestra represented a considerable and unique accomplishment in American music.

The music is challenging and beautiful. Stokowski, the cosmic idealist, was at home with Ives, the New England transcendentalist, and was worthy, I think, of Glenn Gould's tribute to him in *High Fidelity*, that we were once again in debt to this "superb artist" for bringing us into contact with the important and controversial music of our time. (See Gould, "The Ives Fourth," *High Fidelity* 15 July 1965, 96–97).

1965: Ives, *Robert Browning* Overture, included in *The World of Charles Ives*. American Symphony Orchestra. Columbia MS 7015.

The world premiere of this piece was given by Stokowski and the Symphony of the Air in 1956. The American Symphony Orchestra recording, like that of the Ives Fourth Symphony, was made possible by the conductor's efforts at getting grant money to cover recording costs.

**1965:* Mussorgsky-Stokowski, *Pictures at an Exhibition*, and Debussy-Stokowski, "Engulfed Cathedral." New Philharmonia Orchestra. London SPC 21006.

The Stokowski transcription of Mussorgsky is not equal in musical sophistication to that of Maurice Ravel. It is, however, a worthwhile attempt at emotional-musical realization of the romantic, slavic Mussorgsky that Stokowski admired so much. Writing in the *American Record Guide*, Arthur Cohn reminded his readers that in addition to Ravel's transcription of the piece, Lucien Caillet, Alfredo Cassela, Sir Henry Wood, Leon Leonardi, and Walter Goehr had all done like transcriptions. Among such competitors, Stokowski's was a fine and most colorful arrangement of Mussorgsky's music, requiring virtuosi performances from the players (see Cohn, "Mussorgsky-Stokowski," *American Record Guide* 32, March 1966, 604–5).

The Mussorgsky-Stokowski transcription has been rereleased by London in its "Treasury" series as STS 15558 in a coupling with Stokowski's 1969 recording of Tchaikovsky's *1812* Overture.

The "Engulfed Cathedral" at Ys pictured by Debussy as rising from the sea, its bell tolling, becomes for Stokowski, figuratively speaking, the whole city of Atlantis in his larger-than-life transcription and performance. I would think this conception a direct result of Stokowski's musical skills wedded to his fantasy life as romancer, although its performance owes much to Stokowski's peculiar magic with the orchestra. Whether one likes the transcription or not, it is technically masterful in achieving what the maestro was after.

The Stokowski recording of the "Engulfed Cathedral" has now been sumptuously transferred to London compact disc 417 779-2. The transcription has also appeared on CD in Erich Kunzel's set, *The Stokowski Sound*, performed by the Cincinnati Pops Orchestra, Telarc CD-80129.

1965: Tchaikovsky, *Swan Lake* and *Sleeping Beauty*, selections. New Philharmonia Orchestra. London SPC 21008.

**1965:* Josten, Concerto *Sacro I-II*, with pianist David Del Tredici. American Symphony Orchestra. Composers Recording Inc., CRI SD 200.

Wermer Josten—three years older than Stokowski—was a part of the League of Composers circle in the late twenties. When Stokowski premiered Stravinsky's *Les Noces* at the Met in 1929, the second half of the program was conducted by Werner Josten, a performance of Monteverdi's *Il Combattimento di Trancredi e Clorinda*. Stokowski was impressed by Josten as both musician and composer. He had premiered Josten's Concerto Sacro I and his tone poem, *The Jungle*, in Philadelphia in the late twenties. Premiere recordings were not made, however, until the sixties and seventies. Of the five Josten pieces listed in the *Schwann Guide* at the time of writing, four are by Stokowski on the CRI label.

1966: Handel, *Messiah*, Selections, with soloists Sheila Armstrong, Norma Procter, Kenneth Bowen, and John Cameron. London Symphony Orchestra and Chorus. London SPC 21014.

**1966:* Vivaldi, *The Four Seasons*. New Philharmonia Orchestra. London SPC 21015.

This set has been rereleased as London 417072-4 LT.

In an essay on the surfeit of *Four Seasons* recordings—some ninety at the date of writing—Don Vroon, editor of the *American Record Guide*, cited the Stokowski recording as a counter to the increasingly "dry and astringent" recordings of the piece by period authenticists, whom Vroon dubbed "Puritans." Of the contrast Vroon wrote, "I wouldn't give it [the Stokowski recording] up for the entire catalog of period instruments. Stokowski was a greater musical mind (and heart) than all of them put together" (see Vroon, "Four Seasons Glut," *American Record Guide*, 51 September–October 1988, 8).

**1966:* Tchaikovsky, Symphony no. 5 in E Minor. New Philharmonia Orchestra. London SPC 21017.

Here is idiosyncratic Tchaikovsky played with color, precision, and great intensity.

**1966: Stokowski-Wagner, Die Walküre:* "Ride of the Valkyries," *Siegfried:* "Forest Murmurs," *Das Rheingold*: "Entrance of the Gods into Valhalla," and *Die Götterdämmerung*: "Siegfried's Rhine Journey," "Death" and "Funeral Music," London Symphony Orchestra. London SPC 21016.

Beginning in 1957 and running through the sixties into the early seventies Stokowski developed the pattern of recording in Europe during the spring and summer months, thus leaving the fall and winter free for the American Symphony Orchestra season and guest appearances with other American orchestras. Most of his European recordings were made with English orchestras and most of the English recordings were made with the London Symphony Orchestra, to which Stokowski had a special tie dating back to 1957.

This Wagner set, rereleased in 1982 as Treasury series STS 15565, was recorded after only one rehearsal. The recording itself was described by concert master John Georgiadis as singular, in that the recording represented a take of the program piece by piece with Stokowski neither stopping the orchestra nor conferring with the producer or the engineer as to corrections to be made or repeats needed. At the end of the session the maestro told the players he would listen to the takes to see if anything needed to be redone and sent them home. That was it.

While the set as a whole was a good one, the "Siegfried's Rhine Journey" was the finest that Stokowski committed to modern long-play recordings. Of his own work as solo horn in that piece, Barry Tuckwell described himself as "mesmerized" by the maestro into playing beyond himself (see Georgiadis, "Essay," in Johnson (ed.), *Stokowski: Essays*, 34, and Chasins, Leopold Stokowski 227–28, 275).

This set, together with the live *Die Meistersinger*: Prelude to Act 1 from the "Sixtieth Anniversary Concert" (1972) is now available as London CD 421 020-Z on compact disc.

**1966:* Beethoven, Concerto no. 5 in E-flat Major with soloist Glenn Gould. American Symphony Orchestra. Columbia MS 6888.

This is a unique interpretation of the *Emperor* Concerto because it is so deliberate—slow but not ponderous—with the pianist playing obligato to the orchestral portion of the work. Gould, who had the greatest admiration for Stokowski, brought to the conductor an extremely fast conception and an extremely slow interpretation of the concerto as possibilities for their recording. With Gould taking the lead, they settled on a meditative interpretation, which was generally panned by critics at the time, although the concerto was beautifully performed by soloist and orchestra. Gould's later commentary on Stokowski carried in it latent wonder that this eighty-four-year-old could be so daring and so young in spirit. The recording was reissued by Columbia in 1983 in its Masterworks Portrait series as MP 3888 (see Gould, "Stokowski in Six Scenes," 269–76.

**1966:* Stravinsky, *L' Histoire du Soldat (The Soldier's Tale)*, is available in the following versions: Narration with actors and music, done in an English version and in a separate version in French, both versions with Madelaine Milhaud, narrator, Jean Pierre Aumont, the soldier, Martial Singher, the devil, with instrumental ensemble, Vanguard VSD-71165 (in French) and VSD-71166 (in English) and released respectively in two record sets. The French version was released separately in yet two more series: as a Vanguard Cardinal disc, VCS 10121, with text and notes in English; and as Festival Classique FC 442 without text, but with notes in French, German and English, which was intended for general European distribution. Finally, the purely instrumental portion of the work was released in Vanguard's later set, *The Best of Stokowski*, VSD-707-708.

Stokowski had a long affinity for the work, going back to 1918 when he performed it in Philadelphia shortly after its European premiere with Ernest Ansermet conducting. This 1966 set was the first American concert recording to employ the new Dolby noise reduction system. Vanguard's president, Seymour Solomon, produced and supervised the recording (see *High Fidelity*, 17 February 1967, 16, 21). When released it was met by enthusiastic reviews.

1966: Mozart, Serenade in B-flat for Thirteen Wind Instruments. American Symphony Orchestra Wind Players. Vanguard VSD 71158.

1967: "Jesu, Joy of Man's Desiring:" A Baroque Concert, including selections by Bach, Vivaldi, and Corelli. Leopold Stokowski Symphony Orchestra. Vanguard SRV 363 SD.

This set has now been rereleased as a compact disc, Vanguard VBD 363. In a more than positive review, critic Mark Koldys described the set as splended but—with two transcriptions included and modern instruments used—not for everybody. Yet again the litany of Stokowski's mastery of sound and performance was repeated and described as wizardry (see *American Record Guide*, 51 September–October 1988, 116–17).

On a more personal note Mr. Igor Kipnis, who played continuo for these recordings, shared his own reminiscences of Stokowski with me by phone and in a cassette he was kind enough to send me.

Before playing with Stokowski, Kipnis described himself as no fan of the maestro, certainly not in the baroque literature; but in performing with him Kipnis said he was delighted with the unique sense of freedom given him by Stokowski to ornament the works performed beyond simply providing continuo. With Stokowski urging him to play, what Stokowski called, "*im-*

provisato," Kipnis recalled that he felt so free in improvisation that at one point in an early playback of "Jesu, Joy of Man's Desiring", the results sounded like a "concerto for harpsichord." This same sense of freedom pervaded his other performances in the set as well, according to Kipnis.

Kipnis said his ideas about Stokowski had been markedly changed from negative to positive by the experience (Kipnis, telephone conversations with the author and cassette of reminiscences of working with Stokowski in 1967).

**1967*: Ives, *Majority (or the Masses), They Are There (A War Song March), An Election (It Strikes Me That)*, and *Lincoln The Great Commoner*, with the Gregg Smith Singers and the Ithaca College Concert Choir. American Symphony Orchestra. Included in *Charles Ives: The 100th Anniversary*, Columbia M 4 32504 (four records).

Along with Leonard Bernstein and Lou Harrison, Stokowski presided over many of the concert offerings of Ives's music in the fifties and early sixties—although the grand old man of Ives premieres remains Nicolas Slonimsky. Premieres by Stokowski with the Houston Symphony Orchestra, the Symphony of the Air, and the CBS Symphony helped bring Ives's music to general public attention. To conductors' complaints that Ives's scores were too difficult, Henry Cowell noted that those who claimed they needed six or eight rehearsals of the "Washington's Birthday" to make it playable should consider the example of Stokowski, who in 1954 performed it well on CBS radio with but one rehearsal. Cowell and Ives's widow, Harmony, have recounted Stokowski's regular Sunday morning phone calls about the composer's unusual musical touches in the score of the Fourth Symphony, which Stokowski was working on in preparation for the world premiere in April of 1965. That premiere and the subsequent recording of the work by Stokowski were for Mrs. Ives deeply satisfying as another vindication of her husband's career as composer. Of the selections recorded here two years after that premiere, two are recording firsts: *They Are There* and *An Election*. All four are slighter works than the symphonies, but exuberantly Ivesian in spirit and philosophy. Their themes range from the rock-ribbed New England democracy of *Majority* to Ives's idealistic tributes to two of his heroes, Abraham Lincoln and Woodrow Wilson. The performances and engineering are first-rate (see Cowells, *Charles Ives*, 130, 215).

**1967*: Nielson, Symphony no. 2, *The Four Temperaments*. Danish Radio Symphony Orchestra, including interview with Stokowski by Hans Hansen. Poco DLP 8407 (live).

This is a persuasive portrait in sound of the four temperaments—choleric, phlegmatic, melancholic, and sanguine—in which Stokowski showed as positively ferocious in interpreting anger. Gregors Dirckinck-Holmfeld, reviewing the concert for the Danish press, wrote that Stokowski didn't seem to do anything unusual on the podium, but he was told by musicians in the orchestra that Stokowski did something with his eyes that made them grip their bows tighter (see liner notes on Poco DLP 8407).

There is one other thing about this recording very much worth noting. Stokowski's interview with Hans Hansen is so stiff and wooden as to be a parody of the genre with nothing more than the most conventional and banal of facts and sentiments expressed. Why is this worth commenting on then? Because it is not atypical of Stokowski interviews, but rather consistent in interview after interview given by the maestro over the years. The most recent of many I've studied in my own work on Stokowski is one given over San

Francisco radio in 1936 as a part of the Philadelphia Orchestra's transcontinental tour. The interviewer was firmly committed to trying to get Stokowski to talk about himself as a person, while Stokowski turned every question into a blah-blah answer about the tour, the beauties of San Francisco and so forth. So persistent was his questioner, however, that Stokowski, while still answering in cliché, betrayed both agitation and fear at this kind of probing into who he really was. To the end, he told his questioner nothing.

I have read and heard the accounts of those who either knew little about Stokowski or were hostile, who, rather gleefully, have described Stokowski's talk as nothing more than clichés and platitudes, thus in line with many of the public statements and interviews he gave. But research about the man indicates something quite different. Reminiscences of those with whom he felt at home, safe in his differentness, reveal a very different person. Glenn Gould's 1969 conversation with Stokowski, transcribed for later publication, reveals interesting and unusual points of view on the part of Stokowski about life and music as does a portion of his interview with Lyman Bryson. Sylvan Levin, Abram Chasins, and Paul Hoeffler (a Stokowski confidante in the sixties responsible for recording many of the live concerts of the American Symphony Orchestra) all told me that Stokowski could be conversationally fascinating, but only when he chose to be and then only when he felt comfortable with those around him. Elizabeth DeYoung Levin described Stokowski for me as wary and cautious around all those he didn't know, and most cautious around those he distrusted. His reason: personal vulnerability. Paul Hoeffler was more blunt in telling me that Stokowski had been "stabbed in the back" so often that early on he devised the simplistic interview response for self protection.

For me this is a piece in the personal and musical jigsaw puzzle of Stokowski's life that fits perfectly with what we know of his unusual gifts and equally unusual philosophy and identity.

So the Hansen interview in its banal way is important for what it represents, not for what Stokowski said. It is one more example of a facade used by Stokowski to protect his artistic identity and his "inner life" from what he thought of as snoopers, while sometimes in interview creating deadpan mischief to generate the effect of mystification. (Chasins, interview with the author; Levins, interview with the author; Hoeffler, telephone conversation with the author; Stokowski, conversation with Glenn Gould; Stokowski, interview with Lyman Bryson.)

1967: Mahler, Symphony no. 2, *Resurrection*, with soloists Rae Woodland and Janet Baker, the BBC Chorus, BBC Choral Society, Goldsmiths' Choral Union, Harrow Choral Society, and the London Symphony Orchestra. Penzance Records PR 19 N (live).

1967: Stravinsky, *Petrouchka* Suite (live), and Kodaly, *Hary Janos* Suite, performed respectively by the Budapest Symphony Orchestra and the Hungarian State Radio Orchestra. Leopold Stokowski Society. LS 2.

Recorded by Hungarian radio during Stokowski's annual off-season conducting tour, this set includes an interview with the maestro.

**1967:* Beethoven, Symphony no. 9 in D, with soloists Heather Harper, Helen Watts, Alexander Young, and Donald McIntyre. London Symphony Orchestra and Chorus. London SPC 21043

During the last years of his life, Stokowski recorded the Third, the Fifth, the

Seventh, and the Ninth symphonies of Beethoven on the London and RCA labels. Of these only this recording of the Ninth has, so far, been transferred to compact disc on London 421 636-2.

Upon its initial appearance, Harris Goldsmith described this recording of the Ninth as "splendid," with engineering and sound to match, a recording to have for one's own. Upon its rerelease in the London Treasure series in the eighties, Mortimer H. Frank praised the performance, adding that the "tasteless" extrovert of Mickey Mouse fame was capable of doing fine Beethoven, as he did in this performance (Harris Goldsmith, review in *High Fidelity,* 20 August 1970, 74. Mortimer H. Frank's review of the rerelease is from *Fanfare,* 6 January–February 1983, 110).

**1967*: Stravinsky, *Firebird* Suite; Tchaikovsky, "Marche Slav"; and Mussorgsky, "Night on Bald Mountain." London Symphony Orchestra. London SPC 21026.

Demons, princes, and romantic slavicism in general are given a mighty ride in this long-playing vehicle. When it was rereleased by Musical Heritage in 1984 it was described as romantic story telling at its most colorful.

Tempi, dynamics, and orchestration have been altered. The romancer's vision of each piece has been served to the delight of some and the musical horror of others.

John Georgiadis, violinist and section leader of the London Symphony Orchestra for the recording, described working with the conductor as very "exciting." After taking note of Stokowski's alterations in the score, Georgiadis, almost defiantly, discounted the changes, writing that Stokowski's performance with the orchestra forgave everything in the sheer drama of his reading and that he felt it a privilege to have worked with the maestro. (See Teal, ed., *Leopold Stokowski,* sec. 5. Georgiadis, "Essay," in Johnson, (ed.), *Stokowski: Essays,* 35.)

These recordings, coupled with Stokowski's 1968 London recordings of the Tchaikovsky Overture-Fantasy *Romeo and Juliet* and the *Boris Godunov* Synthesis, have been rereleased by Musical Heritage Society in a two-record set, MHS 827052Z.

1968: Mussorgsky, *Boris Godunov:* Symphonic Synthesis, and Tchaikovsky, *Romeo and Juliet.* L'orchestre de la Suisse Romande. London SPC 21032.

The *Romeo and Juliet* seems pale compared to the 1949 recording with the New York Philharmonic Orchestra, even with its poor sound. Nor does the synthesis performance come close to the 1936 Philadelphia recording.

**1968*: Shostakovich, *The Age of Gold:* Ballet Suite and Symphony no. 6. Chicago Symphony Orchestra. RCA LSC-3133.

The Age of Gold, with its satirical line and colorful instrumentation, is a brash statement of the young Shostakovich, akin to the First Symphony. The Sixth Symphony, premiered and first recorded by Stokowski with the Philadelphia Orchestra in 1940—particularly the opening Largo movement—is dark and personally tragic. Stokowski's collaboration with the Chicago Orchestra pops and crackles in the ballet score while empathetically underlining the lyric pathos, the darkness, of the symphony. It is a fine performance by all concerned. The recording has been rereleased on RCA Gold Seal as AGL 1-5063.

1968: Berlioz, *Symphonie Fantastique.* New Philharmonia Orchestra. London SPC 21031.

Somehow one expects more from the combination of Stokowski and Berlioz than this recording delivers. That extra something—call it poetry—can be heard in the maestro's live performance of the work with the youthful American Symphony Orchestra. Noncommercially recorded on 26 April 1970 in Carnegie Hall, the recording on cassette tape only, is available from Classical Recordings Archive of America, El Cerrito, California.

1968: Khachaturian, Symphony no. 3, and Rimsky-Korsakov, *Russian Easter* Overture. Chicago Symphony Orchestra. RCA LSC-3067.

The *Russian Easter* Overture, like Tchaikovsky's *1812* Overture, is an exuberant, quasi-nationalistic, and very sentimental piece of music. Stokowski's fondness for it can be measured in his four recordings. The first recording with the Philadelphia Orchestra was made available for a while in RCA's two-record commemorative package of Stokowski's Philadelphia years. The fourth and last recording is this one with the additional sheen of up-to-date engineering and the Chicago's gleaming virtuosity. The other piece in this set, Khachaturian's Third Symphony, is the album's headliner—yet another Stokowski premiere. But the Khachaturian, billed in the liner notes as a "colossal" work is, to my ears, a colossal bore, albeit beautifully performed.

This set, too, was rereleased on RCA Gold Seal in 1979 as GL 42923, with the added bonus of Anna Moffo's lovely 1964 performance of Rachmaninoff's "Vocalise," with Stokowski and the American Symphony Orchestra.

1968: Kodaly, *Te Deum*, with soloists Joyce Mathis, Ivan Myhal, Arthur Williams, and Alan Ord. The American Youth Performs Chorus and Orchestra. Audio Recording EC 68006 (limited issue, sponsored by American Airlines).

1969: Mozart, Piano Concerto no. 20, with soloist Maria Isabella di Carla, and Bach, Passacaglia and Fugue in C Minor. International Festival Youth Orchestra. AVE 30696.

Stokowski's work with young musicians such as those of the International Festival Youth Orchestra, the American Youth Performs Orchestra and Chorus, and the American Symphony Orchestra of the sixties and seventies was that of gifted mentor working with gifted charges. For me, just as revealing a picture of teacher Stokowski is that provided by David Abel, who covered Stokowski working with New York City youngsters, grades K through twelve, in a 1963 all-city music clinic. While their regular teachers watched, Stokowski approached the student orchestra players with the rhetorical question of what they wanted to play. The Franck Symphony was their answer. This gave the maestro an opening to note that the work was out of fashion at the moment while baroque and modern works were in—foolish faddism that he hoped they would ignore by being alive to the beauty of music of all periods.

Relating his approach to the age and situation of his students, Stokowski next asked his charges to watch him as well as the notes, to relax and leave their nervousness behind as they played. In so doing, he told them, they could achieve poise and tranquility in the beauty of the music. As they played, the youngsters reverted back to playing mechanically, their eyes constantly glued to the music. Stokowski stopped them, noting they must watch the conductor or lose the beat and feel of the music. To illustrate, the maestro noted in his best deadpan manner that they had left him behind in the last passage, adding that they must wait and watch the conductor in order to create ensemble.

Following work with the entire orchestra, Stokowski next concentrated on each section in turn, emphasizing the importance of their contribution to the whole. This then was carried back into performance of the Franck piece by the whole orchestra.

The teachers present agreed at the end of the day that they had watched a "great teacher" at work. Precision, orchestral balance, and phrasing were all improved with a style of teaching that was economical of time and warm in spirit. The observers also noted that Stokowski's obvious respect for the music, his humor, and his interest in the students equated to rapport of a rare kind (see Able, "A Visit with Stokowski," 121).

1969: Tchaikovsky, *1812* Overture; Borodin, *Prince Igor:* "Polovtsian Dances"; and Stravinsky, "Pastorale" (arr. Stokowski). Royal Philharmonic Orchestra, John Aldis Choir, Welsh National Opera Chorale, and Band of the Grenadier Guards. London SPC 21041.

This *1812* has not only orchestra, bells, and cannon, but the Band of the Grenadier Guards and two choruses to join in—a la Stokowski—on the Russian national anthem portion of the overture. It is marvelous romantic fun as are the "Polovtsian Dances" on the reverse side. The Charming Stravinsky "Pastorale" seems to have found itself in roisterous company, out of keeping with its quiet and well-bred mood.

As with many Stokowski recordings of the sixties and seventies, this one was based on works from a program just given publicly, in this case from a concert at Royal Albert Hall the day before recording. As reported in *High Fidelity-Musical America*, 19 (Sept. 1969), to the Borodin and Tchaikovsky pieces earlier played, Stokowski added his own arrangement of the "Pastorale" to fill out the second side of the recording. For recording rehearsal purposes the entire program was played through once. Then on playback Stokowski took notes and shared his ideas about needed corrections with the orchestra and choir. Take two of the entire program then became the recording.

1969: Beethoven, Symphony no. 5 in C, and Schubert, Symphony no. 8 in B. London Philharmonic Orchestra. London SPC 21042.

***1970:* Ives, Second Orchestral Set, and Messiaen, *L'Ascension:* Four Meditations. London Symphony Orchestra and Chorus. London SPC 21060.

Anyone reading both Ives and Stokowski on sound, on music, particularly the future of music, and on life in general must be struck by the similarity of their ideas, by their pioneering independence, and by their idealism. Both are, I believe, transcendentalists in the spiritual sense. Read through and feel the meaning of Ives's *Memos*, his *Essays Before a Sonata*, and the piece he did for Henry Cowell called *Music and its Future;* then read Stokowski's *Music for All of Us*. Then listen to the Second Orchestral Set recording. I am not pedant enough to suggest that the beauty and power of Ives's music and of Stokowski's interpretation won't come through clearly without those readings. But a look at the sources will help identify a striking musical-philosophical bond between these two loners of music, different though they were in temperament and life-style. Stokowski himself calls attention to characteristics of this Ives piece, which, over the years and in a different context, were identified with Stokowski. Consider the importance, the magic, of sound near and sound far, each impinging on the other, blending in air, and layering into something quite startling and beautiful, by way of story telling. Then there is the strange transformation that takes place when several seemingly unrelated harmonies or melodies are played together at the same time, that is, unrelated except in the mind of the composer and eventually in the ears of the music lover.

Before one gets to the climactic "In the Sweet Bye and Bye," which closes the work, the listener has already fallen under Ives's spell as cast by Stokowski in this poignant retelling of New Yorkers' reactions to the 1915 sinking of the Lusitania. While Stokowski's recording premiere of the Fourth Symphony has been, I would venture, the single most important Ives orchestral recording so far, I would judge this an even more beautiful and deeply felt orchestral performance of Ives. It is certainly one of the finest recordings of Stokowski's entire career and should be returned to circulation.

The Messiaen Meditations on the reverse side—recorded once before by Stokowski in 1949—are beautifully played and transcendant in quite a different fashion. Stokowski evokes a level of passion and intensity from the London players that eclipses his earlier recording with the New York Philharmonic as does the sound of this recording.

**1970:* Debussy, *La Mer;* Ravel, *Daphnis and Chloe:* Suite no. 2; and Berlioz, *Damnation of Faust:* "Dance of the Sylphs." London Symphony Orchestra and Chorus. London SPC 21059.

Stokowski's London recordings of the sixties and seventies, including the *La Mer,* were done in Phase 4 stereo. This controversial recording process, using multiple microphones to record the several choirs, sometimes with soloists of the orchestra each on separate channels, centered on remixing the several voices of the orchestra after the initial recording was completed. Many critics have condemned the process for violating the normal mix of sound gained in concert hall performance. Stokowski had used a related—albeit much less technologically advanced—method to record the sound track for *Fantasia* in 1939. For example, the *Fantasia* recording of the *Rite of Spring* had used fourteen channels for recording purposes. In *Music for All of Us,* Stokowski wrote about (perhaps *prophesied* is the better term) the use of such techniques for tomorrow's recordings. Tomorrow came and Stokowski was in the middle of it with Phase 4.

Reviewing the set, critic Edward Greenfield described the *La Mer* as representing a near ideal use of the resources of Phase 4, because it allowed for the projection of performance subleties often lost on record. Stokowski's capture of the inner voices, together with his mastery of the Debussy atmosphere and color, made this recording the pick of current versions then available (see Teal, ed., *Leopold Stokowski,* Sec. 5.). This set together with Stokowski's 1965 recording of the "*Engulfed Cathedral*" and his live 1972 recording of the "Prelude to the Afternoon of a Faun" has been beautifully transferred to compact disc on London 417 779-2.

1970: Franck, Symphony in D Minor, and Ravel, *L'Eventail de Jeanne:* Fanfare. Hilversum Radio Philharmonic Orchestra. London SPC 21061.

Organist Stokowski loved the Franck with its soaring romanticism and, for him, its mystical links to the beyond. It was one of his first showpieces with the Cincinnati Orchestra—before Philadelphia—and his 1927 and 1935 Philadelphia Orchestra recordings of the Franck were mainstays in the RCA catalogue for years.

**1970:* Prokofiev, *Alexander Nevsky* Cantata, with soloist Sophia van Sante, and the Hilversum Radio Philharmonic Orchestra and Chorus (live), conducted by Stokowski, coupled with Concerto no. 1 for Violin and Orchestra, with violinist Igor Oistrakh and the Large Orchestra of USSR Radio and Television, conducted by Gannady Rozhdestvensky. Music and Arts of America compact disc CD-252.

In addition to recording the Franck Symphony with the Hilversum Orchestra during the summer of 1970, Stokowski performed *Alexander Nevsky* for Dutch television. The recording for this compact disc was taken from that live performance as realized by the National Television Company of Holland.

Stokowski had given the American premiere of the work in 1943 with the NBC Orchestra but never had the chance to record it. What a pleasure, then, to have this splendid-sounding set made by a dramatist in music who could fully realize Prokofiev's programmatic score. The sixth movement, "The Field of the Dead," performed with soloist van Sante, is unlike any other recorded performance of this episode that I have heard and seems an attempt to get closer in mood to a peasant girl's grief by moving away from the customary concert style of vocalizing in the movement.

American Record Guide Editor Don Vroon summed up his reaction to the movement as follows: "I'm not sure I like it, but it *is* different!" He finished his review by saying, "If you want an offbeat, really different *Nevsky*, you have come to the right place, who else would have the nerve?" (Vroon, *American Record Guide*, 51 May–June 1988; 51–52).

1970: Panufnik, *Universal Prayer*, with soprano April Cantelo, contralto Helen Watts, tenor John Mitchinson, bass Roger Stalman, three harps, organ, chorus, and the Louis Halsey Singers, all under the direction of Leopold Stokowski. Unicorn RHS 305.

The summer of 1970 was a busy time for the maestro. He had recorded Debussy and Ravel in London, performed Franck and Prokofiev in the Netherlands, and then returned to London for a September recording date of the Panufnik score. In the fifties and sixties Stokowski had given the U.S. premieres of three earlier major works by the composer. In May of 1970 he gave the *Universal Prayer* its world premiere at the Cathedral of St. John the Divine in New York City, thus leading to the English recording for Unicorn.

Andruzej Panufnik, who was present for that recording, would later write a moving tribute to Stokowski's concern for the composer and for the realization of the composer's intent in performance (see Panufnik, "Essay," in Johnson (ed.) *Stokowski: Essays*, 55–57).

**1971:* Josten, *Jungle* and *Canzona Seria*. American Symphony Orchestra. Composers Recordings Inc. CRI SD 267.

Werner Josten's tone poem, *Jungle*, was recorded in March 1971 with Stokowski acting dually as producer and conductor. Born and trained in Europe, Werner Josten emigrated to the United States in 1920 and in 1923 joined the music faculty at Smith College. While composing, Josten staged and conducted productions of near-forgotten works by Monteverdi, Handel, and others. In this context, he and Stokowski became acquainted in the twenties and worked together under the aegis of the League of Composers. Frederick Stock, Serge Koussevitsky, and Stokowski shared the honors of premiering major works by Josten in the twenties and thirties.

By his own account, Josten was drawn to the sensuous and the exotic for composing inspiration for some pieces, and to classical themes and baroque tradition for others. His works in both styles are programmatic. This dualism is represented on the present recording. *Jungle* portrays the impact of the African jungle on a newly arrived white man with the sounds of the jungle itself melded into the emotional states created by the contact of the two worlds.

Canzona Seria, like the Concerto Sacro I-II (recorded by Stokowski in 1965) is neoclassical in style, formal in mood, but with a sensuous tone color range that gives Josten's music an appeal all its own. This idiom was immensely suited to Stokowski's gifts—as was the frankly sensual score of *Jungle*—and he made the most of it. The members of the American Symphony Orchestra provide vivid and alert readings of Stokowski's interpretation.

**1971:* Tchaikovsky, Symphony no. 4 in F Minor, and Scriabin-Stokowski, Etude in C-sharp Minor. American Symphony Orchestra. Vanguard VCS 10095.

This was Stokowski's valedictory orchestral recording with his last youth Symphony. It is a testament to his undiminished abilities as teacher, orchestra builder, and performer thirty years and more after leaving Philadelphia. The first-rate performance and engineering are coupled with a blazing interpretation characterized by accelerations and decelerations of pace and unique turns of phrase, similar to those equally idiosyncratic touches that marked his 1941 recording with the NBC Symphony. Such eccentricities belonged only to Stokowski and the romancer's inner program for the work.

As with the vital and committed reading of the heroic Fourth Symphony, so with Stokowski's transcribed Scriabin etude. It is a moving statement of personal loss and loneliness expressed in the way the maestro communicated best.

New York critic Martin Bookspan, who had lauded many Stokowski recordings over the years, found this recording of the Fourth impossibly far from the Tchaikovsky markings as to phrasing, dynamics, and tempi (see Bookspan, *Consumers Union Reviews Classical Recordings*, [New York: Consumers Union, 1978], 250).

**1972: Sixtieth Anniversary Concert*, including Wagner, *Die Meistersinger*: Prelude to Act 1; Debussy, "Prelude a l'apres-midi d'un faune;" Glazunov, Violin Concerto in A Minor, with soloist Silvia Marcovici; Brahms, Symphony no. 1 in C Minor; and as encore, with spoken introduction by Stokowski, Tchaikovsky, "Marche Slav." London Symphony Orchestra. London SPC 21090/1 (live, two records).

Now permanently resettled in England, Stokowski was the subject of a joyous ninetieth birthday celebration on the anniversary of his 1912 first concert with the London Symphony Orchestra. With subsequent entries for the Brahms and the Glazunov pieces issued separately by London, note here that the whole set is a treasure.

Stokowski has his way with the Debussy Prelude. The once scandalously erotic play of Debussy's faun receives its emotional-musical due from Stokowski in a sensuously phrased and colored interpretation. While the live "Marche Slav" is not quite up to Stokowski's 1967 studio recording, it is rousing and, with Stokowski's introductory comments, moving as well.

**1972:* Brahms, Symphony no. 1 in C Minor. London Symphony Orchestra. London SPC 21131 (live).

This is one of the two major works conducted by Stokowski and recorded live at his ninetieth birthday gala in repeat of his first London Symphony Orchestra concert sixty years before. The performance is vigorous, straightforward, and well played.

1972: Russian Fantasia, including the Glazunov, Violin Concerto in A Minor, with soloist Silvia Marcovici, and Russian selections from other previously released albums. London Symphony Orchestra. London SPC 21111.

The Glazunov Concerto, too, is a live performance from the 1972 *Gala;* its brief twenty-one-minute life on this record is lost among the inclusion of snippets and pieces from other works, plus the "Polovtsian Dances" from *Prince Igor*, all of them previously recorded and released. The whole was then dubbed a Russian Fantasia. The fine Marcovici performance deserved a better fate.

1972: Bach Transcriptions. Czech Philharmonic Orchestra. London SPC 21096 (live).

Released simultaneously on English Decca (London) and on Supraphon for a central European audience, this set, along with the 1974 Bach album for RCA, amounts to Stokowski's last survey of Bach in transcription.

The first Bach-Stokowski transcription was likely made in 1914. The last Bach performance took place in 1975, sixty years later.

Despite the many sincere, and some obviously hostile, criticisms of Stokowski's way with Bach, Stokowski persisted in performing and recording his transcriptions over six decades, which also included transcriptions of music by Chopin, Debussy, Shostakovich, and Duparc among the more than forty composers in all whose works were transcribed.

Signs are that Stokowski, gone for more than a decade, has won, or is posthumously winning, his transcription battle with the critics. After Stokowski's death and before his own, Arthur Fiedler included a Stokowski transcription of Bach in his Deutsche Grammophon recording, *Symphonic Bach* (DG 2584 001). Conductor Robert Pikler has recorded Bach-Stokowski with the Sydney Symphony Orchestra (Chandos ABR 1055). Erich Kunzel has committed Stokowski transcriptions of works by nine composers—including Bach—to compact disc with the Cincinnati Pops Orchestra in a set called *The Stokowski Sound* (Telarc CD-80129). And Charles Gerhardt has recorded a set of the transcriptions with the London Philharmonic Orchestra, which, at the time of writing, has not yet been released. Another generation of conductors is including Stokowski transcriptions on their programs, among them, Francis Madeira, Michael Tilson Thomas, Robert Shaw, Jorge Mester, Zubin Mehta, and George Cleve.

Edwin Heilakka, curator of the Stokowski Collection at Curtis Institute of Music reports increasing numbers of conductors looking over and borrowing transcription scores for study and performance. To facilitate their use they have been microfilmed over a period of time; Stokowski made more than 200 orchestral and band transcriptions. Meanwhile, the Presser Foundation has made funding available to microfilm "all of Stokowski's marked published scores of overtures, symphonies, and concertos" (Heilakka, letter to the author, 22 June 1988, and Heilakka, "Performances and Recordings of Leopold Stokowski Transcriptions and Compositions from the [Curtis] Collection Since 1981," unpublished, 1987).

As to the 1972 *Bach Transcriptions* set at hand, it contains the Passacaglia and Fugue in C Minor, the Prelude in E-flat Minor, "Mein Jesu" (Stokowski's fifth recording), the Chorale from the *Easter* Cantata, and the last Stokowski reading of the Toccata and Fugue in D Minor. The set's joyous highlight is the Chorale-Prelude, "Wir Glauben all'an einen Gott." The set was recorded live in Prague, Czechoslovakia, in good live sound without audience sneezing or shuffling.

The 1972 trip to Prague was planned with live concert recordings of the Czech orchestra in mind, but a bad fall along the way, briefly hospitalizing Stokowski, almost prevented both concerts and recordings. Despite the pain of torn ligaments and the doctor's advice against conducting, Stokowski's will prevailed and his work with the Czechs produced recordings, not only of Bach, but of Elgar, Rachmaninoff, Scriabin, and Dvorak as well (see Daniel, *Stokowski* 878–82).

**1972: *Music of Sir Edward Elgar,* including the *Enigma* Variations. Czech Philharmonic Orchestra. London SPC 21136 (live).

This live performance recording was the second such taping made with the Czech Philharmonic in September 1972. What a September Song it is! Each miniature is shaped with its own emotional-musical frame of reference, and the Czechs play beautifully. The opening statement of Elgar's theme is a moving and elegiac song for strings and woodwinds, which in spirit reminds me of the haunting soprano saxophone of Sidney Bechet. From the opening, through delicate and then explosively humorous portraits to the noble "Nimrod Variation," finally to the pomp of Elgar's own self-portrait, and back to the opening statement, this is a recording to be wondered at, a transcendent performance. As an additional bonus, Stokowski's then protégé, the late Ainsley Cox, conducts the Royal Philharmonic in fine performances of Elgar's Serenade in E Minor for Strings and the *Elegy for Strings* on side two.

Stokowski's own feeling for the *Enigma* Variations is directly related to that strange mix of personal identity and cosmic meaning described in the Appendix. In a 1929 letter to Sir Edward Elgar, Stokowski had described the variations as giving him the sense of infinite life and energy coupled with a buoyancy, a sense of "floating" into a "mystical" plane, both timeless and cosmic (see liner notes to the Elgar set for this letter).

1972: Stokowski Encores, including selections by Rachmaninoff, Chopin, Schubert, Byrd, Tchaikovsky, Clarke, Duparc, and Elgar. London Symphony Orchestra and the Czech Philharmonic Orchestra. London SPC 21130.

With the exception of the "Nimrod" Variation from Elgar's *Enigma* Variations, all of the pieces included are in transcriptions by the maestro. The set might be described as the worst and the best of the Stokowski transcriptions; each category linked to that special and personalized musical world of Stokowski.

In this set the clear misses to these ears are the pieces by Rachmaninoff and Chopin, which seem to bring out the worst of Stokowski's family romance with things Slavic and Polish. The Rachmaninoff Prelude in C Minor is vulgar and ponderous rather than Slavically strong and enduring. The Chopin Mazurka in A Minor is sentimentalized to death, all swooning fiddles and woodwinds—Polish sentiment turned sentimentalism.

Yet this same hand turned, as transcriber and as performer, to the delicacy of Duparc's "Extase" in an arrangement never before recorded, presents perhaps the most chaste example of romantic orchestral ecstasy on record. In short, it is lovely.

The Dvorak "Slavonic Dance" no. 10 in E Minor represents a special case. Most of the transcriptions on this set—and in the Stokowski canon—represent orchestrations of pieces for solo instruments such as piano or violin, or of songs, or of traditional airs or, as in the case of "Night on Bald Mountain," of orchestral pieces Stokowski believed to be flawed in their orchestration and generally recognized as such; but the Dvorak "Slavonic Dance" is a lovely orchestral piece composed by a master, a piece whole and unflawed in its own right.

With neither apology nor explanation, Stokowski provides a matched performance and transcription, which completely change the color and emotional tone of the original, and it works in its own right as yet another moving hymn of loneliness and loss so prominent in the Stokowski repertoire.

Stokowski's audacity in recording this lovely mutation was met on appearance by a predictable and understandable negative reaction from critics—Edward Greenfield called it "grotesque." It further illustrates Stokowski's own search within himself for music's emotional meaning and his willingness to follow the results of that search regardless of tradition or of musical propriety, even if it meant artistic kidnapping.

The other transcriptions on the set are Schubert, "Moment Musical" no. 3 in F Minor; Byrd, Pavane, "The Earl of Salisbury and Galliard" (after Francis Tregian); and Tchaikovsky, "Chant Sans Paroles in A Minor."

The Rachmaninoff and the Dvorak pieces were recorded live with the Czech Philharmonic in Prague. The other pieces were studio recordings made with the London Symphony Orchestra.

**1972–73:* Scriabin, *Poem of Ecstasy* (1972); Rimsky-Korsakov, *Capriccio Espagnole* (1973); and Dvorak, "Slavonic Dance" in E (1972). Czech Philharmonic Orchestra and New Philharmonia Orchestra. London SPC 21117 (all but the *Capriccio Espagnole* are live performances).

The highlight of the album is the erotic *Poem of Ecstasy.* Orchestral colorist and sensualist Stokowski introduced the work to American audiences with his 1916 Philadelphia premiere. The 1972 live recording with the Czech Philharmonic was companion to Stokowski's 1972 Bach album and the *Enigma* Variations recording. All three were recorded in Prague's Dvorak Hall.

The 1973 *Capriccio Espagnole* studio recording with the New Philharmonia Orchestra was his first recording of the piece. It is colorful and exuberant, but the playing is, to my ears, a bit ragged, not up to Stokowski's traditional ability to shape poetically the performance within a technically impressive framework.

The performance of the Scriabin piece, on the other hand, is sheer poetry. Critic R. D. Darrell described this recording of the Scriabin tone poem as one of a kind in its evocations of eros in music (see Darrell, *Records in Review,* 1976, 334).

1973: Beethoven, Symphony no. 7 in A Major and *Egmont* Overture. New Philharmonia Orchestra. London SPC 21139.

Of the last round of Beethoven symphony recordings made by Stokowski beginning in 1967 and ending in 1974, this seems to me to be the least noteworthy. It is competently done and well recorded, but not more than that, at least when compared to his classic Philadelphia recording of 1927 and his Symphony of the Air recording in 1958.

Of greater interest is a late Stokowski project begun with this recording, that is, the first of a series of last-round overture recordings included with works normally taking both sides of a long-playing record. There are four of these: the "Egmont" with the Beethoven Seventh; the "Coriolan" with the *Eroica;* the *Academic Festival* Overture closing out the Brahms Fourth Symphony; and Brahms's "Tragic" Overture included with the Brahms Second Symphony of 1977. An overtures recording made by Stokowski with the National Philharmonic Orchestra for Pye Records in 1976 also included overture favorites as part of the series ended by the maestro's death in 1977.

**1927–73:* Dvorak, Symphony no. 9 in E Minor. New Philharmonia Orchestra. In RCA CRL 2-00334 and coupled with Stokowski's 1927 Philadelphia Orchestra recording of the same work (two records).

After ten years of making his European recordings exclusively for English Decca (London), Stokowski entered a new agreement to make European recordings for RCA as a free-lancer. So angered was Decca's Tony D'Amato that Stokowski's hope of continuing to make records for Decca while recording for

RCA and other labels were dashed. D'Amato cancelled plans for a Decca recording of Rachmaninoff's Rhapsody on a Theme of Paganini with Ilana Vered as soloist, and cancelled Stokowski's contract as well. Quite typically Stokowski was upset that he couldn't do what he wanted to do the way he wanted to do it (see Daniel, *Stokowski* 885–88 for the best account).

From 1973 and the last Decca recordings of the Beethoven Seventh and the *Capriccio Espagnol* up to 1976 and his last recording contract made with Columbia, Stokowski echoed his fifties-sixties practice of free-lancing recordings with several labels and orchestras, with the most recordings appearing on RCA. In addition he recorded with Phillips, Pye, and Desmar.

RCA's first 1973 release was both a reminder of RCA's historic association with the maestro and a commerical collector's item intended to spur interest—and sales—of future Stokowski RCA discs.

This two-for-the-price-of-one set contained not only the 1973 recording of the *New World* Symphony, but also Stokowski's 1927 recording with the Philadelphia Orchestra, which was the first of the RCA Musical Masterpiece sets carrying Red Seal recordings up through the thirties and forties to the LP era. With the exception of the third movement, the Largo, the interpretations differ markedly; that of 1927 was founded in a high-speed performance and dazzling attacks hard on the heels of phrases yet unfinished. For the time when it was made, its sound was first-rate and it was and is a polished virtuoso performance by a great orchestra. The 1973 performance is spacious, more slowly paced, and less well played, yet performed with more feeling for Dvorak's lyrical phrasing and color. RCA retained Stokowski's little 1927 talk illustrating themes from the *New World* and describing their meaning. It is simply awful but historically interesting as an example of Stokowski being conventional and thus very wooden.

When Stokowski actually taught players he was a master. When he conventionally lectured about music he was a pedant, a fact both teachers and students should take to heart whatever their discipline or art.

1973: Brian, Symphony no. 28 in C Minor. New Philharmonia Symphony Orchestra. Aries LP-1607 (live).

This pirated recording was made from an aircheck of the BBC broadcast of the work's premiere by conductor Stokowski in 1973. At the time much was made of the fact that both conductor and composer, Havergal Brian, were ninety-one years old. While the jacket notes ambiguously attribute both the symphony's performance and that of its disc mate, Brian's Violin Concerto, to the Hamburg Philharmonic Orchestra under Horst Werner, neither deserves this legend. Thanks to the detective work of critic David Hall writing in the May 1981 *Stereo Review*, the pseudonyms of conductors and orchestras listed on several Brian Symphony recordings were cleared up, including that of the Stokowski performance. According to musicologist Edward Johnson, the Violin Concerto was played by Ralph Holmes with the New Philharmonia Orchestra in 1969 under conductor Stanley Pope (see Daniel, *Stokowski* 1006).

**1973:* Tchaikovsky, Symphony no. 5 in E Minor and rehearsal of the work. International Youth Festival Orchestra. Leopold Stokowski Society, released on Cameo Classics GOCLP 9007 (two records, live performance in Royal Albert Hall, London).

We are much in debt to the Stokowski Society for making these unique recordings available. Stokowski, one month shy of his ninety-first birthday, was asked to conduct a portion of the final concert of the 1973 International Youth

Festival. Included in the orchestra were 150 players from fifteen to eighteen years of age.

Stokowski's work with the young was as fruitful as in earlier years. The results were quite fine. While some of the attacks are not as clearly delineated as one is used to in Stokowski's commercial recordings, the orchestral color is there as is the peculiarly Stokowski way of phrasing the Fifth. Of particular beauty is the second movement and the third movement, the Valse.

Generous excerpts from the last rehearsal are also included on a second record in the set illustrating Stokowski's economy of approach in preparation for a concert, but most interesting and quite unexpected are his harsh words concerning conducting style. For many years in interview and print as well as in practice Stokowski had championed flexibility, feeling, innovation, and youthful curiosity as keys to orchestral performance, but with never a harsh public word directed toward those of his conducting colleagues or toward critics who chose a more traditional, a more ordered, path to *Euterpe*.

Now in Royal Albert Hall, temporarily exasperated with his charges during rehearsal of the second movement, Stokowski stopped the orchestra with, "No, no, no, watch conductor. You are playing mechanically like a machine. You must look at the music for the notes and look at the conductor for the tempo—notes, conductor—keep watching."

And then by way of explanation, with his voice starting in reasonable and reasoning tone and then—caught up in his own feeling—rising to a harsh and angry pitch, Stokowski said, "Some conductors do exactly what's printed and some conductors—they're all different of course—use their imagination, their flexibility, their ideas. Some conductors are like a machine. Some are flexible, have heart, and feel. You learn about music flexibility and learn also about human beings. If you have the flexible conductor—good. If you have the mechanical one, there's nothing you can do about it [his voice rising and growing more harsh]. Take him out and drown him [in the Thames]? They won't let you [contempt added to anger]. You will have to suffer him! You will have to endure him!"

Then catching himself, anger spent, Stokowski returned to the score at hand; but in the third movement, by way of praising the orchestra for its work, Stokowski said, "If I had a medal I would give it to you, but they took all my medals away because I wouldn't play in strict time." This was said in an uncharacteristic tone verging into pathos.

A lengthy and interesting review of this set by critic Don C. Siebert appeared in the July–August 1981 issue of *Fanfare*.

1973: Tchaikovsky, Symphony no. 6 in B Minor. London Symphony Orchestra. RCA ARL 1-0426.

This is yet another Tchaikovsky score idiosyncratically interpreted by the conductor and not as convincing as his 1946 recording with the Hollywood Bowl Symphony Orchestra.

The 1973 recording can also be found on the Italian I Grandi Interpreti Della Musica label GIM-10, with handsome pictures and extensive notes in Italian.

***1973: Stokowski Conducts Wagner,* including *Die Meistersinger:* Prelude to Act 3 and "Dance of the Apprentices," *Rienzi:* Overture, *Die Walküre:* "Magic Fire Music," and *Tristan and Isolde:* Prelude and "Liebestod." Royal Philharmonic Orchestra. RCA ARS 1-0498.

Here is marvelous playing by the Royal Philharmonic Orchestra in one of Stokowski's two finest Wagner recordings. Highlights include a powerful *Rienzi*

Overture, a majestic performance of the "Magic Fire Music" with exceptionally fine brass playing, and Stokowski's last reading of excerpts from *Tristan and Isolde*. The inclusion of other Wagner favorites may well have prevented Stokowski from presenting the "Liebesnacht" along with the prelude and "Love Death" as he had done in earlier 1937, 1951, and 1960 recordings of this music, but the performance that he gives of the Prelude and "Liebestod" is as remarkable as were the earlier recordings, if differing from them. The 1973 recording is erotically more powerful than either of the earlier recordings, with frenzied climaxes that truly translate absolute musical-sexual abandon, yet which cannot be achieved without the greatest orchestral discipline and, I would guess, Stokowski's peculiar magic. It is a classic tour de force; the Stokowski vision of the music communicated to a hundred players who respond as one but also play with the freedom and excitement that has always been the measure of Stokowski's art at its best. There were yet other recordings to come, but this one could well serve as epitaph to Stokowski's sorcery with orchestra and score.

Of the "Magic Fire Music" critic Martin Bookspan wrote, describing it as " . . . playing of awesome power and beauty . . . which builds to a climax of shattering intensity. . . . One can imagine the musicians in the orchestra on the edges of their seats, mesmerized by the wizard on the rostrum before them" (see Bookspan, *Consumers Union Reviews Classical Recordings* [New York: Consumers Union, 1978], 274–75).

1973: Tchaikovsky, *Nutcracker* Suite, "Capriccio Italien," and *Eugene Onegin:* Waltz and Polonaise. London Philharmonic Orchestra. Phillips 6500 766.

1974: Brahms, Symphony no. 4 in E Minor and *Academic Festival* Overture. New Philharmonia Orchestra. RCA ARL 1-0719.

**1974:* Beethoven, Symphony no. 3 in E-flat and "Coriolan Overture." London Symphony Orchestra. RCA ARL 1-0600.

This was Stokowski's first recording of the *Eroica*, a vigorous, fast, and taut interpretation in sharp contrast to the slower-paced majesty of many recordings. It is persuasive in its own right. The "Coriolan" Overture is dramatically shaped and performed with great intensity. This set has been digitally remastered and released in RCA's "Legendary Performers" series as Gold Seal AGL 1-5247. One can hope for a compact disc rerelease.

**1974:* Mahler, Symphony no. 2 in C Minor, with soloists Brigitte Fassbaender and Margaret Price. London Symphony Orchestra and Chorus. RCA ARL 2-0852 (two records).

Despite repeated Mahler performances—to rave reviews—over the years, Stokowski did not commercially record a Mahler symphony until this recording was made in his ninety-second year. The programmatic themes of life, death, last judgment, resurrection, and eternal life are the stuff of this symphonic requiem. The Stokowski recording is a memorable one dramatically and musically. The last judgment is terrifying.

As reported by Mr. Jack Baumgarten, who was with Stokowski during the recording process, the conductor reacted very personally to the music's message. He felt shades of somberness and blackness in the work that he had never realized before, and, reported Baumgarten, this showed up interpretively in the recording. With the recording finished, Stokowski told Baumgarten that he would conduct no more Mahler (Daniel, *Stokowski*, 899).

This set was digitally remastered in 1986 and rereleased in RCA's Legendary Performers series as Gold Seal GL 85392 (two records).

1974: Stokowski-Wagner: Götterdämmerung Orchestral Highlights, including "Siegfried's Rhine Journey" and "Funeral March" and "Brunnhilde's Immolation." London Symphony Orchestra. RCA ARS 1-1317.

This was the last Stokowski recording of Wagner excerpts and a partial disappointment. Stokowski attempts to concentrate such orchestral power in the "Rhine Journey" climaxes that the shape of the music is distorted and its momentum is lost almost as though the maestro had lost temporary control over his tandem concerns of matching his conception of the work with his control of the orchestra. Furthermore, the players give a more ragged performance than one is used to in Stokowski's recordings. The "Immolation," on the other hand, is beautifully paced and played.

RCA has released a single compact disc (RCA 5995-2-RC) of excerpts from the 1973 and 1974 Wagner albums. From 1973: the *Meistersinger* excerpts and those from *Tristan and Isolde.* From the 1974 set: "Siegfied's Rhine Journey" and "Funeral March."

"That Leopold had failed since his ninety-second birthday was evident . . ." wrote Oliver Daniel (Daniel, *Stokowski,* 898). Many who knew Stokowski or worked with him professionally, who gave their accounts to biographers Oliver Daniel or Abram Chasins or who independently presented their views, could attest by 1974 that while his vigor and energy were ebbing gradually, he had good days as well as bad days, that he was most vigorous and alert when he was dealing with music, and that when he was off the podium his gradually declining vision, his frailty—in short, his advanced years—were clearly in evidence. These good and bad days are likely related to the uneven (for Stokowski) quality of the recordings noted in entries from 1973 forward.

It was in 1974 that he gave his last public concert in England. It was in 1975 that he gave his last public concert ever in Vence, on the Riviera, where Stokowski had built a new winter home. His recording schedule in England was increasingly geared to his physical needs. That this was so is not surprising. What is surprising is how many of the recordings made during, roughly, his last three years of life still show the power of his life force and of his brilliant musicianship.

1974: Tchaikovsky, *Francesca da Rimini* and Serenade for Strings in C. London Symphony Orchestra. Phillips 6500 921.

While sonically an advance over Stokowski's recordings of the *Francesca da Rimini* with the New York Philharmonic (1947) and with the Stadium Symphony Orchestra of New York (1958), the Phillips recording is less dramatic in interpretation and less poetically-programmatically rewarding than the earlier recordings, particularly that of 1947. This is the first recording of the Serenade in C made by Stokowski. It is played with sumptuous string tone and great style.

**1974: Stokowski Conducts Bach: The Great Transcriptions,* including Partita no. 2 for Violin: Chaconne, Partita no. 3 for Violin: Preludio, *Ein Feste Burg,* Orchestral Suite no. 3: Aria. "Little" Fugue in G Minor, Cantata no. 156: Arioso, "Sleepers Awake" and "Come Sweet Death." London Symphony Orchestra. RCA ARL 1-0880.

As to the selections and performance on this, Stokowski's last set of Bach transcriptions, those who do not like Bach-Stokowski on principle will not like this set. Those who have enjoyed some of the transcription performances over the years while finding others too dramatic, mannered, or sweetly sentimentalized will find in this valedictory set Stokowski's finest performances of the

Bach transcriptions since the Philadelphia recordings of the late twenties. Gone is the distortion and the syrupy string playing that marred Stokowski's recording of the Bach Chaconne in 1950 (RCA LM 1133); in its place is a Chaconne of exquisite beauty and power demonstrating clearly what Stokowski had always claimed for the orchestra as a vehicle for interpreting Bach. Gone is the theatrically funereal "Come Sweet Death" recorded in 1958 (Seraphim S-60235); in its place is a straightforward and quietly yearning plea for rest.

As to the transcriptions themselves, closure has finally been achieved as to whether they were Stokowski's work or the work of ghost transcribers. Dr. Edwin Heilakka of Curtis Institute of Music, curator of the Stokowski Collection housed at Curtis, who has gone over the transcriptions again and again since 1981, reports the following: "The myths surrounding the generation of the transcriptions are in no way valid. The mystery is gone. The transcriptions are by Stokowski." Dr. Heilakka has found twenty piano-organ source scores with annotations by Stokowski detailing his desired orchestration.

Conversations between Dr. Heilakka and Stokowski associates Natasha Bender, Albert Tipton, Mrs. Lucien Calliet, Lucille Miller Lynn, Jack Baumgarten and others elicited the following "modus operandi" in the preparation of the transcriptions. An approach which was always the same.

> Stokowski would give them . . . a source score of the work to be transcribed, well marked by him in terms of instrumentation, dynamics, meter changes, style, special effects, . . . doublings, and tempi . . . He would then describe his feelings about the work and discuss the overall orchestration . . .
>
> . . . The orchestrator simply followed his directions, . . .[and] did all the work of preparing a score.

During this process Stokowski regularly checked the progress and the accuracy of his assistant's work. Once the completed transcription was returned to Stokowski, both testimony and internal evidence proves that Stokowski further changed the scores and modified them again and again over the years. (See Heilakka, "The Leopold Stokowski Collection," *Maestrino*, Fall 1987, 3–4, and find it further explored and confirmed in Heilakka's address, "Sights and Sounds." Heilakka, telephone conversation with the author.)

***1975:* Rimsky-Korsakov, *Scheherazade*. Royal Philharmonic Orchestra. RCA ARL 1-1182.

Comment about Stokowski's 1951 and 1964 recordings apply to this 1975 remake. His affinity for and romantic understanding of the program and color of this work make him an outstanding interpreter even as the 1975 interpretation differs from the two earlier LP versions. The set also has fine sound.

RCA rereleased the now remastered set in 1983 in its Legendary Performers series as Gold Seal AGL 1-5213 and in 1988 released it as a Victrola compact disc 7743-2-RV.

**1975: The Stokowski String Sound,* including Vaughan Williams, Fantasia on a Theme by Thomas Tallis; Dvorak, Serenade for Strings in E; and Purcell, *Dido and Aeneas:* "Dido's Lament" (arr. Stokowski). Royal Philharmonic Orchestra. Desmar DSM 1011.

Purcell is represented here with "Dido's Lament" in Stokowski's arrangement preceded by the Vaughan Williams Fantasia. The lovely Dvorak Serenade was recorded here for the first time by Stokowski; indeed, he had not performed it before. As far as sheer sound is concerned, this whole collection is one of the finest recordings of Stokowski's career, which explains why Desmar's engineers in 1982 remastered the tape in "real time" on CrO_2 tape. It is one of the finest-sounding cassette performances I've run across, even superior to the lustrous 1976 disc. It was made available as Desmar SRB 5011 in Dolby B and also in Dolby C, encoded. The performance has since appeared on another LP, Teldec 6 42631 from Germany.

Critic John Bauman, reviewing the performance in its open reel incarnation for *Fanfare* magazine, dealt in superlatives to describe Stokowski's way with the orchestra and his interpretive skills. He calls attention, as had scores of commentators before in reviewing other works with other orchestras, to how the maestro gave the orchestra his sound, that is, the sound of Stokowski's Philadelphia Orchestra of fifty years before (see Bauman, *Fanfare*, 7 November–December 1983, 48–49).

**1975:* Rachmaninoff, Symphony no. 3 in A Minor and *Vocalise*. National Philharmonic Orchestra. Desmar DSM 1007G.

With Sergei Rachmaninoff in attendance, Stokowski gave this work its world premiere in Philadelphia in 1936. Rachmaninoff's assessment of the premiere was that his work was "played wonderfully."

Since its initial recording release the performance has been rereleased on a splendid-sounding German Telefunken disc 6.42613 AW and on reel-to-reel tape by Desmar-Barclay Crocker DSM1007. John Bauman wrote of the later tape release that splendid though the earlier disc was, the beauty and power of the performance was only realized on the later tape, particularly the sonority of the bass underpinning (see Bertonson and Leyda, *Sergei Rachmaninoff*, 330, and *Fanfare*, 6 January–February 1983, 39).

**1975: Stokowski Spectacular*, including selections by Sousa, Ippolitov-Ivanov, Mussorgsky, Johann Strauss Jr., Chabrier, Haydn, Saint-Saëns, Brahms, Tchaikovsky, and Berlioz. National Philharmonic Orchestra. Pye 12132.

Beginning with a rousing, if slightly ragged, *Stars and Stripes Forever* in Stokowski's own transcription, the set's highlights include a sparkling "España Rapsodie" by Chabrier and Stokowski's fifth recording of his transcription of Tchaikovsky's song "Again, as Before Alone," which Stokowski in his transcription called "Solitude." Indeed, the set includes Stokowski short favorites and "rousers" from a lifetime of programming. The "Procession of the Sardar" from *Caucasian Sketches* was included in his first London concert in 1909. Stokowski's demonic interpretation of "Danse Macabre" was a Philadelphia favorite in the twenties and thirties and was first recorded by the maestro in 1925. The Brahms "Hungarian Dance" no. 1 was one of Stokowski's earliest recordings for Victor, made in 1920 with the Philadelphia Orchestra. The Andante Cantabile attributed to Haydn was transcribed for orchestra by Stokowski and offered to audiences and record buyers from the twenties forward as an "18th Century Dance," with recordings made in 1929 and in 1946. The maestro's orchestration of the "Entracte" to Act 4 of Mussorgsky's *Kovanschina* was recorded twice in the twenties and included by him on numerous orchestra programs over the years. Another old favorite recorded four times before 1975 was Strauss's "Tales From the Vienna Woods." The 1975 recording is of a fifteen-minute version, complete with zither, in Stokowski's own transcription of the piece. Rounding out the set is a stirring reading of the "Hungarian March" from Berlioz's *Damnation of Faust*, another Stokowski/audience favorite for years.

This set might well have been called *Stokowski's Old Orchestral Friends* rather than *Spectacular.* Its musical appeal is historical while still listener-immediate, judging by its reincarnations. It was first a remastered 45 RPM long-playing record released by the English company, Nimbus, in 1982 as 45204. Also a splendid-sounding set, but minus the Tchaikovsky and the Brahms pieces. Then in 1985 Precision Records and Tapes rereleased the set in its third incarnation, this time on compact disc as PRT CCDPCN-4, with Brahms and Tchaikovsky restored.

John Bauman in *Fanfare* gave the set a very high recommendation, noting its appeal for both the musical tyro and the music lover of long standing who had not lost his or her taste for lollipops (see Bauman, *Fanfare,* 7 March–April 1984, 327).

1976: Stokowski Conducts Great Overtures, including Beethoven, *Leonora* no. 3; Schubert, *Rosamunde;* Mozart, *Don Giovanni;* Berlioz, "Roman Carnival"; and Rossini, *William Tell.* National Philharmonic Orchestra. Pye PCNHX 6.

With this set Stokowski nearly concluded the overtures series that began several years before with favorite overtures slipped into the final grooves of recordings featuring much larger works.

Stokowski as dramatist-in-music is most tellingly represented here in striking performances of the *Leonora* no. 3, the *Don Giovanni,* and the *William Tell* Overtures. However, the musical drama of the third of these overtures is punctuated for me by a chuckle as Stokowski the musician is confronted by Stokowski the innovator.

In his role as musical innovator Stokowski had over the years spoken and written about the need for the technical improvement of musical instruments generally. A frequently cited example was the need for a valve trombone to replace the traditional slide trombone, for, as he explained, it was impossible for the slide trombone to negotiate the passage work in certain works such as the *William Tell* Overture for example and do so up to tempo. As if to prove his point in this, his only recording of the work, he sets such a pace as to leave the trombones behind, and for several measures it's touch and go. (For Stokowski on the subject of the slide trombone and the *William Tell* Overture listen to the Stokowski interview with Philip Lambro and the Stokowski lecture at Bryn Mawr College.)

This set was rereleased as dell' Arte 9003 in 1981 and transferred to compact disc by PRT in 1985 as *Stokowski Overtures* CDPCN 6.

**1976: Stokowski Conducts Tchaikovsky: Aurora's Wedding Ballet Music.* National Philharmonic Orchestra. Columbia MS 34560.

This recording was the first made by the conductor under the terms of his new 1976 recording contract with Columbia. It ran for six years in order to carry Stokowski to his hundredth birthday and contained a special clause allowing the still independent Stokowski to record with another company should Columbia decline to record a composition or compositions that the maestro wanted to record.

By this time Stokowski was most frail, bent of figure, and sometimes confused by his surroundings, but as Oliver Daniel, who was with Stokowski for his recording session in May of 1976, reported in his biography of the maestro:

> Yet once the music began, he became transformed. He no longer sat but stood, conducting with the old and familiar gestures, his right hand with his long fingers pointing upward, as he had done from the day he first discarded the baton. Rhythm was precise; tempi, vigorous. Little by little the miracle occurred: sonority, shading, pace, balance,

and every musical sublety and nuance fell into place. His capacity to make music seemed utterly undimmed" (Daniel, *Stokowski*, 910).

Critic R. D. Darrell confirmed in print what those present noted of the maestro's transformation when facing an orchestra, at least in terms of the recorded results; he wrote that the performance was one of unbelievable power and "dramatic grip," wrought by a conductor who at his best retained his power undimmed by time or age (see Darrell, *Records in Review*, 1979, 337).

This recording of excerpts from the *Sleeping Beauty* was remastered by Columbia (CBS Records) in 1982 and rereleased as HM 44560. Would that it were released on compact disc!

**1976:* Sibelius, Symphony no. 1 in E Minor and "The Swan of Tuonela." National Philharmonic Orchestra. Columbia M 34548.

Stokowski was a fine, if idiosyncratic, Sibelius conductor. As with the Tchaikovsky symphonies, his readings of Sibelius were highly personalized. I would guess the key reason lay in his romancer's empathy or identification with what he found in the scores of Sibelius's works in addition to the "black notes on white paper," such as the color, the depiction of nature, and the translation of emotion into sound.

Critic Abram Chipman, in a rave review of the set for the 1979 *Records in Review*, invoked the pagan god Dionysus in description of both the performance and the conductor. How appropriate.

* **1976:* Bizet, *Carmen:* Suites 1 and 2 and *L'Arlésienne:* Suites 1 and 2. National Philharmonic Orchestra. Columbia M 34503.

On a memorable CBS 60 Minutes show of 1977, Leopold Stokowski, tired of questions about and commentary on his great age, temporarily aborted his interview with Dan Rather by leaping out of his chair and stalking toward the door. During the same segment, Rather asked critic Henry Pleasants—again mistakenly concentrating on Stokowski's age—if the maestro's advanced years had not, indeed, lessened his musical ability. To the strains of the then newly recorded *Carmen*, "Suites 1 and 2," Pleasants, with a laugh, answered that it didn't sound like it, that his *Carmen* was youthful, vital, and marvelously played. He added that Stokowski's ability to make great music had lasted as long as his "phony" central European accent.

This late recording from 1976 was transferred early on to Columbia's Great Performances series and later was made available on compact disc MYK 37260. As black disc and as CD it was received with generally glowing reviews.

***1976: Stokowski: His Great Transcriptions for Orchestra*, including selections by Rimsky-Korsakov, Debussy, Chopin, Novacek, Tchaikovsky, Albeniz, and Shostakovich. National Philharmonic Orchestra. Columbia M 34543.

How fitting that one of Stokowski's very last recordings would be a final collection of transcribed musical cameos. Recordings such as this one had been largely out of fashion for thirty years when Stokowski made this record. He had, during that time, continued to record such collections in spite of musical fashion. These collections sold well or not so well to people who knew little of musical fashion, or to people who loved music but were less impressed by fashion. I can think of three reasons why Stokowski recorded so many of these relatively short pieces up to and including this collection near the end of his life.

First, Stokowski had an affinity for shorter pieces with a particular color or emotional-musical emphasis reinforced in the transcriptions by the romancer's gifts. Such pieces could be distilled into musical-emotional statements of that artistic thrust. In explanation, the difference between the Shostakovich Prelude in E-flat Minor, included in this set, and the Shostakovich Fifth Symphony is the difference analogically between D. H. Lawrence's eight line poem "At a Loose End" and his epic novel *Sons and Lovers*. In each case the major work, while centering throughout on a major emotional theme, introduces subsidiary themes and changes in mood and tone in the several movements or chapters of the work. The prelude and the poem represent distillations of the major emotional preoccupation of each artist. In the same way, with minimal developmental change in emotional mood, tone, and color to account for, Stokowski could focus a singly charged interpretation into a single musical-emotional statement or state, standing separate and self-contained unto itself, communicate it to the orchestra's members, and achieve, for example, the dizzying sense of motion distilled into Novacek's "Perpetual Motion" and the "Flight of the Bumblebee."

Second, Stokowski's delight in and penchant for sharing the composer's creative process in shaping those states, moods, or emotions, which mark the cameo transcriptions, was served by his very real gift for transcription.

Critic R. D. Darrell put it very well when he wrote that Stokowski's musical taste or judgment could be questioned in individual transcriptions, but that his specialized talent in the art of orchestration and transcription could best be judged by comparing orchestral transcriptions of the same works done by Stokowski and by noted composers and conductors such as Schoenberg, Respighi, Sir Henry Wood, and Eugene Ormandy. When such comparisons were made, wrote Darrell, Stokowski was rarely matched and at no time tanscended. Even in the comparison of Ravel's and Stokowski's transcriptions of Mussorgsky's *Pictures at an Exhibition*, where Stokowski was bested, there was a barbaric power and dramatic slavicism close to the spirit of Mussorgsky in Stokowski's work, well worth the performance and recording. (See Darrell, *Records in Review*, 1975, 531, 533).

The performances—and there are ten of them—on this recording are uniformly vivid and beautifully played. My own favorite is that musical distillation of anguish and resignation that is Shostakovich's Prelude in E-flat Minor. At the opposite end of the emotional scale is a transcription performance so perky and pink-cheeked that I forgot I hadn't liked Tchaikovsky's "Humoresque" since high school, where those of us in the school's orchestra did less than justice to the piece on a regular basis. Albeniz's "Festival in Seville" and Debussy's "Night in Granada" are object lessons in the Franco-Spanish flash and color that Stokowski realized so well. Included in this set are two Chopin transcriptions out of several made over the years, all of which seem wide of the mark to me, but close to the romancer's Polish heritage intuited by Stokowski.

1977: Brahms, Symphony no. 2 in D Major and *Tragic* Overture. National Philharmonic Orchestra. Columbia M35129.

Released in April 1980, three years after it was recorded by Columbia Records, this posthumous birthday present (Stokowski was born 18 April 1882) is accompanied by a touching tribute from Roy Emerson, producer of the last recordings made by the maestro.

**1977:* Bizet, Symphony in C, and Mendelssohn, Symphony no. 4 in A Major. National Philharmonic Orchestra. Columbia M 34567.

This is Stokowski's last recording, posthumously released in 1978. The maestro gives the work of the seventeen-year-old Bizet a performance in which the *joie de vivre* of the youthful melodist is elegantly framed. Mendelssohn's *Italian* Symphony is lean in sound and dramatic in interpretation.

When this set was rereleased on Columbia's Odyssey series, critic Roger Detmer wrote that he couldn't decide which interpretation he was more impressed with, but he was sure that both were evidence of Stokowski's continued growth right to the end of his life (see Detmer, *Fanfare*, 8 July–August 1985, 52).

In a 1982 article on Stokowski for *Toccata*, Nancy Shear, a dear friend of the maestro for many years, recalled Stokowski's last days in terms of his excitement over recording plans for the Rachmaninoff Second Symphony, a piece he loved but had never commercially recorded. For him, it was therefore a new work. In the days leading up to that recording, Stokowski was wholly preoccupied with the Rachmaninoff. At lunch with Stokowski during August, 1977, Ms. Shear remembered that Stokowski's "attention wandered from our conversation. 'I must be with Rachmaninoff,' he said, excusing himself from the table."

That recording cannot be included here because Leopold Stokowski died during the early morning hours of 13 September, 1977; the day scheduled for the first Rachmaninoff recording session.

Addendum

There is now a Japanese Leopold Stokowski Society devoted largely to the rerelease of commercial Stokowski recordings and to making available live performances of Japanese orchestras conducted by the maestro.

Since my knowledge of what recordings have been released and what are available is sketchy, I have not included these recordings in this listing.

Notes

Chapter 1. Of Sonya's Doll, Grandfather's Fiddle, and the Changeling: The Fantasy Childhood of Leopold Stokowski

1. Robert Gomberg, "Recollections of Stokowski," *High Fidelity-Musical America*, 28 March 1978; MA 14–15. Morton Gould, "Essay," in Edward Johnson (ed), *Stokowski: Essays in Analysis of his Art*, (London: Triad Press, 1973), 37.

2. As a classic example of such misleading criticism from a respected figure in the world of musical commentary, see Sigmund Spaeth, "The Barrymores of the Baton," 36 *Theatre Arts*, November 1952; 28. For valuable commentary see Abram Chasins, *Leopold Stokowski: A Profile* (New York: Hawthorne Books, 1979); Paul Robinson, *Stokowski* (Vanguard Press, 1977); Charles O'Connell, *The Other Side of the Record* (New York: Alfred A Knopf, 1949); Preben Opperby, *Leopold Stokowski* (New York and London: Hippocrene Books and Midas Books, 1982); Oliver Daniel, *Stokowski: A Counterpoint of View* (New York: Dodd Mead & Co., 1982).

3. Since so much of Stokowski's life, including his personal idiosyncrasies, was bound up in music, illustrations of the conductor's personality will often center on episodes involving music. However, the music making at this point is not of central interest. The idiosyncrasies are.

4. The epitaph chosen by Stokowski from his own writing to grace his tombstone.

5. As an illustration, note the shock and surprise of Jerome Toobin and Gunther Schuller when Stokowski, with no conversational introduction, asked the two men if either of them had ever made love to a lesbian. Jerome Toobin, *Agitato* (New York: Viking Press, 1975), 67. Sylvan Levin recalls Stokowski's delight in shocking him with outrageous anecdotes or pronouncements during their years together. Sylvan and Elizabeth DeYoung Levin, interview with the author, 6–7 July 1982, New York City.

6. Nowhere outside of Stokowski's recordings is this more clearly illustrated than in his only book, the exuberant *Music for All of Us* (New York: Simon and Schuster, 1943). In the chapter "The Heart of Music," the following words and phrases romantically descriptive of musical works named are all to be found on page 25: "exalted love," "intoxicated orgiastic humor," "ecstatic," "dreamlike ecstacy," "inscrutable godlike utterance," "mischievous gaminlike humor," "stark primitive spirit of the slavic race," "elegiac," "screaming black fury of witches."

7. Nor was Stokowski reticent in advocating such a romantic approach. Noting the similarity between social behavior and musical performance, the maestro derided the proper etiquette of mechanical and correct music making as similar to the social manners of conventional persons, whose conversation and behavior was wholly predictable. How, he wondered, could such an approach in music reach the expressivity necessary to do justice to music, whose

range spanned the gamut of human emotions and whose moods ran from the angelic to the demonic? Leopold Stokowski, interview with R. C. Marsh, January 1958, Chicago, Classical Recordings Archive of America, El Cerrito, California.

8. Gunther Schuller in conversation with Edgard Varèse, in Benjamin Boretz and Edward T. Cone, eds., *Perspectives on American Music* (New York: W. W. Norton & Co., 1971), 36. Louise Varèse, *Varèse: A Looking-Glass Diary*, vol. 1 (New York: W. W. Norton & Co., 1972), 195–96.

9. Joan Peyser, *The New Music: The Sense Behind the Sound* (New York: Delacorte Press, 1971), 156–57. Fernand Ouellette, *Edgar Varèse*, trans. Derek Coltman (New York: Orion Press, 1968), 88–89, 92–93, 95, 97. Varèse, *Varèse*, vol. 1 233–34, 246–47. Richard Schickel, *The World of Carnegie Hall* (New York: Julian Messner, 1960), 243.

10. Herbert Russcol, *The Liberation of Sound: An Introduction to Electronic Music* (Englewood Cliffs, N.J.: Prentice-Hall, Inc., 1972), 50. Varèse, *Varèse*, 233.

11. Sylvan Levin, "Memorial to Leopold Stokowski." Memorial address, 23 September 1977, Curtis Institute of Music, Philadelphia, Pa.

12. Abram Chasins, interview with author, 24 March 1982, Los Angeles, California. Charles O'Connell knew Stokowski's changes of accent well. For him this verbal quicksilver went with a romanticism and sensualism that carried over into Stokowski's love of the exotic in food, drink, and color—indeed all of the senses. One never knew what to expect next in setting off for an evening with the maestro. He delighted in offbeat folk art, ethnic restaurants, and a wide range of music beyond the concert hall. Chasins recalled Stokowski's delight in the gypsy fiddler Bela Babai, a New York attraction in the thirties. Stokowski both attended Babai's performances and bought his records as gifts for women acquaintances. One can perhaps hear echoes of Babai in the violin solos of the 1955 Stokowski recording of the Liszt Hungarian Rhapsody no. 3 rereleased as Quintessence PMC 7023. O'Connell, *The Other Side of the Record*, 278, 280–83. Chasins, *Leopold Stokowski*, 118. Edward Johnson, Notes to *Stokowski: His Great Transcriptions for Orchestra*, Columbia M34543. According to his friend, Sylvan Levin, Stokowski's shrewdness in money and investment matters fully matched his romanticism. Investing his earnings in the twenties, Stokowski avoided the disaster that attended so many in the crash of twenty-nine and came out of the depression an independently wealthy man on the basis of those investments. Levins, interview with the author.

13. Herbert Kupferberg, *Those Fabulous Philadelphians* (New York: Charles Scribner's Sons, 1969), 110–11.

14. Curtis Davis, "Stokowski at 100," *High Fidelity-Musical America*, April 1982, 45. Kupferberg, *Fabulous Philadelphians*, 110. Leopold Stokowski, interview with Aaron Parsons and George Stone, 26 May 1968, Chicago, Classical Recordings Archive of America, El Cerrito, California.

15. Chasins, *Leopold Stokowski*, x. Harold Schonberg, *The Great Conductors* (New York: Simon and Schuster, 1967), 312.

16. Preben Opperby provides yet another variant on the story of the maestro's grandfather, describing him as a Polish aristocrat who, upon immigration to England, was forced to earn his bread as an artisan. See Opperby, *Leopold Stokowski*, 12, Schonberg, *Great Conductors* 312, Toobin, *Agitato*, 43–44, Stokowski, interview with Parsons and Stone, Davis, "*Stokowski at 100*," 45. Gerald Jackson, *First Flute*, ed. David Simmons (London: J. M. Dent and Sons, 1968), 79. Gloria Vanderbilt, *Black Knight, White Knight* (New York: Alfred A Knopf, 1987), 186.

17. Davis, "Stokowski at 100," 45, 82. Chasins, *Leopold Stokowski*, 2.

18. See Daniel, *Stokowski*, 6. Listen to Stokowski's moving and urgent plea for Philadelphians to support their orchestra in the face of depression. This speech was delivered at the end of the last concert of the 1931–32 season. Caught by Bell Telephone Laboratory engineers in their live recording of the concert, it illustrates Stokowski's London accent as softened by years of living abroad but apparent nonetheless. This can be heard in *Early Hi-Fi: Wide Range and Stereo Recordings Made by Bell Telephone Laboratories in the 1930's, Leopold Stokowski Conducting the Philadelphia Orchestra, 1931–32*, vol. 2. For noting the modest improvement in the family's status between grandfather Stokowski's arrival in London in the 1850s and an eighteen-year-old Leopold Stokowski's first employment as choral director and organist in 1899, I am much indebted to my colleague Anthony Brundage, English history specialist. Brundage has related the family's changing addresses to its slowly rising fortune as follows: Grandfather Leopold settled in Oxford Market in Central London. This was a mixed working-class and lower-middle-class area of émigrés, artisans, shopkeepers, and working people. Here his son Joseph Kopernik Stokowski was born in 1862 out of Leopold's union with a Scot, Jessie Sarah Anderson Jones. In turn son Kopernik Stokowski and his bride, the Anglo-Irish Annie Moore, were married in 1881 and set up housekeeping nearby, at 13 Upper Marylebone Street, where conductor Leopold Stokowski was born in 1882. Marylebone, midway between Regents Park and Hyde Park, was a cut above Oxford Market and removed from any concentration of nonEnglish émigrés from the continent. Still in the Marylebone district, the family next moved to 10 Nottingham Street. In 1896 the Stokowskis, together with son Percy John and a fourteen-year-old Leopold, move to 18 Acadia Road in St. John's Wood, some two miles northwest of their old address. Again this new address represented an upward move to a better middle-class neighborhood, but one without the tone of neighboring suburbs like Hampstead. Since even the traditional Roman Catholicism of Poles had earlier been abandoned by grandfather Leopold, his grandson would be baptized into the Anglican faith in 1882. In later life, as part of the fantasy concerning his Polish heritage, the conductor would claim to be Roman Catholic on occasion. See Opperby, *Leopold Stokowski*, 9–15, Daniel, *Stokowski* 1–6, O'Connell, *The Other Side of the Record*, 286.

19. O'Connell, *The Other Side of the Record*, 279.

20. Toobin, *Agitato*, 52.

21. Daniel, *Stokowski*, 7, Chasins, *Leopold Stokowski*, 3, 247–48, Kupferberg, *Fabulous Philadelphians*, 110–11. Opperby, *Leopold Stokowski*, 142.

22. Leopold Stokowski, BBC interview with Sandra Harris, 1974, London, Classical Recordings Archive of America, El Cerrito, California. Stokowski, interview with Parsons and Stone. Leopold Stokowski, interview with Philip Lambro, 1963, n.p., Classical Recordings Archive of America, El Cerrito, California. Kupferberg, *Fabulous Philadelphians*, 111. Eugene Moore, "Fifty Fabulous Years," *Musical America*, 79 February 1959, 17. Chasins, *Leopold Stokowski*, 3–4. Concerning his accidental conductorial debut at twelve, Stokowski told Opperby that he was pianist for an opera chorus at the time, thus upgrading his debut to symphonic status. See Opperby, *Leopold Stokowski*, 12.

23. Stokowski, *Music for All of Us*, 217. Davis, "Stokowski at 100," 46. Chasins, *Leopold Stokowski*, 10–15, 18, 27.

24. Toobin, *Agitato*, 55. "Prince" is the term of endearment Stokowski used

to sign an autographed picture of himself with the salutation, "For Mary with Love," given to Mary Louise Curtis Bok in the 1920s. Mrs. Bok was benefactress of both the Philadelphia Orchestra and the Curtis Institute of Music. See *Curtis Institute of Music, Stokowski Centennial Program, 18 April 1982* (Philadelphia: Curtis Institute of Music, 1982), 1.

According to Sylvan Levin, others during the twenties and thirties called Stokowski "Prince" as well. See Levins, interview with the author. Mabel Dodge Luhan would call Stokowski "Prince" when the maestro and bride Gloria Vanderbilt visited Frieda Lawrence and her circle in Taos, New Mexico, in 1945. See Vanderbilt, *Black Knight, White Knight*, 228–29.

25. Chasins, *Leopold Stokowski*, 13–15. From earliest youth until well past eighty, Stokowski's good looks, his carriage, and his grace of movement were commented on by friends and by enemies whose "glamour boy" label followed Stokowski for nearly three generations. All manner of sobriquets denoting youth, grace, and good looks were used over the years to describe Stokowski. Nor did Stokowski age as most of us do. At ninety he looked aged, but the boyish looking man of thirty maintained his good looks into his sixties and seventies. Upon his marriage to the twenty-one-year-old Gloria Vanderbilt, George Antheil wrote of a sixty-three-year-old Stokowski that of all the people he had known, the maestro had maintained his youthful looks the longest, and added that it might be an unusual glandular condition that kept Stokowski's biological age at least twenty years younger than his chronological age. See O'Connell, *The Other Side of the Record*, 278–79, Schonberg, *Great Conductors*, 310, Chasins, *Leopold Stokowski*, xii, 74. George Antheil, *Bad Boy of Music* (Garden City, N.Y.: Doubleday Doran & Co., 1945), 365–66.

26. Peter Dobson, "Essay," in Johnson, ed., *Stokowski: Essays*, 65. Toobin, *Agitato*, 55. Chasins, *Leopold Stokowski*, 13–14. Long before the charges that Stokowski was not the author of his own orchestral transcriptions, the young Stokowski was transcribing orchestral, piano, and choral works by Beethoven, Mozart, Chopin, Mendelssohn, Tchaikovsky, Elgar, Schubert, Wagner, and Ippolitov-Ivanov for organ. See Daniel, *Stokowski*, 41, 44–45.

27. Chasins, *Leopold Stokowski*, 18–19, 26–27.

28. Chasins, *Leopold Stokowski*, 26–34.

29. Ibid., 18.

30. Andre Previn, "Essay," in Johnson, ed., *Stokowski: Essays*, 59. Martin Bookspan and Ross Yockey, *Andre Previn: A Biography* (Garden City, N.Y.: Doubleday & Co., 1981), 334. The wording of the same quotation taken from Previn's student notes varies in these two sources, but the message and the punch line remain the same!

31. See Daniel, *Stokowski*, 41. Stokowski composed only a handful of works, but one of these, written when he was a young man, is the Dithyramb for Flute, Cellos, and Harp, a deeply emotional hymn to the pagan Greek deity, Dionysus, god of wine and fruitfulness.

32. Chasins, *Leopold Stokowski*, 8, 11, 13–14, 18. Those impressionistically critical of Stokowski's methods during his early rise should take a hard look at the historical realities faced by anyone in Stokowski's position at the turn of the century. Means and ends are very different things to those who are comfortably secure when compared to those whose abilities can only flower through hard-won achievement, as a later Englishman—George Orwell—would so well document.

33. In spite of Stokowski's aversion to the drably plebian characteristics of his background, it is psychologically interesting that he carried over the craft

skills of two generations of cabinet makers into his adult life. For he designed and sometimes built useful and necessary articles for his dwellings, including a fireplace, tables, desk, and cabinets. Josephine Walker, "The Stokowski Only His Secretary Could Know," *Ovation* 3 (Apr., 1982): 18. O'Connell, *The Other Side of the Record*, 283.

34. I think it likely that Stokowski's lifelong concern for bringing the concert hall and great music to millions of people of little or no wealth was not only genuine but shaped by the youthful dilemmas of his own experience. The same could be said of his years of work with youth orchestras, many of whose members were drawn from backgrounds not dissimilar to his own.

35. Davis, "Stokowski at 100," 45.

36. Daniel, *Stokowski*, 28–29.

37. Ibid., 7, 13, 189.

38. Ibid., 212, xxv.

39. Vanderbilt, *Black Knight, White Knight*, 186, 231–32.

40. Ibid., 253–54.

41. Ibid., 255–56, 292–94, 297–98.

42. Daniel, *Stokowski*, 112–18.

43. Ibid., 117.

44. Samuel Grimson, about the same age as Stokowski, would follow the maestro to the Royal College of Music where he, Grimson, became a Gold Medal graduate. While he could not continue a musical career in violin (which was his instrument) because of World War I injuries, he remembered the little Leo Stokes from play time in the streets of London, then as RCM student, Leopold Stokowski; and then as a conductor who "amused" Grimson "by his later posing as a Pole." This information was shared with me by Grimson's widow, psychoanalyst Bettina Warburg, M.D., in letters of 12 and 24 October 1984, from her home in New York City.

45. Stokowski, interview with parsons and Stone.

46. Chasins, interview with the author.

47. See Schonberg, *Great Conductors*, 314 for just such an assumption.

48. I am grateful to psychologist William Fawcett Hill for discussion on this topic and for helping me set it into modern psychological perspective.

49. See *A New Dictionary on Historical Principles (Oxford English Dictionary)*, 1983 ed., s.v. "Changeling." *Encyclopedia of Religion and Ethics*, 1911 ed., s.v. "Changeling."

50. For examples see Bruno Bettelheim, *The Uses of Enchantment: The Meaning and Importance of Fairy Tales* (New York: Alfred A. Knopf, 1976; Vintage Books, 1977). Erich Fromm, *The Forgotten Language: An Introduction to the Understanding of Dreams, Fairy Tales and Myths* (New York: Rinehart & Co., 1951; Evergreen Books, 1957).

51. Bettelheim, *Uses of Enchantment*, 68. I am much indebted to psychoanalyst Martin Silverman, M.D., for his encouragement and help on the subject of the family romance and its applicability to Stokowski.

52. In the context of my work on Stokowski, I put these questions to psychologist Dr. William Fawcett Hill. He answered yes to both questions. Further, in specific reference to Stokowski, he noted that a person with the maestro's constellation of character traits would be the likeliest creator of such a family romance since the only ghastly hole in his sense of identity lay in the accident of his birth. By re-creating that, with his Polish great grandfather and grandfather as his notable family members, he could bring his origins into psychological line with his creation of his own image and success as an adult. In the same

way his assumed accents covered his London origins while lending flair to his self-created image; all of this governed emotionally rather than rationally and strong enough to withstand the skepticism of unbelievers. Dr. Hill warmed to this theme as both psychologist and music lover by noting that his own favorite musician, Edward Kennedy Ellington, was remarkably similar to Stokowski but luckier in family background. The "Duke," nicknamed in childhood for his aristocratic bearing and power over those close to him, including his family, did not in any way disown his prim and moralistic mother nor his easygoing father, but then he did not need to, for while still a small child he substituted his own fantasy identity of himself for the normal reality of a child subordinate to his or her parents. In it he, not his mother and father, played the central family role. Since his family accepted Ellington's conception of himself, the Duke was in charge by age ten as Stokowski, employing his family fantasy, would not be until manhood. Consider Barry Ulanov's biographical picture of the prepubescent school boy Duke coming downstairs on his way to the day's classes demanding—and getting—his family's applause as he left for school.

Ellington's childhood security and happiness were in marked contrast to the Stokowski childhood as were their ways of dealing with childhood memories. However, they were remarkably similar both personally and musically, even to their sense of showmanship and assumption of verbal accent to stress their place in the upper table land of musical aristocracy. Who can ever forget Ellington's "We love you maad-laay."

Master musicians, worshippers of sound, each made his orchestra an instrument to play upon; each created a unique orchestral sound. Both were handsome and particularly attractive to women. Neither was willing to accept human authority, yet both acknowledged the primacy and governing authority of music in their lives—Stokowski with his "Music, the voice of the All," and womanizer Ellington acknowledging his humility to music in the title of his autobiography, *Music is My Mistress*. Each man, by the way, liked and intuitively respected the other; each attended the other's performances.

See Barry Ulanov, *Duke Ellington* (New York: Creative Age Press, 1946), 1, 5–7, 11–13, 16, 188–89. Derek Jewell, *Duke: A Portrait of Duke Ellington* (New York: W. W. Norton & Co., 1977), 65. Ralph Gleason, *Celebrating the Duke and Louis, Bessie, Billie, Bird, Carmen, Miles, Dizzy and Other Heroes* (Boston: Atlantic Monthly Press Book, Little Brown and Co., 1975), 168.

53. For example, Sergei Rachmaninoff, son of land-owning Russian aristocrats, who were also capable musicians, received his degree from the Moscow Conservatory in 1882. In 1909, Stokowski conducted the composer's Second Piano Concerto with Rachmaninoff as soloist. Francis Crociata, *Rachmaninoff: Portrait of a Great and Modest Master* (New York: RCA Victor, 1973), 1. Sergei Bertonson and Jay Leyda, *Sergei Rachmaninoff* (New York: New York University Press, 1956), 163. In 1963, Stokowski recalled that in conversation with Rachmaninoff, he had been particularly interested in Rachmaninoff's account of his own childhood. Stokowski, interview with Phillip Lambro.

54. Cecil Smith, *Worlds of Music* (Philadelphia, Pa: J. B. Lippincott Co., 1952), 242. David Ewen, *Dictators of the Baton* (Chicago: Alliance Book Corp., 1943) 73. Olga Samaroff Stokowski, *An American Musician's Story* (New York: W. W. Norton & Co., 1939), 101, 104.

55. Chasins, interview with the author. Chasins, *Leopold Stokowski*, 22–25. Davis, "Stokowski at 100," 46. Ewen, *Dictators*, 73. Olga Samaroff Stokowski, *American Musician's Story*, 34–37.

56. Clara Clemens, *My Husband Gabrilowitsch* (New York: Harper & Broth-

ers, 1938), 87–91. Olga Samaroff Stokowski, *American Musician's Story*, 146–49.

57. Louisa Miller née Knowlton, interview with the author, June 1984, Claremont, California.

58. Chasins, *Leopold Stokowski*, 99.

Chapter 2. The Eyes and Ears Have It

1. Hector Berlioz, *A Treatise upon Modern Instrumentation and Orchestration*, trans. Mary C. Clarke (Boston: Elias Howe Co., n.d.), 243–44. The size of Berlioz's ideal orchestra was to be 467 instrumentalists with a chorus of 360 for vocal works.

2. Berlioz, *Treatise*, 243.

3. Ibid., 254.

4. Stokowski, *Music for All of Us*, 24–26.

5. Richard Dyer, "Maestro Front and Center," *New York Times* Book Review, 19 Dec., 1982, BR 3.

6. William Trotter, "The Conductor as Musical Hobo," *Toccata*, Winter 1982–83, 7.

7. O'Connell, *The Other Side of the Record*, 275–76.

8. Daniel, 911–12.

9. Ibid., 913–14. *60 Minutes*, 4 Jan, 1977, CBS.

10. Levins, interview with the author.

11. Several sources in this paragraph have been cited earlier and have there received attribution. These I will not note again. Sources not previously cited are noted below.

12. Stokowski, interview with Lambro.

13. Stokowski, interview with Harris.

14. Daniel, *Stokowski*, 675. Leopold Stokowski, interview with Reginald Jacques, BBC, 1959, London, Classical Recordings Archive of America, El Cerrito, California.

15. Nancy Shear, "Stokowski," *Toccata*, Autumn 1982, 20. Daniel, *Stokowski*, xxiii. Andre Kostelanetz, in collaboration with Gloria Hammond, *Echoes: The Memoirs of Andre Kostelanetz* (New York: Harcourt, Brace, Jovanovich, 1981), 182.

16. This orchestral seating layout in Stokowski's own handwriting can be found in Ainslee Cox, "Essay," in Johnson, ed., *Stokowski: Essays*, 22.

17. Elizabeth Neuburg, telephone conversation with the author, 22 September 1988.

18. See Stokowski, *Music for All of Us*, 92–99.

19. See Gustav Janossy, *Leopold Stokowski and the All American Youth Orchestra, Second Tour, 1941* unpublished scrapbook, 1941), 47, 55–56. For further material on the tour see Discography for 1941.

20. Opperby, *Leopold Stokowski*, 127.

21. Ibid., 126–28.

22. O'Connell, *The Other Side of the Record*, 297.

23. Stokowski, *Music for All of Us*, 179–82.

24. Ibid., 53–56.

25. Oscar Levant, *A Smattering of Ignorance* (New York: Garden City Publishing Co., 1939), 45.

26. Stokowski, interview with Parsons and Stone. Stokowski, *Music for All of Us*, 54–56.

27. Stokowski, interview with Lambro.

28. Rosemary Curtin-Hite, interview with Sol Schoenbach, *Maestrino*, Spring 1986, 4, 9. Daniel, *Stokowski*, 302–3. See Discography for 1936 and 1939 for accounts of these recordings.

29. Kupferberg, *Fabulous Philadelphians*, 79.

30. Edna Phillips, Address at the Stokowski Centennial Program, Curtis Institute of Music, 18 April 1982, Philadelphia, *Maestrino*, Spring 1985, 13.

31. Ibid., 12. Levins, interview with the author.

32. Stokowski, *Music for All of Us*, 195.

33. Hans Keller, "Essay," in Johnson, ed., *Stokowski: Essays*, 47. Stokowski, *Music for All of Us*, 194–95.

34. David Measham, "Essay," in Johnson, ed., *Stokowski: Essays*, 50.

35. Curtin-Hite, 9.

36. Daniel, *Stokowski*, 295.

37. Carl Flesch was a distinguished Hungarian violinist who was both a famous soloist and a gifted teacher of violin. In this role he taught violin at Curtis Institute from its beginning in 1924 to 1928. Note that Stokowski led the Curtis Institute Orchestra from 1924 until 1926, when he brought young Artur Rodzinski from Poland to train the orchestra and act as his assistant with the Philadelphia Orchestra.

38. Carl Flesch, *Memoirs of Carl Flesch*, trans. Hans Keller (New York: Macmillan, 1958), 286–88, 334, 342–43. Cellist Gregor Piatigorsky, recalling his premiere with the maestro and the Philadelphia Orchestra, felt there was nothing this orchestra couldn't do. As for Stokowski, his status was that of musical "demigod," whose exquisite recordings had spread the fame of Stokowski and the Philadelphia Orchestra over all of Europe. Alfredo Casella, composer, pianist, and conductor, worked with Stokowski in the twenties both as piano soloist and in the introduction of his own music. Writing in 1941 of Stokowski in the twenties, he described the maestro as "a great conductor" because he combined an unusual memory and a superb understanding of the musical score with an extraordinary command of his musical forces. See Gregor Piatigorsky, *Cellist* (Garden City, N.Y.: Doubleday & Co., 1963), 183–84. Alfredo Casella, *Music in My Time*, trans. Spencer Norton (Norman: University of Oklahoma Press, 1955), 153–54.

39. Morton Gould "Essay," in Johnson ed. *Stokowski Essays*, 37.

40. Daniel, *Stokowski*, 825.

41. Winthrop Sargeant, "Musical Events," 39 *New Yorker*, 19 October 1963, 203.

42. Maestro Szell led the orchestra from 1946 until his death in 1970, a twenty-four year tenure.

43. Schonberg, *Great Conductors*, 337–39.

44. Joseph Wechsberg, "Orchestra," *New Yorker*, 46 30 May 1970, 40–41. Lest one think the orchestra responded to Stokowski in this way out of familiarity with him as guest conductor, note that the same sort of thing occurred at his earliest Cleveland concerts and continued to his last concert in 1971, as attested by F. R. Dixon, "Stokowski in Cleveland," *Toccata*, Spring 1983, 4–12.

45. Dixon, "*Stokowski in Cleveland*," 8–9.

46. For such with the London Symphony Orchestra, New York Philharmonic, Vienna Philharmonic, Berlin Philharmonic, and Danish Radio Symphony Orchestra, see respectively John Georgiadis, "Essay," in Johnson, ed.,

Stokowski: Essays, 33–34. Daniel, *Stokowski*, 668–69. Bernard Hermann, "Essay," in Johnson, ed., *Stokowski: Essays*, 39. Erich Jantsch, "Vienna," *Musical Courier*, 152 August 1955, 19–20. Daniel, 668. Notes to *Stokowski Conducts Nielsen*, Symphony no. 2, *The Four Temperaments*, Poco DLP 8407.

47. Sargeant, "Musical Events," 38 152–53.

48. Lawrence LeShan, *The Medium, The Mystic and The Physicist: Toward a General Theory of the Paranormal* (New York: Viking Press, 1974), 205.

49. Joseph G. Pratt, *ESP Research Today: A Study of Developments in Parapsychology Since 1960* (Metuchen, N.J.: Scarecrow Press, 1973), 169.

50. For religious origins see the *Encyclopedia of Religion*, 1987 ed., s.v. "Charisma." *Dictionary of Religion and Ethics*, 1921, s.v. "Charismata." *Abingdon Dictionary of Living Religions*, 1981, s.v. "Halo" and "Aureole".

51. See Thelma Moss, *The Probability of the Impossible: Scientific Discoveries and Explorations in the Psychic World* (Los Angeles: J. P. Tarcher, 1974), 23–91.

52. Tom Monte, "Healer John Diamond's Soul Music," *East West*, July 1988, 40. Moss, *Probability of the Impossible*, 106–10.

53. LeShan, *The Medium*, 112–13.

54. Ibid., 106–7, 112, 147–48.

55. Levins, interview with the author. Levin, "Leopold Stokowski" *Toccata* (July-Aug., 1981), 13. Chasins, 104.

56. Robert E. McGinn, "Stokowski and the Bell Telephone Laboratories: Collaboration in the Development of High-Fidelity Sound Reproduction," *Technology and Culture*, January 1983, 51–52. Ward Marston, who transferred this recording to modern long-play for Bell, had much the same reaction, describing himself as overwhelmed by this astonishing performance. See Ward Marston, interview with Mark A. Obert-Thorn, *Maestrino*, Spring 1987, 7.

57. John Diamond, *The Life Energy in Music* (Valley Cottage, N.Y.: Archeus Press, 1981), 51, 43–44, 63, 35, 40–41, 46. In reading Dr. Diamond's book I was struck over and over again by Stokowski's perfect match to both Diamond's examples and his paradigm with the notable exception of his stress on the selflessness of the high-energy artist, which Stokowski's sense of mission and egoism precluded. After reading his book I wrote him a note, accompanying it with some of my work on Stokowski and asking permission to cite his book. Diamond later called me from New York, enthusiastic about my findings, and readily granted citation. When on 23 April 1984 I presented an earlier version of "Stokowski and the Family Romance" to a conference of the New York Psychoanalytic Association in New York City, Diamond came down from Valley Cottage, New York, to join us. Once again he supported my findings and enthusiastically joined the discussion, armed with tape recordings of Stokowski that illustrated his multiple accents. See Monte, "Healer John Diamond's Soul Music," 42.

58. Chasins, *Leopold Stokowski*, 103–04.

59. Ibid., 275.

60. Ibid., 138–40

61. Chasins, interview with the author.

62. Levins, interview with the author. Barry Tuckwell, who in another musical context described himself as playing beyond his ability for Stokowski, described Stokowski's initial impact on the London Symphony Orchestra as quite amazing. It was 1957. The orchestra had undergone a major upheaval resulting in the loss of many veteran players and their replacement by young inexperienced newcomers. Tuckwell was one of these. He recalled Stokowski's

first concert with the demoralized orchestra as so extraordinary in the orchestra's improved playing, that the press picked up the theme. As for Tuckwell, it was one of the most memorable concerts of his career. See Daniel, *Stokowski*, 669. In my own view, Stokowski's follow-up recordings with this orchestra during the sixties and early seventies include recordings among the greatest of his career.

63. Levins, interview with the author. In an essay on Stokowski's conducting style, Mr. Levin noted that Stokowski's habit of conducting without a score was dictated not by vanity but by his desire to maintain eye contact with his players. Sylvan Levin, "Leopold Stokowski," *Toccata*, July–August 1981, 13.

64. Joseph Szigeti, *With Strings Attached* (New York: Alfred A. Knopf, 1953), 224. It should be noted that, in memory, Szigeti has confused Stokowski's first London concert of 1909—not 1908-with the maestro's first concert with the London Symphony Orchestra (1912). As mention of "Marche Slav" and the Glazounov Violin Concerto on the program he attended shows, Szigeti attended and remembered the 1912 concert.

65. Daniel Gregory Mason, *Music in My Time* (Freeport, N.Y.: Books for Libraries Press, 1970, 370.

66. Italics mine. It is likely that Stokowski's extra musical gifts were already being used in his years as conductor of the Cincinnati Symphony Orchestra. References from these years cite Stokowski as a "wizard," a "magician," whose "electrical influence," "magnetic influence," and "uncanny virtuosity" mesmerized players and soloists. See Daniel, *Stokowski*, 70–76.

67. Chasins, *Leopold Stokowski*, 107–8.

68. Louisa Miller, interview with the author, 1982, Claremont, California.

69. Daniel, *Stokowski*, 718.

70. José Serebrier, "The Magic Art of Conducting: Part 2 - Stokowski," *Music Journal*, 22 March 1964, 60.

71. Gomberg, "Recollections," 15.

72. Edward Greenfield, "Behind the Scenes," "Watch All the Conductors Please", 23 *High Fidelity-Musical America*, May 1973, 16. Other such accounts from the maestro's later years can be found in Stokowski's radio interview with Aaron Parsons and George Stone, and in his 1974 interview with the BBC's Sandra Harris. In the Harris interview Stokowski, when asked how he established such control over an orchestra, replied, chuckling, that it was a "secret." Obviously flirting with Ms. Harris, Stokowski explained that if he did explain his secret, Ms. Harris might learn the technique and put him out of work. Then relenting, he added that his secret lay in eye contact with the players. To interviewer Carl Bamberger, Stokowski said that he conducted through his eyes and through "inner communication" with his players. See Carl Bamberger, *The Conductor's Art* (New York: McGraw Hill, 1965), 198–99.

73. Nathan Stutch, "Leopold Stokowski: The Sound of Genius—a Personal Reminiscence," included in *New York Philharmonic-Leopold Stokowski*, two records live (New York Philharmonic, WQXR Radiothon Special Edition, 1982).

74. Stokowski, *Music for All of Us*, 214–15.

75. William A. Smith, "Leopold Stokowski: The Eyes Have It," Sonneck Society, College Music Society (Southern chapter) joint meeting, Florida State University, Tallahassee, Florida, 10 March 1985.

76. Dominique-Rene de Lerma, "Stoky in Miami: Informal Memories," *Leopold Stokowski Society Bi-monthly Bulletin*, no. 4, July–August 1979, 9.

77. Daniel, *Stokowski*, 302.

78. Berlioz, *Treatise*, 245–46.

79. Leopold Stokowski, interview with Lyman Bryson in the "Conductor as Creator" series, WGBH Radio, Boston, n.d., Sylvan Levin Stokowski Collection.
80. Daniel, *Stokowski*, 193.

Chapter 3. Stokowski in Philadelphia

1. Nancy Malitz, "Michael Gielen," *High Fidelity Musical America*, 29 October 1979, 5.
2. Ewen, *Dictators*, 74–76. David Wooldridge, *Conductor's World* (New York: Prager Publishers, 1970), 121. Edward Arian, *Bach, Beethoven, and Bureaucracy: The Case of the Philadelphia Orchestra* (Tuscaloosa: University of Alabama Press, 1971), 4–5.
3. It was during these early years that Stokowski began to keep a personal directory of fine musicians he had heard. In addition to auditions, he could rely on the names and addresses in his directory to find capable orchestra players and soloists when needed. This was still his practice fifty years later with the American Symphony Orchestra. It was in this way, during the twenties, that Stokowski, after hearing Joseph Szigeti play in Zurich, Switzerland, invited the violinist to make his American debut, playing the Beethoven Violin Concerto with the Philadelphia Orchestra, 4 and 5 December 1925. After hearing young Artur Rodzinski conduct Wagner in Warsaw, Stokowski brought him to the United States as his assistant for the years 1926 to 1929. The great Wanda Landowska made twin American debuts in Philadelphia and New York during November 1923, at Stokowski's request, playing Mozart on the piano and Handel and Bach on the harpsichord. See Eugene Moore, "Fifty Fabulous Years," *Musical America*, 79 February 1959, 17–18. Robert C. Marsh, "Conversations with Stokowski," *High Fidelity* 11 April 1961, 45.

Stokowski, interview with Lambro. Kupferberg, *Fabulous Philadelphians*, 39. Henry Swoboda in conversation with Stokowski. Swoboda, ed., *The American Symphony Orchestra* (New York: Basic Books, 1967), 117. See Szigeti, 243. Ewen, *Dictators*, 228. Schickel, *World of Carnegie Hall*, 218. Brian Plumb, "Leopold Stokowski and the Philadelphia Orchestra: Season 1923–24," *Toccata*, November–December 1981, 3–4.

Stokowski also, over the years, entrusted the search for just the right performers to a few key and trusted associates such as Sylvan Levin, who helped Stokowski find soloists—often unknown—and orchestral players of topflight ability from 1929 through Stokowski's stint with the New York City Symphony Orchestra, 1944–45. See Stokowski, letters to Sylvan Levin, dated 8 Nov., 1929, 8 Nov., 1930, 21 Dec., 1930, 29 July, 1935, 10 Aug., 1935, 22 Dec., 1938, 1 Feb., 1939, 21 Mar., 1940, 24 Oct., 1944, 20 May, 1945, 20 Sept., 1945, 14 June, 1950. Sylvan Levin Stokowski Collection, New York City.

4. Leopold Stokowski, Lecture at Bryn Mawr College, February 1963, Bryn Mawr, Pennsylvania. Leopold Stokowski, interview with Jerry Bruck and Jerry Fox, 8 April 1970, New York City. Leopold Stokowski, interview with William Malloch, ca. 1964, n.p. All from Classical Recordings Archive of America, El Cerrito, California. Kupferberg, *Fabulous Philadelphians*, 37, 40. Olga Samaroff Stokowski, *American Musician's Story*, 97–98, 166–67. Chasins, *Leopold Stokowski*, 84–85. Chasins, interview with the author. Frances Ann Wister, *Twenty-Five Years of the Philadelphia Orchestra: 1900–1925* (1925; reprint, Freeport, N.Y.: Books for Libraries Press, 1970), 101.
5. Wister, *Twenty-Five Years*, 101.

6. For the most complete account of the Mahler venture see Wister, *Twenty-Five Years*, 99–112. Stokowski also premiered Mahler's *Das Lied von der Erde* during the same concert season. While Stokowski never recorded either of these works, he did at the age of ninety-three record the Mahler Second Symphony, the *Resurrection* Symphony.

7. Wister, *Twenty-Five Years*, 106. Kupferberg, 48. Marsh, "Conversations with Stokowski," 45.

8. Wister, *Twenty-Five Years*, 106.

9. Ibid., 114–15, 132–34. Opperby, *Leopold Stokowski*, 35–37.

10. The new support of such civic lights during those early years amounted to $2 million, raised between 1916 and 1923. See Arian, *Bach, Beethoven and Bureaucracy*, 7–8. Wister, *Twenty-Five Years*, 113, 130–31.

11. Edith Emerson, "The Philadelphia Award," *American Magazine of Art*, 22 May 1922, 156–58. Wister, *Twenty-Five Years*, 158. The casket and scroll can today be seen in the Stokowski Room of Philadelphia's Curtis Institute of Music. The Gold Medal is missing, but Dr. Edwin Heilakka, curator of the Stokowski Collection, has instituted a search for it.

12. Brian Plumb, "Leopold Stokowski and the Philadelphia Orchestra: 1921–1922 Season," *Toccata*, July–August 1981, 3–10.

13. Both Sylvan Levin and Abram Chasins told me that they believed Stokowski had a genuine personal code and sense of values, but that it was unlike the Judaic-Christian code of tradition and was unique in their experience.

14. Kupferberg, *Fabulous Philadelphians*, 103.

15. I recognize in writing the above that many critics and commentators do not fit this description. Not only professional critics, but musicians, historians, novelists, playwrights, conductors, and composers, among others, have written about music, musicians, and performances thoughtfully and often with great humor. Virgil Thomson, Aldous Huxley, Paul Hindemith, George Bernard Shaw, Wanda Landowska, Jacques Barzun, Leonard Bernstein. and many more have brightened the world with their insights. Any yet . . . and yet no consistent concertgoer checking reviews against his or her reactions to recordings and performances over the years can fail to miss what I am getting at in describing a kind of concert hall orthodoxy, and no American conductor ran so afoul of this orthodoxy as did Leopold Stokowski, who got, I believe, more than his fair share of hostile reviews. Since the Stokowski stereotype was in good measure a result of the repetition—over the years and finally over generations—of review clichés based often on preconception rather than on performance, I know of no way to deal with the situation except to call attention to it while attempting to redress the balance for a clearer view of Stokowski, the man and the musician.

16. Chasins, *Leopold Stokowski*, 113–19.

17. To the end of his life Stokowski concerned himself with the possibilities of the future, never with the memories or accomplishments of the past. The personal side of this trait was often less praiseworthy since it was linked to Stokowski's almost compulsive abhorrence to references about his age. As Jerome Toobin recalls it, the Stokowski of the fifties and sixties had a positive distaste for talk of the past and the good old days. He was not averse to noting the advancing years of others, but never in relationship to himself. See Toobin, *Agitato*, 44–45.

18. Clair R. Reis, *Composers, Conductors and Critics* (New York: Oxford University Press, 1955), 86–87.

19. Reis, *Composers*, 87–89.
20. Several of these recordings from the late twenties and early thirties have been rereleased: Dvorak's Ninth Symphony on RCA; Stravinsky's *Le Sacre du Printemps* and *Firebird* Suite on dell' Arte; and an explosive Brahms Third Symphony on RCA Camden. Beethoven's Fifth and Seventh Symphonies are coupled on a disc from the English Stokowski Society. See Discography for the late twenties and early thirties for listings of these and other recordings transferred to long-play.
21. Chasins, *Leopold Stokowski*, 158–59.
22. Reis, *Composers*, 92–94.
23. Chasins, *Leopold Stokowski*, 204–05.
24. Reis, *Composers*, 94–100.
25. Ibid., 109.
26. Olin Downes, *Olin Downes on Music* (New York: Simon and Schuster, 1957), 162–66.
27. Harvey Sachs, *Toscanini* (Philadelphia and New York: J. B. Lippincott Co. 1978), 198–202. Roy Harris, "Problems of American Composers," in Henry Cowell, ed., *American Composers on American Music* (New York: Frederick Ungar Publishing Co., 1962), 158. Edgard Varèse in conversation with Gunther Schuller in Benjamin Boretz and Cone, *Perspectives*, 37.
28. Chasins, *Leopold Stokowski*, 128–30.
29. Ibid., 130–31.
30. Robinson, *Stokowski*, 119.
31. Not until the late 1940s would long-playing records reappear, this time successfully revolutionizing the recording industry, a change predicted by Stokowski fifteen years earlier. See Chasins, *Leopold Stokowski*, 136 and Robinson, *Stokowski*, 126.
32. For further material on these experiments, see Discography items on the Bell Laboratories recordings of 1931 and 1932 and comment on the *Parsifal*: Prelude to Act 1 recording of 1936.
33. In 1979 the Bell Laboratories released the first of two long-playing records commemorating these sessions. Included on it are complete performances or excerpts of the following: Berlioz, "Roman Carnival" Overture; Weber, "Invitation to the Dance"; Mendelssohn, Scherzo from *A Midsummer Night's Dream;* Wagner, "Liebestod" from *Tristan and Isolde;* Scriabin, *Prometheus;* and Mussorgsky-Ravel *Pictures at an Exhibition*. While all of these recordings are of historical-musical interest, the Berlioz, Wagner, and Scriabin live recordings are intrinsically marvelous. These records may still be available from Bell Telephone Laboratories, New York, under the wordy title, *Early Hi Fi: Wide Range and Stereo Recordings Made by the Bell Telephone Laboratories in the 1930s, Leopold Stokowski Conducting the Philadelphia Orchestra, 1931–1932*, vols. 1 and 2.
34. O'Connell, *The Other Side of the Record*, 297–98. Among these treasures are: the Bloch *Schelomo* with soloist Emmanuel Feurmann (1939); the Debussy Nocturnes (1937–39); the Dukas "Sorcerer's Apprentice" (1937); the Franck Symphony in D Minor (1935); the Mussorgsky-Stokowski *Boris Godunov* Synthesis (1936); the Rimsky-Korsakov *Scheharazade* (1934); the Saint Saëns *Carnival of the Animals* (1939); and Stokowski's Symphonic Synthesis of Wagner's, *Tristan and Isolde* (1935–37). See Discography.
35. RCA rereleased this concert performance on long-play in its Legendary Performances series as RCA AVM 2-2017 (two records).

36. Virgil Thomson, *American Music Since 1910* (New York: Holt, Rinehart and Winston, 1970), 113. Robinson, *Stokowski*, 31–32. Reis, *Composers*, 132–147.

37. Chasins, *Leopold Stokowski*, 103–4, 117–18. O'Connell, *The Other Side of the Record*, 279–86.

38. Kupferberg, *Fabulous Philadelphians*, 87. Chasins, *Leopold Stokowski*, 131.

39. Robinson, *Stokowski*, 40. Chasins, *Leopold Stokowski*, 8–9.

40. Halina Rodzinski, *Our Two Lives* (New York: Charles Scribner's Sons, 1976), 76.

41. This sound track recording can still be enjoyed musically and sonically in *Fantasia*, Buena Vista Records 101 (three records), however, in 1982 the score was rerecorded by Irwin Kostal and a Los Angeles pickup orchestra to take advantage of recording advances. That set, Buena Vista Records 104, is now to be superceded by the digitally remastered rerelease of the original Stokowski recording. The new recording is scheduled to appear in 1990 as part of the fiftieth anniversary rerelease of *Fantasia*.

42. Reis, *Composers*, 151–52.

43. Three RCA Victor recordings were made by Stokowski with the New York City Symphony: the Beethoven Sixth Symphony; Richard Strauss's tone poem *Death and Transfiguration;* and an absolutely splendid *Carmen* Suite. During 1982, Stokowski's centennial year, the Leopold Stokowski Society rereleased *Death and Transfiguration* on its own label as LS 5. Also to celebrate the centennial, Town Hall Records released the Hindemith (1939) Violin Concerto with Robert Gross as soloist, accompanied by Stokowski and the New York City Symphony in a live performance dating from 1945. For more on Stokowski and the New York City Symphony see Discography.

44. Robinson, *Stokowski*, 54–56.

45. Odell Shepard, ed., *The Heart of Thoreau's Journals* (New York: Dover Publications, 1961), 16, entry for 30 June 1840.

Chapter 4. Leopold Stokowski: A Reevaluation

1. Irving Kolodin, *The Musical Life* (New York: Alfred A. Knopf, 1958), 207–8.

2. Stokowski, interview with Harris. Greenfield, "Watch All the Conductors Please" 16. Levin, "Leopold Stokowski," 11.

3. Stokowski, interview with Malloch. Stokowski, interview with Parsons and Stone. Stokowski, interview with Bryson. Stokowski, conversation with Glenn Gould, December 1969, New York City, in Robert Chesterman, ed., *Conversations with Conductors* (Totowa, N.J.: Rowman and Littlefield, 1976), 123. Daniel, *Stokowski*, 637.

4. Harry Ellis Dickson, "Running the B.S.O.," in George Seltzer, *The Professional Symphony Orchestra in the United States* (Metuchen, N.J.: Scarecrow Press, 1975), 357. Jackson, *First Flute*, 79.

5. Glenn Gould, "Stokowski in Six Scenes" in Tim Page (ed.), *Glenn Gould Reader* (New York: Alfred A. Knopf, 1984), 262–64.

6. Originally released in 1966, this recording has been digitally remastered and is now available in Columbia's Masterworks Portrait series as MP 38888.

7. Geoffrey Payzant, *Glen Gould: Music & Mind* (Toronto: Van Nostrand Reinhold, 1978), 7, 34, 68.

8. Payzant, *Glenn Gould*, 68.

9. O'Connell, *The Other Side of the Record*, 290–91.

10. Phillips, Address, 14.

11. H. L. Mencken, "Wind Music," in Lewis Cheslock (ed.), *H. L. Mencken on Music* (New York: Schirmer Books, 1961), 122–24.

12. As examples of this last—of pathos as youth past/passed, of love lost, of yearning, of lost hope—here are a few recorded examples that are exceptional, even when controversial: the "Modinha" from *Bachianas Brasileiras* no. 1 by Villa-Lobos included in Everest SDBR-3016 (from the late fifties); the opening theme in Elgar's *Enigma* Variations in London SPC 21136 (from the seventies); the Dvorak "Slavonic Dance" in E Minor, op. 72, no. 2 (from the seventies); and the exquisite poignancy of *The Plow that Broke the Plains* by Virgil Thomson in Vanguard VSD 2095 (recorded in the late fifties).

13. B. H. Haggin, *Music in the Nation* (New York: William Sloane Assoc., 1949), 159. Rodzinski, *Our Two Lives*, 109. Stokowski recorded his transcription of *Pictures at an Exhibition* with the New Philharmonia Orchestra in 1965 (London SPC 21006). His transcription is quite unlike that of Maurice Ravel and without the subtlety of the French composer's transcription. Yet his conception of the music is a valid musical alternative as well; it is powerful, emotionally compelling, and as ferociously slavic as Mussorgsky. Compare it to Toscanini's 1953 recording of the Ravel transcription (RCA LM 1838) and you not only have two valid orchestral approaches to the same piano score, but in Toscanini and Stokowski you have performance approaches that are poles apart—Toscanini, the literal photographer in sound, Stokowski, the larger than life muralist—representing wholly different approaches to interpretation as well as to music generally.

14. Schonberg, *Great Conductors*, 313–14.

15. Haggin, *Music in the Nation*, 161.

16. Stokowski, *Music For All of Us*, 46–49.

17. Swoboda, *American Symphony Orchestra*, 116–17. Chasins, *Leopold Stokowski*, 233–42.

18. Robinson, *Stokowski*, 79.

19. Ibid., 77. One can judge the range of orchestral color, the sonority, the solo skills of first desk personnel, and the ability of American Symphony players to catch and, as one, to follow Stokowski's vision of a work in several fine recordings made from 1962 to 1971: William Dawson's *Negro Folk* Symphony, Varèse Sarabande VC 81056; Werner Josten's Concerto *Sacro I–II*. CRI SD 200, and Josten's *Canzona Seria* coupled with the tone poem *Jungle*, CRI SD 267; Charles Ives's Fourth Symphony, Columbia ML 6175; a controversial Mozart, Serenade for Thirteen Winds, K. 361; and an idiosyncratic last recording of Tchaikovsky's Fourth Symphony—both Stokowski's last recording with the orchestra and his last recording of the symphony-which is unique in interpretation and represents the orchestra at its musical and sonic best, Vanguard VCS 10095. The Mozart Serenade is, by the way, included in a two-record set from Vanguard VSD 707/8, which also includes Thomson's *The Plow that Broke the Plains* and Stravinsky's *L'Histoire du Soldat* as well as music from the Baroque period.

20. Bernard Jacobson, *Conductors on Conducting*, (Frenchtown, N.J.: Columbia Publishing Co., 1979), 159–60, interview with José Serebrier.

21. John Kirkpatrick, ed., *Charles E. Ives Memos* (New York: W. W. Norton & Co., 1972), 66. Henry and Sidney Cowell, *Charles Ives and His Music* (New York: Oxford University Press, 1969), 105.
22. Kirkpatrick, *Ives Memos*, 67.
23. For Associate Conductor José Serebrier's comments on this mammoth task in connection with his own recording, see Jacobson, *Conductors on Conducting*, 176–77, 162–63.
24. Cowell and Cowell, *Charles Ives*, 130, 208–9.
25. RCA ARL 1-0589.
26. Jacobson, *Conductors on Conducting*, 162, 165–66.
27. Ibid., 160, 164–65.
28. Ibid., 171–72.
29. Ibid., 171–72.
30. Included in *Charles Ives: The 100th Anniversary*, Columbia M 4 32504, released in 1974. The "Robert Browning" Overture is included in Columbia's *The World of Charles Ives*, recorded through a grant from the Edgar Stern Foundation, Columbia MS 7015.
31. Leopold Stokowski conducted the London Symphony Orchestra and Chorus, London SPC 21060. This may well be the greatest Stokowski recording of them all.
32. Stokowski's understanding of and emphathy with Ives's music and ideas can be clearly established by comparing Ives's essay, "Music and Its Future," in Cowell, ed., *American Composers*, 128–45, to Stokowski's writing, interviews, and experiments over the years. Further confirmation can be found in Kirkpatrick, *Ives Memos*, and in Charles Ives, *Essays Before a Sonata and Other Writings* (New York: W. W. Norton & Co., 1961).
33. Robinson, Stokowski, 81.
34. *Sixtieth Anniversary Concert: Leopold Stokowski and the London Symphony Orchestra*, London SPC 2109/1 (two records, live).
35. Stellar examples drawn from nonagenarian Stokowski's work during the last three years of his life are: Stokowski's last recording of Bach transcriptions, RCA ARL 1-0880; Mahler's Symphony no. 2, the *Resurrection* Symphony, RCA ARL 2-0852 (two records); Rachmaninoff's Symphony no. 3, Desmar DSM-1007G; Stokowski's fifth and last recording of Rimsky-Korsakov's *Scheherazade*, RCA ARL 1-1182; one of two last Wagner sets, RCA ARL 1-0498; and a dazzling final set of Stokowski transcriptions for orchestra of works by Chopin, Debussy, Albeniz, Novacek, Rimsky-Korsakov, Shostakovich, and Tchaikovsky, Columbia M 34543.
36. Stokowski, *Music For All of Us*, 321.

Appendix

1. Sigmund Freud, "Family Romances," in James Strachey, ed. and trans., *The Complete Psychological Works of Sigmund Freud*, vol. 9 (London: Hogarth Press and the Institute of Psychoanalysis, 1974), 238–39.
2. Phyllis Greenacre, "The Childhood of the Artist," in *Emotional Growth: Psychoanalytic Studies of the Gifted and a Great Variety of Other Individuals*, vol. 2 (New York: International Universities Press, 1971), 488. Also see in the same collection, "The Family Romance of the Artist," 531–32.
3. Stokowski, *Music For All of Us*, 69.
4. Greenacre, "The Childhood of the Artist," 494–95.
5. Ibid., 498–99. Greenacre, "The Family Romance of the Artist," 529, and,

also in *Emotional Growth*, "The Relation of the Imposter to the Artist (1958)," 533, 542. I was delighted when psychiatrist John Diamond, upon reading an earlier draft of my work on Stokowski, confirmed the likelihood that two or more identities were a part of Stokowski's psychological makeup. He did so in a telephone conversation with me early in 1984.

6. Greenacre, "The Family Romance of the Artist," 506.

7. Ibid., 506–8.

8. Drs. Leo Stone, David Beres, and Robert C. Bak, commentators at the Ernst Kris Memorial Meeting, Academy of Medicine, New York City, 24 September 1957, cosponsored by the New York Psychoanalytic Society and Institute and by the Western New England Society. I am grateful to psychoanalyst Dr. Martin Silverman for calling my attention to the commentary and for providing additional annotation on the subject.

9. Greenacre, "The Family Romance of the Artist," 530.

10. Stokowski, *Music For All of Us*, 21, 46, 52.

11. O'Connell, *The Other Side of the Record*, 286. Vanderbilt, *Black Knight, White Knight*, 186. Chasins, *Leopold Stokowski*, 153. Stokowski, *Music For All of Us*, 11, 321–22.

12. Stone, commentary on Greenacre's "The Family Romance of the Artist," New York, 1957.

13. Stokowski, *Music For All of Us*, 320.

14. Stokowski, in conversation with Glen Gould, 124.

15. Stokowski, *Music For All of Us*, 192.

16. Daniel, *Stokowski*, 27.

17. Greenacre, "The Childhood of the Artist," 499; "Play in Relation to Creative Imagination," in *Emotional Growth*, 568–71; and "Relation of the Imposter," 543–44.

18. Vanderbilt, *Black Knight, White Knight*, 298, 213, 210, 222–29, 207.

19. Ibid., 230.

20. Ibid., 269.

21. Ibid., 270, 273.

22. Greenacre, "The Childhood of the Artist," 499, "Play," 568–71, and "Relation of the Imposter," 543–44.

23. Nancy Shear, telephone conversation with the author, March, 1989, Marguerite Friedeberg, telephone conversations with the author, February and March, 1989. Mrs. Friedeberg née Rockhold met Stokowski during the filming of *The Big Broadcast of 1937*. They were friends until Stokowski left Los Angeles in 1939 and returned to the east coast permanently. She never saw the maestro again.

24. Stokowski, interview with William Malloch. Daniel, *Stokowski*, 191.

25. Greenacre, "Relation of the Imposter," 543–44.

26. Levins, interview with the author.

27. Levins, interview with the author.

28. The note from Stokowski to Levin was undated and was written at sea, Sylvan Levin Stokowski Collection. Chasins, *Leopold Stokowski*, 98. Daniel, *Stokowski*, 27.

29. Stokowski, *Music For All of Us*, 320–22. When I first presented the thesis of "Stokowski and the Family Romance" as a paper before the New York Psychoanalytic Association at its April 1984 meeting in New York City, commentator Jules Glenn, M.D., P.C., was kind enough to provide in advance a typed copy of his commentary on the paper. Given the evidence, he agreed that Stokowski was indeed the creator of a family romance.

Selected Sources

I have left a number of items included in notes to the text out of this listing for the sake of brevity. They include innumerable concert reviews, record reviews, notes on recordings and the like. They are attributed in notes to the text to the following periodicals: *American Record Guide, Christian Science Monitor, Consumers' Union Reviews Classical Recordings, Fanfare, Gramophone, High Fidelity, High Fidelity-Musical America, Los Angeles Times, Musical America, Musical Courier, Music Educators' Journal, Music Journal, New Yorker, Stereo Review, Theatre Arts, Time, USSR,* and *Virtuoso*.

There is no source collection of Stokowski's papers and correspondence, since the cargo container holding Stokowski's papers as well as much memorabilia was washed overboard on the trip from England to the United States, following the conductor's death.

Stokowski: Writings, Correspondence, Rehearsal, Material, Lectures, Interviews, and Conversations

Stokowski, Leopold. *Music for All of Us*. New York: Simon and Schuster, 1943.

———. Correspondence with Sylvan Levin, 1928–51, varied places.

———. Interview over San Francisco radio with anonymous broadcaster. San Francisco, 1936. Stokowski Society of America Collection.

———. BBC interview with Roy Plomley. London, 1957. *Toccata*, Winter 1985, 25–33.

———. Interview with R. C. Marsh. Chicago, 1958. Classical Recordings Archive of America, El Cerrito, Calif.

———. BBC interview with Reginald Jacques. London, 1959. Classical Recordings Archive of America, El Cerrito, Calif.

———. Interview with J. W. Keeler, n.p., 1962. Classical Recordings Archive of America, El Cerrito, Calif.

———. Dialogue with Frank Merkling. "Whats Wrong with Opera." *Opera News* 26, 24 February 1962, 8–13.

———. Interview with Philip Lambro. n.p., 1963. Classical Recordings Archive of America, El Cerrito, Calif.

———. Lecture at Bryn Mawr College. Bryn Mawr, Pa., 1963. Classical Recordings Archive of America, El Cerrito, Calif.

———. Interview with William Malloch. n.p., 1964. Classical Recordings Archive of America, El Cerrito, Calif.

———. Interview with Carl Bamberger. Bamberger, C., ed. *The Conductor's Art.* New York: McGraw Hill, 1965.

———. In conversation with Henry Swoboda. In "Innovations." Chap. 11 in *The American Symphony, Orchestra*, edited by H. Swoboda, 115–25. New York: Basic Books, 1967.

———. In conversation with Hans Hansen. Copenhagen, 1967. Poco Recording DLP 8407.

———. Interview with Lyman Bryson, WGBH Radio. Boston, ca. 1968. Sylvan Levin Stokowski Collection.

———. In rehearsal with the American Symphony Orchestra. New York City, n.d. Sylvan Levin Stokowski Collection

———. Interview with Aaron Parsons and George Stone. Chicago, 1968. Classical Recordings Archive of America, El Cerrito, Calif.

———. In conversation with Glenn Gould. New York City, 1969. In *Conversations with Conductors*, edited by Robert Chesterman, 121–28. Totowa, N.J.: Rowman and Littlefield, 1976.

———. Interview with Jerry Buck and Jerry Fox. New York City, 1970. Classical Recordings Archive of America, El Cerrito, Calif.

———. *In Rehearsal with the American Symphony Orchestra.* National Educational Television *Fanfare* production. New York City, 1970.

———. In rehearsal with the International Festival Youth Orchestra, 1973. Cameo Classics GOCLP 9007.

———. BBC interview with Sandra Harris and Michael Oliver. London, 1974. Classical Recordings Archive of America, El Cerrito, Calif.

———. Interview with Dan Rather on CBS's "*60 Minutes*," London, 1977.

Stokowskiana: Including Author's Interviews, Conversations, and Correspondence, Psychological and Parapsychological Material, Biographies and Other Analyses Bearing on Understanding the Man and the Musician

Abel, David W. "A Visit with Stokowski." *Music Educators' Journal*, 50 September–October 1963, 121.

Arian, Edward. *Bach, Beethoven, and Bureaucracy: The Case of the Philadelphia Orchestra.* Tuscaloosa: University of Alabama Press, 1971.

Bettelheim, Bruno. *The Uses of Enchantment: The Meaning and Importance of Fairy Tales.* New York: Vintage Books, 1977.

Brundage, Anthony. Conversations with the author. Claremont, Calif, 1983–84.

Chasins, Abram. Interview with the author. Los Angeles, Calif, 1982.

———. *Leopold Stokowski: A Profile.* New York: Hawthorn Books, 1979.

Curtin-Hite, Rosemary. "A Conversation with Sol Schoenbach." *Toccata*, Spring 1986, 2–9.

Curtis Institute of Music. *Stokowski Centennial Program*. Philadelphia, 18 April 1982.

Daniel, Oliver. *Stokowski: A Counterpoint of View*. New York: Dodd Mead & Co., 1982.

Davis, Curtis. "Stokowski at 100." *High Fidelity-Musical America*, 32 April 1982, 45–48, 82.

Diamond, John, M.D. *The Life Energy in Music*. Vols. 1 and 2. Valley Cottage, N.Y.: Archeus Press, 1981, 1983.

———. Telephone conversation with the author, 1984.

———. Conversation with the author. New York City, 1984.

Dixon, F. R. "Stokowski in Cleveland." *Toccata*, Spring 1983, 2–12.

Freud, Sigmund. "Family Romances." In *Complete Psychological Works of Sigmund Freud*. Vol. 9. Translated and edited by James Strachey, 237–41. London: Hogarth Press and Institute of Psychoanalysis, 1974.

Friedeberg, Marguerite. Telephone conversations with the author. February and March, 1989.

Fromm, Erich. *The Forgotten Language: An Introduction to the Understanding of Dreams, Fairy Tales and Myths*. New York: Evergreen Books, 1957.

Glenn, Jules. Commentary on William A. Smith "Stokowski and the Family Romance." New York Psychoanalytic Association meeting, 1984.

Gomberg, Robert. "Recollections of Stokowski." *High Fidelity-Musical America*, 28 March 1978, MA 14–15.

Gould, Glenn. "Stokowski in Six Scenes" in Tom Page (ed.), *Glenn Gould Reader* (New York: Alfred A. Knopf, 1984), 258–282.

Greenacre, Phyllis. *Emotional Growth: Psychoanalytic Studies of the Gifted and a Great Variety of Other Individuals*. Vol. 2. New York: International Universities Press, 1971.

Heilakka, Edwin. Correspondence with the author. Philadelphia, 1982–88.

———. Conversation with the author and tour of the Stokowski Collection. Curtis Institute of Music. Philadelphia, 1982.

———. "Sights and Sounds." An address to the 1988 Stokowski Conference at Andrews University, Columbus, Ohio, 1988.

Hendl, Walter. Interview with Robert M. Stumpf and Susan Betz. Columbus, Ohio, 1984. *Maestrino*, Spring 1985, 2–11.

Hill, William Fawcett. Conversations with the author. Calif. State Polytechnic University, Pomona, Calif, 1983–84.

Hoeffler, Paul. Telephone conversation with the author, 1988.

Howard, Richard. Conversations with the author. Fullerton, Calif., 1982; and Oxford, Ohio, 1983.

Janossy, Gustav. *Leopold Stokowski and the All American Youth Orchestra: Second Tour, 1941.* Unpublished collection of articles & reviews.

Johnson, Edward, ed. *Stokowski: Essays in Analysis of His Art.* London: Triad Press, 1973.

Kipnis, Igor. Telephone conversations with the author, 1988.

———. Recollections of Stokowski. West Redding, Conn., 1988. Cassette recording

Kupferberg, Herbert. *Those Fabulous Philadelphians.* New York: Charles Scribner's Sons, 1969.

Lerma, Dominique-Rene de. "Stoky in Miami: Informal Memories." *Leopold Stokowski Society Bi-monthly Bulletin* no. 4 (July–August 1979): 8–12.

Le Shan, Lawrence. *The Medium, The Mystic and the Physicist: Toward a General Theory of the Paranormal.* New York: Viking Press, 1974.

Levin, Sylvan. *Memorial to Leopold Stokowski.* Philadelphia: Curtis Institute of Music, September 23, 1977.

———. "Leopold Stokowski." *Toccata,* July–August 1981, 10–16.

———. Correspondence with the author. New York City, 1982–84.

Levin, Sylvan, and Elizabeth De Young Levin. Interview with the author. New York City, 1982.

McGinn, Robert E. "Stokowski and the Bell Telephone Laboratories: Collaboration in the Development of High-Fidelity Sound Reproduction." *Technology and Culture,* 24 January 1983, 38–75.

Miller, Louisa. Interviews with the author. Claremont, Calif., 1982.

Monte, Tom. "Healer John Diamond's Soul Music." *East West: The Journal of Natural Health & Living* 18 (July 1988): 38–45.

Moss, Thelma. *The Probability of the Impossible: Scientific Discoveries and Explorations in the Psychic World.* Los Angeles: J. P. Tarcher, 1974.

Neuburg, Elizabeth. Telephone conversation with the author, 1988.

Obert-Thorn, Mark A. "An Interview with Ward Marston or Zen and the Art of 78 Transferring." *Maestrino,* Spring 1987, 2–9.

O'Connell, Charles. "Leopold Stokowski." In *The Other Side of the Record.* New York: Alfred A Knopf, 1949.

Opperby, Preben. *Leopold Stokowski.* New York: Hippocrene Books, 1982.

Phillips, Edna. Address at the Stokowski Centennial Program, Curtis Institute of Music. Philadelphia, 18 April 1982. In *Maestrino,* Spring 1985, 10–14.

Plumb, Brian. "Leopold Stokowski and the Philadelphia Orchestra." An ongoing listing of Philadelphia Orchestra programs and soloists directed by Stokowski. *Toccata,* 1981 to date.

Pratt, Joseph G. *ESP Research Today: A Study of Developments in Parapsychology Since 1960.* Metuchen, N.J.: Scarecrow Press, 1973.

Robinson, Paul. *Stokowski*. Canada: Vanguard Press, 1977.

Schuller, Gunther. "Conversation with Edgard Varèse." In *Perspectives on American Music*, ed. Benjamin Boretz and Edward T. Cone, 34–39. New York: W. W. Norton & Co., 1971.

Serebrier, José. Interview with Bernard Jacobson. Bernard Jacobson, *Conductors on Conducting*. Frenchtown, N.J.: Columbia Publishing Co., c. 1979, 157–83.

———. "The Magic Art of Conducting: Pt. 2—Stokowski." *Music Journal*, March 1964, 60, 81.

Shear, Nancy. "Stokowski." *Toccata*, Autumn 1982, 16–21.

———. "Stoki' Would Have Flipped His Baton." *Toccata*, Summer 1982, 7–10.

———. Telephone conversation with the author. March, 1989.

Silverman, Martin, M.D. Correspondence and conversation with the author. Maplewood, New Jersey, and New York City, 1983–84.

Stutch, Nathan. "Leopold Stokowski: The Sound of Genius a Personal Reminiscence." In *New York Philharmonic-Leopold Stokowski*. Two records, live. New York Philharmonic, WQXR Radiothon Special Edition, 1982.

Tall, David, and John Bird. "Stokowski and the 1952 Grainger Settings." *Toccata*, September–October 1981, 12–19.

Toobin, Jerome. *Agitato*. New York: Viking Press, 1975.

Trotter, William. "The Conductor as Musical Hobo." Serialized in *Toccata*, November–December 1980 to date, First episodes of 1980–81, are titled "Sorcerer-The Life and Times of Leopold Stokowski."

Walker, Josephine. "The Stokowski Only His Secretary Could Know." *Ovation*, 3 April 1982, 18–19.

Warburg, Bettina, M.D. Correspondence with the author. New York City, 1984.

Warkow, Stewart. Interview with Martin Bookspan describing Stokowski and the American Symphony Orchestra. Intermission feature of American Symphony Orchestra broadcasting, 1967–68 season, New York City. Sylvan Levin Stokowski Collection.

Diary Material, Memoirs, Autobiographies, Letters, and Criticism

Antheil, George. *Bad Boy of Music*. Garden City, N.Y.: Doubleday Doran & Co., 1945.

Berlioz, Hector. *A Treatise upon Modern Instrumentation and Orchestration*. Translated by Mary C. Clarke. Boston: Elias Howe Co., n.d.

Carter, Elliott. *The Writings of Elliott Carter*. Edited by Else and Kurt Stone. Bloomington: Indiana University Press, 1977.

Casella, Alfredo. *Music in My Time: The Memoirs of Alfredo Casella*. Translated and edited by Spencer Norton. Norman: University of Oklahoma Press, 1955.

Chapin, Schuyler. *Musical Chairs: A Life in The Arts*. New York: G. P. Putnam's Sons, 1977.

Davenport, Marcia. *Too Strong for Fantasy: A Personal Record of Music, Literature, & Politics in America & Europe Over Half a Century*. New York: Avon Books, 1979.

Downes, Olin. *Olin Downes on Music*. New York: Simon and Schuster, 1957.

Flesch, Carl. *Memoirs of Carl Flesch*. Translated by Hans Keller and edited by him in collaboration with C. F. Flesch. New York: Macmillan, 1958.

Graffman, Gary. *I Really Should be Practicing*. Garden City, N.Y.: Doubleday & Co., 1981.

Haggin, Bernard H. *A Decade of Music*. New York: Horizon Press, 1973.

———. *Music in the Nation*. New York: William Sloane Assoc. 1949.

———. *35 Years of Music*. New York: Horizon Press, 1974.

Ives, Charles E. *Essays Before a Sonata*. New York: W. W. Norton & Co., 1961.

Jackson, Gerald. *First Flute*. Edited by David Simmons. London: J. M. Dent & Sons, 1968.

Kirkpatrick, John, ed. *Charles E. Ives Memos*. New York: W. W. Norton & Co., 1972.

Kostelanetz, Andre. *Memoirs of Andre Kostelanetz*. In collaboration with Gloria Hammond. New York: Harcourt Brace Jovanovich, 1981.

Luening, Otto. *The Odyssey of an American Composer: The Autobiography of Otto Luening*. New York: Charles Scribner's Sons, 1980.

Mason, Daniel Gregory. *Music in My Time and Other Reminiscences*. Freeport, N.Y.: Books for Libraries Press, 1970.

Mencken, H. L. *H. L. Mencken on Music*. Edited by Louis Cheslock. New York: Schirmer Books, 1975.

Menuhin, Yehudi. *Unfinished Journey*. New York: Alfred A. Knopf, 1977.

Piatigorsky, Gregor. *Cellist*. Garden City, N.Y.: Doubleday & Co., 1963.

Primrose, William. *Walk on the North Side - William Primrose: Memoirs of a Violist*. Provo, Utah: Brigham Young University Press, 1978.

Reis, Clair R. *Composers, Conductors and Critics*. New York: Oxford University Press, 1955.

Rodzinski, Halina. *Our Two Lives*. New York: Charles Scribner's Sons, 1976.

Rosenfeld, Paul. *Musical Impressions: Selections from Paul Rosenfeld's Criticism*. Edited by Herbert A. Leibowitz. New York: Hill and Wang, 1969.

Stein, Leonard, "Stokowski and the *Gurrelieder* Fanfare: Further Correspondence." *Journal of the Arnold Schoenberg Institute* 3 (October, 1979): 219–22.

Stokowski, Olga Samaroff. *An American Musician's Story*. New York: W. W. Norton & Co., 1939.

Szigeti, Joseph. *With Strings Attached.* New York: Alfred A Knopf, 1947.

Thomson, Virgil. *The Art of Judging Music.* New York: Greenwood Press, 1969.

———. *Music Right and Left.* New York: Henry Holt & Co., 1951.

———. *The Musical Scene.* New York: Greenwood Press, 1968.

———. *Virgil Thomson.* New York: Alfred A. Knopf, 1966.

———. Virgil Thomson Reader. Boston: Houghton Mifflin Co., 1981.

Vanderbilt, Gloria. *Black Knight, White Knight.* New York: Alfred A. Knopf, 1987.

Varèse, Louise M. *Varèse: A Looking-Glass Diary 1883–1928.* Vol. 1. New York: W. W. Norton & Co., 1972.

Volkov, Solomon, ed. *Testimony: The Memoirs of Dimitri Shostakovich.* New York: Harper & Row, 1979.

Wechsberg, Joseph. "Orchestra." *New Yorker,* 46 30 May 1970, 38–69.

Wister, Frances Anne. *Twenty-Five Years of the Philadelphia Orchestra 1900–1925.* Freeport, New York: Books for Libraries Press, 1970.

Secondary Sources: Books, Monographs, and Biographies

Appleton, Jon H., and Ronald C. Perrera, eds. *The Development and Practice of Electronic Music.* Englewood Cliffs, N.J.: Prentice-Hall, 1975.

Battcock, Gregory, ed. *Breaking the Sound Barrier: A Critical Anthology of the New Music.* New York: E. P. Dutton, 1981.

Bertonson, Sergei, and Jay Leyda. *Sergei Rachmaninoff.* New York: New York University Press, 1956.

Bookspan, Martin, and Ross Yockey. *Andre Previn: A Biography.* Garden City, N.Y.: Doubleday & Co., 1981.

———. *Zubin: The Zubin Mehta Story.* New York: Harper & Row, 1978.

Chotzinoff, Samuel. *Toscanini: An Intimate Portrait.* New York: Alfred A. Knopf, 1956.

Clemens, Clara. *My Husband Gabrilowitsch.* New York: Harper & Brothers, 1938.

Cowell, Henry. *American Composers on American Music.* New York: Frederick Ungar Publishing Co., 1962.

Cowell, Henry, and Sidney Cowell. *Charles Ives and His Music.* New York: Oxford University Press, 1969.

Eaton, Quaintance. *The Miracle of the Met: An Informal History of the Metropolitan Opera 1883–1967.* New York: Greenwood Press, 1976.

Evans, Mark. *Soundtrack: The Music of the Movies.* New York: Da Capo Press, 1979.

Ewen, David. *Dictators of the Baton.* Chicago: Alliance Book Corp., 1943.

———. *The Man with the Baton: The Story of Conductors and Their Orchestras.* New York: Thomas Y. Crowell Co., 1936.

Gerson, Robert A. *Music in Philadelphia.* Westport, Conn.: Greenwood Press, 1940.

Gleason, Ralph J. *Celebrating the Duke and Louis, Bessie, Billie, Bird, Carmen, Miles, Dizzy and Other Heroes.* Boston: Little Brown and Co., 1975.

Griffiths, Paul. *A Concise History of Avant Garde Music from Debussy to Boulez.* New York: Oxford University Press, 1978.

Jewell, Derek. *Duke: A Portrait of Duke Ellington.* New York: W. W. Norton & Co., 1977.

Kolodin, Irving. *The Metropolitan Opera 1883–1966: A Candid History.* New York: Alfred A. Knopf, 1966.

———. *The Musical Life.* New York: Alfred A. Knopf, 1958.

Levant, Oscar. *A Smattering of Ignorance.* Garden City, N.Y.: Garden City Publishing Co., 1939.

Ouellette, Fernand. *Edgar Varèse.* Translated by Derek Coltman. New York: Orion Press, 1968.

Payzant, Geoffrey. *Glenn Gould: Music and Mind.* Toronto: Van Nostrand Reinhold, 1978.

Pearton, Maurice. *The LSO at 70: A History of the Orchestra.* London: Victor Gollancz, 1974.

Peyser, Joan. *The New Music: The Sense Behind the Sound.* New York: Delacorte Press, 1971.

Riesemann, Oskar von. *Rachmaninoff's Recollections.* Translated by Dolly Rutherford. Freeport, N.Y.: Books for Libraries Press, 1970.

Roussel, Hubert. *The Houston Symphony Orchestra, 1913–1971.* Austin: University of Texas Press, 1972.

Russcol, Herbert. *The Liberation of Sound: An Introduction to Electronic Music.* Englewood Cliffs, N.J.: Prentice-Hall, 1972.

Sachs, Harvey. *Toscanini.* Philadelphia: J. B. Lippincott Co., 1978.

Schickel, Richard. *The World of Carnegie Hall.* New York: Julian Messner, 1960.

Schonberg, Harold. *The Great Conductors.* New York: Simon and Schuster, 1967.

Schwartz, H. W. *Bands of America.* Garden City, N.Y.: Doubleday & Co., 1957.

Seltzer, George. *The Professional Symphony Orchestra in the United States.* Metuchen, N.J.: Scarecrow Press, 1975.

Shanet, Howard. *Philharmonic: A History of New York's Orchestra.* Garden City, N.Y.: Doubleday & Co., 1975.

Smith, Cecil. *Worlds of Music.* Philadelphia: J. B. Lippincott Co., 1952.

Stuckenschmidt, H. H. *Schoenberg: His Life, World and Work.* Translated by Humphrey Searle. New York: Schirmer Books, 1977.

Taylor, Deems. *Walt Disney's Fantasia*. New York: Simon and Schuster, 1940.

Teal, Anthony R. *Leopold Stokowski: Off the Record—a Compilation of Record Reviews*. London: Leopold Stokowski Society, 1982.

Ulanov, Barry. *Duke Ellington*. New York: Creative Age Press, 1946.

Thomson, Virgil. *American Music since 1910*. New York: Holt, Rinehart and Winston, 1970.

Walker, Robert. *Rachmaninoff: His Life and Times*. Bath, England: Midas Books, 1980.

Wooldridge, David. *Conductor's World*. New York: Praeger Publishers, 1970.

Secondary Sources: Periodical, Journal, and Newspaper Materials

Dyer, Richard. "Maestro Front and Center." *New York Times* Book Review, 19 December 1982.

Emerson, Edith. "The Philadelphia Award." *American Magazine of Art*, 22 May 1922, 156–58.

Greenfield, Edward. "Watch All the Conductors Please" *High Fidelity-Musical America* 23 May 1973, 16–18.

Heilakka, Edwin E. ". . . To the Advancement of Fine Music." *WFLN Philadelphia Guide to Events and Places*. 22 April 1982: 11–13.

Malitz, Nancy. "Michael Gielen." *High Fidelity-Musical America*, 29 October 1979, 4–6, 22.

Marsh, Robert C. "Conversations with Stokowski." *High Fidelity* 11, April, 1961, 45–47, 162–63.

Moore, Eugene. "Fifty Fabulous Years." *Musical America*, 79 February 1959, 16–18.

Spaeth, Sigmund. "The Barrymores of the Baton." *Theatre Arts*, 36 November 1952, 26–29.

Leopold Stokowski Societies Publications

Bi-monthly Bulletin of the Leopold Stokowski Society. Various editors. London. March–April, 1979 to November–December, 1979

Maestrino. The journal of the Leopold Stokowski Society of America. Robert Stumpf, ed. Columbus, Ohio. 1983 to date.

Toccata: The Journal of the Leopold Stokowski Society. London. March–April, 1980 to date.

Index

Index to Discography

Content notes appearing in discography can be found in general index.